HER
SECRET
LIFE

BOOKS BY ANNA E. COLLINS

Love at First Spite
These Numbered Days
A Life in Bloom

Anna E. Collins

HER
SECRET
LIFE

bookouture

Published by Bookouture in 2024

An imprint of Storyfire Ltd.
Carmelite House
50 Victoria Embankment
London EC4Y 0DZ
Uniter Kingdom

www.bookouture.com

ISBN: 978-1-83525-365-6
eBook ISBN: 978-1-83790-974-2

To Sara and Elisabeth—faraway but always near

ONE

LEAH

Would they expect her to wear black?

Leah frowned into the closet, where knitted turtlenecks embraced sheer camisoles, and Neil's old jeans smothered her summer capris. Where was that dress? Or did a dress scream "trying too hard"? She dug beneath scarves and button-down shirts until her hands grazed the silky-smooth satin she'd been after. With a tug and a grunt, she pulled it free. Shook it out. Held it up.

Nope.

Her fingers twisted in the dark material before she tossed it to the floor. It was beyond her why she'd even kept it. Once a funeral dress, always a funeral dress.

Leah sighed, hands on hips. Gray blouse, dark-blue slacks maybe? Surely no one would fault her for being disrespectful in that. She pulled her unruly curls into a tight ponytail and dressed quickly, allowing herself no time to reconsider. Lord knows if she did, she'd miss the assembly altogether.

It was always a relief to shut the closet door, as if *that* was her deepest darkest secret—the piles, the mess, the sheer assortment of garments amassed over the course of a nineteen-year marriage. Admittedly, it used to be organized. His to the right, hers to the left. Shoes on racks below, seasonal items on the shelf above. Neil color-coordinated his side lights to darks, and he'd frowned upon her not following suit. She'd been *such* a rebel.

"How do you like it now?" she whispered to the closed door. It was a stupid question—obviously he wouldn't like it one bit. But allowing the mess was progress. Finally.

Leah shrugged off the cold, spectral hand at her neck and hurried to the kitchen, closing the door to the bedroom behind her. She had forty minutes until she'd take her seat in the gym with her colleagues at Aspenwood Middle School for the last time this school year. As the librarian, she wasn't required to participate in all assemblies, but this one was as much for her as for the outgoing class of eighth graders, so here she was, sweating over her oatmeal. A celebration of life, they'd said. An "In Memoriam" on the anniversary of his death. "The greatest principal we ever had here at Aspenwood." Rah rah rah.

It was fortunate she'd had a lot of practice over the past year accepting people's sympathies, gracefully bowing her head as condolences were bestowed upon her. Poor Leah Sloane, the young widow. Without Neil, surely her light had gone out. They did everything together and now she's all alone in that big house, daughter off to college...

At the thought of Hannah, the tension in Leah's shoulders eased. Eight more days and Hannah would be with her again. Home for the summer. They'd go hiking and shopping, watch movies together, read in the sun. She'd laugh. Hannah had her summer job at the YMCA too, but still. She could do eight more days. No biggie. One foot in front of the other.

She put her bowl in the sink and almost left it there to dry before thinking better of it, instead rinsing and placing it in the dishwasher. No need to be sloppy.

. . .

Leah's cheeks heated as she hurried to her office with the swell of students at her back, post assembly. She'd underestimated the overzealous impulses of a vice principal struggling to fill much bigger shoes. They even had the choir sing "Amazing Grace". Unbelievable.

She clasped the grocery-store bouquet of assorted flowers they'd gifted her, nearly dropping it when she fumbled with the key to her door. They meant well. She tossed the flowers on her desk and loaded the coffeemaker with a pod, before collapsing in her chair. It protested loudly, mostly due to its respectable age.

Leah closed her eyes and inhaled deeply. Today was Wednesday—only two more days of work after this. She'd miss the kids; they weren't the problem—it was the adults she no longer knew how to be around. As the thought crossed her mind, the library assistant, Mags, poked her head in the door, brows knitted.

"How're you holding up, dear? Not a dry eye, I think. Not one." She made a sad little *tsk* sound and shook her head. "A fitting tribute."

"Mm." Leah pressed her lips together in what she hoped would come off as a smile.

"It must be so hard. So. Hard. I swear I don't know how you do it."

"Well..."

"If Carl went before me, I'd die myself, I'm sure." She held up her hand, middle finger and index finger crossed. "Like this, we are. Like one. Just like you and Principal Sloane. Such a darling couple." She was tearing up now, splotches of red blooming on her neck.

Leah got up and put a hand on Mags's arm. "Hey now."

"Whoo." Mags fanned herself. "Look at me, a hot mess. And you such a picture of grace in the midst of this hardship. You poor thing."

She caressed Leah's cheek, and Leah had to focus all her willpower not to pull away. *She means well,* she thought again. *They all mean so* darn *well.*

She allowed Mags a few moments to collect herself then said, as gently as she could, "I have a heap of paperwork to do," hoping the older woman would take the hint. When she didn't, Leah added, "Would you be able to shelve the books on the gray cart? I didn't have time yesterday."

Mags startled as if she'd forgotten where they were. "The books. Yes." She grasped Leah's hand and squeezed. "Say no more. It's done. And if you need anything at all, let me know. I'm *here* for you."

Leah smiled, because how could you not? "Thank you. Now, let's get some work done. No time like the present."

"Oh." Mags's hand went to cover her mouth, and her eyes grew red again. "That's what he used to say."

Did he? Leah supposed it did sound like something he'd tell her. *You're starting to look your age. Go work out or something. No time like the present.*

She made a mental note never to use the expression again.

"Want me to find a vase for those flowers, dear?"

"Huh?" Leah followed Mags's gaze to the bouquet. "Oh. Sure. And you know what? Let's put them on the check-out desk. That way everyone can enjoy them."

"Always so considerate." Mags grinned at her and accepted the flowers, but she lingered in the doorway still.

Leah glanced at the clock on the wall. This day was slower than a snail in molasses. "Was there something else?" She had to get some work done, but maybe it was only fair to indulge those who needed to dwell on Neil's demise today of all days. Wasn't that the least she could do as his widow? After all, it wasn't Mags's ribs he'd fractured. Twice. He *had* been a great principal.

"No." Mags blinked her watery eyes a few times. "I'm all right. You stay strong, you hear?" And with that she left.

Leah reached for her coffee mug and drank deeply, burning off every taste bud in the process.

To Leah's credit, she kept it together the whole day thanks to the kids. Their curious minds, day-to-day conundrums, and unapologetic opinions were warm turquoise oceans to dive into, forgetting the world above. Plus, they couldn't care less about her late husband. To them he'd been an adult in a sea of other adults who told them what to do and how to behave. To them, he was lost to the past already. As he should be. Heck, the sixth graders had never even met him.

To be so lucky.

But now she was home again. She parked on the right side of the garage because Neil's sedan still sat in its spot to the left, and she made sure to bring the mail straight to the office and not leave it on the kitchen counter. *I've tried to tell you—each thing has its place. I refuse to live like some fucking hobo.* Some habits die hard.

The itinerary for her ticket to Seattle still sat on the printer, and she eyed it warily as if it had appeared there by magic. Her fingers twitched. To rip it or not to rip it? No, her therapist was right; it was time. A quick trip before Hannah came home. She'd manage.

She snatched the papers up and took them with her back to the kitchen. She'd need to get a suitcase down. Where did they keep that weird attic key again? It was always Neil who'd gone up there.

Leah stood in the middle of her kitchen, island at her back, surrounded by cabinets and drawer banks. Her mind prodded each space, testing them. It wasn't with the cooking utensils.

Not in the junk drawer. She was about to check the cabinet in the foyer when her cell lit up next to her hand. *Hannah.*

"Do you have any idea where we keep the attic key?" she asked by way of greeting.

Hannah chuckled. "Hello to you too. And I think on the top shelf in the bathroom closet."

Ah, that's right. Next to where Neil kept his gun safe. That's why she'd never gone close. She didn't want to remember those times, but her treacherous mind conjured thoughts that bounced like skipping rocks, testing the dark surface to find a weak spot.

No. Not today. He was no longer here, and neither were the firearms.

Leah cleared her throat. "How are you, hon?" she asked, moving on to safer waters. "Ready to come home?" She toed off her flats and made her way into the living room. One of the throw pillows was askew at the end of the chaise, so she picked it up and tucked it back into its corner. There —better.

Hannah was a sophomore at the University of Mass-achusetts, working hard to become a veterinarian. Her finals were done and aced, but she'd stayed in Amherst with her boyfriend, Chase, while he finished up his thesis.

"Yeah, about that..."

Leah froze right as she was about to sit down. Straightened again. "What?"

Hannah sighed. "Look, before you say anything... I have this opportunity, okay, that everyone thinks I'd be stupid not to take."

"Who's everyone?"

"And it's only for the summer, but I've always wanted to travel more, and—"

"Hannah."

"I know I said I'd be home, but Chase really wants me to

come. I have enough money, and this could be my last chance before I graduate."

Leah sat down at the edge of the couch, steeling herself. "Start from the beginning please."

"Chase is going to Brussels for the summer. He has an internship with some animal rights lobby organization, and he wants me to go with him."

"But you have a job here."

Hanna was quiet for a beat. "I already told them I can't do it this year. They'll find someone else."

"But..." Leah pinched the bridge of her nose. *But what about me?* she wanted to say. Eight days. That's what the calendar on the fridge promised. Her reward after Seattle. "It sounds expensive," she said instead. "And without a job..."

"Grandma gave me some money." Hannah's voice was low and quick, brushing past the words.

"She did what?"

"I told her I wanted to go, and she offered me some money."

"You told *her*..." Leah's jaws clamped shut. Jealousy wasn't a good color on anyone.

"Mm-hmm."

"How much?"

"She said she'd always wanted to summer in Europe, but that it was too late for her. She insisted."

"How much money, Hannah?" The room was suddenly too hot, that stupid gray blouse clinging to Leah's back.

"Five grand."

Leah sagged back in her seat. "Five... She gave you five thousand dollars? No strings attached?"

"Do you have to get all weird about it? Yes, she gives me money sometimes. I'm her only grandchild. Maybe she appreciates that at least one person in the family calls her regularly."

Leah ignored the stab. "And now you're going to Europe?" A dry chuckle forced its way up her throat. "I haven't seen you since Christmas." Ugh, she hated how whiny she sounded. But the words were already out.

"Mom."

"No, it's your life."

"Mom, I'm really sorry. But Chase needs me there. It'll be too hard to be on separate continents."

"Is that what you think or what Chase thinks?"

"Both of us. Jeez."

A long silence stretched between them. Longer than the physical distance between Leah's Chicago suburb and her daughter's apartment in Massachusetts.

Leah blinked against the late-afternoon sun cutting through the plantation shutters. It was so much easier pretending things were fine when Hannah was here. And now she wouldn't be.

"You could come out this weekend," Hannah said finally, the excitement of an epiphany in her voice. "Yes, that's perfect. I'll fly you out Friday, we'll hang, and you can help me pack."

Oh, the sweet child. "I can't. I'm going to see Mom, remember?" It would be hard not to bring up those five thousand dollars, but she'd have to try since the point of the trip was making amends.

"You're actually going this time?"

"I bought a ticket."

"Good for you."

"Well," Leah mumbled after a long moment, "it's not like anyone is here to stop me anymore. And I should apologize while there's time. Tell Mom the truth." Then as an afterthought, "I wish you'd come with." Thoughts of her past in the Pacific Northwest always jostled Leah's equilibrium. It was an undefined tremor at the earth's core that broke open cracks to another world and forced glimpses of it upon her. Some good, some bad. All bigger and brighter than what she'd lived since. Would it even be possible to reconcile the two?

"Oh, Mom."

Leah waved a hand in front of her face as if Hannah could see her. "No, I know."

"You're a strong, independent, forty-year-old woman." Hannah chuckled. "You can do this."

"Almost forty-one."

"Whatever. I'm proud of you."

Leah rested her head against the cushion and closed her eyes. "You know today is the anniversary, right?"

Silence. "It's only been a year? Feels longer." Hannah's voice was clipped.

"Do you miss him?"

"Fuck no."

"He was your dad."

"I don't have a dad."

Leah didn't have the energy to argue. Maybe Hannah was right to look at it that way. It seemed to work for her.

"You should forget about him too, Mom. Move on. I don't know how you still live in that house."

"Is that why you're not coming home?"

"What? No."

Leah wasn't convinced. Seeing your dad throw your mom down the stairs at the tender age of nine was bound to leave marks. "I'll miss you. A whole lot."

"I'll be back before you know it."

What choice did she have? Leah forced a smile. "So, Europe, huh? What places do you think you'll see? Tell me everything."

Leah hadn't left Chicago since she'd toured colleges with Hannah, and that time they'd driven. Plane travel? Not since her honeymoon. Sea-Tac Airport wasn't as confusing as O'Hare, but she still didn't fully exhale until she sank into the driver's seat of her rental car and closed the door behind her.

"I'm going to take five," she whispered to herself, a cue she'd learned in therapy that allowed a moment's stillness to center a frazzled mind. With each breath, the stress of the day drained off her. She was solid underneath. It was a miracle every time because that hadn't always been the case.

Traffic was light even for a Friday night at 9 PM, so it only took her forty minutes to get into the Eastside suburbs where she'd grown up. Nothing looked the same, and not only due to the waning light of day. If not for the 520 plotting a straight line to her destination, she might have gotten lost. Redmond had more than doubled in size since she was there last. Even far up Avondale—a road that used to be a pathway to nowhere—there were now subdivisions and businesses.

Leah viewed the changes with growing interest. She'd spent the first twenty years of her life in this corner of the country, but with Neil, she'd had to cut the cord. Their life was in the Midwest—he'd made that crystal clear. Driving the familiar old road now was like rediscovering a derelict building that had morphed in both shape and size from the ivy taking over. She glimpsed the masonry beneath the green, and the potency in the recognition surprised her.

Her mom's house was located in the back corner of a subdivision that was well past its heyday. There were signs of effort here and there—fresh paint on one split-level home, a porch added to another, a cherry-red front door on a third—but most were still dressed in the drab camouflage palette of the 1970s and showed little evidence of owners who prioritized curb appeal. The canopy of evergreens didn't help, rendering everything in night-time shade. It had been a bright and bustling place when Leah grew up, kids running all over, all day long, but now the swing sets sat rusty, only dreaming of a child's touch.

"They're probably in bed," Leah muttered, as if to console the abandoned playground.

She made the turns without having to think—so odd to know intimately a place that no longer knows you—and pulled into the driveway a few minutes later. Her childhood home and the three neighboring ones stood out in the mishmash of seventies construction since they were the first four built here by at least fifteen years. Each lot backed onto Cottage Lake and sported a large two-story home with a deep wraparound porch in the front and a deck in the back. The slight elevation they were on gave a stately impression—noble rulers to their smaller minions below.

The Brady house was a shade of blue that over the years had turned leaden, but unlike the neighbor's flat gray sibling, Leah's childhood home still held on to its original beauty. With white corners and window trim to contrast the siding, the house stood out amidst the untamed landscaping.

Leah frowned. Normally, the yard was impeccable with mulched flowerbeds, trimmed shrubs, and seasonal flowers adding splashes of color. Though who knew what normal looked like these days? She hadn't been back in so long.

She opened the car door and stepped out into the pine-crisp June evening. Warm cypress and lilacs. She inhaled deeply, hand still on the car as if she needed steadying against the onslaught of memories the scents invoked. Bare feet on cedar needles, flashlights in a tent, hide-and-seek.

The sky was a kaleidoscope of colors over the lake behind the house, but evening crept closer by the minute. With one last pat on the car roof, Leah closed the door and made her way up the path to the front door. She deliberately left her suitcase in the car. She hadn't told her mom she was coming, and after all this time, it would be foolish to presume she was welcome.

Echoes of the past rang through her mind. Mom had thought Leah too young to marry, too naive to commit, too inexperienced to know for a fact Neil was the one for her. They'd fought fiercely. Repeatedly. It was the only time in her life Leah remembered something *she* did eliciting in her mom a response beyond moderately fond, everyday parental engagement. Attention and expectations were usually reserved for her older sister, Alison, who was carted from one activity to the next as soon as her *potential* became obvious. Which was fine with Leah. What middle child isn't okay with playing second fiddle?

In response to her mom's novel attention, Leah had done the only thing that seemed logical at the time. She'd eloped and moved to Chicago. Neither one of them had attempted to mend the rift, and by the time Leah mistakenly ordered chocolate cake instead of vanilla for Hannah's first birthday and learned the dire consequences of that from Neil, she was already so far removed from her past, all she could picture Mom saying was "told you so."

They'd had meager contact over the years, and as soon as Hannah was old enough, she'd more or less taken over all communication with her grandmother, but now it was finally time to change that. If Mom wanted to gloat about how she'd been right all those years ago, Leah could take it. After a year in therapy navigating a treacherous climb from rock bottom up, she was confident she'd be able to say she was sorry. Sorry she didn't listen. Sorry she was too proud. Sorry for running away and being a shitty daughter. Sorry for attaching herself to someone like Neil. She only hoped her mother would listen.

Lost in thought, Leah stumbled over the edge of a paver but caught herself on the porch railing. She cursed under her breath and grimaced as pain shot from her toe up her shin.

"Calm down," she muttered, stepping onto the wooden deck. She looked up to face the shadowed corner where the doorbell was, but the sight that met her made her freeze. What on earth?

Across the door, like a garish forgotten Halloween decoration, was a large X in yellow tape. POLICE LINE, it said. DO NOT CROSS.

TWO

ALISON

"It's not often one of these homes becomes available. A yard this size so close to downtown? Unheard of." Alison Brady smiled at the young couple in front of her. They already had starry eyes over the property in Seattle's Magnolia neighborhood. "You could bike to work, Mark. And the elementary school is excellent and within walking distance."

The woman—Charlotte—grasped her husband's arm. They were pregnant with their second child and moving up from California. Money wasn't an issue. The offer was as good as a sure thing, but making her clients excited was like a shot of espresso straight into Alison's bloodstream. She pictured them staying up at night, making plans, dreaming big. It's what made her one of the most sought-after realtors in the greater Seattle area. If she could improve the clients' experience at all, she would.

"If you have some time, I'd like to show you Discovery Park. It's right around the corner. Miles of walking trails, gorgeous views, playgrounds, a lighthouse..."

Charlotte laughed. "You're like our own magical house fairy."

That was a new one. Alison grinned. "I truly want you to be happy here." She turned and pointed in the direction of the park. "It's a few minutes that way. We'll take the car today, but you can walk there once you move in." The language was strategic. Let them picture it a done deal. She knew they wouldn't be the only bidders, but often those who wanted it the most ended up the winners. Alison would make it happen this time too.

They'd just started driving when a call came in over the speakers—415 area code. It had to be Gladys Malone's office. Alison had been interviewed by the prolific media maven a while back for an Entrepreneurial Women magazine feature in conjunction with the fundraiser she was spearheading for Stepping Stone Foundation—a women and children's shelter. They'd gone back and forth with publishing dates. Perhaps it was finally set.

She glanced at the couple in her backseat. To pick up or not to pick up? Gladys wasn't Oprah but still a big deal and known by many West Coasters. It couldn't hurt to flaunt the connection as a way of further reassuring Mark and Charlotte they were in the best of hands.

"Sorry, I have to take this. It'll be quick." She put the call through on speaker.

The news was good, and she could tell by the look Mark and Charlotte exchanged when she hung up that it had been the right decision. She had this one in the bag.

As soon as she dropped her clients off at their hotel, Alison pulled out her phone and started returning calls. Traffic was a beast downtown with all the construction in South Lake Union, and she cranked the air conditioning on high to keep her cool, both literally and figuratively. Her assistant, Peter, was supposed to have forwarded her the Queen Anne property paperwork, but he'd let that slip again. She should start utilizing

Bess, her office manager, more—give her more of the meat and have Peter do the back-end stuff. He wouldn't like it, but she needed the business to run smoothly.

The office was empty when she finally got there. It was past noon according to her Fitbit. Everyone would be out to lunch. She should eat too, but there was another client meeting at 1 PM, and she still had to draw up the offer paperwork for Mark and Charlotte. A protein bar from the shared pantry would have to suffice.

Alison was deep into the contracts when an instant message appeared on her monitor. She tried to ignore it, but two others followed in rapid succession.

"What now?" she muttered through her teeth. Tyler knew she didn't have time for chit-chat during the day, but lately that hadn't stopped him. Her husband was between jobs and burdened with more free time than he (or she) could handle.

Ding! *When will you be home?*

Ding! *I'm making chili.*

Ding! *Are you still mad at me?*

Alison was still mad. Though to be fair, this was no longer a flaring emotion when it came to Tyler but a constant state that needed little kindling to swell and stir beneath her skin—the sight of his old tennis shoes next to her suede ankle boots, a soda can left on the kitchen table, his timid snoring. She couldn't even remember what they'd fought about last night, but she did know she was glad she had to leave for a conference tonight so she'd get a break. This was her busiest season, and he didn't get it. And chili? She almost reached for the antacids in her desk drawer at the thought of it. He knew she had a sensitive stomach.

Ding! *Let me know if there's anything you need me to do this afternoon.*

Ding! *Anything from the grocery store?*

If he didn't get a job soon, she didn't know what she'd do.

How hard could it be with every tech company in the western hemisphere squeezed into a few square miles?

Her private cell rang in her purse, interrupting that line of thought. He never stopped! She kicked the bag further under her desk and smoothed her brow with her fingertips. There'd been a time when his easy-going, fly-by-the-seat-of-his-pants approach to life was endearing. The way he'd drop whatever he was doing to make her happy, how easy he was to please...

For their first wedding anniversary, she'd panicked and bought him a knitted sweater. In mid-July. He'd worn it around the house every evening that week, insisting it was perfect with the thermostat lowered a few degrees. She smiled at the memory, twisted the gold braid on her right ring finger that had been his gift to her that day. Maybe they should see that marriage counselor again—Dr. Wezniak. Then *she* could hold Ty accountable for getting his life back on track, and Alison could go back to being his wife instead of his minder. She made a mental note to schedule an appointment.

She closed her eyes for a moment, willing her pulse to slow, then she erased the snarky response she'd started to type and wrote instead: *Lime seltzer would be great. Thanks. Home to pack in a bit. See you then.*

After a moment's hesitation, she added a kiss emoji too.

The front door to the office jingled, announcing her next appointment. Inhale on a count of four. She rose, smoothed the front of her slacks, and squared her shoulders. *Three, two, one.* Out into the hallway she went, heels clicking against the tile.

"You must be the Dhawans." She smiled warmly at the couple in front of her and extended her hand. "I'm Alison Brady—we spoke on the phone. Ready to find your dream home?"

· · ·

Later that afternoon, Alison had her suitcase open on the ottoman in their walk-in closet and she was paying it full attention, ignoring Tyler's downturned brows by the door. "I've told you before—I must attend these conferences if I'm to have any chance at nominations for the NAR awards. The networking, the leads... It's indispensable." She folded two skirts into one bundle and placed them into the bag.

"But you've been working so hard lately, hon. You're gone all the time. I was looking forward to hanging out." Tyler's voice turned up at the end. Hopeful.

Alison paused what she was doing and gestured in the general direction of their home office. A tired wave. "This trip has been on the calendar for over a month, Ty. Would it hurt you to look at it once in a while?" Damn, that came out more patronizing than she'd intended. She stood and brushed a wayward strand of her auburn hair off her forehead.

He nodded slowly, lips pursed, jaw tight.

That expression was the worst. Like she'd failed him. She walked over to him, placed her hands on his chest, and used his T-shirt to pull herself into his space. He was still in good shape underneath the saggy casuals. Still smelled like her Ty. Like home. "Sorry, that was... Sorry. I'm just stressed."

It took a moment, but then the tension across his shoulders eased, and he placed a kiss on her forehead. "But why?" He leaned back, brows knit. As if he really had no idea. "Business is great. You're great."

"Only *because* I work hard. Maybe in a couple years, if I'm able to hire one or two junior agents, I can take a step back, but until then..."

Her phone beeped with an email notification, and she held up a finger as if to pause Tyler while she checked it. "You've got to be fucking kidding me," she muttered while scanning the lengthy message.

"What?"

She stepped away from him, her eyes widening in exaspera-tion. "Everything. I have to do *everything* myself. This is the third time in two weeks Peter's fucked up the broker agreement. The clients need to sign those documents, and they shouldn't have to contact me to get them." She shook the phone to under-score each word then inhaled deeply. "Now I'll have to run by the office on my way to the airport. Everyone's already left for the day."

"Can I help?"

"No, I'll do it." She pushed past him into the bathroom and grabbed her hairdryer off its hanger. "Dammit."

"You're going to give yourself an ulcer. It's just work."

Alison came to a halt. "*Just* work?"

Tyler stared at her for a long moment, something indefin-able moving behind his steady gaze, but he didn't respond.

She let his silence hang above them while she continued packing, knowing any moment now he'd apologize, say he understood. But as she tossed the hairdryer into her bag, Tyler turned on his heel.

"I'm gonna go for a jog," he said, walking away. "I guess I'll see you Monday."

Tyler's abrupt exit chafed against the back of Alison's mind as she finished packing. She dropped her suit jacket on the floor while trying to fit it into the garment bag, bumped her knee into the corner of the ottoman, and chipped a nail on the zipper when she closed the bag. Her insides were like the liquid in a level swooshing from side to side, trying to stabilize.

Get it together. There was so much to do, so much to think of. She didn't have time for Ty to throw temper tantrums about her job. Her wanting something wasn't a bad thing. Ambition wasn't ugly; it was necessary. It made her better, made them better. People wanted to work with her, she and Tyler got invited places, she'd made a name for herself (and for him by association), and she liked that. She thrived on seeing her name in *Top Agent Magazine* or hearing it announced at conventions. It was her lifeblood. Better than sex.

She left the house in a huff of righteous indignation, now even more stressed since the driver she'd called was the honking kind. Smaller tip for him.

She gave him her office address and hoped the papers she needed were at least still on Peter's desk so she wouldn't have to search for them. She'd scan and email them from Atlanta as soon as she arrived. It would be fine.

"I'll be right back," she told the driver at the curb. "Don't go anywhere."

She ran into the building, keys in hand, and crashed straight into two police officers on their way out as she rounded the corner. One of them reached out to steady her when she threatened to stumble backwards.

"So sorry, ma'am," the other officer said. "You all right?"

"Oh no. I'm sorry," Alison sputtered, drawing up straight. "I didn't expect anyone to be here." She made to start moving, and the officers parted for her. "Have a nice evening." She walked on, willing her heart to stop racing. She still had time. Everything was still fine.

"Ma'am," the first officer called after her.

No, no talking. Maybe if she pretended not to hear. She reached the door, was about to put the key in the lock.

"Ma'am, you dropped this."

Alison pressed her lips together and turned, and now the officer was coming toward her, something aloft in his hand. What were the police doing here anyway? Did they want to buy a house?

He held out the pen she usually kept tucked in an exterior pocket on her purse.

"Thanks." She reached for it, but when she tried to take it, he didn't immediately let go.

"Wait a minute," he said, staring at the pen. "Brady Real Estate. Are you by chance Alison Brady?"

Well, how about that? Maybe he *was* in the market. Alison decided she could spare a minute after all. She launched her biggest smile and extended her hand. "That's right. How did you hear about us, Officer...?"

"Durham."

"Officer Durham." She waited for the usual—a referral from someone who'd been pleased with her services; one of the TV ads; that article where she had been featured. But instead he called his partner over.

"Hey, Nate, this is Alison Brady," he said in a low voice.

A look passed between them, and then something shifted in their expressions. For a brief moment, Alison was certain they'd caught her breaking a dozen laws.

"Is there somewhere we can sit down and talk, Mrs. Brady?" Officer Durham asked.

"It's Ms. Brady. I've never taken my husband's last name." Alison's forehead twitched. She had papers to collect and a plane to catch. Not to mention an Uber waiting. "Now isn't a good time." She reached into her purse and pulled out a business card. "Here. If you give the office a call Monday, my assistant can put something on the schedule."

"We're here on official business, ma'am," the other officer said. "We'd appreciate a moment of your time."

Alison looked from one to the other. "Have I done something wrong? Am I under arrest?"

"No, of course not."

Alison unlocked the door and reached for the handle. "Then you'll have to excuse me. If I don't leave now, I'll miss my flight." She opened the door and was halfway across the threshold when Officer Durham spoke again.

"Ms. Brady, please."

Oh, for God's sake!

He continued in a hurry as soon as she turned, as if sensing she was about to lose it. "There's been an incident with your mother."

Her gaze snapped to his face, another objection catching in her throat. She shifted her weight from one foot to the other. "What do you mean?"

"We've been trying to reach you and your sisters." His expression softened. "Ms. Brady, I'm very sorry to have to tell you this, but your mother has been found dead."

THREE

LEAH

Leah's brain wasn't working. She stared at the yellow tape, caught between the urge to still ring the doorbell and to run away.

"Can I help you?"

She flinched and spun to find an older woman peering at her from the neighboring yard, straight-backed and alert but with hair like white cotton balls.

"Are you with the police?" the woman asked. "You don't look like police."

As the woman spoke, Leah saw past the aged exterior and found someone she'd once known well.

"Mrs. Carlisle?" She took a couple of steps toward her old neighbor. "I didn't know you still lived here."

The woman's face crinkled, first in confusion then in recognition. "No, could it be?" She paused for a moment before a wide grin bloomed on her face, erasing ten years at least. "Leah Brady, as I live and breathe." She approached Leah with open arms and reached her in a few long strides. She laughed and hugged her close. "My, my, my. Aren't you a sight? I barely recognized you, girlie."

"It's been a long time."

"Oh, Malcolm will be tickled to see you. He's out tonight, but—"

"Mrs. Carlisle..."

"Oh, we're both adults now—call me Ruth."

"Ruth." Leah gestured toward the door. "Do you know what's going on with the tape?"

Ruth sucked in a quick breath. "But of course, you're here because of Marion." A shadow crossed her face as she squeezed Leah's hands. "Terrible business that. I'm so sorry."

"Sorry for what?" Leah took a step back, freeing herself, and glanced again at the tape. "Has something happened? Where's Mom?"

Ruth's hand went to her heart. "Oh dear." She looked about her as if hoping for rescue. "Oh my."

Leah blinked, thoughts churning. What was she not getting? "Is Mom okay?"

Ruth's face fell, and she covered her lips with her fingertips as if to nip emotion in the bud. "This is not—" Her voice broke. "You'd better come inside with me, dear. Let's get you something to drink."

Leah held on to the glass of amber liquid in front of her as if letting go would send her floating away into the abyss. Her heartbeat thumped sluggishly in her ears, and she stared unseeingly at Ruth next to her in the Carlisles' kitchen. Surely, she'd misheard. Mom wasn't dead. She took a sip, letting the whiskey burn proof of life down her throat. Then another. Ugh, she hated whiskey.

"What happened?" she asked eventually, her voice barely a whisper.

Ruth wrung her hands, her gaze out the window toward the lake. "Oh dear. Well, Malcolm was on his morning walk. With the dogs. We have two labs now—old Barney who you used to play with died many years ago—and they walk a good two miles every morning come rain or sunshine.

"Well, yesterday, he wasn't able to call Sheppy back. He tried for a long while, but the darn dog had got hold of something in the wind down by the shoreline. Malcolm followed her and that's when he saw it. Her," she corrected. "Marion."

Ruth put her hand on Leah's arm, but Leah barely felt it. Her skin had gone clammy.

"Of course, he didn't know it was her at first, but when he got closer, he saw her washed up in the reeds. Real peaceful looking he said. It was a terrible shock. Not what you expect on a Thursday morning."

Leah shook her head slowly. This made no sense. They must be mistaken. She'd come all this way and she still had unfinished business. Besides, Mom had been a great swimmer. How could she have drowned? Had someone...? She shivered as the word *murder* skittered across her mind. What was going on?

"Oh, that's right, I have the number for the officer who was here," the older woman said, rising from her chair. "Said to call if we thought of something that might be important." She held out a note to Leah, who took it. "Do you have a phone? Or you can use the landline."

Leah stared at the digits on the paper as they swam together into abstract shapes. A phone. Did she have a phone?

"Leah, dear?"

"Huh?"

"Do you want me to call?" Ruth's chin trembled. She probably regretted stepping outside in the first place. "I think we should let them know you're here. I gave them Alison's number —I had one of her business cards from several years ago—but I know she's busy..."

Alison. Oh my God, Alison and Jillian. And Hannah! Leah

stood abruptly. The whiskey was a warm lead weight in her belly. She couldn't just sit here—she had to do something.

"It's okay. I'll call," she heard herself say from afar. And she must have, because thirty minutes later, two uniformed police-women showed up to erase any doubt she was still holding on to. No mistake had been made. Her mother was, indeed, dead.

FOUR

JILLIAN

It was too early to wake up. Jillian rested her hand over her phone on the nightstand as if that would prevent it from going off again in five minutes. She'd slept well, only not enough. As usual. This side of her thirties definitely felt closer to middle age than she was okay with. Next to her, someone stirred. A long, lithe arm draped across her waist, and then a puff of warm air swept across the skin between her shoulders. Jillian opened her eyes and smiled to herself.

"You don't have to get up yet, do you?" a voice mumbled against her neck. "It's still dark out."

Jillian rolled over, forcing her companion to scoot back. What was her name again? Audra? Aubrey? Something like that.

"I've got places to be." Jillian hesitated for a moment then reached out and traced the bridge of the woman's nose. In the murky room, she appeared a grayed-out shadow against the white hotel sheets, the freckles Jillian remembered from last night only visible in her memory. Audra/Aubrey kept her eyes closed, but Jillian thought she saw the corner of her mouth twitch.

The phone alarm sounded again.

"You can stay if you want. Sleep in." Jillian reluctantly pulled her hand away then sat up and silenced the phone. "Thanks for, you know. It was a good time."

"The best," Audra/Aubrey mumbled into the pillow. "You've got my number."

That's right, she did! Jillian smiled as she grabbed her phone to check. She glanced briefly at the missed-call notification that popped up—why on earth was Alison trying to reach her? As usual, her oldest sister hadn't bothered to leave a message. Well, too bad, so sad—she'd have to wait until Jill got back home then. She probably wanted to brag about another achievement or award or something anyway.

Jillian opened the contact list and scrolled through *A*. There she was—Audrey Guinness. It was coming back to her— how she'd joked that Audrey's last name was unfortunate since Jillian didn't drink. Not the best pick-up line perhaps, but it had worked.

In the contact entry was also another nugget of information that was useful; by *city* she'd entered *Dublin*. At this point, all the hotels she stayed at blended into each other. Some had better beds, others nicer bathrooms, but essentially, they were all the same. She'd stopped beating herself up about losing track of where she was—especially before the first cup of coffee of the day. Occupational hazard, she supposed. But now she knew where she was—Dublin, Ireland.

Jillian moved through the room as quietly as she could, wheeling her overnight bag into the bathroom. She still had an hour before she had to report to work—plenty of time, and that's how she liked it. After a warm shower, she dressed and re-emerged into the bedroom in her uniform.

Audrey was awake now, sitting up in bed with the comforter pulled up to her neck, checking her phone. Her eyes widened when she spotted Jillian, then a wide grin broke out on her face.

"You didn't tell me you're a pilot."

"You didn't ask." Jillian smirked and picked up the keycard from the dresser. "I'll leave this here. Give them my name when you check out—the room is paid for already."

Audrey's eyes narrowed. "Um, Jill... This is a bit awkward, but I don't think you told me your last name."

Jillian moved over to the bed and sat down, folding one long leg beneath the other. It was getting lighter out, a sliver of daylight peeking through the gap in the curtains to reintroduce those lovely reddish hues to Audrey's hair she remembered from the pub last night. She reached out and wrapped one of the curls around her finger.

"It's Brady."

Audrey grabbed Jillian's wrist and pulled her closer. "Stay a while?"

A heavy heat spread low in Jillian's belly. It would be so easy to crawl back into Audrey's arms and sink slowly into heavenly oblivion. But it was better this way. Not that she hadn't tried relationships before, both with women and men—they just didn't last. It was her job, or her addiction to freedom, or her short attention span. Not for her.

"I can't." She placed a quick kiss on Audrey's lips, then pulled away before she could change her mind. "I have a flight back to New York in less than two hours."

"Fine." Audrey pouted, but there was still a twinkle in her eyes. "Fly safe, I guess. Look me up if you're ever in town again."

Jillian was already at the door. "Will do," she called over her shoulder.

She might.

Or she might not.

· · ·

"Ladies and gentlemen, we are starting our descent toward New York's JFK Airport. The local time is 10:30 AM, and the weather seventy-eight degrees with an abundance of sunshine. We hope you've enjoyed your flight with us, and that we see you again soon. Cabin crew, please prepare for final approach."

Jillian turned off the intercom and rested her head against the seat back. It was good to be home. The trip had only been five days, but it stretched much longer in her mind. She knew exactly what she'd do with her three days off—catch up with her roommates Dixie and Carla, go to the park, cook food from scratch. That was it.

"Home sweet home," she said to her first officer, Colum. Her grin reflected in his sunglasses.

"For you maybe. I don't get to Raleigh until tomorrow."

"Still." The sun glinting off the city's metal structures far below never failed to fill her with a sense of elation. She'd moved here at seventeen, ready for anything that wasn't Seattle. Never looked back. Sure, she lived modestly and shared her space, which, at thirty-seven, you could reasonably frown upon. But it worked for her. She was gone so much of the time anyway; it didn't make sense to pay full rent for some studio apartment in Brooklyn when a room in a brownstone on the Upper West Side was up for grabs.

"I might not bump into you for a while actually," Colum said. "I've requested domestic only for the time being, since the baby is due soon."

Jillian's anticipatory fantasies of her imminent homecoming dissipated. She tried to conjure them again but failed. "Right," she said instead. "Is it your second or third again?" Her voice sounded tight. Somehow Colum had ended up her first officer three times in the past year—an almost unheard-of thing when there were over 800 possibilities. She should have known the answer to her question.

"Third." Colum scrambled to pull up a photo on his phone

that showed his very pregnant wife and two daughters in front of a swing set. "Want to know what it is?"

"That's not ne—"

"It's a boy."

Jillian pressed her lips together and nodded. Tried to make it into a smile. "Congratulations."

She ran through the landing procedures, hoping that would keep them both occupied enough that the subject would be forgotten. Most of her colleagues were older and past the baby years, so usually she didn't have to contend with reminders about her biological clock at work. Among friends was another story. She hated to admit it, but there were people she'd known, and liked, since college who she avoided nowadays because they'd never shut up about their spawn. That's why Dixie and Carla were so great—voluntarily childless and not swayed by either infants dressed up as pumpkins or the cuteness of a three-year-old teaching their sibling the ABC song.

Because Jillian was.

Every time someone mentioned babies, her chest hurt. Every time she got Christmas cards in the mail with photos of happy families, she wanted to cry. It was out of reach for her. It didn't fit with her lifestyle. She didn't want to get married and move to the suburbs. *She'd make a terrible mother.*

And yet, there were moments.

Jillian pulled back on the throttle, and the wheels touched the ground.

She wouldn't think about it anymore. This was New York, city of opportunity, home. Her life was rich already. Think of all the freedoms she'd be giving up if she had Colum's life. Domestic flights only? No thank you.

Jillian was met by a dozen yellow roses and a card on the kitchen counter when she entered the house, carry-on in tow.

She smiled. This was a tradition Carla had started several years ago if ever they weren't home when Jillian returned from one of her longer trips.

Hey, Goose, Staying upstate tonight, the card said. *Catch up tomorrow. Sushi and Cheetos, baby!*

The flowers infused the whole space with a crisp, fruity scent. Jillian inhaled deeply as she walked over to the fridge to grab a bottle of water. On the top shelf was another note, this one in Dixie's bulky handwriting: *Got you stuff for chicken parmesan ;)*

Man, those two knew her well. She closed the fridge door and stretched. The sunlight streamed through the windows and slanted off the wooden floors. Somewhere, a car honked, and another responded in kind. Ah, home.

She hauled her luggage into her room to unpack—a quick venture since she never took much with her. She smiled when she pulled out the shirt she'd worn at the pub with Audrey. She'd whooped her butt at pool—her and everyone else who was game to play. The flirting across the table, the brogue voices surrounding them, the easy banter, a possible promotion on the horizon... It had been a great night.

In a moment of nostalgia, Jillian brought the shirt to her face only to quickly pull it away. Nope. Nothing but sweat and smoke. She shook her head at her folly.

Maybe she would text the lovely Audrey after all. They'd had a good time—if nothing else, they might at least be friends. Friends were the icing on *her* cake. All she needed.

She returned to the kitchen, blinking against brightness that promised a perfect day for the park. A nap, a cup of coffee, and a good book. That was all she wanted.

Except as soon as she turned on her phone to see what she'd missed while in the air, it wouldn't stop dinging. She groaned. If it was work, she would not call back. She'd earned these days off. Ever since they'd approached her about the check airman position, they'd been looping her in in a way they never used to. It was flattering, of course, that they thought her qualified. Her dad hadn't made that transition until he was well into his forties. Still, higher pay aside, she wasn't yet a hundred percent sure she wanted the responsibility.

With a sigh, she glanced at the screen. Eleven missed calls. She frowned and unlocked it. Why were both her sisters calling her? Alison had finally left one voicemail, but it was only a curt "Please call me back." Jillian scoffed. How about, *"Hi, Jill, it's been too long. How are you?"* It always baffled her how her bull-dozer of a sister had ever managed to grow a successful business that relied heavily on customer service. Did people no longer care about niceties?

So, who to call back first? She hadn't spoken to either of her sisters in months, so it was about time. Growing up, she'd been closer to Leah, but as soon as Leah married and had Hannah, everything had changed. Over the years, talking to her had become something akin to treading through mud. Like she no longer cared about Jillian's life at all.

A flare of something sour poked beneath Jillian's ribcage. *No one cares,* echoed inside her head. *No one cares about you.*

But then she spotted the roses again, and, if she thought about it, Hannah was a pretty great niece. And poor Leah who was widowed now. It was coming up on a year soon, wasn't it? Or had the date passed already? A burst of shame sent heat to Jillian's face. She really should make a greater effort there.

She grabbed a yogurt from the fridge before she dialed Alison's number. This had better be good.

"Where in the world are you?" was Alison's greeting. "I've been calling you since last night."

"I'm home now. Just got back. How's it going? It's been, what, eight months?"

"Are you sitting?"

"What?"

"You should be sitting. That's what they told me."

Jillian didn't like the tone of Alison's voice. High strung was normal for her, but there was something else behind it this time. Something strained. "Okay." She sat down. "Who's 'they'?"

"The police came to see me yesterday."

"The police? Are you in trouble?"

"Stop interrupting me." Alison's voice shook. "Sorry." She sucked in an audible breath.

"Ali, you're scaring me. What's going on? Is Tyler okay?"

"It's Mom," Alison spit out. "Mom's dead."

In that split second of the words entering Jillian's ear, swirling their way into the intricate pathways of consciousness, the room went stark white around her. An image of their mother from years ago forced its way into her mind, where she was standing in the kitchen with her back to Jillian and her sisters. It had been one of those rare moments where all three girls had been getting along, and Marion had whipped her head around to look over her shoulder. She'd opened her mouth at first, as if she might on impulse ask them to quiet down, but then she'd watched them for a long while, as if she'd forgotten what she was doing. Jillian had never thought of that moment before, but it was the first thing that came to mind upon finding out their mother was gone. The parted lips, the straight shoulders, the pensive gray of her eyes. It might have been the only time Marion had looked directly at Jillian with something other than disdain in her eyes.

A chill skated across her skin. She hadn't talked to her mother since last summer. Her schedule was so different from everyone else's, and she was often in different time zones. It was hard to find the right time. Or so she told herself. "How?" she asked.

Alison was quiet for a beat. "The neighbors found her in the lake."

Jillian sat up straighter. "What?" She'd expected a heart

attack or cancer or something, not this. She should have known better—their mother would never voluntarily go to the doctor. She was the champion of pulling herself up by the bootstraps and expected everyone around her to do the same. In second grade, Jillian had once gone a whole week with a broken wrist, not daring to complain, until her PE teacher had called home.

"But she was a great swimmer. That doesn't make any sense. Did you talk to the police?"

"Yeah, they're calling it a suspicious death at the moment. We'll know more after the autopsy. I'm heading over to the hospital in a bit."

"But... So..." Jillian tried to find the right words, the right thoughts. "Wait, they think someone killed her?"

"That's not what I said. They don't know what happened."

"Did she go for a swim and get confused?"

"I don't know. They said she was dressed though, so probably not."

"So maybe an accident? Like she fell in?"

"Jeez, Jill, I said I don't know."

Jill clamped her lips shut at Alison's exasperated tone.

"Sorry." Alison sighed at the other end of the line. "I'm just... Anyway, you should probably come out here."

"Of course."

"She was your mom too. I'm not going to do everything with the police and the funeral and the house and whatnot myself." Alison's voice cracked. "This is an extremely busy time for me. I'm supposed to be in Atlanta right now. I don't have time for this."

"Ali, chill. I said yes."

"Oh." A flustered breath came over the line. "Well, good. Just so we're on the same page. Never know where you're off to with your job."

"They'll accommodate me. Death in the family." Her

tongue stumbled across the word. She had to ask. "And you're sure—I mean, they're sure it's her?"

At that, Alison remained silent for a long while. When she finally spoke, her voice was softer and more sympathetic. More like Leah's. "They're sure."

Jillian blew out a slow breath. Steady now. "I'll try to get out there tomorrow. When's the funeral?"

"As soon as they release the body to us. Depends on how long everything takes and what they find."

Body. Jillian shuddered.

"Oh, another thing." Alison was back to sounding like she was talking to a client. "I think it would be in everyone's best interest if you called Leah instead of me."

"She doesn't know?"

"I don't even know if I have her current phone number."

Jill wished that wasn't the state of things, but Alison was right again; Leah might not even pick up for a Seattle area code on the caller ID.

"Fine, she's tried to reach me anyway. But if we're all going there, you two will have to get your shit together. I'm done playing the middleman."

FIVE

LEAH

Leah jolted awake in an unfamiliar room at the first hint of daylight. After trying, and failing, to reach Jill and Hannah the night before, she'd lain awake counting bubbles on the popcorn ceiling until well past midnight, and it took her a minute to get her bearings. Crocheted throw across the back of a wooden chair near the window, floral curtains, potpourri in a bowl next to a family portrait in the IKEA bookcase.

Ruth. The police. Being offered the guest room.

Mom was dead.

She pressed her fingers into her eye sockets until it hurt. She'd come for closure, and she was too late. Not that she'd been under the illusion life was fair for quite some time, but this? This was jab-to-the-gut, spit-in-your-face ridiculous.

A strange snort escaped Leah's nose. Oh, Mom. A well of regrets inside threatened to overflow, but Leah didn't have time for that right now. She had to try to get ahold of Jill and Hannah again before the appointment at the morgue for identification. Alison she'd have to seek out in person; there was little chance of her older sister picking up the phone, considering they hadn't been on speaking terms for years.

Before the thoughts pulled her under, she sat up, pushed the comforter aside, reached for her phone, and dialed her daughter's number.

Hannah cried all the tears Leah couldn't. Thank goodness her daughter was normal where Leah was not. A blog she'd consulted once after Neil had died suggested too many years of compartmentalization trained your brain to have atypical emotional responses to traumatic events. So basically, that was her. Faulty wiring.

"She wasn't even that old," Hannah lamented. "How can she be dead? I talked to her last week."

"We don't know the details yet, sweetie." It wasn't the full truth of course, but she'd do anything to protect her daughter from more distress. The police were investigating it as a suspicious death, but they'd know more after an autopsy. "I'm still trying to reach Jill. I'm hoping she can coordinate your flights. If not, I'll pick you up any time. Just let me know when."

Hannah's sobs subsided, and she blew her nose long and loud. "But, Mom, we leave for Brussels tomorrow. You know that. The tickets are non-refundable."

What? Leah almost stomped her foot where she stood in front of the window in the Carlisles' guest room. "You can't be serious. You're still going?"

Hannah sniffled. "Grandma wouldn't care one way or the other if we were there. She wanted me to travel. At least this way we're doing something I know she'd like."

"But…"

"You'll have Aunt Jill and Aunt Ali—you'll be fine. Chase only has me."

But you're the one they like, Leah wanted to say. Instead, she bit down hard on the inside of her cheek until she tasted blood. If that's how it was going to be, she might as well prepare.

But how on earth would she get through this without her daughter?

. . .

After hanging up with Hannah, Leah tried Jillian yet again, still only getting her voicemail. Dejected, she wrapped the throw from the chair around her and headed out into the hallway instead.

Trying not to make a sound, she tiptoed across the carpet, sneaking a quick glance over the railing to where Ruth and Malcolm were busy cooking breakfast. She'd have to go down there eventually. Make conversation. Accept more condolences. Nothing she wasn't well versed in, but she was so tired of it. She wanted to talk *to* Mom, not about her as if she wasn't there. "Except she *isn't* here," Leah mumbled, her throat achy.

Preoccupied with how best to avoid a lengthy conversation over breakfast, she pushed open the door to the bathroom without much care—and barreled into it nose first when it stopped short midway against the backside of a half-naked man.

"Ow! Fuck!" he yelped, dropping whatever he was holding into the sink with a splash, while Leah sank into a crouch, covering her nose in her hands. She groaned, eyes watering.

"Dammit," the man muttered. Then: "Hey, are you okay?"

"Nuh-uh," Leah managed through a groan. She was very far from okay. Mom was dead, she was in a strange house, she'd just inadvertently assaulted someone in their bathroom, and now her nose was probably broken.

"Here, let me get you something."

Leah sensed more than saw the man opening the door to a tall cabinet in one corner of the bathroom. She leaned back against the doorjamb and focused on the throb of her heartbeat between her eyes. Something warm and tangy coated her lips.

"Oh shit, that doesn't look good." The man returned, pressing a towel into Leah's hands. "Tilt your head back."

"I'm scho schorry," she mumbled, blinking against the bathroom's original fluorescent tube lights.

A square-jawed face, half covered in shaving cream moved into her line of vision. Was that…?

He broke into a wide grin. "Gotta say—of all the ways I've pictured running into you again, none of them involved a bathroom assault and a nose bleed at seven o'clock on a Saturday morning. It's good to see you again, Leah. But what the hell are you doing here?"

Oh my God, it was. "Andrew?"

He let out a deep guffaw, which, paired with the white suds on his chin, evoked more than a fleeting resemblance to a fit Santa.

"Ruth didn't tell you I stayed over?"

"They were out with the dogs when I got in."

"Well, it's a long story," Leah mumbled, looking away. "But you? What are *you* doing here?" She pushed herself up to standing, removing the towel from her face. "I mean, I know it's your house—your parents' house—but—"

"Whoa there." Andrew grabbed her hand and moved the towel back in place. "Still bleeding."

His hand was warm and calloused against the back of hers. She swallowed, suddenly more aware of his state of undress. "You too," she said.

"What?"

She gestured to his cheek. "You're bleeding too."

"Oh." He turned to the mirror. "Right. I cut myself when you barged in." He dabbed at it with another towel. "Eh, it'll stop. *'Tis but a flesh wound.*"

And like that, Leah was back in junior year of high school, watching *Monty Python's Holy Grail* with the gang in Carl Loomis's basement. She and Andrew stared at each other for a long moment, then they both started laughing.

The heaviness that had kept Leah up most of the night slid off her like a shadow at noon at the pitiful sight of the two of them in the bathroom mirror. Between bouts of laughter, she took in the tall, solid shape of her childhood friend—the way his eyes now crinkled when he smiled, the salt-and-pepper seasoning at his temples, a torso that—it had to be said—belied his four decades on earth. He'd done both cross country and swim team in high school. Clearly, he'd kept up his active lifestyle.

"What?" Andrew asked.

"Huh?" Leah's gaze snapped back up to his. Her cheeks heated. "No, sorry, it's the... my nose. It's making it hard to um... look up." God, she was a terrible liar.

He took a step closer. "Can I see it?"

She removed the towel and closed her eyes as he gently prodded her face with his fingertips. She winced when he touched a particularly sensitive spot.

"Sorry." He grimaced as if he felt it too. "I don't think it's broken. You do look a bit like someone used you as a punching bag though."

Leah flinched at his words, her heart seizing. She took a step back.

He doesn't know. Just a joke.

She gave a small shrug, forcing a smile to her lips. "Anyway, I should probably let you get back to... whatever you were doing."

His eyes narrowed briefly, but she kept her face even until he smiled again. "It's sort of become a tradition that I do my morning run out here around the lake and have breakfast with the parents on Saturdays. You caught me during my post-shower shave." He smirked.

"Again, so sorry."

"How about we both get ready, and I'll meet you downstairs for coffee? I think I'm owed some kind of explanation here." He shook his head in bewilderment. "Leah freaking Brady."

His expression triggered the peal of another chuckle. "Andrew freaking Carlisle," she countered.

Once upon another time, in what felt like another universe, he'd been her first kiss.

From the look on his face when she came downstairs a little later, Leah knew Ruth must have filled him in as to why she was there. Gone was the lighthearted merriment, replaced instead with what could only be described as pity.

"Why didn't you tell me?" he asked after they'd sat down outside on the deck.

"I said it was a long story." Leah stirred her coffee. A buttered scone sat on a plate next to her mug.

Andrew frowned toward the house. "I mean, obviously my parents should have called me right away when it happened. Not that we talk every day, but you'd think that..." His voice trailed off. "I'm really sorry. Marion was a nice lady."

Leah choked on her coffee. Of all the ways to describe her mother, "nice lady" was definitely not the first thing that came to mind. Capable, driven, and intelligent? Yes. Beautiful and intimidating? Sure. But nice? Mom was cordial at best, and only when circumstances required.

"Thanks," Leah said. "It's all very confusing right now." She looked out across the lake, hoping he'd take the hint.

For a while they sat in silence, then Andrew cleared his throat. "So, it's been a while."

"Half a life."

"Well, you look... great. I mean, all things considered..." He sighed.

Leah smiled. "You too."

"Again, I'm really sorry."

"Thanks, Andrew." She broke off a piece of her scone and chewed slowly. The scent of his cologne mingled with cut grass and coffee. Such grown-up flavors. She had to admit, this new version of the boy she'd once known intrigued her.

"I like that you still call me Andrew," he said after a long moment. "Everyone else calls me Andy."

"Oh yeah?" Leah smiled and put her mug down. "Andrew," she said, lengthening the vowels. "It suits you better than Andy. Especially now. Andy is a little, I don't know..."

"What?"

"Juvenile."

His hearty laugh broke through the quiet yard. "And I'm all man now, is that what you're saying? I'd better let my friends know."

The hard core in Leah's stomach softened again. She had so many questions for him all of a sudden, but the timing was terrible. No need to add to this already complicated situation... Besides, she had to leave for the morgue soon.

"How's your nose?" he asked, interrupting her thoughts. "Does it hurt a lot?"

She waved off his question. "I'm fine." Her gaze caught on the way his lips pulled sideways as if he was skeptical of her answer, then wandered up to his eyes. Something in them made her stay there a moment too long. "Um... but I should get going. It's... Mom..." She pushed her chair back and stood.

He did the same. "Okay. But if there's anything I can do, let me know. Do you have your phone? I'll give you my number."

She wouldn't call him, but she entered it all the same, not wanting to be rude. She was passing through, that was all. Their lives were twenty years different, and her mother had just died.

"It was really good to see you," she said as he walked her to her car. "Could have been better circumstances, but..."

"At least you'll think of me when you look in the mirror later." He smiled.

"What? Oh. Yeah." She brought her fingers to her nose. A purple bruise was already growing underneath her left eye. The skin on her upper arms prickled. Perhaps that was her lot in life

—always associating men with contusions. She'd better leave. Now.

After waving to Ruth in the window, she got in the car and grasped the steering wheel hard. Then she sped off, trying but failing at not looking in the rearview.

Andrew freaking Carlisle.

SIX

ALISON

"Everything okay?" Tyler glanced at Alison when she entered the kitchen after calling Jillian. He poured a second cup of coffee and handed it to her. She took it without comment and swallowed a scalding mouthful, ignoring the burn.

"Yeah, Jill will try to get here tomorrow. Today I have to get over to the hospital, then I have a showing after lunch, and since I'm missing Atlanta, I can make the Portland dinner tonight instead. I'll only be gone one night."

When Tyler didn't respond right away, she looked over to find his eyebrows bunched together. "What?"

"I wasn't asking about today's schedule; I was wondering if *you* are all right?" He came toward her, head cocked to the side. "Your mom died. Unexpectedly. If you need a break, people will understand."

His words tugged at the safety pins that had been holding her together since she'd received the news. She turned away. "A break is the last thing I need. And I already cancelled a showing this morning. Mom would be the first to tell me business as usual." She put her cup in the sink and ran the tap. For a moment, the swirl of the water down the drain made her light-headed, and she closed her eyes, gripping the edge of the counter tightly. She was fine. She was *fine*.

Okay, she wasn't entirely fine.

"Maybe you could come with to the hospital?" she said, her back still to Tyler.

"Of course. I thought that was a given."

"Oh. Well, good."

"Leave in ten?"

Alison exhaled through her nose. "Yeah."

Alison walked through the parking garage, the lobby, the elevator vestibule, and the waiting room clutching Tyler's hand and doing her best to pretend she was someplace else, but the hospital smell permeated every surface. Surprisingly, the morgue was no worse than the other areas. She'd pictured an abundance of metal and tile with stark lights illuminating the cold space, but instead, they were shown into a gold-toned office, where three chairs in muted blue were set out before a desk. Nondescript floral prints adorned the walls.

"The counselor will be with you shortly," the aid said. "Can I get either of you a glass of water?"

They declined, the aid left, and the room was overtaken by silence. How had she gone from packing for a business trip to this alternate universe in less than twenty-four hours? Had she been a good sleeper, she'd be inclined to ask Tyler to pinch her so she might wake up from what seemed more like a surreal nightmare than reality.

No sooner had the thought crossed her mind than the door opened, and a deep voice said, "Right through here."

Alison turned, a greeting on her tongue, but it caught in her throat when not one but two people entered. The grief counselor came first, taking up a significant part of the doorway, but behind him was her sister. The sight made her tongue release from her palate with a soft *tick*.

"Leah?" She forced her hands to remain still across the folds of her impeccable royal-blue sheath dress. "You're... here."

Leah froze, one foot across the threshold, her purse strap slipping down her shoulder with the sudden inertia. "Ali?"

The two stared at each other until Tyler got up with a "Well, this is a surprise." He pulled Leah into a tight hug then held her at arm's-length. "We didn't know you'd be here. When did you get in? And what happened to your face?"

"Um... long story." She gave a dismissive wave in front of what looked like a painfully darkened eye socket then turned to Alison. "I went to the house after I got in yesterday. I didn't know. Mrs. Carlisle told me..." Her voice trailed off.

The counselor had followed their sparse exchange from behind the desk, and now he cleared his throat and suggested they all take a seat. "Do I understand the situation correctly— the two of you had not arranged for a joint meeting?" He looked between Alison and Leah.

This dream was growing more surreal by the minute. Leah was here? Now? After all these years? And she hadn't bothered telling anyone? "We had not," Alison said, not hiding the pique in her voice.

"But it's fine, right, hon?" Tyler added, placing his hand on her arm.

"It's okay with me," Leah said, leaning forward to peer around Tyler at Alison. "I didn't have your number. I was going to look you up afterwards when I was sure that... You know."

"Afterwards..." Something clenched painfully between Alison's ribs. "But if you didn't know then why are you in Seattle in the first place? A little far from home for you, isn't it?"

"Ali..." Tyler cautioned.

"No, I want to know. Am I supposed to believe it's a coincidence?"

Of course it was a coincidence. Leah didn't have a sinister bone in her body. But Alison still said the words and ignored the foul taste they left on her tongue, because with Leah that had become a knee-jerk reaction borne by old hurts.

Leah shrank back at Alison's insinuation. She looked as if an explanation was on her tongue, just beyond reach, her eyes shifting sideways as she flushed red, but all that came out were a few disjointed syllables, at which point the counselor cut in, coming to her rescue.

"Okay," he said, raising his hands off the desk. "Perhaps this conversation can be tabled for now to let us focus on the present moment?"

Both Leah and Alison snapped their attention to him.

"Sorry," Leah mumbled.

"Yes, fine." Alison leaned back out of Leah's sight. There'd be time later for answers.

"First of all, I'm deeply sorry for your loss," the grief counselor said, his tone softening. He went on to explain in detail what would happen during their meeting and to offer resources should they need more support afterwards.

"We don't actually get to see her?" Alison asked when he was done talking. How was she ever going to be convinced this was real?

"No, all identifications are done by photo. In fact, I have it right here." He gestured to a clipboard with a print pinned to it upside down. "When you're ready, you may look at it. Take all the time you need."

Oh. Alison swallowed, resisting the urge to reach for it that instant. If this was a mistake, if it wasn't Mom, she wanted to know now. Then again if it was...

She squeezed Tyler's hand tighter and looked at her sister, but Leah was staring blankly ahead, offering no help.

"Will she look very different? Because of the drowning?"

Alison asked. She'd looked it up in a weak moment, regretting it instantly.

The grief counselor consulted his papers. "While she was found in the water, the cause of death wasn't actually drowning, which means there was no submersion. So, to answer your question, you'll find her features intact, though we all do change somewhat in death."

"She didn't drown?" Leah asked, eyes alert once more. "Then what happened?" She shifted in her seat, angling her legs toward the door as if getting ready to sprint off at an undesirable response.

"We'll know more once the toxicology report is complete, but preliminary findings suggest she may have succumbed to an opioid overdose."

Alison pulled her hand from Tyler's. "That's absurd. Mom wasn't a druggie." She crossed her arms over her chest. Now surreal was veering into the bizarre. "Your findings must be wrong."

"You're right, there's no sign of addiction." The counselor exchanged a look with Tyler.

Alison recognized something in them—a warning perhaps, a heads-up. Tyler straightened.

"Then what?" she demanded. Why was no one saying things that made sense anymore?

Suddenly, Leah let out a strangled noise before covering her mouth with one hand. "Are you saying it was intentional? Mom killed herself?"

Alison balked. "What? Why on earth would you say that? She'd never."

Leah blinked at her. "Well with the lake and an overdose... And she recently gave Hannah five thousand dollars."

"So?"

Instead of responding, Leah looked to the counselor, who inclined his head.

"Death by suicide is the coroner's preliminary conclusion," he said. "Again, I'm very sorry."

"No, that's ridiculous." Alison stood up. "I saw her a few weeks ago and she was fine."

"You said she looked older," Tyler inserted.

"The fuck Ty? Whose side are you on?" Out of the corner of her eye, Alison registered Leah flinching at the curse, which only intensified her anger. Why was Leah *not* swearing? Shouldn't they all rage at this ridiculous notion that their mother—their strong, opinionated, intransigent mother—had chosen to end her life?

"Okay, maybe—" the counselor started, but Tyler spoke over him.

"Come on, hon, sit back down. We'll figure this out." He reached out and touched Alison's arm. The connection was what finally pierced through the red haze and made it settle enough that, after a moment's hesitation, she allowed him to guide her back into her seat. *For now*, she thought. She'd have more to say about this later. She was just getting so tired from the strangeness of it all.

Tyler looked to Leah, who nodded. Compliant as always.

"All right," he said. "Sorry about that. I think we're ready now."

The June sunlight was so bright and cheerful it offended Alison when they emerged at ground level again a little later. She wanted to scream at it, rage at the people enjoying it, close her eyes and hide to make it go away. Or maybe she should stare directly into the sun? Would that burn off the image of her mother's lifeless features from her inner vision?

"Yes, that's Mom," Leah had said as soon as they turned the photo over. And somehow that, too, had offended Alison. At least give it a minute. See if it still rang true.

Unfortunately, one minute hadn't made a difference, and neither had ten or twenty-five. Leah was right.

"Now, will you tell us why you're here?" Alison asked when they reached the garage. Leah wouldn't get off that easily.

"Ali, come on," Tyler tried.

"No, I want to know. I haven't seen her in Lord knows how many years and then she shows up here the day after Mom *allegedly* decides life is no longer worth living." She turned back to Leah, surfing a fresh wave of aggravation. "Did you say something to her?"

"Ali, that's enough! She's your sister. You've both lost your mother. Please."

Alison glared at him, weighing her options. Tyler hardly ever raised his voice, but when he did, one had little choice but to listen. She stood down.

"She didn't know I was coming," Leah said, her voice the same soft cadence Alison remembered from their childhood. "I had... things I wanted to talk to her about. Personal things," she added as if sensing the follow-up question on Alison's tongue. She went on to explain the events of the previous evening, her shock, and her intention to get in touch with both her sisters as soon as she had confirmation. "Jill's phone's been off, and I should have guessed the police had already contacted you," she concluded. "That was stupid of me."

"I talked to Jill. And I *did* tell her to call you," Alison said, a pang of something suspiciously like regret shaving off the edge of her annoyance. "In case you thought I forgot."

Leah waved her explanation away. "It doesn't matter. Is she coming? We need to tell her about... this." She gestured toward the hospital.

"Tomorrow hopefully. And I can call and let her know what they said."

Leah nodded.

She'd aged, Alison thought. Not necessarily in a bad way,

but she was stretched out, more angular, skin almost diluted. The black eye didn't help. She'd been the cute one of the three. Jill was hot stuff, Alison more classically good-looking, and Leah the ringlet-headed doll. The flatness of Leah's eyes at the moment belied that epithet. She'd been through things—that much was clear. Neil's death must have been such a blow. Another pang in Alison's core as they reached her car.

"Okay, well..." Leah backtracked a few steps. "I guess I'll see you tomorrow?"

Alison sighed inwardly. Now there would be arrangements to make and she was already overbooked. The three of them together wouldn't make things *less* complicated. "Yeah, I'll text you once Jill gets in. Where are you staying?"

"Um... oh." Leah's face went blank. "I hadn't thought of that. I'll figure it out."

"Okay." Alison opened her door ready to enter but paused, the onward motion impeded by once-upon-a-time shared things —inside jokes, scrunchies, a love for Val Kilmer movies... However distant those memories, however great the chasm, Leah *was* her sister. She rolled her fingertips against the metal of the door then pressed her lips together briefly. "You know... we have a guest room you could use."

Leah's mouth opened on a short "Oh." She shifted her stance.

No, perhaps it was vain to think all these years of unraveling sisterhood stitches could be so easily mended. "Unless you'd prefer a hotel," Alison hurried to add.

But Leah only seemed to assess the offer a moment, then her shoulders rolled back, and her chin lifted. "No, that'd be great. Thank you."

How about that? Alison got in her seat and buckled with the same snap as after closing a house sale.

SEVEN

LEAH

There was no way Leah was going to spend all day at Alison's sitting around, but after a few hours at a mall in Bellevue, she made her way through the winding streets of her sister's neighborhood, bracing for impact. The Alison Leah had known growing up may have been opinionated, but she'd never bitten people's heads off like she'd done with Tyler earlier. Then again, it made sense that Mom's death had affected her the most; of the three of them, she was the one who'd been closest to her. The only one.

It was the first time Leah had ever set foot in Alison's home. She'd seen it in pictures on social media and knew it was valued in the several millions, but walking through the door, the first thought that struck her was how it's possible to spend your childhood with someone and still have no idea who they are.

They hadn't struggled financially growing up by any means —Dad was a pilot and Mom a professor of linguistics at the University of Washington, both decently paying jobs—but Alison had clearly reached another level of affluence.

"Sorry Alison isn't here." Tyler took Leah's suitcase from

her. "She's in Portland for the night. Some last-minute dinner she 'couldn't miss.'" His nose wrinkled.

Leah paused her stride. She would've never pegged Tyler for the bitter type.

"Sorry," he said, before she could ask. "It's probably a good distraction for her. I'm just worried—she works all the time."

Sounded like her sister. "She loves her job."

A wry chuckle. "I suppose."

The wide foyer opened into a sprawling two-story living room with floor-to-ceiling windows that Leah would have never been able to clean to Neil's standards. A rustic two-sided stone fireplace divided that room from the kitchen, which sported ten-foot ceilings, sleek gray cabinets, and open wood shelving with decorative dishes on display. Leah resisted the urge to run her fingers across the behemoth marble island. It was a magazine spread, not a home. Beautiful but cold. A house befitting Alison.

"Sorry," Tyler said again. "Don't get me wrong, I am proud of her for what she's built. But there has to be more, you know?" He pressed his lips together briefly, then waved his hand as if to erase what he'd said. "Anyway. Can I get you something to eat?" He opened the double-wide stainless-steel fridge and peered inside. "Or a drink?"

Leah's gaze found the breakfast nook at the other end of the room. Though "nook" was the understatement of the year. Her dining room back in Chicago wouldn't even have been able to accommodate the round trestle table. She swallowed. Here, she was the smudged IKEA glass in a collection of polished crystal. "Maybe just some water for now."

"Coming right up." Tyler busied himself fetching Leah a glass. "I have the basement guest room ready for you. If you need anything at all—food, drink, whatever—help yourself. The pantry is over there." He pointed. "Everything else is pretty self-explanatory. If you want to watch TV, there's one in your room, or you can use the one up here."

Leah followed him down the stairs to the walk-out basement. There were the standard staples—a pool table, a ping-pong table, a wet bar—but in another room beyond, Leah also glimpsed a small movie theater. What a life.

"There are clean sheets on the bed, fresh towels in the bathroom." Tyler turned the light on in a room that was bigger than Leah's master suite at home. "Instructions for the TV and the Wi-Fi password are on the nightstand."

At last Leah found her voice. "Thanks, that's very thoughtful. It's... really nice." She put her purse down on the bed. "Oh, do you know when Jill is landing tomorrow?"

"Afternoon sometime, I think. Ali said she'd get her."

Leah nodded.

"Well, I'll let you get settled. I'll be upstairs, but holler if you need anything, and I'm usually up by eight in the morning."

Leah thanked him again, and, once he was gone, she sank onto the bed, expelling a breath that held the tension of a thousand impressions. Alison was rich and she'd had no idea. Everything was so... perfect. Perfect house, perfect career, perfect husband. Compared to Neil anyway.

"Don't know why I'm surprised," Leah muttered.

Alison had always been the ultimate Brady sister. Straight As, always in the right clothes, popular with both peers and their parents, juggling work and school ever since freshman year in high school. If Leah had a quarter for every time her mom had asked why she wasn't more like Alison, she'd perhaps be able to afford a place like this too.

She yanked open the zipper of her bag and pulled out the T-shirt she always slept in—the UMass one Hannah had given her the first time she'd come home from college. She still couldn't believe Hannah wasn't here with her. Nothing was right anymore. Mom was dead, Hannah was on her way to Europe, and here she was, staying in Alison's guest room of all places. Was it only yesterday she'd come here to take charge of her future with Mom only to have to confront the fact that no such thing existed? Only yesterday someone had pushed her onto this moving train toward the unknown? Because she already couldn't wait to get off. If only she knew how.

EIGHT

ALISON

It might have been a blessing in disguise after all, not being able to go to Atlanta. Alison had been trying to get one-on-one time with the top broker in Oregon for months now, and last night he'd been at the same venue in Portland, and he was just as interested in her proposal to collaborate on buyer recruitment as she'd known he'd be.

Her Tesla glided smoothly north on I-5, sunroof open, and, without thinking, she hummed along to some song or another she recognized. As if nothing was amiss. When the music ended, she turned off the radio and checked her phone. Jillian's flight wouldn't land for another two hours so Alison was in no hurry. There was plenty of time to prepare mentally for the Brady sister reunion. In hindsight, she'd had time to mull over inviting Leah to stay. Not that it wasn't still the right thing to do —everything was just so complicated. So... emotional.

Would the reason they were here matter? The suddenness of it all?

No sooner had the thought crossed her mind than a whiff of that stale, chilly hospital air forced its way into her nostrils. It swept over her like a tidal wave that threatened her balance.

She grasped the steering wheel tighter to correct an inadvertent swerve then rolled down her window, not caring that it would mess up her blowout.

Not now, not now, not now.

She fought an impulse to close her eyes. Save crying for the funeral. That face in the photo hadn't borne much resemblance to Mom anyway. If she tried hard, she could almost forget what she'd seen. Forget her mother was gone. Forget the questions that still needed answers. Forget the predictable balance of things was now skewed. The tug of war that had spurred her on since childhood—Mom on one side urging focus, strength, perseverance, and Alison on the other alternatively yielding and exerting herself—that game was over. She was left standing. Alone.

She sniffled and closed the window, something sharper rising through her chest with edges and corners that made her jaw set. If she was to believe the hospital, Mom had thrown the game. That was so unfair, especially in light of the fundraiser Alison was working on for the Stepping Stone Foundation. She'd pictured her mother in attendance, perhaps even uncharacteristically moved by what Alison had done with the knowledge of which they never spoke. They might have had a moment, forged a bond. As equals. But apparently, Mom had been in a hurry to leave.

Another car passed her and pulled in too close ahead. Alison honked and hit the gas, reveling in leaving it behind with noiseless speed. She didn't have time for these *feelings*. She didn't have time for any of it. Mom had made her choice and Alison wasn't it. And now she had her sisters to deal with too.

She gave a gloomy chuckle.

Alison was in the middle of a text thread with Bess when a shadow fell across her corner near baggage claim at Sea-Tac.

She'd proposed via email that Bess take on a few more administrative tasks, and now Bess had requested a sit-down to discuss this expansion of roles more in depth. Alison was both annoyed with and proud of Bess for doing so. It showed spine.

"Working hard as usual, sis?" Jillian's melodic voice cut through the buzz of conversations around them, and Alison startled. She'd completely lost track of time.

"I've been looking for you for a while. Didn't realize hide-and-seek was on the table." Jillian smirked, but it wasn't an angry one.

Alison tucked her phone into her purse and stood. "Work's busy." A quick embrace. "It's good to see you."

"You too." Jill's brow lowered slightly. "Did you hear anything new?"

Alison didn't have to ask what about. "Not since yesterday." She had called to inform Jill about the likely cause of their mother's death after the meeting. Jill had been quiet for a long moment before asking in her detached way, "Why would she do that?" like she was asking why their mother had put up Jack-o-lanterns in May or decided to buy a motorcycle. Her ability to keep emotions reigned in on command was at times both enviable and extremely irritating. But Alison knew her little sister had her reasons.

"Okay," Jillian said now in that same unruffled way. "Hopefully tomorrow then." She gripped the handle of her bag and gestured toward the escalators as if waiting for Alison to lead the way.

And since the last thing Alison wanted to do was talk about anything related to hospitals, autopsies, and causes of death, she dropped the subject for something more innocuous.

"You're looking well," she said as they started walking.

It was true. Even in plain skinny jeans and a soft white button-down blouse, her youngest sister looked like a million bucks. Something about those lanky, modelesque legs and square shoulders maybe. She towered at least four inches above Alison's five-six and did so with a natural grace to her movement that immediately made people assume she'd been a dancer, when in fact it was Alison who'd toiled away at the barre for years. Jillian couldn't dance to save her life, but she sure could enter a room and draw everyone's attention.

"Thanks. You too."

Right... Nearing forty-three, Alison was on a regular Botox schedule, she'd cut carbs almost entirely, and she owned more creams and lotions than a mad scientist. Whenever she looked in the mirror these days, the problem areas vastly outweighed the rest. Jillian probably didn't even have to brush her hair in the morning. Her understated earrings and that ever-present charm necklace looked better on her than Alison's diamond ear studs and Tiffany necklace ever could.

Alison shook off the sneaky green feeling when they got to the pay station. So what if Jillian was the more striking sister? She didn't even own a car. Or a house for that matter. This was Alison's turf. She got her receipt and turned, stumbling over Jillian's small wheelie bag.

"Is that all you brought?" she asked, after regaining her balance. Her own suitcase for the one night in Portland had been twice the size.

"Tricks of the trade." Jillian winked. "Plus, I'm not staying long."

"Well, you'll have to be here for the funeral, and we have no idea when that will be yet."

"If it gets delayed, I'll leave and come back. Are Leah and Hannah staying with you?"

"I don't think Hannah is here." Alison fished her keys out of her pocket. Where did she park again?

Jillian slowed. "What?"

"Leah didn't mention her." Maybe she could summon the

car? It was a feature she still hadn't tried. It seemed irresponsible somehow, driverless cars.

"Ali." Jillian stopped. "How do you not know?"

Alison turned, the frustration over the complexity of the garage shifting to her sister. "Why is this a thing now? I saw Leah briefly yesterday, then I've been away. I came straight from Portland." She glanced at Jillian, who was doing a perfect impression of their mother at her most irked. "Meetings," she explained.

Jillian pursed her lips further. "Right. So you weren't avoiding Leah or anything?"

Alison's neck heated. "No, I legit had to be there." *Legit.* She cringed at her word choice.

"Mm-hmm."

"Whatever," Alison muttered. "I offered her a place to stay, and she should be there when we get home."

Ah, finally, there was the car. Alison sped up and practically threw Jill's bag into the trunk. They circled the exit ramp in heavy silence.

Once on the expressway, Jillian turned toward her. "Don't you think it's time?"

Alison didn't take her eyes off the road. "For what?"

"To bury the hatchet. So she didn't come to your wedding. That was eight years ago."

"That's not all there is."

"Then what? I've seriously never understood this. Leah is the most harmless person."

Alison scoffed for lack of a better response. If she was honest, she could no longer recall every transgression she'd once found Leah guilty of. Yes, there was the wedding—that was the big one. Who doesn't go to their own sister's wedding? Then there were all those unreturned phone calls, how hard she'd made it for Alison to see Hannah when she was little, the lack of enthusiasm for any of Alison's career achievements. Leah didn't care about her, didn't even pretend to be happy for her. Period. So why make an effort?

"You didn't go to Neil's funeral."

Of course she'd bring that up. "Because—"

Jillian put her hand up. "I don't care why. But try to look at it from both sides. A wedding and a funeral. You've both let the other down."

"She barely even talked to me at Hannah's graduation. Remember? She was glued to Neil the whole time. And I sent a card for the funeral." Alison swallowed, hands slick on the steering wheel. As much as she liked to pretend otherwise—had convinced herself Leah preferred she didn't go—that nipped at her heart still. Neil had been her sister's husband. What would it do to her if Tyler died suddenly? A lump formed out of nowhere in her throat. No, sending a card had been an inadequate response, and she knew it.

"All I'm saying is—Marion's dead. There's just us now."

Alison's hackles rose again, pushing conscience away. "Do you have to call her that? Why can't you say *Mom* like a normal person?"

Jillian's gaze burned a hole into the side of Alison's head for a long moment before she turned away. "All I'm saying is, play nice."

The urge to push further was overwhelming, but Alison held her tongue. Like it or not, she knew why Jill was the way she was. She'd play nice. It was a role she knew well.

NINE

LEAH

Leah was pacing the living room when the garage opened, and a car pulled in. She wrapped her sweater tighter around her. The air conditioning was set too high for any normal person, especially those with images of their mother afloat in the shallows stuck in their head. Leah hadn't been able to get warm since she'd found out.

She sat down on the couch, gaze fixed on the door, then stood and moved back to the windows.

"They're your sisters," she whispered to herself. "Get it together."

Jillian was first through the door, bag in hand, but she didn't immediately spot Leah.

"I don't know why you don't use my discount when you travel," she was saying. "I've offered before."

Alison entered behind her. "You're not the easiest person to get a hold of, you know. Besides, I can write off business travel."

Jillian set her bag down and pulled a hand through her shoulder-length brown hair. "Just saying."

They were halfway to the kitchen when Leah cleared her throat. "Hi."

Alison stopped dead in her tracks, hand to her chest. "Oh my God, you scared the bejesus out of me."

"Leah!" Jillian flew across the room and wrapped Leah in her arms.

Leah returned the surprising hug. They'd never been close, but unlike with her and Alison, there was no animosity behind it, only three years in age difference. It didn't sound like much now, but when one is eleven and the other fourteen, that could be an eternity.

When Jillian let go, she laughed. "You always were the best at hiding in plain sight. I'll never know how you keep that still." She jerked her chin back. "What the hell happened to your face?"

Leah's hand flew up to her eye. She kept forgetting. "I walked into a door," she mumbled, before Alison approached them, face inscrutable.

"Hi again. Did Tyler set you up downstairs?"

Leah forced herself to meet Alison's gaze. "Yes. Thanks for having me."

"It's no problem."

"Still."

Jillian rolled her eyes. "Seriously, you two. Stop it."

"I'll let you guys catch up. I'm going to go unpack." Alison turned on her heel and disappeared up the stairs.

Leah's heart sank. No change there then, not even in light of Mom's demise. Despite opening up her home, Alison still wanted nothing to do with her. Not that she blamed her. She should apologize for everything. But what would she say? *I avoided you because I was a doormat, and I didn't want you to know*? How could she possibly explain in a way that would make sense, a way that didn't lay bare every crevice of her naive choices and their consequences when she knew how much Alison loathed weakness?

· · ·

The four of them sat at the round table in the breakfast nook, an assortment of boxes of Thai takeout scattered between them. Jillian was on her third helping of Pad Thai—where she put it all, Leah didn't know—and Tyler had polished off all the orange chicken with impressive speed once his attempts at conversation failed. Alison was busy saving the world, judging by her attachment to her phone. She'd barely touched her plate. The panoramic windows offered breathtaking views of a golf course.

For their tenth anniversary, Neil had taken Leah to a resort in Wisconsin where they'd spent three days in the most gorgeous setting. Neil had golfed every day while Leah read on the patio or visited the spa, and in the evenings, they'd had dinner at one of the restaurants and gone for walks. It was one of the best memories of her marriage—enough to remind her, at the time, that there might still be something inside Neil worth fighting for. They'd never gone back, and she'd never again made that foolish assumption, but this view still brought about a pang of nostalgia.

Leah moved her broccoli pieces to one part of her plate, the rice to another, and the chicken with cashews to a third, making sure they didn't touch. She'd pushed it around for fifteen minutes already, stalling for time so that maybe the others would leave and let her eat in peace without this knot in her stomach. She much preferred eating alone where no one could comment on greens stuck in her teeth or how loudly she chewed. Or, in Hannah's case, pointing out how little she ate.

Hannah.

Her sisters weren't happy Leah had come alone. As she'd predicted.

"She knows her grandma is dead, right? You did tell her?" was Alison's reaction.

Leah stabbed her fork into a broccoli spear and the tines made a loud squawk against the china. Her face scrunched together in discomfort, but before she had time to apologize, the loud melody of a phone interrupted her.

Alison pushed her chair away from the table with a curt, "I've got to take this," and disappeared into the family room only to return a moment later, now gesturing to the phone. *The sheriff's office,* she mimed. Leah stood, fork still in hand.

"Mm-hmm. Okay. What does that mean?" Alison sat down at the kitchen island.

"What are they saying?" Jillian whispered.

Alison put her hand up to silence her. "And you're sure about that? Uh-huh. I'll contact them tomorrow. Yes, thank you."

She ended the call and sat for a moment, staring down at the counter.

"What?" Jillian asked.

Alison looked up, her normally bright complexion suddenly pale beneath the carefully applied make-up. "As suspected, no signs of foul play, but"—she gnawed at her lower lip—a nervous tic Leah had forgotten plagued her older sister when they were little—"apparently Mom was recently diagnosed with lung cancer."

The word seemed to echo off the walls in the stunned silence that followed. Leah sank back into her chair. Tyler went to Alison's side. Jillian finally stopped chewing.

"She didn't tell you about the cancer?" Leah asked. "You didn't know?"

"Are you saying it's my fault?" Alison spat. "Because last time I checked, there's three of us."

"That's not what she meant." Jillian looked from Alison to Leah. "Right?"

"Of course not," Leah said, massaging her temples. This conversation was bringing on a massive headache. "But you were closest to her. If she was going to tell anyone, it would be you."

"Well she didn't."

"A cancer diagnosis could explain why she did it." Jillian shrugged.

"Maybe." Tyler turned to Alison. "Didn't you say she stopped returning calls a while back?"

Alison scoffed. "That was every other month with her."

"No, I remember. You'd been named *Greater Seattle Realtor of the Year*, and it was like two months before you got hold of her to let her know."

"Doesn't matter now," Alison said. "Clearly, she didn't want us to know."

"Mom keeping things to herself? How unusual."

Jillian's snide remark sparked another silence, but Leah's head was pounding now, and she didn't have the energy to call it out. The tension in the room wasn't helping. "So what do we do?" she asked.

"I can call the funeral home tomorrow," Jillian offered, perhaps to counter the acidity in her earlier comment.

"No, I'll do that—I've already talked to them." Alison typed something on her phone.

Jillian's eyes widened. "When did you have time for that?"

"I called them right after I spoke to the police on Friday." She glanced up from her phone. "I made a tentative booking for Saturday. In case."

Leah and Jillian exchanged a look. *Typical.* But also, thank goodness this would soon be over. One week to handle the funeral, the house, and everything else that came with this type of thing, and then she'd go back to the predictable confines of her own home. Jillian would head out on her next adventure, and Alison would be free to chase her next success without them here to cramp her style. She could do one week.

"Okay, fine." Jillian plucked a piece of leftover chicken from one of the takeout containers. "What about a lawyer?"

Alison made her way back to the table, seemingly placated by their lack of objections. "What about one?"

"Did she have one? Is there a will? What happens to the house?"

Alison's lips parted as if to answer, but she quickly closed them again.

"Maybe the Carlisles know," Leah said. "Or maybe there's a..." A wave of unease flushed over her. "A note."

Both her sisters stared at her.

"I can't believe I didn't think of that," Jillian said.

"I did." Alison had a sip of her wine. "The police searched the house. Nothing."

"But we should look again," Jillian said, new determination in her voice. "Who kills themselves without leaving a note?"

Their mother, that's who, Leah thought. She'd been eight the first time Mom had gone to one of her academic symposiums without telling them. She remembered, because as a pilot their dad had been away on one of his long hauls, so it had been up to Alison to babysit her younger sisters. Jillian had only been five at the time, but Alison had taken charge as if she was born to do it, so Leah had suffered no physical hardships, but not knowing where Mom was and why she wasn't coming home—that had made a lasting impression. Mom had swept back into the house Sunday evening, a smile on her face, and when Leah had dived into her arms, she'd actually held her for once.

"Now," she'd said. "Did Ali take good care of you?"

Leah had nodded, heartbeat too far up her throat to speak.

"I knew you girls could do it." And she'd patted Leah's shoulder and pried her off her lap.

Pride and relief had mixed with terror at the prospect of it ever happening again. Which, of course, it had. But she'd never complained.

"Leah?" Jillian asked. "You still with us?"

"Huh?"

"Nine AM tomorrow? House of horrors?"

"Do you have to call it that?" Alison asked, lips tight.

"Sure." Leah started clearing her plate, but Tyler, who'd kept to himself for most of the conversation, took it out of her hands. "There's ibuprofen in the hallway closet if you need it," he said out of the corner of his mouth. "I've got this."

It wasn't lost on her that in the midst of this family crisis, it was that small act of kindness that nearly brought tears to her eyes.

TEN

JILLIAN

It rained the following day, a steady downpour swayed by no wind as was so typical of the Pacific Northwest. Jillian cursed when she opened her blinds, and the expletive lingered in her subconscious throughout every mundane task of getting ready for a new day. She should have stayed in New York. She could be taking off for Rome this evening. God dammit!

Alison was in her home office looking like she'd been up for hours already when Jillian came down the stairs—coffee mug at hand, frenetically typing something on her laptop. No change there.

"Oh, hey, Jill," she called upon seeing her. "I spoke to the coroner's office and the funeral home. They need some paperwork signed so I'm heading there first and then to the office real quick. I'll have to meet you at the house."

Or we could stay here. "Fine."

"What's up with you?"

"Nothing." Jill forced a yawn. "Tired. Stupid rain."

Alison looked out the window as if she hadn't noticed. "Yeah, traffic will be horrible. I should head out soon. Can you make sure Leah is up?"

All Jillian wanted was some caffeine in her system, stat, but she continued down into the basement without grumbling. It was easier that way. She made her way through the large space and knocked on Leah's door. Waited.

"I'm up."

Leah's voice came from behind her, and Jillian spun round. She was on the small couch near the pool table, wrapped in a blanket, feet pulled up under her.

"I woke up early." Her eyes returned to the windows and what lay beyond. "I love the sound of the rain," she said. "It doesn't sound like this in Chicago. I'd forgotten about it."

Something in Leah's face made Jillian pause. In the gray morning light, her skin was almost translucent—like a faded Renaissance painting—and she was too still.

Jillian took a few steps closer. "Everything all right?"

Finally, Leah turned to her fully. "It doesn't make sense. Mom killing herself." She rested her chin on one of the cushions.

Jillian walked around and sat down. "She was sick."

"Recently diagnosed. She didn't even start treatment." Leah squinted. "Do you remember when her appendix almost burst?"

Jillian's eyes widened. "No."

"Yeah, maybe you were too little. I caught her doubled over in the kitchen, but when she saw me, she straightened, and she said nothing about it while we were getting ready for school. She went to work as usual. I only found out later that a colleague had made her go to the hospital."

"Sounds like her. God forbid any signs of vulnerability. The show must go on."

"You see my point then?" Leah asked. "She wouldn't give up that easily. I feel like we're missing something, but I can't put my finger on what."

Jillian nodded. "Maybe she'd changed?"

Leah raised a pointed eyebrow.

"No, you're right," Jillian conceded. "Could be it was her way of avoiding needing help though. Either way, we'll find no answers here." She stood, offering a hand to Leah. "Let's get this over with."

Alison had left without giving them her key to Mom's house, so Jillian waited in the car while Leah ran through the rain to get the one from the neighbors. She glanced up at the window that had been hers but found the curtains drawn. The fleur-de-lis-patterned fabric was one Jillian had picked out herself in seventh grade, hoping Marion would transform it into the same style drapes Leah had in her room. But after a few months, she'd resorted to hanging the material up using thumbtacks instead. It was better than seeing it in a pile on the office floor.

"Got it," Leah hollered outside. "Come on."

They ducked through the wet and onto the covered porch. June could be perfectly lovely here, yes, but it was just as likely to revert to March temperatures on a dime. Jillian pulled her hands into her shirtsleeves and shivered. She should have brought a sweater.

"Did we always get this much debris onto the porch?" Leah asked.

Jillian frowned at the dried pine needles and dusty leaves that littered the floorboards. It was messy. The broom Marion had always used to sweep the steps was in the corner, but with spiderwebs clinging to its bristles, it couldn't have been used much as of late. There were even footprints on the welcome mat, presumably left there by whoever had searched the house.

Leah unlocked the door, and they stepped inside. Jillian turned the hallway light on.

And there it was. The past.

"Wow." Leah toed off her shoes.

Jillian couldn't move. She'd spent her whole adult life

leaving this place behind—had almost succeeded—and yet...
"It's exactly the same," she mumbled. There was the storage
bench underneath the large mirror with a cracked corner. The
portrait of their dad in uniform next to a large aircraft. Mom's
scarves on the hook closest to the wall. The closet door that
wouldn't close all the way. Her throat felt dry. Maybe they
should wait for Alison. She could brush off the porch in the
meantime, get some fresh air. The rain wasn't so bad.

"It smells weird though," Leah said, moving toward the
kitchen. "Musty."

Jillian followed her, dragging her feet. "Smells like old
person to me."

"Mom wasn't that old."

Jillian shrugged, taking in the room. Same pale-blue valance
in the window, the stack of old Christmas cards in a tray on the
buffet, two checkered towels on hooks near the sink. She was
thirteen again, doing dishes. Doing them wrong. Either too
much soap, or not enough scrubbing, or taking too long and
wasting water. She'd objected to the criticism only that once.
They're cleaner now than before, aren't they? Marion hadn't
spoken to her again for several days. As if she didn't exist.

Leah had moved to the family room but was already on her
way back into the hallway when Jillian caught up.

"Do you see it?" Leah asked. She didn't wait for Jillian to
respond before she headed upstairs.

"What?" Jillian trailed Leah into their mother's bedroom.
The white coverlet was new, but everything else remained as
Jillian remembered it, down to the folded nightgown on the
stool in the corner. The one with small yellow flowers. A shiny,
black leather-bound book sat on top of it.

Leah dragged a finger along the top of the dresser and
frowned. Then she folded back the coverlet and the comforter
and turned to Jillian. "There are no sheets on the bed."

"So?"

"You don't think that's weird?"

Jillian considered this. "Maybe she tidied up before she—"

"No." Leah shook her head rapidly. "She didn't. This place hasn't been cleaned in months. I know—I used to do it weekly."

Jillian peeked into the bathroom. Neatly folded towels, spotless mirror, a fine layer of dust not only on the counter but also in the sink. Leah was right.

"But that makes no sense. Mom hated dirt. *Messy house, messy character.*"

"I think that was Dad's saying, not hers."

Jillian frowned. "Really?"

"Hello?" Alison's voice rang loud through the house from the foyer.

Jillian leaned toward the hallway "Upstairs," she called.

"All arrangements with the funeral home are set—Saturday 11 AM. We're allowed to pay our respects an hour earlier," Alison said without preamble, entering the bedroom where they were gathered. "Why are you guys in here? Ugh, smells like this place needs an airing." She moved to open the window.

"Wait." Leah's forehead wrinkled. "Something's not right—I can feel it."

Alison snickered. "Of course it doesn't feel right. Mom's dead and we're standing in her bedroom. She'd have a conniption if she knew we'd even opened the door."

Leah's face reddened. "Then why does this place look like a museum? How are you not seeing it?"

For the first time since she'd arrived, Alison stopped to really look around.

"I agree with Leah," Jillian said. "It's kind of spooky." Something was nagging at the back of her mind.

Alison didn't respond, but after a long moment she headed out of the room, down the hall. "Are you coming?" she called. "Let's check the office."

Jillian and Leah hurried after her, and together they entered the doorway to the central sanctum of the house. Jillian saw it clear as day in her mind. Walls lined with bookcases, the two overflowing filing cabinets—wooden ones with a roll top—a desk covered in stacks of research and papers to read or grade or edit. Reading glasses, cords, coffee mugs. On a warm day, there'd be a quiet hum from the air-conditioning unit outside, but that was also the only sound allowed in there. It may have been the only room in the house where Marion tolerated this particular kind of chaos, but that didn't mean she'd also condone needless noise.

Except, this time, the space looked nothing like that.

"What the..." Even Alison's jaw dropped.

Every book was neatly stacked on a shelf, the filing cabinets were closed, the desk bare.

The hair on Jillian's arms rose. "Leah's right," she said. "Something's up."

ELEVEN

ALISON

They'd grown up in this house. It was part of the fabric that made them who they were. And the office was supposed to be a mess.

Alison didn't know where to start. Seeing the bare surfaces and the neat rows of books and periodicals, her chest tightened for the second time since getting the news. Mom had erased herself from the house. But not only that... "Are you thinking what I'm thinking?" she asked.

Leah nodded. "It's like it's not lived in."

"Maybe because she was retired?" Jillian tried. "It's not like she needed the office anymore."

"Except the bedroom is the same way." Leah lifted an engraved paperweight off the edge of the desk and blew on it. A cloud of dust dissolved in the air.

"And she was still doing research. When I stopped by in December, it wasn't like this." Alison turned slowly in place. She was pretty sure. When Mom hadn't returned her calls after the award, Alison had stopped by instead, and they'd talked for a while in the kitchen. She hadn't been inside the office, but she'd glimpsed its innards through the door in passing.

"What the hell?" Jillian crossed her arms. "It's like she's been gone for months."

Leah walked over to the desk and began checking the drawers. "In case there's a note," she explained. "Seems odd she'd go to the trouble of tidying the house and not leave instructions for a will or anything."

Alison was still shaking her head. "I don't get it." Was she remembering things wrong?

"There's nothing here." Leah's arms fell to her side.

Jillian had been scanning the bookcases but turned, equally empty-handed. "Not here either."

"How are we supposed to make it right without knowing what she wanted?" Alison said, the threat of failure billowing closer like an approaching sandstorm. Mom was particular.

"Did she have a priest or someone else she trusted?" Leah asked.

Alison cocked an eyebrow. She'd wanted so badly to do the first communion classes with her friends in second grade—it was a sign of maturity she couldn't possibly miss. Add to that the pull of those beautiful white dresses they all got to shop for of course. Her mom had said no. Bradys didn't do church. And Dad, who'd been home for once, had given Alison a long speech about the folly of organized religion and warned her not to talk of such things again. No, there would not have been a priest.

"Oh." Jillian straightened suddenly then ran out of the room.

What now?

"Do we go after her?" Leah asked, as if she needed permission.

Sometimes Alison wondered how she and Leah were even related.

Jillian returned with a book in her hand. "I knew something was off," she said. "In the bedroom. This was on her nightgown,

but it wasn't dusty like everything else. And it's a Bible. Look."
She held up the thick tome and pulled a note from its pages.

Leah and Alison crowded close. "What does it say?" Leah
asked.

"Not much." Jillian read aloud. *"My will is with J.R. Dunn
& Sons. It's time. To quote Roosevelt, 'The light has gone out of
my life.' I'm sorry. Marion."*

They looked at each other in silence for a long moment,
then Jillian turned the small piece of paper over and scoffed.
"Someone else's words and a phone number. That's it."

But for Alison it was finally something to go on. She didn't
hesitate before pulling her phone out.

They crammed into J.R. Dunn's office later that day, which was
barely the size of Alison's walk-in closet. Since this was the only
office in the small suite, Alison assumed the *& Sons* part of the
firm name was more an expression of hope than actual reality.
Leah sat behind Alison and Jillian on a folding chair the secretary had pulled out from a nook in the waiting area. Alison tried
not to let the deference annoy her, but surely it would be better
for the three of them to show a strong united front in this situation. Who knew what this lawyer had in store for them?

"Let me start by expressing my condolences," J.R. began. "I
didn't know your mother long, and saw her only briefly on two
occasions, but she seemed a fine lady."

"When was this?" Alison asked.

"Oh, about six months ago or so. Janie can get you an exact
date if you wish." He nodded toward the secretary.

Too long ago to make a difference. A lot could happen in six
months. This was most likely a dead end as far as facts were
concerned. Alison sighed. "No, that's okay."

"Is there a note with the will?" Leah asked from behind
them. "Like a letter?"

J.R. pushed his glasses higher up on the bridge of his nose and squinted at them. "No, it's a standard document. Why?"

Jillian leaned forward. "What she's wondering is, do you know if she planned to kill herself all along? Is that why she wrote the will?"

J.R. blinked, his saggy cheeks paling. "Oh. I had no idea. I never inquire as to my clients' personal reasons unless it's pertinent to my job."

This man was no help. Alison shifted in her seat. It was already 3 PM. She needed to get back to the office before Bess left for the day. They had a showing the next morning that she wanted Bess to attend, but they needed to go over the specs first.

"Let's get to it then. What does it say?" she asked, ignoring how Jillian turned sharply toward her at the question. Tiptoeing around things never made them better. This was why they were here after all.

"Oh. Hmm. Well." J.R. pulled the document in front of him and scanned it. "Marion—your mother—is leaving the house and a sum of $55,000 to be split equally between her three daughters." His eyes flicked up. "That would be you. She had a TODD, or Transfer on Death Deed, in place, so you're already the legal holders of the property. She's further leaving $10,000 plus what remains after any debts are paid, as well as her car, to her granddaughter, Hannah Sloane. She specifies no course of action for the estate—you may keep it or sell it."

"Hannah should have been here," Leah said quietly.

Alison ignored her. "We'll sell it of course." The market was especially strong in the suburbs right now.

J.R. went on to explain some details of legalese in the paperwork, and when he was done, he looked at them over steepled hands.

"Do we have to sign anything?" Jillian asked.

"You'll need to record the death certificate with the county. And I'll be happy to set up a time to help you navigate the process. Right now, I imagine you have other things on your minds."

"Yes, we should get going," Alison said. She'd have to hire cleaners and probably replace the drafty windows in the family room before she put the house on the market. She shook hands with J.R. "I'll be in touch." Fitting this into her already full schedule wouldn't be easy, but that's why she was training Bess. And she knew the house well—it wouldn't be a hard sell.

Her thoughts were interrupted as Leah suddenly stood, causing her chair to collapse with a clang. Before anyone could react, she'd mumbled a vague excuse and fled the room.

What now?

TWELVE

LEAH

Another death, another lawyer, another house that was no longer home. Leah sucked in deep breaths in the half-full parking lot outside the office. This was what was left when you died. Things. Money. Sign here, sign there. Done. At least Hannah would care when it was Leah's time, she thought. Her daughter wouldn't sit in an office and talk about estate value, dry-eyed and impatient to get back to her real life. Or so she hoped.

Leah's hands shook as she dialed her daughter's number. What time was it in Europe now? Midnight? When voicemail finally picked up, she ended the call and turned her face toward the setting sun. Let it paint yellow spots inside her eyelids.

How was it this hard to *feel* something about Mom's death? Her mind was working overtime sorting through images and impressions, but it was more like shuffling cards to keep your hands busy than anything else. She was emotionless. Cold-hearted. Maybe she deserved to lose Hannah to the world.

"Are you okay?" Jillian approached the car, concern written on her face.

Leah had the white lie on the tip of her tongue—a headache, no worries. But this was Jill. And she wasn't supposed to lie anymore. She forced half a smile. Small steps. "Ha. No, not really. This is so..." She shook her head. "I needed air."

Jillian gave a slow nod. "Yeah, it's weird, right?"

Leah was about to lean into that long-lost realm of sisterly accord when Alison joined them, her mouth a tight line of disapproval. "What happened to you?" she asked Leah. "We still have things to discuss."

Leah's face heated. "I didn't..." The words caught, halted by the command in Alison's voice.

"It's fine, Ali," Jillian chimed in. "What's the next step?"

Alison turned from Leah to Jillian as if momentarily thrown. "Well, we'll need to let people know about the funeral."

Leah sent Jill a look of thanks. This was new—having someone in her corner.

"I'll call the university," Alison continued. "But we need neighbors, friends..."

"I can talk to Mrs. Carlisle," Leah offered tentatively. "She might know who to contact." She wouldn't mind seeing the old neighbor again. And maybe Andrew. She did have his number... Something fluttered in her belly at the thought, but she pushed it aside. As friends only of course.

"And we have to deal with the house," Alison continued.

Jillian put her hands up and chuckled. "Not me. Do whatever you want with it."

Alison let her palm fall onto the roof of her car. The sudden noise made Leah's shoulders tense again.

"What?" Jillian's smile tightened, the irreverently drawled question lingering between them.

Alison glared. "You're not going to help at all? I'm up to my neck already."

"Which you love."

"Well, I run my own business."

Jillian's eyes narrowed. "And that's good for you. But you're not the only one with a career. I'll have you know I'm about to be promoted at work. Just because Marion favored your job over mine doesn't mean I don't also have things to do and places to be."

"I didn't say that. And for God's sake, call her *Mom!*"

Jillian cocked her head, gaze now menacing. "Tell me you didn't think it."

Leah held her breath. The air around them seemed to have cooled several degrees. It wasn't like Jill to call Alison out like this.

"Whatever. I'm heading up to a friend in Vancouver tomorrow," Jillian said after a long moment's silent stand-off. "I'll be back Friday."

Alison's fair complexion flamed crimson. "You've got to be joking."

"Come on—it's okay." Leah swallowed hard when both her sisters turned her way, but she kept going. "I'll arrange for the house to get cleaned. In fact, I'll do it myself." Saying it lifted something off her shoulders, and she straightened. "I have no other plans. I'll get my stuff and take it over there so I'm out of your hair, Ali. I don't mind. Then you can focus on work, and Jill can do whatever she's got planned. Everyone's happy. Plus, if there's something we overlooked at the house that could shed light on all of this, I wouldn't want a cleaning service to accidentally dispose of it."

It would feel good to be useful while they awaited Saturday. The more she pictured leaving Alison's overwhelming house, the easier she breathed.

After a beat, Alison threw her arms up in resignation. "Fine."

Jillian made her way to the other side of the car. "Works for me."

Alison pulled out her car keys and turned to Leah. "I'm heading to the office. You'll have to drive her home."

Leah nodded.

"And let me know if you need cleaning supplies or anything. If we're going to put it on the market ASAP, it needs to be shining. Windows, baseboards, everything."

"For fuck's sake. She knows how to clean a house." Jillian got in the car and slammed the door.

Leah didn't say anything. It was usually better that way.

Late that night, she lay in her childhood bed, staring at the crack in the ceiling like it was an old friend. Whispers of long-ago voices still echoed in the walls. *Have you seen my blue sweater? Be quiet, Dad's sleeping. Dinner's ready.* The air duct that always banged when the heater started up in the winter, the two creaky steps in the stairs, Jillian on the phone in the room next door.

A lifetime ago.

Leah rolled over on her side and traced the loose seam in the wallpaper. To be young again. Make different choices. Though if she had, Hannah wouldn't be here. Hannah who carried her heart around on the other side of the world. Hannah who still hadn't called her back. She was probably busy getting settled. Leah shouldn't worry.

She reached behind her for the phone on the nightstand and typed quickly: *At Mom's house now. Miss you. Everything okay? Call soon.*

She rested her forehead against the screen, willing a response to appear.

Nothing.

"Well then..." She turned out her light and blinked against the darkness that followed. Something about the safety of "life before" surrounding her allowed her to drift quickly, peacefully for once. Sleep hadn't been her friend in years, so this was a particular blessing in light of what tomorrow would bring. If Alison wanted a shiny house, that's what she'd get.

THIRTEEN

LEAH

By noon the next day, Leah's forearms ached from scrubbing the tile in the foyer and bathrooms spotless. She'd dusted the whole house and brought out all the bedding to air, so her progress was good enough to warrant a break. She'd bought a few pre-packaged salads at the nearby grocery store and took one of them onto the porch to eat.

It wasn't as warm today—a cool breeze whipped around the corner—so she pulled a blanket off the porch railing and wrapped herself in it. It made eating messier, but it wasn't like anyone was there to judge her. Or so she thought.

"Hi there."

Leah froze, fork halfway to her mouth. She'd recognize Andrew's baritone anywhere.

"Um, hi." She lowered her hand and shook the blanket down past her shoulders to avoid looking like a complete cave troll.

He was dressed in white coveralls today, his hair on end. The sun hit it at an angle that made his strawberry blond strands glint rose gold.

"Sorry, didn't mean to scare you. Mom sent me over. She

saw you out here and said to tell you she's made pierogis in case you'd prefer that to your 'rabbit food.' Her words, not mine." He smiled, his teeth matching the color of his outfit. "How's the nose?"

Leah's fingers went to the tender patch beneath her right eye. It wasn't bothering her anymore, as long as she avoided the mirror. Memories and such... "It's fine. Thanks."

He looked older today than he had Saturday morning— maybe being fully clothed helped. His jaw was stronger than when they'd been friends, rough with morning stubble that certainly hadn't been there during that game of seven minutes of heaven in seventh grade. Ruby Mallard's closet had smelled of floral body spray and well-worn sneakers, and Leah had been so nervous she'd almost blacked out. The kiss had been over long before the seven minutes were up, and they'd both pretended nothing had happened once they'd been let out, but it was common knowledge Andrew had had a crush on her for years afterwards.

He bobbed his head, peering up at her. "So... what—" Before he could finish the sentence, he jumped backwards with a startled "Ah!", brushing at his sleeve in a panic.

Leah stood to peer over the railing and found him doing a curious imitation of a dog chasing its tail.

After a moment, he turned back to her, a sheepish expression on his face. "Um... Spider." He scratched the back of his head. "Wow, yeah. Sorry you had to see that."

Leah tried hard to hide a grin. There was something endearing about a grown man bested by a creepy-crawly. "Is it gone now?" she asked.

He examined his sleeve again and a small shiver ran through him. "Dad's back is bad, so they needed help checking the traps in the crawlspace. Since I'm on vacation this week, I volunteered. Foolishly. Should have known better."

"Ah, hence the get-up." Leah nodded toward his outfit.

"What these?" He struck a pose, hooking his thumbs into the fabric as if he was wearing suspenders. "No, no, these are my Sunday bests. Didn't you know coveralls are all the rage?"

A laugh rolled up Leah's chest, taking her by surprise. She'd forgotten how funny he could be.

"Anyway." He did a little drum roll against his thighs. "Pierogis? Fresh batch?"

It was tempting. The salad left much to be desired, and she wanted to chat with Mrs. Carlisle again. Wouldn't mind chatting more with Andrew too, to be honest. And yet... "I still have a lot to do today. Maybe I can stop by this evening. If it's not inconvenient, I mean."

"I'm sure that's fine."

"Tell her thank you. And if tonight doesn't work, please let her know I'll be staying here this week to get the house ready."

"Oh." Andrew's face brightened. "Okay, well then I guess I might... see you around?" His mouth pulled sideways as if trying to stifle a smile.

"Maybe," Leah conceded, a mirrored expression tugging at her own lips. It wouldn't be the worst thing.

He raised one hand in parting and started off toward his house. "Enjoy the rest of your leafy greens."

Leah watched his back retreat, but when he reached the property line, she had a thought. A nutty, impulsive one with no logical explanation other than his coveralls. "Wait!"

He turned, came back a few steps.

"You don't happen to know anything about plumbing by chance?" she asked. "Because the upstairs bathtub has some drainage issues."

He shaded his eyes and glanced toward the second-floor window instead of answering.

She shouldn't have asked. Just because he was helping his parents didn't mean he'd want to get his hands dirty with an old neighbor's bathroom. What was she thinking?

She was about to take it back when he asked, "The pink one?"

His question stumped Leah for a moment until she remembered he'd been over countless times when they were younger. Their group used to roam from house to house on the weekends, and since Mom was often away working, they'd spent a fair amount of time at the Brady house.

"The very same."

"Yeah, sure. I'll take a look."

The tension in Leah's shoulders eased. "Really? That would be so great. I'll pay you of course."

He frowned. "I insist you don't. Just come over for dinner and make Mom happy."

"That's hardly an even trade for you."

He leaned forward and mock whispered, "Negotiations were never my strength." He started backing away. "Dinner at six. I'll tend to the vintage tub after."

As he walked away, Leah wasn't at all sure what to make of him. He was so much more self-assured than she remembered—not at all the scrawny nerd she'd tried to pretend didn't have a thing for her back then. Was he still in touch with other classmates? Did Dave become a journalist like he wanted? Did Lou end up going to France for a gap year? And what happened with that Kenmore girl Andrew dated senior year? Not that it mattered. Except, she had just invited him into her house. What if he was married? Neil would have... Her hands gripped the railing tighter. Yes, she knew all too well what Neil would have done.

"He's not here," she whispered. Then louder, chin up: "He's *not* here."

FOURTEEN

JILLIAN

Jillian was driving too fast. Past Marysville, Burlington, Bellingham. She didn't actually have plans in Vancouver—it had slipped out—but as luck would have it, her Canadian friend Greg had responded right away when she'd texted him last night. With excitement even, in spite of them not having seen each other in close to a year. She shouldn't be surprised; Greg was always up for hanging out. They'd dated for a while years ago before deciding they were better off as friends, and now he was happily married to an American accountant named David.

Jillian allowed each passing mile to drain the tension from her shoulders. She wasn't *really* mad at Alison. That, more than anything, was what was so frustrating. But Ali was such a big sister, always expecting everyone to do things her way. Plus, Alison wanted to be here. She'd settled here, near their mother, of free will. Alison had never understood Jillian's love for New York.

Jill leaned her head back, loosened the grip on the steering wheel, and eased off the gas pedal. It was a decent car, now that the scent of vanilla air freshener that had initially overwhelmed her had faded into the background. Marion's car.

"It's just sitting there," Leah had said. "No point in you renting one too. Mom wouldn't mind."

Jillian wasn't so sure.

Maybe if Dad hadn't died when she was nine, things would have been different. From the beginning, she'd been his girl. She'd idolized him, maybe even more so because they saw him so rarely. His job had seemed the epitome of glamor—flying all over the world, meeting new people, people who respected his uniform. She grinned at the thought. She wasn't quite so wide-eyed these days, but she'd still never regretted taking her place in the cockpit in his honor. The job suited her, as it had suited him, and she took pride in being John Brady's daughter. Only her looks betrayed she was also Marion's.

Jillian sniffled, surprised to find a tear had found its way down her cheek.

"Wow." She wiped her face with the back of her hand. "Huh."

She shook her head rapidly and rolled down the window. The breeze knocked some sense into her. It was good that Alison was taking charge. She'd make arrangements better than anyone else. As usual. Give Marion a proper service. Jillian didn't begrudge her that. Even though she'd been an afterthought to their mother, things could objectively have been worse. They'd had friends growing up whose parents were both alcoholics and belt aficionados. And she'd had her dad's attention until he'd passed. It wasn't nothing.

No, she'd text Ali when she got to Greg's and apologize. If her sisters needed her to come back sooner, she would.

There were people in Jillian's life she'd consciously cut out, and also those she'd drifted from involuntarily. It was in her nature and in that of her job that people came and went, and she didn't always take time to reflect on it. Greg could have easily been one of them. A shared history that didn't work out, lives lived far apart, and vastly different career interests didn't exactly conjure the most stable ground for a friendship, and yet here they were, splayed across the sectional in his living room overcome by fits of laughter at the memory of a double date gone wrong. They'd tried to match up their friends only to discover the two were second cousins halfway through the main course.

David was the calm to Greg's lively persona. He sat in his armchair off to the side, sipping his wine, an indulgent smile flickering across his lips every so often. Jillian had only met him once before—at their wedding—but she'd liked him instantly. He obviously loved Greg, he was well traveled, so they had plenty to talk about, and his very presence calmed everyone around him.

During a temporary lull in the conversation, Greg got up to fetch "the best damned dessert British Columbia has to offer" and returned with two pints of Ben & Jerry's Salted Caramel Core ice cream and three spoons.

Jillian was never one to decline sweets, so she accepted and tore open the lid. "Thanks for this," she said. "And for letting me crash. It was getting claustrophobic down there with my sisters."

Greg and David shared a glance. "You're heading back to New York after this then?" Greg asked, digging deep into the center of the pint.

David elbowed him gently. "Hey, save some caramel for me."

"As soon as possible. The funeral is Saturday."

The men looked at each other again. Longer this time, with David giving Greg an almost imperceptible nod.

"What?" Jillian put her spoon down.

"Well..." Greg's lips twitched, as if he was struggling to control them. "I was really glad you called actually. I'd been meaning to get in touch."

Jillian dove back into the ice cream. "Yeah, for sure. It's been too long." She pointed at both of them with the back of her spoon. "And you know if you're ever out my way, let me know. We can put you up. Have you ever been to New York, David?"

His eyebrows rose. "Um, yeah. But I was fifteen and with my parents. So, Statue of Liberty, Empire State, and a Broadway show."

Jillian chuckled. "You'd like it better now, I promise."

"Anyway." Greg leaned forward. "There's something we wanted to talk to you about."

He glanced quickly at David, who filled in, "And we know this is kind of strange timing. You have a lot on your plate already."

Greg continued, "But then you called, and that seems like kismet."

David nodded.

Jillian frowned. This was convoluted even for Greg. "Okay..."

Greg wiped his palms on his thighs. "Well, you know we've been married over a year now."

"Happily married," David interjected. "

"And we've been talking about it for a while—about a next step."

"Mm-hmm." Jillian pretended to follow along. The ice cream was melting in its tub.

"And we have friends who've been able to, you know... quite successfully, but we've always felt we didn't want to go the anonymous way."

Anonymous what?

Jillian put a hand up. "I'm afraid you've lost me. What are we talking about?"

"A baby," Greg said, as if that was a given. "We want to start a family, and we're wondering if you'd consider being the mother."

FIFTEEN

ALISON

The house was dark and quiet. Only the desk lamp in the office offered a sphere of light in which Alison remained tethered. Tyler had gone to bed several hours ago, but she had work to do. She'd gone from finalizing an offer to preparing her keynote for a local scholarship awards dinner, and one thing had led to another. The pitch for Mom's house sat half written on the screen in front of her. The cursor hadn't moved in a long time.

Alison's heart was a mob of horses galloping across a dry plain, wildfire chasing it, and every time she tried to finish the last sentence, the wild animals picked up speed. Her fingers trembled on the keyboard. Why couldn't she finish the paragraph? She'd written hundreds of these before; from a business standpoint, there was nothing special about this house and she was a pro—she should be able to handle this as a transaction only. She didn't want the house. Selling was the only thing that made sense.

She had a sip of water and refocused. Deep breath in.

"It's two thirty in the morning. Why are you still up?" Tyler stood in the doorway, hair on end, nothing but boxers and a T-shirt on. His bare legs turned him into a gangly teenager in the dim light.

Alison pulled her hands into her lap as if he'd caught her red-handed. "I wanted to finish... I mean, I had work—" Her voice broke. *What the hell?*

"Hey." Tyler made his way across the room to her. "What's going on?"

She turned her face so he wouldn't see and blinked away the hotness in her eyes. Swallowed. "Nothing. It's fine. Tired." She rubbed at her neck.

"Here, let me." He moved to stand behind her.

Alison allowed her shoulders to sag. His hands were warm, hypnotizing, as he worked the knots beneath her skin. Strong, familiar fingers playing a relentless waltz across her nerves.

"You're so good at that," she mumbled, drowsy from his ministrations. "Don't stop."

Tyler obeyed for a minute then paused to pick up a letter from her desk. "What's this?"

She opened her eyes. "Oh, I was nominated for the North American Women's Business League's Education and Leadership award. Forgot to tell you."

"Really? That's fantastic. I didn't even know you'd applied."

"Yeah, the conference is in Toronto in August. To be honest I'd forgotten about it myself." It was a little disconcerting. She pulled the letter out of his hand and tilted her head forward. "More massage please."

For a long while, neither of them spoke. They were allied again, lock-stepped in the golden glow of the small room. Perhaps tonight they would even—

"You know," Tyler said. "There's a lot going on for you right now. It's okay to take a step back."

Alison's eyes snapped open. Not now. "A little to the right," she said, clinging to the feeling that was already dissipating.

He complied but pressed on. "I don't think it's good for you to be working this much."

Alison's jaw tightened. He was really going there then. She shrugged away from his touch and leaned back over her keyboard.

Tyler huffed. "What? Are you mad that I care?"

"Even if I wanted to—which I don't—I actually can't take a step back, because I run my own business. And ever since you lost your job, that seems to be a growing thorn in your side."

She ignored his stunned expression. She didn't need pity or coddling. She needed to get her work done without a guilt trip. Was that so much to ask? If Mom was here, she wouldn't want them grieving—she'd want action taken, results, forward motion. *Your work ethic will take you places, Ali.* They'd had that in common. Mom had been one of the youngest female professors to get tenure at UW and Alison was sure that had been the happiest day of her mother's life. *Don't settle for less than excellence, Ali.*

"It's not. I only want what's best—"

"I'll be up in a little bit," she said, interrupting him with a voice flinty enough to not invite rebuttal. She returned her focus to the screen, shutting him out. Held her breath as he turned.

As soon as he was out of sight, she sagged back in the chair, hands pressed tightly to her aching chest. Tyler was making this so much harder than it needed to be. She needed to get him a job, get him out of the house, stop the hovering. If not, she wasn't sure how they'd make it.

SIXTEEN

JILLIAN

Jillian stared at Greg, the pulsing of her heartbeat blocking all other sounds. She must have misheard. A fist clutched her stomach abruptly and she stood.

"Excuse me a second."

If they responded, she didn't hear it.

Alone in the bathroom, she closed her eyes and buried her face in her hands—a game of hide-and-seek to delay the battle that threatened inside.

A baby, a baby, a baby.

Impossible, impossible, impossible.

Her schedule was too demanding, like her father's had been. She was too selfish, too young, too old, too alone. She looked too damn much like her mother.

And yet...

They'd stabbed her in her weakest spot. Her yearning was bleeding out of every pore.

A soft knock on the door. "Jill?"

"Just a minute." She should leave now. Should never have come at all. She stood, ran the sink, splashed cold water across her throat. She'd run from her sisters—from her family. If that didn't tell her everything she needed to know, what did?

Greg and David hunkered in the hallway outside the bathroom. David had his hands wrapped around Greg's arm. So close—already a family. A child only had to come into their lives and take its place. They were so lucky.

"Um..." Jill pushed her hair behind one ear. *There's no way. I have to go. Find someone else.* "Why me?"

Greg tilted his head. "Because we love you. And you're smart, and beautiful, and funny, and great with kids."

A jab behind her ribs. "No I'm not."

"Oh, come on. You had them eating out of your hand at the wedding. And remember that time my sister brought her family to the cabin. You were the only one who could get Lois to sleep. My sister almost kidnapped you."

Jill remembered. But that had been a long time ago and other people's children. It's one thing to borrow them for a few hours and hand them back—another entirely to mess them up full-time and permanently.

"Can we sit?" Greg asked.

Against her better judgment, Jill agreed. This was a non-starter. She'd never. Couldn't. Wouldn't. Shouldn't.

She sank back onto the couch and found the same depressions that had held her fifteen minutes ago.

"You can say no," David said, voice soft. "You don't have to explain."

"Do you not want kids then?" Greg asked.

Jillian sighed. "Fucking A." She pressed her lips together; she hadn't meant for that to come out. "I mean... This is me not knowing what to say." She made a self-deprecating little noise.

"You can think about it too," David added. "If there's a chance."

"I guess I don't get it." Jill leaned forward. "How would this work exactly? I'm in New York, you're here. Would I only be the oven? Like a surrogate? Because that's a hard no."

"No, of course not." Greg put the glass he'd been sipping from down. "We're hoping that whoever… agrees… will want an active role."

"And we'd move to New York."

Jillian's gaze cut to David as he spoke.

"I have several contacts there. Getting a job wouldn't be hard."

Jillian let out a chuckle. "You guys have really thought this through."

"We want to start a family. Badly. More than anything."

"And what? We'd share custody?" Something warm spread throughout the hollow in her stomach as she said the words. Was it so impossible after all? Marion *had* fed her, clothed her, kept a roof over her head. It could count as "nurture-adjacent" if she was feeling generous. "I don't know…"

"What don't you know?"

"If it's for me." Jillian twisted the ring she wore on her right middle finger. "My mom was a single parent for half of my childhood and not exactly a role model as such."

Greg moved to sit next to her. "You're not her. And if we do this, our kid will have the attention of three parents who love them."

Our kid.

"Greg, hon." David's voice was a call for restraint.

Greg leaned back, out of Jillian's space. "Fine," he said. "You're right." He offered Jillian a small smile. "But please think about it."

Jillian nodded slowly. "I wish I could tell you what you want to hear. But this is big. And I have a funeral in a few days. I can't…"

"Take your time," David said.

But not too much, Greg's eyes filled in.

He'd always been an immediate kind of person. No delayed gratification there.

Jillian stood. "I think I'm going to go to bed. I will give it some thought, but I'm not making any promises. I hope you understand that. And know that whatever I decide, I really hope you two find a way to get what you want. You'll be amazing parents."

How she wished she could say the same for herself.

Once in bed, the memory reel gave her no rest.

It was her tenth birthday, and she came home to money on the counter to buy herself a present.

She was twelve and had to hitch a ride with a friend to her seventh-grade orchestra concert because Alison had a recital Marion couldn't miss. Again. Never mind Jillian had the only solo of the night.

She was fourteen and got her first period, and Leah was the one to make sure she had pads.

She was seventeen and moving across the country to neither a chorus of hand-wringing nor maternal cautions to stay safe.

"Let me know your address when you get there," was all Marion had said, already moving past Jillian up to the office, or out the door, or somewhere. Always moving past.

No wait, that wasn't completely true. When Jill arrived at her destination, she'd found a roll of three hundred dollars tucked into a small pocket on her backpack. The money wasn't from her sisters—she'd asked—so it must have been from her mom. A gesture, however small.

Jillian kicked her legs free of the blankets in Greg's guest room, frowning at the memory. The money had helped, but she'd have chosen a hug over it any day. Still, should the gift have meant more to her than it did?

Her eyes had adjusted somewhat to the dark, and now they

traced each texture of snagged shadows. An open shelf at the foot of the bed that held carefully curated vacation mementos; a plant on the windowsill; the crown molding encasing the ceiling boards. No answers there.

With a groan she turned her head sideways toward the nightstand. The clock blinked to 3:35 AM. Another groan. Every time she tried to assess the situation rationally, she ended up with nothing but bad memories and inane quotes like *The apple doesn't fall far from the tree* or *Like mother like daughter*. She needed a different angle. A new perspective. But everyone was asleep.

Except maybe...

She sat up and yanked her phone from its charger. It would be noon in Brussels. Hannah would be awake. Hannah who was the only kid she'd known her whole life. Hannah whose mom had grown up exposed to (almost) the same mothering Jillian had.

She waited with bated breath for the line to connect.

"Hi, Aunt Jill." Hannah's voice had a slight echo to it.

"Hannah banana." It was their inside joke—something she'd called her niece since she was three and couldn't pronounce the fruit. It had stuck.

"Ha-ha very funny. You're up late."

"Can't sleep. How's Europe?"

"Oh, you know. Good. Seems like Chase will be working a lot."

"There's lots to see. You'll have no problem keeping busy."

"I should be getting a ton of reading done, that's for sure. There's a small park outside our building—so pretty. Chase just prefers us going places together. It's safer that way."

"Okay..." Jillian frowned. Maybe they were in one of the less savory parts of Brussels. It had always seemed pretty clean to her when she'd been there.

"So what's new?" Hannah asked. A rattle sounded on the

line as if a window was being closed. "Where are you? Is my mom there?"

Jillian squeezed her eyes shut. *I left your mom behind to deal with Ali and the house alone.* "I took a day to visit friends in Vancouver. Heading back in the morning." Yeah, she should head back. What had she been thinking? Selfish was the word. Too selfish to be a—

"Gotcha." Hannah was quiet for a beat. "How's everyone doing?"

Jillian picked at a hangnail on her left hand. "All right, I guess. I think everyone's been a little shocked. We miss you."

"Yeah, me too."

"Marion didn't... I mean, I know you talked to her on the regular. Did she ever mention anything?"

"About not wanting to live? No. For *sure* no. She seemed a little tired maybe the past few months, but she was pretty old. And anyway, she never really talked about herself. She mostly interrogated me about my life."

At least she cared.

"Yeah, no—it was a complete surprise. Still doesn't feel real."

"You miss her?" Jillian asked.

Hannah was quiet for a moment. "I do. Like, she was family and everything. But is it bad if I'm not crying all the time? Don't tell Mom I said so. It still feels like she's there. Like it's not real."

Jillian understood what she meant. It hadn't felt real until they'd walked the empty rooms of the house.

"Hey, can I ask you something?" she said. "Would you say you had a happy childhood? Was Leah a good mom?"

This time, Hannah was quiet so long Jillian thought the connection had been lost.

"Hello?"

"Um..."

The sudden restraint in Hannah's tone made Jillian

straighten. Oh no—here it was. The Bradys' faulty mothering. Maybe that's why Hannah had grown less communicative as she became a teenager, not really reconnecting with Jill until she'd gone to college a few years ago. Jillian braced herself.

"Yeah," Hannah said. The word pitched across ocean and land. "Yes." Stronger, now, gaining momentum. "She was a *great* mom. The best. She did everything she could." Her voice trailed off. "Why do you ask?"

Jillian's shoulders slumped forward with an exhaled breath. It wasn't genetic then. That was something. Not that it meant she was in the clear. Leah was older, and even if she'd not been as prized as Alison, she'd still had her place at the table with their mother. She'd been visible.

"No reason."

"Hold on, someone's calling." Hannah disappeared for a minute, then returned, sounding flustered. "I've got to go. Chase's on the other line. We're going out with his colleagues tonight."

They ended the call with a promise to talk soon, but Jillian remained sitting with the phone in her hand long after. Leah and Marion had done things in the right order: found a great guy, got married, had a kid. And Neil had been so much like their dad—a real man's man, a career guy, proud of his work, doting on his daughter. And both had died too young, leaving single mothers. So what had made Leah succeed where Marion had come up short?

Of course, Hannah had been a young adult when Neil had his accident. Leah wasn't stuck caring for three young kids like Marion had been. Was Jillian judging their mother unfairly? Did grief get in the way?

No matter how she turned things around in her mind, Jillian still ended up with memories of a mother that left her wanting. One she didn't want to become.

SEVENTEEN

ALISON

Alison woke up Wednesday morning on the couch in the office, feeling only slightly better than she looked. A shower took care of the external remnants of her restless night, but she'd never wished so much for intravenous caffeine as she did walking into the kitchen a little later to find Tyler scrolling through the news on his phone. *News, not job listings.*

"Good morning." She went straight for the espresso maker.

"You never came to bed."

Tyler's voice was factual, not accusatory, but Alison still bristled at the comment. She was a grown woman—she didn't need him to keep tabs.

"Did you sleep at all?" he asked.

She took a sip of the bitter brew and allowed it to spread its energizing warmth through her system before she answered. "A bit." Around four in the morning she'd finally managed to wrap up the pitch for Mom's house. She didn't know if it was any good yet, but at least she had something to work with.

Tyler put his phone down and pinned her with his gaze. "I know you don't want to talk about this, but I'm worried about you." He articulated each word.

She turned away from him to put her cup in the sink. "Not necessary."

"About us."

She stilled, a silent alarm going off in her head, buzzing its way down her spine.

"I've made an appointment with Dr. Wezniak for Friday. Noon. Please be there."

She spun around. This was all wrong. If he made the appointment, it would suggest she was the one in need of an intervention, not the other way around. Alison opened her mouth to object, but the words got stuck in her throat. They needed this meeting—she already knew that. If only she hadn't put off calling Dr. Wezniak; now she'd have to spend precious minutes setting the record straight as to why they were there.

"You don't have anything to say?"

The way he looked at her. Sad, unimpressed. *Disappointed.*

No. She had worked so hard in her life to avoid exactly that expression on people's faces.

She squared her shoulders, lifted her chin. "Let me check my planner. I'll do my best to make it." She marched out of there, the burn from his gaze propelling her forward. She stumbled on the second stair but caught herself on the railing. She needed to go. Somewhere. Anywhere. The office maybe. Although there she'd have to juggle the new tensions between Peter and Bess that had arisen the moment she'd given Bess more to do.

Ty wasn't supposed to be worried about the two of them. He was supposed to be worried about his career.

She grabbed her hairbrush and a pair of sandals from the bedroom and shoved them into her purse, then she ran down the stairs hoping he wouldn't intercept her.

This wasn't her fault.

She got in her car and closed the door, and only in that muted silence did she release the breath she'd been holding.

You shouldn't have to change for other people. She was in the right here. Wasn't she?

The sun pierced her eyes as the garage door opened, so she flipped down the visor and blinked to clear her vision. She didn't have showings until later in the day, and Bess could cover the office and let her know if something new came up. Alison could just drive. Anywhere and nowhere. Or... She glanced at the laptop bag next to her in the passenger seat. What if she checked up on Leah and the house—how much progress she'd made on the cleaning? Maybe if they put the house on the market and were done with it, things would go back to normal again. Yes, new plan on the agenda.

She crossed the 520 bridge and headed east.

"Hello?" Alison closed the door behind her and hung her purse on one of the hooks by the door. A slight breeze drifted from the kitchen through the hallway and into the family room—open windows presumably—and the air smelled crisp and citrusy. A vast improvement from Monday.

"Leah, you here?" She peeked into the kitchen, where breakfast dishes remained on the table and her sister's sweater lay bundled on one of the chairs. Maybe she'd gone outside.

Alison continued through the dining room and out onto the deck, where a trill of laughter made her look up toward the open bathroom window on the second floor. She hurried in and up the stairs. Was Jillian back already?

"Hello?" she called, going down the hallway.

Leah poked her head out the opening to the bathroom. Her hair was in a ponytail, and she was wearing Mom's robe. Her mouth made a small O when she spotted Alison.

"Um, hi. What are you—"

"You didn't hear me come in?"

"No, we were talking."

Alison came around the doorway into the room and stopped short at the jeans-clad legs stretched out on the floor.

Leah stood, pulling the robe tighter around her. "You remember Andrew Carlisle, right?"

Andrew emerged from underneath the sink, wrench in hand. "Hiya, Alison."

"Sure. Um, hi."

"The bathtub had issues, and one thing led to another." Leah blushed violently. "I mean, not led to another as in... I mean he was helping his parents, and I thought... I asked..."

"After I fixed the tub last night I noticed a drip under the sink, so I came back this morning." He held up a round plastic thingamajig. "Coupling nut had a crack. Easy fix."

"Ah. Gotcha." Alison nodded slowly. At the edge of her vision, Leah was squirming like a kid forced to hold still for pictures. She must have known she should have checked in before making costly repairs. "Then thanks, I guess."

Andrew did a small salute and disappeared back into the sink cabinet.

"Hey, can I talk to you for a sec?" Alison asked Leah. She didn't wait for an answer before she strode out of the room. "So," she continued once they were back downstairs.

Leah shifted in place. "I wasn't sure what to do about the tub and he had coveralls on and seemed like he... God that's pretty presumptuous, right? What was I thinking?"

Alison stared at her. What *was* she on about? "All I want to know is how much he's charging. Everything involving the house should go through the estate, so I wish you'd have called me before hiring him."

Now it was Leah's turn to look confused. "But I didn't hire him. He's helping out for free."

Alison's chin retracted. "Oh." How odd. Not a great way to run a business.

"Yeah, for old time's sake. He's not actually a plumber—he

does some techie stuff, web design or something, for Amazon. He just also happens to be handy."

"Oh." Alison's shoulders lowered an inch. Maybe that was okay then.

"Why are you here anyway?"

"I... um..." Clearly, Leah had things under control. But the office already knew she'd be out, and she didn't want to go back home. Alison's eyes skimmed the surfaces in the room for a hold. There it was in the glinting glass. "I thought I should help with the windows. There are a ton of them."

Leah stared at her. "You're going to clean windows in that?"

Alison started rolling up the three-quarter-length sleeves on her blouse. "Sure. Why not?"

"Okay." Leah studied Alison for a moment then started up the stairs. "I'm getting dressed." She walked a few steps then turned, looking like she was about to start speaking. She gnawed at her lip for a moment. "Never mind. The squeegee is in the laundry room."

Alison nodded. She waited until Leah had disappeared before she pulled out her phone and quickly typed *How to best wash windows?* into the search engine. Success was part hard work, part tools and strategy, and there was nothing you couldn't learn with the help of the internet.

EIGHTEEN

LEAH

Leah hurried past the hallway bathroom on her way to her room, cringing at the clangs and grunts coming from under the sink. She closed the door behind her, mortified. What must Ali have thought finding Andrew here—and her half-dressed? Not to mention what might be going through Andrew's head. Through the lens of Alison's eyes, she'd seen their interaction in a different way. He couldn't possibly still have feelings for her, could he? At least he wasn't wearing a ring.

With jerky movements, she undressed and changed into the jeans and T-shirt she'd worn the day before. Neil's voice echoed in her head—*Let's just say, he's not talking to you because he's interested in your mind.* Another time, another place, another friendly guy. She should have learned her lesson.

Perhaps she ought to pay him to make sure he understood this was about the house, nothing else. She shook her head. No, she was being ridiculous. She wasn't exactly in her prime—not a woman men were likely to chase. Which was fine. She'd known when Neil died that she'd spend the rest of her life alone, and there were worse things.

Taking one last strengthening breath, she went back to the

bathroom where Andrew was now packing up his tools. He looked up when she entered.

"Everything okay?"

"Yup. A-okay." Leah smiled, though the corners were stiff.

"Did Alison leave already?"

"She's washing windows." Saying it aloud further underscored how odd that was. She'd never helped when they were kids, busy as she'd been with school, student council, debate club, ballet, and the list went on and on. A clean house made no one applaud.

"Gotcha."

Andrew stood, towering a head above Leah. When he smiled, a dimpled crease appeared in his left cheek. She'd never noticed that before.

"I should get going. Vacation days or not, I still have some work to get done."

Leah hadn't thought about that. He was foregoing other responsibilities by being here. Foregoing his days off. The realization made her scalp heat. "Thanks again," she said, forcing her gaze away from the dimple. "We really appreciate it."

She walked him out, but before he headed down the porch steps, he paused and glanced up at the house. "You've got my number already, right? I'm only fifteen minutes away. In case you have more issues, I mean."

Leah patted the pocket holding her phone. "Yeah, I've got it."

"Or"—Andrew hesitated—"if you want to grab coffee or something one day? I know you have other things on your mind, but I'd love to catch up more."

Oh. Leah swallowed. Coffee with him sounded nice. *Very* nice even. But the reality was, she knew nothing about him aside from who he'd been more than two decades ago. Yes, he seemed as kind as she remembered, and yes, he made her smile, but so had Neil—the nicest, most polite, caring guy she'd ever met. Until he wasn't.

She feigned interest in the quiet neighborhood behind him, not meeting his gaze. "Thanks, but..." But what? It was a sentence with no ending.

"Yeah?" he asked, drawing her attention back. The dimple was out again.

When she didn't respond, he let out a low laugh. "It's fine. You're busy." He jogged down the steps, then turned. "See you around, Leah."

She watched him leave like she had the day before, this time without calling him back.

"That's that," she muttered, entering the kitchen. She had chores to do. Dishes, baseboards, curtains. But as she filled the sink with soapy water, her mind still went there. Because who knew? It was a pretty old house. It couldn't hurt to check all the sinks and drains on the property an extra time. Due diligence. And if there was a problem, he'd offered. She might make him coffee as a thank you. That would be different, wouldn't it? Less intimate.

With that thought, something popped in Leah's chest; a beautiful fault forming in the armored shell she carried around her heart. Like sun on cold muscles, air to constricted lungs, it eased something at her center, and for the first time in years, she started to hum as she worked.

One room at a time, the Brady house revealed its original hues. Yellowed became white again, blue-gray turned back to light azure, the inky sheen of the piano appeared from beneath months of dust. Through the windows, the deep greens of summer imparted life onto all the spaces ill-suited to dormancy.

There were memories in every corner—the faint scent of beef stew lingering in the drapes, the dent in the floor from when Jill's chair tipped over, the dimpled side of the fridge, the notches on the pantry door Dad put up as they grew. Leah paused there, fingertips to the pencil smudges. They stopped when she was eleven.

She didn't remember their dad much. She had pictures of course, so she knew his face, but she couldn't recall his voice. Couldn't place him in these rooms. She saw him on the porch, carry-on in hand (coming or leaving she didn't know), on a ladder putting up Christmas lights, down by the dock showing Jill how to bait a worm, disappearing behind the sheets while Mom was hanging them to dry. Never inside.

Leah closed the door to the pantry, creases deepening between her brows. How odd that he'd been here, had been part of the family, and yet her mind wouldn't let him be pinned down within these walls.

A crash and yelp coming from outside startled her out of her reverie. She rushed to the open window, and there was Alison sprawled in the grass, the bucket of soapy water tipped over next to her. Her blouse was streaked dark from the spilled liquid.

"Are you okay?" Leah's gaze roamed across her sister, looking for blood and bruises.

Alison shook her hands as if to rid herself of the wet. "Fuck," she hissed.

"Hold on—I'm coming out." Leah ran through the house and out onto the deck.

"I'm fine, I'm fine." Alison had pushed herself up to sitting when Leah reached her. "I slipped on the bottom rung."

Leah followed Alison's gesture toward the ladder that stood leaning against the house then back again. "Well, you are wearing dress flats," she said.

For a moment they stared at each other, measuring goodwill and judgment, then Alison started laughing. "Yeah, what the hell was I thinking?"

Leah smiled and shrugged. "Are you sure you're okay?" Her sister didn't look injured—aside from her pride—but not everything shows on the outside.

Alison pulled her soaked blouse from her skin. "I'm wet. And my hip will be bruised tomorrow." She extended a hand to Leah. "I'll live."

Leah helped her up with a reach that bridged more than the feet between them. This was her chance. "Maybe it was time for a break anyway? Come on—I'll get you a dry T-shirt." She picked up the empty bucket and started walking toward the door, holding her breath. *Please follow.* She made it up the steps, set the bucket down. The board behind her creaked.

"Do you have any coffee?" Alison asked.

Alison looked younger in one of Mom's old UW sweatshirts. The casual garment softened not only her form but also her posture, and she sat with one leg pulled up underneath her on one of the kitchen chairs.

Leah poured them coffee and added creamer to her own cup. Alison took hers black.

"Thanks for helping today," Leah said when she'd stirred her cup long enough.

Alison nodded. "It's weird to be here, isn't it? Without her." She studied the room. "Strange to think of someone else living here."

"Maybe I should move in," Leah said, the words materializing unbidden out of dust particles and that unspoken longing for something—anything—new. At the upwards flicker of Alison's eyebrows, she laughed to smooth over the absurdity of her words.

Alison let out a brief cackle. "Right. Can you imagine? That would be *way* too much for you to take on."

Leah coughed, the laugh catching sideways in her throat.

Her grip on the cup tightened. Those had been Neil's exact words when she'd suggested she go back to school. She'd ended up waiting five more years.

They sipped in silence another few minutes. Leah searched for the right words to say now that she finally had Alison across from her, but her mind snagged on a cobweb in one of the corners by the ceiling. She would have to take the broom to it later. How could she have missed it? Ali was probably right.

"I'm sorry I didn't come to the funeral," Alison said suddenly. "I should have. I've been meaning to tell you, but I—"

"No, that's okay." Leah put her mug down, the words she'd wanted to get out now tumbling over each other in her throat. "You didn't miss anything." She put fingers to her brow. "I mean, it was fine. I was fine." She faced Alison. "I'm sorry too. I know how disappointed you were when we didn't go to your wedding. But with Hannah and Neil... I wanted to go—I just couldn't."

Alison's hands circled her mug. "Then why didn't you tell me?" She cocked her head. "An RSVP card in the mail?"

Was this the time? Leah's palms turned slick, and she hid them under the table. Could she say the words? *Neil made me. He had ways.* No, she wouldn't understand. She had Tyler. It would sound like a poor excuse. "I... I don't know. I was a coward I guess." A sigh. "A card was easier."

Something tightened inside of Leah at how easily the lie escaped her lips. So many years she'd made excuses for Neil, taken the blame, sugarcoated—and she was still doing it. The force of habit was too strong to break. She knew what questions would follow: Why didn't you leave? Why didn't you fight back? Report? Why didn't you protect your daughter? What kind of mother are you?

Leah pressed her lips together. "If it was now, I'd be there." It was the best she could do.

Alison nodded slowly. "Maybe we should consider it the

past. If not for us, then for Mom. She never said it out loud, but I think it bothered her we weren't talking."

"How so?" Leah thought back to her sporadic calls with their mother. She'd never said anything about Alison, had she? Mostly they'd talked about Hannah, and once Hannah was old enough to talk to her grandma herself, the calls had grown shorter—little more than status updates.

Alison shrugged. "I don't know. Sometimes I'd catch her staring at that picture of us in the hallway—the one from Chelan."

"The sandcastle one?"

"If that's what you'd call it." Alison raised one brow, smiling.

"Fine—the mud-cake one." Leah smiled back.

"Yeah. I stayed over every now and then, and at times she'd stop in front of it and this haze would come over her. She'd touch the frame. Pause. Touch it again."

"Are you sure she wasn't straightening it?" God forbid things were out of place in the Brady house. Mom had been almost as bad as Neil. She got a little better when they were older, but still.

"This was different."

"Did you ask her about it?"

"No. You know Mom."

Leah wasn't so sure. Do kids ever really know their parents? Mom was Mom. Not particularly warm and doting perhaps, but a provider. A focused matriarch enmeshed in home and career. An adequate single parent. She'd pulled the weight of their family even before Dad died. She'd been stronger than Leah, that was for sure. "Do you think she was depressed?"

Alison shrugged. "I don't know. I'm not sure she was ever truly happy if that's what you're asking, but whether it was clinical..." She squinted out the window. "I keep wondering—why the lake? Why take the pills and go into the water?"

"She loved the lake."

"Which is why it feels like a statement. Not desperate, not impulsive. Determined. Like it meant something."

Leah nodded, but then her phone beeped in her purse, and she pulled it out. "Jill's wondering where we are. She's in Everett."

Alison's brows shot up. "I thought she wasn't coming back until Friday."

"Another pair of hands can't hurt." Leah started typing a message. If she and Ali could start mending fences, they might as well include Jill too. In some ways this must be hardest on her. Mom may have been a decent parent to her and Alison, but Jill was a different story. It was the elephant in the room. While Leah didn't fully understand why this had been their family dynamic, she knew all about burying someone you were supposed to love but didn't—how it made you question your very humanity. Death was supposed to come with sorrow. No one ever taught you its companion could be relief.

NINETEEN

JILLIAN

Jillian slowed her car as she approached their childhood house. She'd driven from Vancouver without stopping after an awkward morning with Greg and David, breathing easier with each mile. They'd been appropriately tactful—she'd expected no less—but the question had still loomed like a smothering cloud above lattes and frittatas. Right before she left, she'd assured them again she'd think things over and let them know, but that was the only mention any one of them had made of the previous night's conversation.

So far, she'd been able to keep the thoughts at bay with eighties hair metal playing at ear-numbing volume, and now she was about to face Alison again.

"Out of the ashes, into the fire," she muttered to herself, parking. She hadn't expected her sisters to be together when she texted Leah, but perhaps it was best to get apologies over with. It wasn't their fault Jillian couldn't wait to go back to New York. It wasn't their fault Marion had been the way she was, that she'd tuned out her third daughter. Yes, Jillian had inherited their mother's looks, but Alison owned the same detached focus that only ever skimmed Jillian's contours as a child. It was no wonder her oldest sister pushed her buttons so easily. But again, not her fault.

No, Jill would take back the harsh words, help with whatever, sit through the funeral, and be done with it. She opened the car door and stepped out, then slammed it closed.

"Hi there," came Alison's voice out of thin air.

Jillian spun, searching for the source.

"Up here."

She tilted her head back and shaded her eyes from the sun, and there, perched on the windowsill outside the office on the second story, was Alison with a sponge held aloft. What on earth? And what was she wearing? "Um... hi?"

"Just washing some windows."

Jill stifled a smile. "I can see that." Alison's hair was in a sloppy ponytail and her face was shiny from the effort. She looked beautiful. Real somehow.

"How was Vancouver?"

Intense—a real mind fuck. "It was interesting."

"You're back early." Alison wiped the edge of the squeegee on a rag. Since when did she know how to do this? The scene was definitely a close runner-up for the weirdest thing Jillian had encountered in the past twenty-four hours.

She walked closer to the house, so she came to stand right beneath Alison. "Yeah, I shouldn't have left. That was childish. And I'm sorry about what I said."

Alison waved off the apology and went back to polishing the window. "Leah's in the kitchen. She might need a hand."

Well then, so much for worrying about this conflict dragging out. Jillian shook her head and went inside.

She found Leah with her head in the oven, scrubbing furiously at something. "What's Ali's deal?" she asked.

Leah jumped back, bumping the bowl of soapy water at her knees. "Oh, hi."

"Sorry—I didn't mean to scare you."

Leah dropped the scrub pad in the water. "How was Vancouver?"

Jillian repeated the answer she'd given Alison.

"Interesting? Did something happen?"

Damn. Leah always was the more perceptive of her sisters. Then again, talking about the whole thing with someone might be helpful. Not now though. Definitely not now.

"Nah, some stuff with Greg's job." Jillian's voice trailed off. "Anyway—Ali? Did you hypnotize her or something?"

The side of Leah's mouth quirked. "Weird, right? Between us, I think she needed a break from the office. Tyler says she works too much."

Jillian scoffed. "Old news."

The devil conjured, Alison's cell rang on the table where she'd left it. Jillian glanced at it. "As if I needed help proving that point."

Leah wiped her palms on her jeans and held out her hand. "I'll go up there."

"Or"—Jillian pursed her lips even as she handed Leah the phone—"we could pretend we didn't hear it?"

"Not our place."

"You're no fun."

Jillian sat down, waiting for Leah to come back down and assign her some chores. Every surface had been wiped, polished, and scrubbed. Gone was the closed-up smell, and with the breeze from the window caressing Jillian's skin, she almost didn't mind being there. Coming back early had been the right thing to do. See, she *was* capable of making mature decisions. Maybe she'd take after her dad instead of Marion. He'd always been so put together, such an adult. Always with a little gift for her after his trips, taking time to teach her about the plants and critters in their yard on his days off. Sure, he was gone a lot, but she had nothing but fond memories of the time he had spent with her. It was worth considering.

Leah returned, weighed down by the filing box she was carrying. "I found these in the office closet." She set the box on the table and took off its lid. In it was a jumble of loose photographs, small albums, and sleeves for negatives. "We'll want to split them between us so it would be helpful if you'd start sorting."

"Wow." Jillian reached into the box and took out the top handful. The photos were in no particular order—school graduations mixed with Christmases and beach days. She chose one she hadn't seen before and held it up. In it, three-year-old Leah was holding a newborn Jillian on the couch in the family room. The toddler beamed at the tiny, wrinkled face of her new sister, who gazed up with equal fascination. But that's not what caught Jillian's eye. Marion was also in the picture, sitting next to Leah. She wasn't looking at the baby though—her face was angled toward the window on her right, away from her children, lost somewhere far away. There was a sadness so profound in her lax jaw and hollow eyes, it made Jillian's stomach clench. Here it was, right in front of her—proof their mother hadn't wanted her from the beginning.

"What is it?" Leah asked, watching her.

Jillian handed her the photo.

"Aw, how cute," Leah cooed. "My God, I looked just like Hannah at that age."

"But look at Marion," Jillian said.

Leah did and fell quiet.

Jillian cleared her throat against the constriction that lingered there. "Greg and David want me to have a baby with them."

Leah's head jerked up. "What?"

Just then, a door slammed upstairs followed by a loud string of curses as Alison came running down the stairs.

TWENTY

ALISON

God dammit all to hell. She'd fire Peter. Alison had taken *one* day off—not even a whole day—and now he'd called to inform her (*inform* not ask) that her four o'clock had been moved to three because the client was already in the neighborhood. She could cancel of course, but this was a Microsoft bigwig— commission aside, the word of mouth would be priceless. You didn't cancel on clients like that—especially not when she'd already invested so much time showing him several other properties already. Peter was probably doing it on purpose as revenge for having a few responsibilities taken away. That was it. Last straw.

Alison flew into the kitchen and found her sisters staring at her, wide-eyed. Leah was holding a photo, and Jillian looked like she'd swallowed something bitter.

"I've got to run," Alison said, reaching for her purse. Where was her blouse? She asked Leah, who pointed to the laundry room.

"I can wash it and bring it to you later," Leah offered, following Alison into the small room.

"No, I've got it."

"You sure?"

Alison spun on her sister. "I said I've *got* it."

Leah shied back, jumpy as she was. Like a bunny, ears always twitching, ever ready for flight. Alison pulled in a steadying breath. *Careful*, a voice said in her head. *Don't ruin everything again.* "Sorry, didn't mean to yell." A sharp pain was gaining momentum behind her brow.

"Anything we can do?" Jillian asked.

"No." Alison hurried to the door but stopped with one hand on the handle. "I'm working late tonight. Jill, are you coming back to the house? I'll need to let Tyler know about dinner."

Jillian looked at Leah, something Alison couldn't put her finger on passing between them. "Actually, I think I'll stay here —help get things in order."

"Fine." Alison yanked open the door. "Talk to you later then."

They've got things under control, she told herself, speeding through the neighborhood. If they kept the windows, maybe offered a credit to replace them, the house was as good as ready. She should ask the lawyer to meet them after the funeral on Saturday, sign what needed to be signed. That would clear them to move ahead.

A glance at the clock told her she had ninety minutes. Thirty minutes home, twenty to get ready, thirty to the property, ten to prep. If anyone could pull it off, it was her—Alison Brady, Seattle Realtor of the Year.

She pressed harder on the gas pedal, her heartbeat well on its way toward an incessant buzzing rather than a steady beat.

TWENTY-ONE

LEAH

The Alison tornado had briefly knocked their conversation off course, but as soon as she swept out the door, Leah sat back down at the table. What Jill had said a minute ago was huge. A little cousin for Hannah. But she was getting ahead of herself. "Do you want to have a baby?" she asked. "I've never heard you mention it."

Jillian fiddled with the edge of the photo box. "Well, you know—I'm single, work a lot. All that travel... It's not exactly the best starting point." She picked at an old price tag near the bottom corner, pulling off minuscule slivers one at a time.

Leah wanted to reach out and steady her little sister's hand. Jill's normally straight back was hunched, her brows furrowed. This was weighing on her. Having Hannah was the best thing Leah had ever done. She'd do all of it over—even marry Neil—for her girl. But motherhood wasn't for the faint of heart. Not a decision to take lightly. Knowing Jill's track record for spontaneous adventures, Leah didn't know what surprised her more—the baby question itself or that Jill was taking it seriously.

"But aside from that, do you *want* kids?" she asked.

Jillian leaned back in her chair and sighed. "That's the thing. I do."

"Really?"

"Don't hide your disbelief or anything." Jillian smirked. "I know you probably think I'd be a shit mother. Hell, that's sort of the core of the issue, isn't it?" She flicked a stray crumb off the tabletop onto the floor.

"What is?"

"That I'm not cut out for motherhood."

Leah's brain churned at this. Why on earth? "And I was? At twenty-one, with no degree, no job?"

Jillian pouted. "Hannah turned out great."

Leah laughed drily. "Dumb luck, nothing else. You love them, that's all."

Jillian's gaze wandered out the window and rested there. "Not all parents do."

Leah had been about to keep poking holes in Jill's argument, but now she snapped her mouth shut. So that's where the shoe pinched.

"I know it wasn't the same for you and Ali," Jillian continued. "But you know I'm not making it up. She hated me."

"Hate is a strong word."

Jillian's face reddened. "Can you think of a better one?"

Leah didn't respond. It was usually best to avoid defending ghosts in favor of the living. Besides, in this case, Jill wasn't wrong.

"What if there's something about me, in me—something from her? And she knew it and it made it too hard for her to love —" Jillian's voice broke, and she pulled in a long breath. "I don't want to have a baby only to discover I want nothing to do with it. That wouldn't be fair."

"I really don't think that would happen." Leah reached for her sister's hand, and they sat in silence for a long moment.

"Ah crap, now I'm all mushy." Jillian freed herself from

Leah and got up to grab a paper towel. She blew her nose then sat down again. "So it's not as simple as whether I *want* a baby. It's also—*should* I have one? And I don't have the answer to that." She sniffled and wiped at her nose one more time.

Leah nodded, knowing she had to tread carefully if she was to convince Jill of how wrong she was. "No, I get it. And I feel terrible Mom was the way she was to you. I never understood it. But for the record, you're nothing like her. I mean, you're gorgeous like she was—but I think Alison got all the other traits. And she doesn't want kids, so..."

"Maybe." Jillian shrugged. "Maybe not. Don't tell Ali by the way. I don't need her opinions at the moment."

Gently now. "What are you going to tell them?"

"Who the heck knows?"

"Yeah, take your time. There's no rush."

"Not getting any younger."

"I guess," Leah conceded.

They lapsed again into silence, and this time it stretched with the shadows on the floor until Jillian declared introspection was done and she needed food.

Some things never changed.

Finally, late that evening, Hannah called. Maybe her ears had been burning when Leah talked about her earlier—whatever the reason, Leah pressed the phone close to her cheek as soon as her daughter's name lit up the screen. The Atlantic Ocean had only separated them for four days, and it already felt like a lifetime.

"Hi, sweetie, how are you?"

"Hi, Mom. Hold on, I'm putting you on speaker. I'm making breakfast." There was a clank and then the cavernous reverb of an open line took over. "Chase finally has a morning off so we're doing a picnic in the Bois de la Cambre."

Leah smiled at Hannah's enthusiasm. "I have no idea what that means."

"It's a gorgeous park."

"Hello, Mrs. Sloane," came Chase's voice on the line.

"Hi, Chase. How's the internship?"

"Great."

"You taking care of my girl?"

"You know it."

There was some giggling that Leah tried to ignore, then Chase's voice farther away, "Are you wearing those shorts?"

More giggling.

Leah waited.

"Sorry," Hannah said. "Please tell my boyfriend this is Europe. He's being such a prude."

Leah could practically hear her stick her tongue out. Oh, to be young again.

They talked a while longer while Hannah prepared sandwiches and scoured the small apartment for towels and sunscreen. *She's all grown up*, Leah thought. It sometimes seemed like only yesterday that her days had been consumed with scraped knees, packing lunches, and driving to soccer practice, and now she was no longer needed. At least not like that.

After they hung up, Leah went outside onto the deck and sat on the steps with her comforter wrapped around her. The light in Jillian's room was out, and the only sound around was the gentle lapping of the lake through the reeds at the far end of their property.

I could live like this, she thought. What if Ali was wrong? Maybe it wouldn't be too much to take on. If she moved here, there'd be no more Chicago, no more tiptoeing around colleagues and friends grieving someone they didn't really know. No more bad memories at every corner. She'd thought she needed to stay for Hannah—to maintain a home base, a constant, as her daughter tested her wings, but now that seemed silly.

"She's not coming home again," she whispered to the fluttering moths. "Not to stay." And that was both unbearably sad and okay.

Maybe it was finally time to be brave.

TWENTY-TWO

ALISON

"Remember, we have counseling at noon," Tyler called after Alison as she headed out the door Friday morning.

Shit! She'd completely forgotten. If it wasn't in her planner, it didn't exist. Already on edge from still not having heard back from the big client about the showing on Wednesday, she didn't answer, pretending instead she'd already reached the garage.

She'd be there. She knew they needed it. But did he have to make the appointment for midday Friday? All it did was underscore how far removed he was from the concept of working hours. *You cleaned windows instead of working the other day*, a small voice in her head whispered, but she brushed it away. She'd been available on her cell phone the whole time. This was different; she hadn't been consulted. Tyler had simply commandeered her time as if she had nothing else to do.

The more she thought about it, the tighter her grip on the steering wheel, so when her cell rang over the speaker in the car, she answered with a brusquer than normal "Hello."

"Alison? It's Steve Orturo."

Mr. Microsoft. Alison straightened against the seat belt. *Finally.* "Steve, what can I do for you?"

"Well, we really liked the last property."

Yes. And...

"So we'd love to have another look at it."

Alison almost drove into the car in front of her. "I see."

"I know it's coming up on the weekend and we're heading out to the coast in the morning. Any chance we could meet up today around eleven thirty?"

Alison cursed under her breath. Of all the times... "I absolutely want you to have that extra look—unfortunately, my schedule today is all over the place. Any chance we could do eleven?" It would still be cutting it close, but she'd hurry them up. And Dr. Wezniak wasn't too far from Laurelhurst.

"Hmm, I don't think so. My wife will be coming from Everett. How about one o'clock? I have to be in the office by two, so that's the latest I can do."

Alison's knuckles whitened. "Give me one moment, Steve— let me check." She didn't wait for him to respond before she muted the line. "Fuuuuck," she groaned. This sale would be a huge feather in her hat, but she'd have to leave couples counseling early. Tyler would kill her. Maybe Dr. Wezniak could help him understand.

She unmuted the phone. "Sure, I moved some things around. One o'clock is great. See you then."

Dr. Wezniak's office was located in a multi-suite office building north of University Village with ample parking outside. Alison was early to the appointment, so she maneuvered the Tesla into a shady spot and sat for a few minutes with the windows rolled down, going over the things she wanted said. Tyler might have made the appointment, but she wouldn't have the conversation taken over by his gripes about her job. That's not why they were here.

At five minutes to noon, she headed inside and took a seat in the small waiting room. The first time they'd come, she'd nearly left at the sight of the faux stone garden waterfall that sat propped in one corner. No therapist worth this exorbitant hourly fee could possibly stoop to such New Age lows. But Dr. Wezniak had come out to greet them before she'd had a chance to retreat, and, after that initial session, Alison had decided the decor was likely a remnant from a prior tenant.

When Tyler walked in a few minutes later, Alison couldn't help but feel smug at the surprise on his face at seeing her already there.

"Hey." He settled in the chair next to her and leaned over to kiss her cheek.

"Hi."

"How was your morning?"

"Good."

He nodded.

"Yours?" Alison asked.

Dr. Wezniak's door remained closed. *Any moment now.*

"Fine."

Silence.

Alison fought the urge to pull out her phone, fiddling instead with the nail she'd chipped on her suitcase the week before. She'd meant to go to the salon and get it taken care of, but life had got in the way.

"Maybe we should get one of those for the patio," Tyler said.

Alison looked up. "One of what?"

He pointed to the fake stone sculpture. "A waterfall. It's kind of peaceful, right? Listening to the water trickle."

She laughed. "Right."

"No?"

His earnest face made the chuckle stick in her throat. "Oh, you're serious." As if they needed something else to disagree on.

His brows pinched, but he didn't have time to respond

before the door to the inner office opened and Dr. Wezniak appeared in all her six-two glory, beaming down at them as if they were long-lost friends.

"Alison, Tyler. It's been a while." She gestured for them to come inside.

Alison chose the left side of the couch, closest to the window. Also closest to Dr. Wezniak's chair.

"How've you both been? What's new? How can I help?" She smiled. Warmly.

"Well, my mother died a week ago," Alison said. "She killed herself apparently. No one knows why." The words hanging in the air, she pressed her lips together and fought an impulse to touch her throat. Where had that come from? She'd had no plan to discuss Mom at all.

"Oh," Dr. Wezniak said, with a quick glance at Tyler. "I had no idea. My condolences."

"It's not why we're here though," Alison added, reclaiming control of the situation. "I assume Tyler told you we're having some issues." She crossed her legs, straightened. There. Now they were on track. She had forty minutes.

"Okay..." Dr. Wezniak narrowed her gaze. "You're sure this isn't something we need to address first? The death of a parent often throws us for a loop—questions of mortality, legacy..."

"No, I'm okay. The funeral's tomorrow. Each thing has its own time, right?" Alison smiled.

"See, this is what I was talking about on the phone," Tyler said. "That's not a normal response. You can't push emotions away like that and decide to put them off for another day." He turned to Alison. "It's like you're playing a role and deciding what to display at any given time. It used to be only for work, but now it's even with me."

Alison stared at him. "You think I'm abnormal?"

"Let's pause there for a moment." Dr. Wezniak tilted her head. "Grief responses do look different for different people.

This compartmentalizing you're describing is not necessarily—"

"But it's all the time. Not only with Marion's death." Tyler turned back to Alison. "When we disagree on something, you can tell me. You don't have to worry about my feelings. Or when you're stressed about work—let me know how I can help."

"But you can't help." Alison was starting to sweat. How was she under fire here? "You don't know the first thing about real estate. And I certainly don't keep things in to spare your feelings."

"Hm." Dr. Wezniak settled further into her chair. "It sounds to me like you're a bit out of sync with each other. Alison, you said you're having some issues. Could you elaborate? And as usual, let's keep in mind that when Alison talks, she's describing her experience, and when you talk, Tyler, you're describing yours. We're not stating indisputable facts."

Alison took a deep breath. She'd been resistant to this type of nuanced dialogue navigation the first time they'd come. It was all "I feel that…" and "It would work better for me if…" And it was so difficult to listen to Tyler do the same without being able to rebut. It had helped some though, so it couldn't hurt to give it another go.

"Fine. I'm worried about his lack of purpose. His *seeming* lack of purpose," she corrected, turning toward Tyler. "This stint of unemployment is dragging on, and I *feel* like you're not motivated to find another job. And because I do care about mine, you're giving me a hard time about it."

Dr. Wezniak jotted something down on her notepad. "Tyler?"

He took a moment to fold his hands in his lap. "I love that you're driven and care about your job. I've always known that's a big part of you. But we haven't really talked in months. We're hardly ever intimate. I eat dinner alone most nights. Actually, I don't even think she eats dinner. Look at her."

Alison's face heated at being talked about and put forth for observation in such a way. How dare he?

Tyler continued. "I'm worried about your health, and I'm worried about our relationship."

"But not about your unemployment?" Alison couldn't keep the snark out of her voice. "I mean, that's the root of all of this, isn't it? When we were both working, things were fine. We were both busy, we had things to talk about over dinner. Now I'm the sole provider, and quite frankly, I have enough people to manage at work—I don't need more of it at home."

"Is that how you feel—like you have to manage your husband?"

"Maybe *manage* is the wrong word, but I'm constantly reminding him to check listings and send in applications." She looked at Tyler. "You were great at your job. I don't understand how you're still unemployed after eight months."

"You feel like he's not trying," Dr. Wezniak said.

"Yeah."

"And, Tyler, what do you think about that?"

"I guess to me there's no hurry. I want to make sure I don't take the first thing that comes along."

"The first thing?" Alison crossed her arms. "How many interviews have you had?"

"I don't know. A few."

"Three." She stabbed the air with her hand. "Three interviews in eight months."

"And one callback," Tyler mumbled.

"One... what? You never told me that."

He swung his head toward her. Defiantly. "Because I didn't go."

Alison was about to launch another volley of disbelief when Dr. Wezniak put a hand up to silence her. "Is there perhaps more to this than you're sharing, Tyler? Could you talk more about what's holding you back in regard to finding a new job?"

"I'll tell you what it is," Alison bit out. "He likes being home. It's comfortable, floating around—"

"Fine!" Tyler near shouted. "Maybe I haven't been trying very hard. Maybe I don't actually know what I want to do anymore." His voice broke. "Not everyone has a clear path they're destined to follow like you. And I would have told you if you'd been around. I tried—several times. But let's face it, I'm not that important in your life anymore. You could care less what I want."

Couldn't, Alison thought. *You* couldn't *care less.* But since she wasn't sure he'd ever raised his voice to her before, she kept her mouth shut.

A pressing silence enveloped them. Tyler now sat as far away from her on the couch as possible, his eyes averted. Alison expected Dr. Wezniak to pounce on this new information, but instead she homed in on Alison.

"How does hearing this make you feel?" she asked.

"That he doesn't know what he wants to do?" Alison shrugged. "I mean, it's not rocket science. You figure it out."

"No, that this is something he's tried to share with you before. That his experience is one of not being valued in your relationship."

Is that what he'd said? That's not what she'd heard.

"Well, it's not true. I value him."

"Oh yeah?" Tyler said. "When was the last time you asked about my day? I offer input when you vent about yours, but it's in one ear out the other, and as soon as you're done, you're off to your corner of the house. Never mind if I have things to say."

Alison crossed her arms. "But you don't. 'They trimmed the green today' or 'the O'Neils got a new car' doesn't count. That's filler. I have actual responsibilities, and I can't believe you don't get that."

Tyler groaned. "Not every single thing you do needs to have productive outcomes and performance measures. We're not business partners; we're married. Husbands and wives are supposed to talk to each other about silly things. Day-to-day stuff. And they're supposed to care what the other person did that day even if it didn't involve closing a multimillion-dollar sale."

His pained expression made Alison's rebuttal fizzle on her tongue. Was there something to what he was saying? It was rare that he got this close to crying. There was so little time in her day for chit-chat—maybe she'd fallen out of practice. She was about to voice this small concession, but as she leaned toward him, she also caught sight of the clock on the wall. *Fuck*, she barely had ten minutes left.

"Alison?" Dr. Wezniak said.

"Yeah."

"What do you think?"

"I think..." She pressed her lips together. This was obviously important to Tyler, and she didn't want him to be upset with her. Usually, she was enough for him. He was the only one who didn't demand *more* and *better*. Until now anyway. Maybe she could admit some fault if it meant focus returned to the real problem—Tyler not having a job. As soon as his days were busy again, she was sure he'd realize she was only being efficient. But for now, she supposed she'd have to adjust and coddle a bit. Make sure he got the quality time that newlywed personality test had suggested he needed to feel most loved. Because she did love him. How could he think otherwise? "I'll try to listen more, okay? And to sit down to dinner. Most nights."

Tyler nodded once.

"But I really think you need to figure this work stuff out. That's key." Alison pulled her purse into her lap. "Here's my suggestion. Use the rest of our hour to work on that, the two of you. And then you fill me in tonight. Over dinner. Sound good?" She looked at them expectantly.

When they didn't respond, she stood. "Thanks, Dr. Wezniak. I'll see you later, Ty." She made her way to the door.

She was about to open it when Tyler spoke. "You have a meeting, don't you?"

She stiffened at the disdain in his voice. Steeled herself. Put on a smile. Turned.

"No," Tyler said. "I don't want to hear it. Just go."

And what else could she do? She had a one o'clock.

TWENTY-THREE

JILLIAN

They'd decided on casual summer wear for the funeral, but come Saturday morning, Jillian stood in her childhood room, hesitating in front of the deep-blue dress Leah had helped her pick out the day before. It looked great on her—that wasn't the problem. The issue was it didn't match her insides. Her insides were colored wrong, like a jagged Picasso, setting her on edge.

They were burying Marion today. *Mom.* No, that still wasn't right. Tomorrow she'd return to New York and her life. Everything would go back to normal. Alison would sell the house. It would be as if they'd never existed in this place. She should be relieved, but it was more complicated than that. No one is anyone without a past.

She averted her eyes from the dress and looked out the window at the lake. It was a gorgeous summer day. The sun glittered off a barely rippling surface, and in the distance two kayaks glided toward the shore. This is where she'd sat, in this window, season after season, writing in her journal, studying, chatting with friends, strumming the guitar she'd had high hopes of conquering. She'd plotted mischief against her sisters one moment, then watched the next as they grew up, one after the other, and left. She'd raged against the unfairness that was cancer taking Dad away, waiting a whole winter through frost-nipped panes for it to come for her too. She'd tracked Marion's path through the garden—clipping raspberry bushes, planting seeds, mowing—for hours, hoping at some point, surely, she'd look up and wave. But she never did.

Jillian walked up to the glass, placing her fingertips against it. She traced the outline of the raised garden bed at the edge of the property. There—right there—was where Marion would kneel and root around for the first new potatoes of the season. And that one year when Leah had brought home several cherry-tomato shoots from school, which grew into the largest tomato plants they'd ever seen in that rich soil near the water, she'd harvested them with growing panic as the fruit abounded. They'd eaten them sun-warm, right off the plant like candy that whole summer. There were no tomatoes that fresh in New York.

A cloud obscured the sun, and for a moment the outside darkened enough that Jillian caught her reflection in the pane. There, too, was Marion, eyes startlingly dry.

A soft knock fell on the door. "Jill, are you ready? We have to leave soon."

Leah had been up early. Through a sleepy haze, Jillian had heard her go up and down the creaky stairs since seven in the morning.

"Be right there," Jillian said, eyes still on that long-ago world. Then she breathed a cloud onto the glass and traced with italicized flourish *The End.*

The funeral took place at a funeral home near Bellevue. Alison and Tyler were already there when Jillian and Leah arrived, though lingering in different parts of the room. Tyler was arranging wreaths around the casket while Alison studied the pictures of Marion displayed in frames along the back wall. She seemed more tightly wound than usual, Jillian noted as they approached. Shoulders bunched tight, hands fluttering across pictures, adjusting them just so, her eyes not settling on anything for extended periods of time.

"You guys are late," she said. No friendly "hi there" today. "The officiator had questions about the eulogy, so I had to tell him something."

"I thought he knew Mom through the homeowners' association," Leah said. "Should we go talk to him?"

"I told you—I already did." Alison's gaze flicked to the front of the room, and her lips tightened before she said with a slight quiver, "I think everything's in order."

Jillian studied her. Alison was the one who'd feel their mother's absence most, so this must be what grief looked like. That ripple of emotion beneath the skin. An alien force searching for a way out.

"I'm going to... um... say goodbye before people get here." Leah turned, setting course toward the closed casket up front.

Alison blinked, a shadow stealing across her face.

"Hey." Jillian brushed her fingers against her sister's sleeve. "Can I help with anything?"

"You don't want to pay your respects too?"

Did she? At the front of the room, Leah's head was bent, her right hand resting on top of the polished wood. What was there to say now? Though she supposed for once Marion would have no choice but to listen. "No, I'm okay."

In an uncharacteristic moment of solicitude, Alison reached for her hand and squeezed it. She didn't say anything, and she didn't need to; Jillian got the message—Alison understood. Marion's death might have left a void in other people's lives, but for Jillian that void had always been there. What was gone was the hope to ever fill it, and she wasn't sure how to mourn something so abstract.

"Did you get hold of her colleagues?" she asked after releasing Alison's hand.

"I did. And I think Mrs. Carlisle rallied the neighbors."

Jillian nodded. "It's hard for Leah that Hannah isn't here."

"A little odd, isn't it?" Alison lowered her voice as if Leah would be able to hear her from afar. "Considering how often Hannah talked to Mom."

Jillian shrugged. "She's young. In love."

"Have you met this Chase guy?"

"I talked to him on the phone once."

"And he's nice?"

"Seems like it."

Alison pursed her lips.

"Why?" Jillian asked. "Leah is okay with him. That probably counts for more than our aunt opinions anyway." Jillian smiled.

"Think she'd say anything if she didn't approve?"

Jillian made a *tsk* sound with her tongue. "That's pretty cynical even for you. So she's not the most outspoken person we know—that's a skill too, parsing your words."

Now it was Alison's turn to smile. "I wouldn't know."

"And what does Tyler say about that?" Jillian cocked an eyebrow. "I have eyes—you're dealing with something there."

Alison sighed. "Not today we're not. Today we're burying Mom, so we've called a truce."

"A truce? That bad?"

"You don't want to know."

And with that the doors to the room opened and the first mourners trickled in, led by the lawyer, Mr. Dunn.

"What's he doing here?" Jillian asked.

"I invited him." Alison waved to get his attention. "He called yesterday to say he needed to speak with us, and I figured since we'd all be together today anyway..."

As he approached, Jillian steeled herself for what she knew

was going to be a minefield of propriety. To grieve or not to grieve? Her sisters may understand her predicament, but no one else would, and so she had a role to play here that she hadn't ever thought to practice for. Then again, apparently so did Alison and Tyler, if cast somewhat differently. And who knew what other secrets dwelled beneath the surface of every single person here. Maybe no one had it together. In some strange way, that notion was a small, but real, comfort.

TWENTY-FOUR

LEAH

Leah ran her fingers across the glossy casket one last time then backed away. She'd told herself she wouldn't bother Hannah with the sadness of the service, but faced with this goodbye, she couldn't help herself. She needed her daughter. It was all kinds of sideways that she wasn't here.

Miss you today, she texted once seated.

As if she didn't all the other days.

It was thanks to Hannah that Leah had maintained as decent a relationship with Mom as she had. Neil had made it hard, but he'd never deprived Hannah of anything. All she'd had to do was start asking questions about her other "nana" and he'd flown Mom out once a year and made sure the two of them spoke regularly. Those annual visits had been little compensation for a real mother–daughter relationship as far as Leah was concerned, and she was always aware of Neil lingering in the periphery as they caught up. But seeing Mom with Hannah was better than nothing, almost allowing her to pretend there was no Neil-shaped wedge between them.

Mom loved Hannah in a way that was wholly different from how she'd been with her own three daughters. Not even her devotion to Alison's childhood endeavors compared. With Hannah, she was unwound, uncomplicated. During those visits, she was the steady center to Hannah's spinning top, content to be pulled in different directions, climbed on, and barraged with questions. Words Leah would have never used about her mother growing up came to mind—patient, indulgent, present. Though admittedly only when Hannah was around. When Hannah got older and took off with friends for a few hours at a time during those weeks, Mom would go back to her regular aloofness. She'd converse politely for a few minutes then disappear into her work or a book. Not that Leah complained. She wouldn't have stomached the attention bestowed upon Hannah —not while expending all her energy keeping the truth about Neil from view. What a cruel trick this was, then, to rob her of even a chance to once and for all bridge the divide.

Her phone vibrated with a message.

I'm thinking of you and Grandma. *sad face emoji*

The room was starting to fill up, and the officiator lingered near the pulpit, poised to start. Quickly, Leah typed back, *I can conference you in for the service.*

She waited for a response.

Sure.

Leah took a seat in the first row of chairs and sent a video-call request through the Interweb. And there was Hannah on her screen.

"Hi, sweetie." Leah kept her voice low. "What time is it there?"

"Almost eight in the evening. Hold on, I'll go into the bedroom. Chase is watching a movie."

The screen blurred, and then a new light source illuminated

her beautiful girl's face again. "Can you show me the room?" Hannah asked.

As inconspicuously as possible, Leah held up the phone and did a slow pan of the space.

"Wow, there are a lot of people there. Do you know them?"

Leah hadn't been paying much attention to her surroundings up until then, but now she examined them in earnest. There *were* a lot of people there. Many more than she'd expected.

"I know some of them," she said. There was Mr. Dunn, the Barkers, the Hillwoods, and several others from the neighborhood, a group of colleagues, the Carlisles... Oh, and Andrew too, standing next to them. A thrill shot through her chest. She hadn't expected him to show up. "But most of these people must be more recent acquaintances and people from work I've never met."

"Students too, you think?" Hannah asked. "Some look kind of young to be friends."

"Maybe." Leah glanced again at the spot where Andrew and his parents stood. Jillian had joined them, and Mrs. Carlisle had her hand on Jillian's arm. Suddenly, Andrew looked her way, and their eyes met across the room. He smiled and raised his hand. She did the same before turning away, cheeks hot. That dimple.

She bit down hard on her lip before telling Hannah, "I think it's about to start. I'll mute you, but you should be able to see and hear just fine."

As if on cue, the officiator tapped the microphone and urged everyone to take their seats.

Jillian and Alison—with Tyler trailing a few feet behind—took their seats either side of Leah.

"Hannah?" Jillian nodded toward the phone Leah was holding.

"Yeah."

"Good." She took Leah's free hand and squeezed it. Didn't let go.

Daughter in one hand, sister in the other, Leah kept her eyes fixed on the casket a few yards away. It was the closest she'd come in a long while to feeling anchored in a place not by weighty obligation but by human connection—strange perhaps since Mom was gone, Jillian would leave for New York in the next day or two, Alison preferred being a solo act, and Hannah was a face on a screen. Still, there was a traceable line between them all and it formed a circle. A circle she was part of.

A sudden epiphany: She should go visit Jill in New York sometime. Why not? She'd travelled here, hadn't she?

Her thoughts were interrupted by the officiator's greeting.

"Welcome, all. If you're in the back and you'd like to sit, there are still a couple of seats up here." He pointed to his left.

Leah turned. Standing room only. Who were all these people, and how had they known her mother?

There were a few coughs coming from the back, but soon everyone settled, and the eulogizing began.

"... a devoted friend..."

"... a loving mother..."

"... the smartest person I knew..."

"... a quiet life..."

"... a full life..."

"... a life cut too short..."

For a brief moment, the room spun as memories from a year ago settled like a semi-opaque fog, overlaying the scene. One of Neil's best friends—also the superintendent at the school district they worked for—had said similar things about him. Leah squeezed her eyes shut and focused on Jillian's hand, on Alison's shoulder against hers.

There was one big difference between that day and this one.

Today she cried.

TWENTY-FIVE

ALISON

If Alison had known the whole department from UW would show up, she'd have booked a larger venue for the wake. Bannerman Bistro's event room had a head count restriction of forty-five people, and while not everyone who'd been to the funeral had joined them, they were still at least fifteen over and spilling into the bar and dining area.

She waited as the hostess went to find the manager to see if accommodations could be made. Tyler had offered to figure things out, but she'd rather he mingle and make sure everyone was comfortable. He loved that stuff; was great at it too. Alison was able to fake it well enough on a good day, but right now she feared if she sat down and tried to converse with people, the engine that kept her running would shut down. Stand, walk, organize, coordinate, troubleshoot. As long as she kept doing what she did best, she would hold it together.

In truth, her insides were like that creaky branch when you climb a tree. You step onto it, and it protests, but you figure it will still hold you, at least for a while. She'd cried at the service —she blamed that. Caving to emotion always rattled her, and today it had been hard to catch a solid breath even before all that blubbering. Mom would not have approved.

Alison tried again for a long inhale. Good, she was breathing better now. *Another one. Shoulders down.* Only that low-pitched tone ringing in her ear remained. On their way over, she'd almost told Tyler to drive them home. She would have, if they'd been on speaking terms. It had felt like such an impossibility to not only get into the car but also exit it, walk places, talk to people. She didn't want to. She wanted to go home, crawl under the covers, never emerge.

Her eyes drifted toward the groups of socializing mourners at the other side of the room. Tyler was engaged in an animated conversation with Andrew Carlisle, as if nothing was amiss. Problems were for fixing, but she didn't understand Tyler anymore. He'd chosen to sleep in the guest room the night before. First time ever in their eight years of marriage. Alison had done it many times of course, but then it had been on her terms. This was new. She'd dozed for only a couple of hours, kept at the cusp of consciousness by his glaringly empty side of the bed, and the complete confusion at not knowing how to put things right.

The hostess returned, a solicitous smile on her face. "Thank you so much for waiting. We can set up some extra tables in front of your space—that way everyone is near each other."

Alison fought another lump in her throat at the kindness. "That would be fantastic. Thank you."

On her way back to the guests, Mr. Dunn intercepted her halfway. "Do you think we might find a corner for a chat with your sisters per our talk yesterday?" he asked when she stopped. "I know you have guests to attend, but it won't take long. I've got the papers ready."

Alison scouted the bar area and found an empty table near the far wall. "How about over there. I'll go get Jill and Leah."

With leaden feet, she moved through the crowd, accepting

condolences and kind words as she went. She tried to circum-vent Tyler's spot, but as luck would have it, Leah had joined him and Andrew in conversation, so she had no choice but to approach.

"Leah, do you have a minute? Mr. Dunn is about to leave, and he needs us. Over there." She pointed.

Leah was pale, her eyes red-rimmed, but for once she didn't flinch at the interruption. In fact, there was a calm about her when she nodded that Alison vaguely recalled from their child-hood. Over the years, that unflappability had been replaced by skittishness. Until now. But maybe Leah was simply as tired as Alison and it was low energy she sensed, not a personality shift.

"I'll be right back," Leah told Andrew. "I want to hear more about that hike. It sounds amazing."

She joined Alison as they went further into the room.

"Have you seen Jill anywhere?" Alison craned her neck to scout.

"I think she went to the bathroom a while ago."

"Let's check so we can get this over with."

"What does Mr. Dunn want anyway?"

"I asked him to bring the house paperwork. It seemed like a good idea at the time since we're all together."

They pushed open the door to the ladies' room, and there was Jillian in front of the mirror, dabbing wet tissue under her eyes to clean up half-moons of sooty goop. When she saw her sisters, her hands fell to her sides, and her face contorted.

"I can't stop crying," she sobbed. "I'm wearing waterproof fucking mascara, but I've cried so much it's now lodged itself underneath my eyes."

Alison and Leah stood frozen for a moment, then something released in Alison's chest, and she did something she hadn't done in years. She started giggling.

"It's not funny," Jillian whined, but her lips quirked up first a little, then with the full force of a grin. Eyes still glittering with tears, she joined in the laughter, and soon, so did Leah. The three of them clung to each other for a long while, balancing together on the crisp edge between mirth and despair, but eventually they emerged from the vortex, storm weathered.

"I have make-up wipes in my purse." Alison fished them out. "Here."

Jillian proceeded to clean herself up. "I don't even know what my deal is. Maybe there's a full moon or something."

Alison shrugged. "It's your mom's funeral. It's supposed to mess you up."

"Well, I don't like it, and I certainly didn't sign up for it." Jillian examined her face in the mirror. "People are going to think that..."

"What?" Alison asked.

"Nothing. Is this better?" Jillian turned toward them.

Leah took a wipe and removed something off Jillian's temple. "Who cares what people think?" she said quietly. "Most of them don't know you, and you won't have to ever see them again. To them, you're a grieving daughter. They don't need to know all the other stuff." She took a step back. "There."

Jillian smoothed her hair in the mirror and took a deep breath. "It's kind of messed up right, that I don't want to be sad. As if she wins if I am."

"Very," Alison said.

Jillian's lip quirked.

"You're hardly alone." Leah held open the door. "Everyone's different shades of messed up." She offered them a sad smile. "Now, come on—let's go see Mr. Dunn."

There were two stacks of papers and a yellow envelope on the round table in front of the lawyer. After exchanging greetings and complimenting the service, he placed a hand on top of one of the piles and paused. "I brought the papers for you to sign, but I also have some news," he said, brows knit. "I only learned of it late yesterday or I would have reached out sooner."

Alison turned the yellow envelope toward her to read the address. "Is that Mom's handwriting?"

"It is," Mr. Dunn confirmed. "It appears it was mailed to the office shortly before she... um..."

"Killed herself," Jillian filled in.

"Um, yes." He pushed his glasses higher on his nose. "Because it had no sender's address, my secretary left it in the inbox on her desk before she took off for a few days. My sincere apologies for the delay."

"What is it?" Jillian asked.

While they were talking, Alison had pulled some of the paperwork closer to her. Was this the letter they'd been looking for? The explanation? She scanned the top document; flicked to the next page. "It's the deeds to another property," she said, frowning.

"Right." Mr. Dunn nodded. "For some reason, she never told me about this when we first drew up the will. If she had, I would have divulged it when we first met. But everything is in legal order. She hadn't owned it long, but the property was hers and is rightfully part of the estate."

"That would explain why her house didn't look lived in," Leah said.

"Did you know about it, Ali?" Jillian asked.

Alison ignored Jillian's question while studying the paperwork. "185th Avenue. Isn't that on the other side of the lake?"

"Yeah, Max used to live there," Jillian offered, referring to an old boyfriend.

"But why would Mom need a second house?"

All three of them turned as one to Mr. Dunn as if he'd have the answer.

He blinked. "That I can't tell you."

"And still no note?" Jillian leaned closer to Alison and the documents.

"Not in the sense you're hoping for I'm afraid," Mr. Dunn said. "Here, it might still be in the envelope."

Alison beat him to it and fished out a slip of paper from its yellow confines. "'*I should probably give you this too*,'" she read. "'*The key is under the blue planter on the north side of the deck.*'"

"That's it?" Jillian looked decidedly less teary now, arms crossed in front of her.

"That's it," Alison confirmed.

"Maybe she left a note in *that* house," Leah said. "There has to be something more than what we found in that Bible."

"If I could get your signatures here, here, and here." Mr. Dunn flipped over a couple of pages, pen at the ready. "I know you have guests, so I'll get out of your hair. If you have any questions, anything at all I can assist with, don't hesitate to call."

"What's with all this secrecy?" Jillian asked after he'd left. "The cancer, the suicide, now this house..."

"That's what I keep saying," Leah said. "We're missing something. We need to get to that house."

"It would look bad if we left now." Alison gestured to the people around them. "But I agree, we need to see it in person. Especially since this means we'll now have two houses to sell." She sighed. She didn't need another thing added to her list. Two houses? What was Mom thinking? Sure, real estate was a solid investment, but she was hardly a property flipper. Like so many other things these days, it made little sense.

"I... was actually going to talk to you both about that," Leah said. Then before they could respond: "Never mind—we should get back. We can talk tomorrow. It's not important."

Too much talking, Alison thought. She needed a drink and fast. "Yeah, I think tomorrow is better. Why don't we meet at this new mystery house at ten and go from there?"

TWENTY-SIX

LEAH

Leah and Jillian returned to Mom's house late in the afternoon. The tab for appetizers had far exceeded their budget, but Alison had picked it up without a word in spite of being thoroughly tipsy. It wasn't like her to overindulge, and Leah was worried. She'd never known her oldest sister to succumb like that—like her buttresses were failing. She'd always carried herself and whatever was on her plate unfazed.

"Give her a break," Jillian said when Leah voiced her concern. "She's not superhuman."

Leah conceded that was true but couldn't shake her unease.

They'd decided to go for a walk to shrug off the lingering cloak of sadness. The sun was still high enough in the sky that kids played in the water as if time was abundant, but the shadows were growing longer by the minute.

While Jillian changed out of her dress, Leah ambled through the yard, passing azaleas just out of bloom, fragrant Spanish lavender, and the waxy green of Mom's favorite, the honeysuckle, beginning to show off its orange flowers. All the growth was bigger than she remembered, mature now, like her.

She turned toward the house when she was halfway down

the lawn, shading her eyes with one hand against the sun reflecting in the upstairs windows. The view pulled at something deep within again. A tugging siren call. She wrapped her arms around herself. Could it be that it was meant for her?

Jillian came bounding down the deck steps, interrupting Leah's yearning. She was in shorts and had put her shoulder-length hair up in a ponytail. In that light, she could have easily passed for a version of her fifteen-year-old self. It gave Leah a dizzying sense of déjà vu.

"Ah, that's better." Jillian stretched her arms high above her head as she approached Leah. "Where do you want to go?"

"The beach trail?"

A trampled path meandered through the tall grass near the water's edge all the way from the Carlisles' property to the park. As kids they'd run it daily in the summers to get to the small patch of sandy gravel that served as a launch pad for kayaks, inflatable floats, and kids who were not yet old or daring enough to jump into the water from the communal pier. They'd affectionately named this path "the beach trail", making it sound much fancier than it was.

"Lead the way."

They walked in silence, single file, until they were past the last property and the trail widened. As if on cue, they both stopped by the willow that grew at an angle in the marshy border of the lake, reaching its arms longingly toward the deep.

Jillian spoke first. "Which house do you think it is?"

Leah scanned the row of homes on the far side of the lake, wishing she'd brought binoculars. It was impossible to make out much else than the size of the buildings.

"I have no idea, but there'd better be some answers there."

"Hi there."

They turned at the greeting to find Mr. Carlisle and his two dogs approaching from the other direction. He'd changed out of the suit he'd worn at the wake and into jeans and a T-shirt.

"Man, for a moment there I thought I was seeing a ghost." He faced Jillian with a pained expression. "Spitting image of your mother if I ever saw one. What a day, huh? Sunset will be gorgeous. How are you girls holding up?"

Leah practically heard steam shooting out of her sister's ears at the comparison, so before Jill could say anything, she thanked him for coming earlier. "We weren't expecting such a turnout."

He waved it off. "We'll miss her dearly, that's for sure. Hadn't seen her in a while, but then again, she was always so busy with this and that. It kind of feels like she might still turn up in the garden at any moment."

Leah and Jillian shared a look.

"Um, Mr. C, do you know if she was thinking of moving or anything?" Leah asked.

"Or investing in real estate?" Jillian added.

His eyebrows jumped. "Huh? I can't say I do. But Ruth would be a better person to talk to about that. Why do you ask?"

"Oh, no reason." Jillian grabbed Leah's arm and took a step backwards. "We should let you continue your walk. Give our thanks to Ruth too, for coming today."

"Will surely do." He raised a hand in goodbye.

When he was out of earshot, Jillian half whispered to Leah, "Did you hear that? He hadn't seen her 'in a while'. I'll bet you anything Mom wasn't living in the house anymore. This other place—that's the key."

Leah nodded. Was that the answer to Alison's question too? Why the lake? If their mother was living in this other house no one knew about, maybe she was worried her death would go unnoticed.

"We should go find it now. I mean it's right there. Some-where." Jillian pointed. "Why wait until tomorrow?"

"Ali will literally kill us if we do it without her."

"We can call her."

"I doubt she's able to drive considering how much she drank."

"Dammit, I forgot about that. What's going on with her and Tyler anyway?"

Leah's step faltered. "Is that why she was drinking? I thought it was because of Mom."

Jillian shook her head. "I don't think so. At least that wasn't the only reason. She said they'd called 'a truce' so by definition there must have been a fight."

They crossed the short bridge that spanned the creek feeding into the lake. Was the issue only Ali working too much, or was there more? Her sister was an intense kind of person; once she set her sights on something, she was 110 percent in. That sort of focus could be both intimidating and exhausting. But Tyler appeared to be the perfect mellow counterpart to balance her out... Or maybe he wasn't. Leah was the last person who should argue you always knew what you were getting into when you married someone.

"You got quiet," Jillian noted, after a few minutes passed.

"Just thinking. Sharing your life with someone is weird."

Jillian's mouth pulled sideways. "I wouldn't know."

"Well, yeah, but... you like it that way, right? Or no?"

Jillian shrugged. "It has its moments."

Leah hesitated, then went for it. "Have you thought any more about Greg's question?"

They reached the park and continued away from the water into a lush grove of maples interspersed with a few tall evergreens. Jillian kicked a stray pine cone off the paved path. "When am I not thinking about it?" She glanced at Leah. "Not getting anywhere though. There's the promotion and... I mean, you heard Mr. C—'spitting image of Mom.'"

This again. Leah's jaw tightened. "So you look like her. Big deal. Hannah looks mostly like Neil and that doesn't mean shit." She spat out the last word then sucked in a quick breath as if it had taken her by surprise.

Jillian stared at her. "Whoa, where did that come from?"

"I..." The words were on the tip of her tongue. *He hit me.* "He..." Her fists tightened at her side. "Never mind." She sighed, throat tight. Soon. "My point is—you are you. You've always been a great aunt to Hannah. I think you'd be an amazing mom. Don't sell yourself short."

They reached the end of the trail where the path crossed a busy road and stopped. "Turn around?"

They did and backtracked their footsteps. Jillian was deep in thought.

"Can I tell you something?" she asked eventually.

"Sure."

"When I start thinking about having a baby with Greg and David, doubting myself isn't the only thing on my mind."

"No?"

"I mean, I know they said they'd move to New York and all that, but honestly—when I think about having a baby, I kind of want it to be mine. All the time. I don't want a... a time share. Sure, it would be handy to have a second person around for when I have to travel, but I think if I did this with Greg and David, they'd be number one and number two, and I'd be the odd person out. I'd rather hire a nanny then, or bring the kid with me when its older."

Leah stopped short at that, forcing Jillian to turn around.

"What?" Jillian asked.

Leah smiled. "Don't you realize what you just said? You're planning, thinking things through, looking for ways to make it work. All things a parent does."

"Maybe."

"Not maybe."

They started walking again. "There's kind of a major problem though," Jillian said. "If not Greg and David, then who? Last time I checked, we hadn't yet solved the reproductive glitch of needing a male."

"One-night stand?"

"Um, no. Totally unethical. Would never."

"Good—that was a test." Leah bumped shoulders with her little sister. The topic was alleviating some of the heaviness from earlier. The idea of new life in the wake of loss perhaps. "How about a donor then?"

Jillian frowned. "Isn't that weird?"

"Hey, whatever works. My point is there are options."

The sun was getting low, painting the treetops in gold and orange, the sky in pink, as they made their way back to the house.

"I'm going to miss you when I leave tomorrow," Jillian said after a while. "I was dreading coming out here, but it actually hasn't been too bad."

"Yeah, we have our moments," Leah said wryly.

"You know what I mean. We need to be better at staying in touch. And Chicago isn't that far—I'll come visit."

If I'll still be there, Leah thought. That was the next thing she needed to figure out. Jillian may have made it clear she laid no claim to their heritage here, but Leah still needed to convince Alison to let her have Mom's house.

TWENTY-SEVEN

ALISON

Alison woke up alone in their king-sized bed. Had Tyler slept in the guest room again? Was he really avoiding her the weekend of her mother's funeral? The questions swirled through her foggy, hungover mind as she drifted on the threshold of sleep, until she managed to turn toward his side of the bed and found the sheets bunched and the pillow dented. She reached out a hand and caressed the spot where his head had rested. No, of course he'd stayed with her. If she focused, she could vaguely recall coming home and Ty tucking her in. How classy of her— getting drunk at her mother's wake.

More thoughts like cold water droplets against a bare neck. Her husband was a good man. She didn't deserve him. Why were they even fighting? She squeezed her eyes shut against the threatening tears. The move intensified the pounding behind her forehead.

Alison's phone chimed with a message, jarring her compromised senses like the squeak of Styrofoam against cardboard. She groaned, rolling back over. Her mouth was vinegar and sandpaper, but the tap was all the way in the bathroom. She contemplated this problem until she slowly drifted off again, unconsciousness promising more heavenly numbness.

Her phone beeped again, pulling her back out. Leah.

Hope you're feeling okay this morning. Just reminding you we're meeting at 10 (in case you forgot)

Alison fake-sobbed with dramatic flair and flopped onto her back. What time was it? Almost 9 AM. She had no choice. She had to get up and get on with her day. Her head throbbed with each step as she staggered toward the bathroom. The light was too bright. Her heartbeat too loud. The world too real. She stopped with her hand on the door handle, startled by unexpected noise. The shower was already running. She pushed the door open a crack, a cloud of steam escaping as she did. Tyler had his back to her in the glass enclosure, his bare skin fractured in the water-slick panes. Her husband. Her husband who'd tucked her in and slept next to her all night.

Something softened inside her at the sight of him like this— not naked and alone necessarily but bared. Unexpected.

She stepped into the bathroom and out of yesterday's skirt in a move that should have made her stumble but didn't. She pulled off her shirt next, her bra, her pride. Being near him would make this feeling in the pit of her stomach go away. She knew it, even through the fog.

She paused outside the stall and sucked in a breath. "Do you mind if I join you?" Her voice came out hoarse, forty-two years of not smoking for nothing.

Tyler spun, eyes wide. "God, you scared me. I thought you were still asleep."

She took his lack of protest as an affirmative and slid open the door. The steam was thicker inside, billowing toward the ceiling. He'd always liked his showers piping hot, and this morning she didn't mind. The funeral sat like an icy rod through her core.

"Leah texted me." She slid the door closed behind her, allowed the heat to chase across her skin.

"How are you feeling?"

The spray of the water was a deluge down Tyler's shoulders, ricocheting off his skin onto her. First her feet, her calves, then her thighs and hips as she stepped further into his space.

"Like I drank too much." She tried for a smile but struggled to make her muscles cooperate. "Sorry about that."

He shrugged, and for a brief moment, she thought she'd misread things. What if he did nothing—or worse, stepped back when she reached him? But then he ran a hand across his face as if to wipe the water away and lowered his gaze to her breasts. Her shoulders softened from the combined effect of this warm cocoon and his visible approval. He was right—it had been a long time. She used to love it when he looked at her like that.

"Want me to do your back?" she asked.

His eyes returned to her face, gray storm clouds analyzing her. After a long moment, he turned around and handed her his loofah.

Long ago, when they'd first started dating, they'd mapped each other, and she knew every birthmark, every scar, every turn of muscle on the expanse before her, yet she hesitated before daring to touch him. Without heels on, she only reached the nape of his neck, but his impassive back made her shrink even smaller. She'd forgotten how to read it. Didn't know what he wanted from her. Her throat tightened. When had they stopped claiming each other?

"Is the water too hot?" he asked when she didn't move.

She blinked then let her palm make contact with his shoulder blade. A visible shiver ran across his shoulders. Her thumb skimmed across the small scar near his spine, left over from a childhood tree-climbing accident. A familiar landmark. She clung to it. "No, it's good."

She let her hand holding the loofah mimic the other's circular movement, first up to his neck and down his triceps, the soapy suds competing for the drain in a mesmerizing race. Then back down his sides and down past his narrow waist until she reached the dimpled crest of his pelvis. Repeat and rinse.

On the third round, his head tipped forward beneath the spray and his hands reached back for her, making ginger contact with her hips. She dropped the loofah and stepped close to him, skin to skin, slipping easily around to his front to face him.

"My turn?" he said, voice thick.

She nodded, reaching up to meet his lips. She'd be late for her sisters, but this couldn't wait any longer. Since words didn't work for her and Tyler nowadays, they had to find other ways to communicate.

With her back to the tile, Alison gave in to the possibility that this was the solution they'd been looking for. Or at least a temporary remedy.

TWENTY-EIGHT

JILLIAN

Jillian sat at the edge of her bed, phone in hand. Greg's name was still on the screen even though five minutes had passed since they'd hung up. She'd made the right decision. Talking to Leah the previous evening had told her that she'd already known the answer to her friends' proposal, as tempting as it had been. It was the first time she'd had to confront the thought of having a kid as a real possibility and not as a flight of fancy to dismiss.

Greg was disappointed of course. An understatement. Being the bearer of bad news was the worst. No amount of "if anyone, then you" soothed the sting in such a rejection. She was selfish, that was all. If she was going to have a kid, she would do it full out. That was the takeaway after these past few days of inner turmoil—at least now she knew she wanted to give it a serious shot. She'd already started looking into what using a donor would entail and had decided a visit to her OB/GYN would be a good first step.

"Will you be ready to go in five minutes?" Leah hollered from downstairs.

"Coming!" Jillian tucked the phone into her purse and

pulled her hair up into a ponytail without brushing it. Soon enough she'd be back to work where making good impressions was part of the deal. Her small suitcase was already packed and ready at the door. She'd stripped the sheets off the bed and aired out the room. This afternoon she'd pack up what few belongings she'd left here in a box to be shipped. There wasn't much—a few books, some photos, a bag of childhood memorabilia Leah had pulled out from the attic.

Jillian's fingers sought out the necklace around her neck, its charms a rare solid connection to that time. She'd loved the vintage bookcase and diminutive flea-market-find desk that had once stood in her room, but, true to form, Marion hadn't kept any of her furniture once she'd moved out. She wanted nothing from the rest of the house. Well, except for the framed picture of their dad by his plane; she'd claimed that one. The rest of the furnishings could be sold off separately or go with the house—it didn't matter to her. She'd be glad for her share of the money from the sale, but that was it. Let someone else move in here and make happier memories.

On a whim, she pulled out a pen from her purse, opened her empty closet, and crouched down on the floor. There, in the farthest bottom corner, she found the markings she'd made as a child when counting the days until Dad would get home from his trips. Numerous notches made in blue, black, and red pen. Now, she drew a tiny heart next to them, then considered what other profound legacy she might leave to mark the end of an era. In the end, nothing came to mind, and she settled for simply scribbling, *Jill was here*. That's all she'd ever wanted the house to know anyway.

TWENTY-NINE

LEAH

If Marion's neighborhood was a fairly uniform 1970s suburban creation, the homes along 185th were a more eclectic jumble of modest ranch homes wedged between the mansions that had popped up as the old lots were sold off and their buildings torn down in the 1990s and early 2000s. This was prime real estate, right off the lake, and each home—old and new alike—had some form of lakeside recreational set-up, whether a modest pier or a full boat house.

Leah's fingers tapped the steering wheel as she drove. Whatever was at the end of this ride, some of their questions had better get answered. "It's 20324," she muttered. Then to Jillian: "Do you see any house numbers?"

The road curved up a hill where several well-manicured homes sat partly hidden behind picket fences, sloping willows, and towering cedars, then narrowed to a quaint lane, adorned with quirky mailboxes, old rhododendrons, and occasional glimpses of the water through the foliage.

Jillian leaned close to the window and scanned the houses they passed. "That's 20320. It must be around here."

"Is that it?" Leah stopped next to a mailbox overgrown with

ivy. "Can you go look?"

Jillian got out and pushed the leaves out of the way. "Yeah, this is it," she hollered. She hurried back into the car and pointed down a long, sloped driveway that ended somewhere behind the neighboring house. "Down there."

Leah backed up and took the turn. The closer they got, the faster her pulse. Ten-year-old, Nancy Drew-loving her would have been jumping up and down at this bona fide treasure hunt. Come to think of it, didn't Andrew and his brothers used to have a detective agency when they were little? Then, unexpectedly: she wished she could tell him about this quest. A shake of the head to disperse that notion. This was no time to get sidetracked.

They parked in front of a white, cottage-like home with dormers, a chimney, and a well-kept front yard streaked in bright green from the sunlight.

"That's cute." Leah opened her door, shading her eyes.

"Like a house Little Red Riding Hood's grandma might live in," Jillian said.

The property was lined with a hedge in need of pruning, but the grass was neat, and the flowerbeds burst with colors. Clearly, whoever lived here had green fingers.

She corrected herself—no one lived here. This house belonged to them now. Had Mom planted these flowers?

Before Leah had time to ponder this further, Alison pulled up next to them, exiting her car with a large to-go mug in her hand, a pair of sunglasses firmly planted on her nose, and wet hair in a bun on top of her head. "So, what have we got?" she asked.

"How are you feeling?" Leah countered.

"Fine."

Jillian offered a teasing smile. "If you remove the shades too?"

"Yeah, yeah. Yesterday wasn't my best." Alison eased her

stance and took a sip from her mug. When she raised her arm to drink, her collarbone stood out in sharp relief beneath her navy blouse.

Leah frowned at the sight. "You know you can talk to us if something's going on, right?"

Alison blinked at her. "Um, no, I'm okay. It was the funeral and... everything. I'm much better now." She held her cup up toward the house. "Shall we?" Her tone didn't invite argument.

If that's how it's going to be... Leah led the way through the gate in the hedge. "The key is in the back," she said, veering off the stone path. "Blue planter."

"Might as well check out the exterior first," Alison said.

They marched single file around the right side of the building and found the overall structure larger than their first impression had suggested. Because of the gradient of the lot, the building had a walk-out basement and a large deck that was partially glassed in to create an additional three-season room. The emerald lawn stretched at least fifty yards down to a neat little dock and a decent-sized shed. The hedge was taller back here, offering privacy from the neighbors, and a large patch of blueberry bushes took up the whole left side of the property next to the house.

"Wow," Jillian said, scanning the water. "That's gorgeous."

"It must be close to an acre," Alison said. "That's huge for these lots. I suppose since the house itself is a little smaller, it leaves more space for outdoor living."

Jillian craned her neck. "I can almost see our house from here."

Leah carefully tilted the large planter that sat next to the door. Bingo! "Found the key." She held it up.

They looked at each other.

Alison pushed her sunglasses up on her head and rubbed her eye. She wasn't wearing any make-up. "All right," she said. "Let's do this then."

THIRTY

LEAH

Undefined tension permeated the air as the three of them rounded the corner to the front and made their way past the flowerbeds. Small glass ornaments glittered among the plants, enforcing the initial fairy-tale impressions, and so did the hand-painted garden gnome next to the front step.

"No Man's Land," Leah read aloud off the sign above the front door. The lettering was burned into a polished woodcut. "What do you suppose that means?"

Alison scoffed. "Some people like to name their houses. They think it's cute."

"Could be left from the previous owner," Leah suggested. It wasn't Mom's style. "Didn't Mr. Dunn say she hadn't owned it very long?"

"Just unlock it." Alison shifted her stance. "We don't have all day. Jill has a flight to catch."

The key was cold in Leah's hand. She wasn't sure why she wanted to drag out this moment. Maybe she sensed there'd be a before and after, and that the leap between the two would require an elasticity of mind she wasn't used to employing. This past week had already brought so much change. She drew a breath. "Fine."

The door swung open.

From the foyer they could see straight through to the other side of the house where a row of windows overlooked the backyard and lake. The view was stunning of course, but disappointingly similar to that of their old place. Some of Leah's anticipatory jitters dwindled. Maybe it was nothing more than a house after all.

Alison pushed past her, nodding approvingly. "They've done some work here. I'll bet anything there was a wall here when it was first built." She marked the space with her body.

Faint notes of *Dune* by Dior mixed with something earthier in the air as they started moving through the room. "It smells like Mom," Leah said.

Alison stopped what she was doing. "You think?" She sniffed the air. "Maybe a little."

"Hey, guys?" Jillian called from down a short hallway to the right. She was standing in the doorway of a room beyond.

Leah and Alison joined her, and together they surveyed the odd mix of furniture before them. With bookcases lining the walls and a desk shoved into a corner, it was clear the space had once been an office. Now, however, that desk was covered with empty vases and in the middle of the room stood a state-of-the-art hospital bed, its head end elevated.

Leah was the first one to enter the room, making her way around the bed to the desk to pick up two stray cards that still sat next to the vases.

"Mom had just been diagnosed," Alison said. "Why would she have a hospital bed?"

Leah held up the cards. "I don't think it was hers. Both of these are for someone called Catherine." She frowned. The name didn't sound familiar, but what did she know?

"This is getting weirder and weirder," Jillian said with a shudder. "Let's get out of here."

They returned to the foyer and proceeded into the open living area. The house footprint may have been modest, but the pine floors gleamed in the sunlight, and the decorating was tasteful. The juxtaposition of the old building and the modern color scheme—muted warm gray with an occasional pop of orange and teal—shouldn't have worked, but Leah walked through the room feeling as if she'd been there before, even though it wasn't long before the differences outweighed the similarities to their childhood home. There was an intention at work here—in layout, hue, and ambiance—that was lacking in the other place.

"These paintings are fantastic," Jillian said, admiring the wall opposite the windows. She turned to Alison. "Is everything in here ours? Like, if I want to bring one of these with me home, I can?"

"We should do inventory before we start dividing things up. But yeah, I guess."

"Look." Leah pointed to one of the end tables next to the couch where several books sat stacked in a neat pile. "*The Power of Babel: A Natural History of Language*; *Social Linguistics and Literacies*; *Transformational Grammar*. These must have been Mom's."

"Not this." Alison toed a basket full of yarn and knitting needles. "I've never seen her knit anything."

Leah spun in a circle in the room. Mom had made herself comfortable here, that much was clear. But someone sick had been with her. Her mind churned. "Maybe she was a caretaker," she said.

Jillian frowned. "Like a personal assistant? Nah."

"Yeah. Think about it—if this Catherine person got worse, she might have needed full-time care. Maybe that's why Mom moved in."

Alison dragged a finger along the windowsill. Examined it. "It's possible, but it hardly answers everything. For one, why retire from the university and start another job? She would have told me."

"And it's a messy job." Jillian drifted toward the kitchen. "No, I don't buy it."

Leah followed. "But what else is there? We know she wasn't living at the house. She owned this place. Someone in need of medical assistance also lived here..." She stopped short at the sight of the farmhouse sink in hammered copper. It was the first thing she'd ever added to her Pinterest board for home ideas, but obviously that dream had never been realized. Here, it sat as the crowning glory of a space that begged for fresh herbs, sizzling pans, and long Sundays of baking. The countertops were white quartz and the cabinets a weathered gray with uppers sporting metal mesh inlays instead of glass. It was the same mix of modern and rustic found in the living room, and for some reason it filled Leah with a longing that made her want to cry.

"Nice reno," Alison commented, touching the sink. "These things aren't cheap."

Her words made Leah's hackles rise. "Do you have to look at everything as objects of revenue?" she asked. "Can't we just take in the space and appreciate it? It's a dream home. I don't blame Mom for wanting to live here."

"It's a little quaint for me," Alison said.

"Way to miss the point," Jillian muttered to Leah, who gave her an appreciative smile.

Leah sat down in one of two chairs at the small kitchen table and ran her palms over the smooth wood. An idea was already taking over, filling her with anxious elation that was highly premature. Alison may have shot down the notion of her taking over Mom's house (and deep inside Leah knew she was right—that house was much too big for one person), but this one, this adorable cottage, was perfect. It was move-in ready, as far as she was concerned; she wouldn't even have to bring her furniture from Chicago. Everything here was better.

"Huh," Alison said after opening a door to a small bathroom. "The bedrooms must be downstairs. Not ideal…"

Leah and Jillian exchanged another wry look before following Alison down the open staircase to the bottom floor.

The walk-out basement was steeped in light, glassed-in as it was along the whole lake-facing wall. The left side of the room was a de facto library, complete with filled bookcases, two easy chairs, and a reading lamp. The right side was meant for entertaining, its focal points a long slab table with eight chairs and a console that served as a combined bar and buffet. It resembled the living room upstairs in style; however, you didn't need Alison's expertise to deduce this part of the house had yet to be updated. The wood paneling on the walls was probably older than all of them, the laminate flooring either a hack job or simply old and creaky, and a distinct smell of mold trickled from the area near the bathroom.

"Yikes," was Alison's judgment.

Leah ignored her in favor of scanning the spines of the books on the shelves. Mysteries mingled with historical romances, biographies, and the classics. They were in alphabetical order, which, if Mom's office in the other house was anything to go by, wasn't her doing, and Leah was about to comment on it when two photographs at the end of one shelf caught her attention. One was of a woman Leah had never seen before, paintbrush in hand, in front of a half-finished canvas. Judging by the style of her hair, Leah guessed it was taken sometime in the 1990s. Leaning closer, Leah realized the work in progress was one of the paintings currently hanging on the wall upstairs. It was a candid photo, but the photographer had failed to completely sneak up on his or her subject—the woman was looking straight into the camera with a wide grin on her face.

The second photo was one Leah had seen many times before. It used to sit in the kitchen window at the other house when they were growing up, and it featured her and her sisters crammed into the backseat of the station wagon Dad used to drive. The photo was taken from behind the car with the hatch open, showing three serious little faces peering over the backrest. Jillian's hair was on end, as if she'd just woken up.

"What are you looking at?" Jillian came up behind Leah and looked over her shoulder.

Leah handed her the frame and waited for a reaction.

"I don't remember this," Jillian said, staring at the photo.

"You can't have been more than two."

Jillian handed the frame back, forehead creased. "Why would she keep this here?"

Yet another question to add to the list. "No idea." Leah placed it back on the shelf. "If she had to move in, maybe she brought a few things over to make it feel like home?"

Jillian arched her brows. "A random photo of us as kids?"

"I don't know. You have a better explanation?"

"I think Mom slept in here," Alison said from the doorway to the larger of the two bedrooms that flanked the common area. "There are sheets on this bed."

Jillian and Leah joined her, continuing the exploration.

"It smells even more like her too," Leah said. That and old carpet. There was a distinct possibility cats had lived here at one point. She slid open one of the double closet doors, expecting it to reflect the temporary stay of a guest, and found instead every hanger taken, every shelf filled. Tops and bottoms, hats and sweaters. Several pairs of shoes lined the floor, along with small storage boxes and a vacuum cleaner. Leah grabbed a pair of shoes and checked for a size—7.5. Not Mom's then—she'd always been a nine.

But as Leah browsed through the garments, something red caught her eye—a parka she knew was Mom's because she'd been with her when she'd bought it on Michigan Avenue in Chicago a few years back. And there was her blue shirt dress with the woven belt and a familiar floral-print top.

Mystified, Leah headed to the other bedroom and opened the closet in there. Winter coats, formalwear in garment bags, extra comforters and pillows, more boxes: a storage closet. Something about this wasn't sitting right with her, but she couldn't put her finger on what. She returned to the first bedroom and turned a slow circle in the space, willing her mind to connect the dots she felt were there, but the out-of-reach feeling persisted. She was about to leave the room when her eyes snagged on the wall above the bed. "Guys," she called. "Come here."

Jillian joined her. "Did you find something?"

"Where's Ali?"

"She got a call." Jill nodded toward the backyard. "What's up?"

"Look at that." Leah pointed to the empty space where a large, discolored square marred the wallpaper. "A whole house full of paintings, but this one is missing."

Jillian frowned. "Maybe she moved it to a different room."

"Without hanging something else to cover the spot? No. Mom didn't stand for imperfections. It would have grated on her. She took this one down recently and I don't remember seeing anything that size on the walls upstairs."

"Recently as in right before she died?"

Leah shrugged. She knew it was speculation, but as with so many other things in this house, there was a gut feeling guiding her. Whatever had adorned this wall mattered, and if it was still here, she would find it.

Jillian's phone chirped, and she pulled it out. "Ugh, my flight is delayed an hour."

She stepped out of the room, and Leah followed her into the brighter common space.

"Well, the airport *is* like a second home to you."

"Ha-ha."

Leah looked at her watch. "What time do we need to get going?"

"We still have twenty minutes."

"Okay good." The missing picture would have to wait. This was her chance to address that other thought that had been percolating in her mind. Both her sisters in one place. Now or never. "I want to talk to you and Ali about something. An idea."

Just then, Alison returned, face red.

"What?" Jillian asked her.

"Nothing. A sale that fell through. Client went with someone else." Her voice was clipped, distracted.

"That's a bummer," Leah said. "Hey, can you sit for a minute?"

"I might have to run actually."

"It won't take long."

Finally, Alison looked up at Leah. What she saw must have convinced her it was important because she pulled out a chair next to Jillian and sat down.

"Okay." Leah took a deep breath. Rip off the Band-Aid. "I've decided to leave Chicago." Saying the words out loud gave her vertigo.

"You have?" Jillian's eyes widened.

"What about your job?" Alison asked.

"I'll find a new one." Leah leaned back in her chair, forced her shoulders to unclench. "I need a new start, and now seems like a good time." She made herself meet their curious stares, both wanting and not wanting them to probe further.

"Where will you go?" Jillian again.

"Well…" Leah looked at them both in earnest. "I know it might sound a little out there, but I'm thinking maybe here?"

"Seattle?" Alison frowned. "Why?"

"No, I mean *here* here. This house." A nervous chuckle. "Maybe."

Alison put a hand up. "Wait—when you mentioned moving into Mom's house the other day, you were serious?"

"No. I mean, not really... But I guess something about this area feels like home, and our old house was... there. But you're right, it's way too big. This, however..."

"It would be perfect for you," Jillian agreed. "It's small but not too small, super cute, right on the lake."

Leah nodded, eagerly. "Right?"

"Well I hate to be a party pooper, but I think you're forgetting something here." Alison clasped her hands together on the table in front of her. "Even as is, this will go for over a million if we sell it, and since we each own a third, you'd have to buy us out. Can you afford that? And still have money left over for renovations? Sure, upstairs is great, but this"—she gestured around them—"needs work."

"Oh, come on, Ali," Jillian snapped. "It's not like either of us are hurting financially."

"You're telling me you can't use an extra $300,000?"

Leah looked down at the table. If Jill was going to try for a baby on her own, take time off work, hire a nanny, and who knew what else, that would definitely help. "She's right, Jill—especially considering, you know..." The rose-colored image of lazy breakfasts on the deck dissipated like smoke before Leah's eyes. "It was a stupid idea. I don't know what I was thinking."

"No." Jillian slammed her palm down on the table, making both Leah and Alison jump. "Why do you always back down like that? Maybe there's a way. I think it's a *great* idea. You fit here."

A small kindling of hope. "I do?"

"And, Ali, this is what you do for a living—we can help figure stuff out, can't we?"

Alison mulled this over for a moment, and in the end, she

conceded that yes, they could at least look into it. "It might come down to how much we get for Mom's house and your house back home. I have no idea what the Chicagoland market is like, but I can't imagine it's as inflated as here."

"See?" Jillian squeezed Leah's arm.

"I have to go into the office anyway, so I'll start researching what's reasonable out here." Alison looked at Leah. "If you're serious about this, you'll have to contact someone locally in Chicago and find out what yours might go for. Also, this place needs to be inspected. Top floor looks good, at least at a first glance, but this floor?" She wrinkled her nose. "You'll definitely want to make sure it doesn't have issues you can't handle. Also, not sure how old the roof is. These old cedar-shake ones aren't the most reliable. I'll call one of my guys and have them contact you since you're out here anyway."

"Sure, no problem." Leah grinned. She'd do anything for the mere possibility of this becoming a reality.

"When are you leaving anyway?" Alison asked.

"It's an open ticket. I didn't know how long things would take, and I have the summer off so..." Leah sent a thought of thanks to the airline rep who'd let her refund her original return ticket because of Mom's death.

"Okay good. Well, I'm out." Alison gathered her purse and stood.

"Yeah, we've got to go too," Jillian said. "Plane to catch, life to get back to."

The three of them climbed the stairs with Leah lingering a few steps behind.

It was silly, she knew that, but walking out of that house, she was overcome by the need to assure it, and herself, she'd be back soon.

THIRTY-ONE

ALISON

Mr. Microsoft had shafted her. Five properties, eight showings, and one botched marriage counseling session, and there was nothing to show for it. Alison could scream. And the worst of it was, it was her own fault. She *knew* what Peter was like; she should have never let him handle the exclusivity agreements after the first time he'd messed up, but afraid as she'd been to lose their business, she'd rushed things, had given Peter the benefit of the doubt, and now here she was—all that work for nothing.

"Other fish in the sea," she muttered through her teeth, turning into the office parking lot. "Other. Fish. In. The. Sea." She willed it to be true. She'd find a different account, a better one. If she got a head start reaching out to potential referrals today, she might even have something in the bag by the end of the week. You push on. Got a broken pinky toe, guess what? You can still pirouette. It's all in how much you want it.

She'd work for a couple of hours, go get groceries, and then head home. She'd had to leave Tyler rather abruptly after their shower that morning and she needed to talk to him, tell him they'd do more sessions with Dr. Wezniak. She'd try harder.

Maybe they could go out to dinner and celebrate her N.A.W.B.L. nomination. Good Lord, she'd almost forgotten about that. You win some, you lose some. That award was more important than another millionaire client in the grand scheme of things. As long as she won.

She parked and texted Tyler her plan and an ETA of 7 PM.

The clock on the dashboard showed 10:48 PM when she finally pulled into the driveway at home. The house was dark, and the night air smelled like rain. Where had the day gone? The hours had disappeared as she'd dug deep through client records, catalogued neighborhoods and listings, cross-referenced all of it. She'd reformatted her newsletter to include the award info and links to new properties for sale that might generate clicks. She'd done research on the property values for Mom's houses and even some basic digging on Leah's house. She'd brainstormed new lines of revenue, the possibility of hiring another agent for the team. And now it was late.

She was late.

With some trepidation, she pushed open the door from the garage to the mudroom and closed it as quietly as she could. If Tyler was asleep, there was no point in waking him up. The kitchen smelled like popcorn, and it made her stomach churn. Had she eaten at all today? She couldn't remember.

She tiptoed into the kitchen and placed her purse on the island, then headed for the fridge. The cool light spilled out in a rectangle on the floor as she opened the door to examine its insides. Finding nothing appealing, she grabbed a banana from the fruit bowl and fetched the bread and peanut butter from the pantry. She'd always preferred mashed banana over jelly. Too tired to make a big production out of her improvised meal, she scarfed it down standing at the island and washed it down with half a glass of milk. She'd just put her dishes in the sink when a movement to her right made her yelp in surprise. Tyler was in the doorway.

"Oh my God, you scared me half to death." Alison leaned against the counter, one hand pressed to her chest. "Sorry if I woke you. I was trying to be quiet."

Tyler tilted his head. "No, I was up." He pushed off the doorjamb and entered the room. "Had a lot of thinking to do."

An unfamiliar edge in his voice gave Alison pause. "Oh?"

"That's it? You're not even going to apologize?"

"It's... I lost track of time. Of course I'm sorry. It won't—"

"Happen again?" A bitter scoff.

Tyler's eyes sought hers, but his gaze was too penetrating for comfort. Instead, Alison studied the woodgrain of the floor. "Look, it's been a rough weekend," she said.

"Weekend?" Tyler crossed his arms. "It's been a rough year."

"I know, I know. The unemployment, and—"

Tyler's hands flew to his head. "Oh my God, this again. I thought after this morning..." He paced a few steps into the living room and returned. "No. *Not* the unemployment. You."

He stared at her as if expecting a rebuttal, the air swelling between them. Alison blinked. Her mind had ground to a halt, the words she normally wielded like weapons departed. There was nothing. In the face of his disapproval, *she* was nothing.

Finally, Tyler's shoulders sagged. "I know you're still in there. You came to me... I thought maybe things would change, that we'd..." His voice hitched. "You know what? I can't do this anymore. Not like this. I'm going to go stay with my sister for a bit. And maybe that's shitty because Marion just died, but honestly you don't even seem upset about that. People don't matter to you anymore, and I won't play the role of not-good-enough, dead-weight husband in this farce of a life you're creating. Not on your terms. I'm not perfect; I've never pretended otherwise, but you—you have some serious issues, Ali. And until you see how messed up your priorities are, it's not healthy for me to be here. So I'm leaving in the morning."

That word, *leaving,* stirred a shiver up the dark well of Alison's mind. He was right—this morning had brought them closer, and she'd been too careless with that fragile peace. She'd known she was out of bounds as soon as she'd seen the late hour in the corner of her monitor.

"How long?" she croaked.

Tyler shrugged. "Depends. I highly suggest you call Dr. Wezniak."

He turned to leave but stopped and looked back at her one more time, his face softening for a brief moment. "I still love you, you know. But you're a one-woman show these days, and I'm not sure I can be with someone who doesn't have room for me in her life. So, your call. Get your shit together, Alison."

With that, he disappeared into the dark of the living room, leaving her alone in the airless space created by his words. On her first sputtered breath, she sank to the floor where she stood, her knees flopping listlessly to the side. Her husband was *leaving.*

How had it come to this?

THIRTY-TWO

LEAH

"Where are you off to?" Leah asked as she navigated the circular entry of the Sea-Tac parking garage.

"Looks like a 7 AM flight to Frankfurt Tuesday morning, one-night stopover, then deadheading to Paris Wednesday, return to New York Friday morning."

"When's the doctor's appointment?"

"Saturday. Should be fine."

"Let me know how it goes, okay?"

"It's only a check-up."

"Still. I'm excited. I've never been an aunt."

"No pressure."

Leah found a parking spot and turned the engine off.

"You don't need to come inside with me," Jillian said. "I'm a big girl; I know where to go."

Leah smiled. "No, I'm coming with you. I'm squeezing everything out of these last few minutes."

"Ha! Very funny."

"I mean it—it'll be weird here without you."

Jillian fell serious. "You know I don't care what you guys do with either of the houses, right? Sell them, demolish them, move into them—whatever is fine with me. If you want *No Man's Land*, I want you to have it. I'll tell Alison as much if she gives you a hard time."

"I'd forgotten it had a name." Leah opened the door. She locked the car after Jillian got her bag out. "But I won't take your share. That wouldn't be fair."

"Fair, schmare. I liked you there. Don't take this the wrong way, but I'm starting to see some of the Leah I remember. I can't even begin to imagine what it must have been like to lose Neil, but maybe this is the new start you need, you know?"

Leah used the escalator as an excuse to fall behind and ignore the comment. Again, it was tempting—more so than ever —to say the words she'd kept to herself for so long. But Jill was leaving. And what difference would it make? No one would ever be able to ask him why. Leah was the only one left to hold accountable. *Why did you stay? What did you do to provoke him?*

"Andy was being very helpful yesterday by the way."

Jillian did a decent job of sounding casual as she dropped him into the conversation, but Leah knew what she was getting at. She'd spent quite a bit of time at the wake talking to him, and she'd enjoyed every minute. He was a welcome contrast to the drama surrounding the estate and the general melancholy that had cloaked the week, and he reminded Leah of who she'd once been. Plus, he was interesting. And funny. And—a burst of warmth through her chest—pretty cute.

"I heard he helped at the house too. Always was a great guy." Jillian glanced at Leah, who kept her eyes straight ahead.

"Sure, yeah," Leah said. It was too soon to have this conversation.

"Didn't he use to have a major thing for you?" Jillian's eyes were wide, innocent, but a smile tugged at the corner of her mouth.

"Oh, stop it," Leah muttered, cheeks heating. Yeah, she

should definitely not tell Jill that yesterday, Andrew had repeated his invitation to grab coffee sometime and asked for her number. Or that she'd given it to him.

They reached the security line, and it was time to say goodbye.

Leah's tight-lipped responses must have discouraged Jillian from pursuing Andrew as a topic, and instead she said, "I'll call more often. And you'll come visit?"

Leah promised, and they hugged.

"Oh, I almost forgot." Jillian released Leah abruptly. "Just an idea, but Paris isn't that far from Brussels. If you want, I might be able to check in on Hannah while I'm there."

As usual, the mention of her daughter made something snag in Leah's throat. That eons-old compulsion to protect was a permanent structure in the territory of motherhood. "You'd do that?" It would be a relief to have eyes and ears on her baby again.

"Of course."

They hugged again, and when Jillian joined the throngs of people being corralled toward the checkpoints, Leah didn't linger. Usually not in a hurry, today she was propelled forward by something new, or at least something she hadn't felt in a long time—that December 1 feeling of something on the horizon. A promise, a wish. Anticipation.

She had a house calling her name.

After a waterlogged drive and a measly sandwich eaten while the rain pelted the surface of the lake in a deluge of gray, Leah spent hours going through the cottage and ended up cross-legged in one of the reading chairs on the lower level. She'd hoped to find Mom somewhere within these walls. Answers. How *had* she come to live here? Was Catherine a colleague? A friend from the gardening club? An altruistic whim? Why had she chosen an early death over fighting the cancer? But even the hidden spaces had been quiet, the missing picture nowhere in sight, and it was now dark enough outside that she no longer saw the wet. Only a steady smattering coming from the deck let her know the skies had not yet cleared.

In front of her was a notepad full of scribbles, and she tapped the eraser end of a pencil against her chin. She looked up and met her reflection in the window: a pale round face with dark eyes. There was a lot to do here—more than she'd originally thought. She read through the handwritten list again starting with "mold in bathroom?" and ending with "ants." She'd found a colony of the tiny insects by the baseboard in the smaller bedroom.

Thankfully, not all items on the list were must-haves. New carpet would be nice but wasn't a priority; the same for repainting the walls. The wood paneling, however, was more urgent—she'd need to pull it out to make sure none of the drywall was compromised, but maybe that was something she could do herself. No one so resourceful as a librarian who knows how to do research, right? Still, Leah didn't need Alison there to tell her the walk-out basement was a fixer-upper.

She was getting ahead of herself of course. She didn't have $750,000 or however much she'd need to buy her sisters out lying around. Even if she got $400,000 for her Chicago home and Mom's sold for close to a million, she still needed renovation money. Who'd give her a loan if she was between jobs? She did have some savings, and Neil's life insurance, but she'd hoped to save that for a rainy day.

At that thought, the downpour increased in intensity, as if to hammer home that's exactly the kind of day this was. There had to be a way. A small loan perhaps, dipping into the savings? Alison must have contacts who could help out. Maybe Andrew...

She rested her lips against the pencil. What was the deal

with Andrew? Jillian's insinuations had stayed with her. She was intrigued by him and who he'd become, that much she could admit, and for the next few minutes, she replayed their few interactions so far. She really had no reason not to have a coffee with him. Why shouldn't she be a little impulsive?

She looked down at the notepad in her lap. She'd doodled abstract swirls while thinking, patterns of rising and falling waves. On paper she'd been alone for a year, but in reality, it was so much longer. Maybe the tides were turning in her favor for once.

She pulled her phone out of the pocket of her hoodie and dialed his number. He picked up after the second ring with a cheerful "Well hello!"

A bubbly thrill summersaulted in her belly. "Um, hi. It's Leah Brady. I mean Sloane." She cringed.

"Yeah, I can tell." Andrew's smile was audible.

"Um, so what's up?" *What's up?* Ugh, this was getting worse by the second. She hid her face in her free hand.

He let out a warm chuckle. "Not much, but this is a nice surprise. How are you holding up today?"

Leah lowered her hand. "Oh, I'm okay. It's been an interesting day. You?"

He ignored her question. "Interesting how?"

Turns out Mom had a secret house that I want to live in. Leah smirked. No, that was too long a story to relay right now. She chewed at her lip for a moment. What to say? Hannah's voice in her mind yelled, *Dare a little!*

"Some stuff with the will. It's complicated. But... how about I tell you over coffee one day this week?" She squeezed her eyes shut, insides fluttering. He probably hadn't meant it when he'd suggested it yesterday. He'd think she was too forward, too presumptuous. He'd regret their convers—

"I'd love that."

She could tell he was smiling again, and it made her do the same. She inhaled deeply. Okay.

"How about tomorrow after work?" he asked.

That's right—tomorrow was Monday. "You sure you have time?" The last thing she wanted was to make him feel stressed and pressured at work.

"For coffee with Leah Brady?" He laughed. "I sure do. How about Ground Beanz in Woodinville? Pick you up at 5:30 PM?"

Holy crap, she had a date.

THIRTY-THREE

ALISON

Alison spent the night on the living-room couch, guarding the stairs with wide-eyed vigilance. If she was here and awake when Tyler got up, he couldn't leave. He'd never walk away while she was watching.

As the minute hand on the clock on the mantel moved incrementally forward, Alison struggled against sleep. She counted spines in the bookcase, barely discernible in the low light, braided and unbraided the fringe on the throw slung across the armrest, listened for the coyotes they could sometimes hear hunting on the golf course at night. Again and again, her gaze returned to the photo next to the clock. She'd left one spotlight on low, and it glinted in the silver frame. It was a picture from Italy taken three years ago when she and Tyler had toured the Amalfi Coast with their expat friends Lola and Charles. A once-in-a-lifetime trip with yachts, cerulean waters, sunhats, and midday mimosas.

How lucky she'd felt. Not only that they were in paradise, but that she had Tyler. Charles drank too much. Not to the point of being obnoxious or in danger, but enough for Lola to acknowledge it when she and Alison browsed the stores of some small harbor town. *Tyler would never do that*, she'd thought. By not settling, she'd truly found the best.

They'd made love that evening, and there'd been a moment right after when she'd even flirted with the idea that if a child happened, it wouldn't be the worst thing. The moment had passed of course. Alison had known from a young age she would be content without kids—better off even. But there *had* been a handful of such moments in their years together, mostly because of Tyler. If he'd wanted them, which he didn't, she knew she would have had a hard time saying no, because with him, she could do anything.

How times changed.

Alison resisted an urge to get up and turn the photo around so her old smugness would quit staring her in the eye, but her limbs were too heavy, and it wasn't like the recent contention would go away by moving a silly picture.

Besides, Lola and Charles were still going strong.

"All couples have their issues," Alison muttered, in an effort to reassure herself. She knew *that* to be true. And who was to say Tyler intended to leave at all? It could be an empty threat. When he came down in the morning, they'd talk, and he, too, would remember Italy. Alison blinked at the moon outside the window, willing conviction into the thought. All she had to do was stay awake and they'd be okay.

But as the sky changed outside from black to slate, fatigue got the better of her and she drifted off. When she awoke fully a few hours later, there was no sign of Tyler aside from the blanket covering her. He'd been there, and she'd missed him. An involuntary sob rose through her chest. This was exactly what Mom had always said—you couldn't rely on anyone except yourself, not even the one who was supposed to love you the most. Now she was completely alone.

She showered and brushed her teeth, avoiding the mirror as much as possible. She wanted to be mad at Tyler, but like last night, a nagging needle prick in her conscience whispered about her own role in this, and she didn't want to risk catching its reflection. If she held tight to her indignation, ignoring all else, she'd push forward. This was no time to falter.

"I'm stronger than this," she muttered under her breath, straightening her collar just so. "Chin up."

THIRTY-FOUR

LEAH

Leah almost backed out of the date twice during the course of Monday, but each time she'd picked up the phone to cancel, she'd thought of how comfortable and familiar Andrew's company was, and how nice it would be to already know someone if she ended up moving here.

They'd had friends, she and Neil, but they were friendships driven by him, and, as such, they'd grown distant when he died. No one wanted a widow over for couple's brunch. She'd never formed close friendships with other women in Chicago; Neil didn't like her going out by herself, wanted time outside of work to be *their* time, which at first was cute and chivalrous but later turned into the root cause of her isolation and dependency on him. No one would have believed she was lonely—the problem was, her "friends" were his too. Teachers and admins in the district, golf buddies, neighbors. And their tag-along wives. She'd liked some of them fine, but conversations never got far past work and kids. Leah didn't remember the last time someone had asked her about her likes and dislikes, her goals, what had brought her to this point. Andrew had cut through to that the second time she'd seen him.

"What's your fondest memory of this house?" he'd asked, forcing her to think. And when she'd responded it was summer evenings on the deck with a book, he'd asked "Why?"

No one ever asked her why.

Hence, come five o'clock, Leah was ready. Nauseous with jitters but committed to going through with the plan. It didn't have to mean anything. They'd have coffee, maybe a sandwich since it was close to dinner time. They'd chat.

Preparation was key to avoiding any awkwardness, so while she waited for him to pick her up, she listed ten, twelve, fifteen possible questions to ask in case the conversation dwindled. She also planned to feign a call from someone if she sensed him getting antsy. It would give him an out and allow them both to save face. She didn't consider the possibility *she* might want to end things early.

He pulled into her driveway at 5:25 PM.

"Sorry I'm early," he said after she'd buckled in. "I used to be the world's biggest time optimist, but in college it got so bad my friends often told me the meetup time was fifteen minutes earlier than it was, so they wouldn't have to wait for me. When I found that out, I decided to prove them wrong." He shrugged, making a left onto Avondale. "Since then, I'm early everywhere."

"Fewer complaints that way, I imagine." Leah scanned his profile, the smattering of stubble along his jaw, the long ridge of his nose, the healed piercing in his earlobe. Wait, what? A strangled laugh spilled out of her. "When on earth did you have earrings?"

His hand flew to his ear as if to hide the evidence. "Ah. Ha-ha. Yeah, that would be from my freshman year of college. Pretty badass if you ask me. A friend did it with ice and a needle."

Leah shuddered.

"Yeah, turns out I'm super allergic to nickel. In fact, I was close to doing a van Gogh, so, you know, you should count your-self pretty lucky to be going on this date with a guy who still has two ears. Just saying."

Leah blinked but stayed angled toward him. "So it's an offi-cial date? Not just two old friends grabbing coffee? Good to know."

Andrew's fair skin flushed as he bumbled several incoherent syllables.

She laughed again. What was this buoyant feeling that kept rising to the surface of her mind? This unrestrained urge to *be*? She should be ashamed of herself, Mom just put to rest, but instead, she put her hand on his arm to feel the muscle tense beneath her fingers. "It's fine. I'm teasing. Carry on."

He glanced at her, a curious glint in his eye. "No, that was it. It's all I got."

They drove on in silence, a smile still lingering on Leah's lips, until they parked and joined the line at the counter at Ground Beanz.

"Oh awesome—paninis! I'm starving." Andrew's whole face lit up, his earlier sheepishness now gone. "I hope you don't mind if I eat. I didn't get lunch today—someone scheduled a meeting. I swear, sometimes I'm convinced the people I work with are undercover aliens who get their sustenance from capsules washed down with soda."

Leah giggled at the image. "I'm eating too," she admitted. "Though I did eat lunch."

"Rabbit food doesn't count." Andrew winked.

Leah's chest expanded. If he said so.

They ordered and found a table near a window that over-looked the busy parking lot.

"So, what exactly is it that you do?" Leah asked after they'd both had a bite. First question on her list, check!

"I'm a UX design manager."

"UX?"

"User experience." Andrew went on to describe in broad strokes how he'd traversed the field of web design from college to present day, taking breaks every now and then to answer Leah's follow-up questions or take a bite of his panini. "But that's enough about that," he said eventually. "Work is work. I don't mind what I do, but I'd rather leave it behind when I go home for the day."

Leah nodded, mouth full of her own sandwich. She'd chosen turkey and avocado with sun-dried tomatoes. It was the best thing she'd had in a while.

"What about you?" Andrew asked before she could finish chewing and launch her next question. "You said librarian, right?"

Leah wiped her lips on a napkin. "At a middle school."

"Yikes." He laughed.

"Yeah, it has its moments. But I love it. Love the kids, their curious minds..."

"I don't know if you remember, but I was a terrible reader in school. I would have made you want to bang your head against the wall."

She smiled at his contrite expression. "I doubt it. I actually have a lot of kids like that. But then, one day, you find the right book for them, and everything changes. They find themselves... somewhere else, transported, and it's almost as magical to me as it is to them."

Andrew had stopped eating and was eyeing her with a curious expression on his face.

"What?" Leah asked. "That's it. That's my job."

He gave a brief shake of the head before lifting his mug to his lips again. "It's fascinating, that's all. It's not often you meet someone who likes what they do. Good for you. Kind of makes me wish you'd been my school librarian." He said it while still holding her gaze, and even though the words were innocent enough, the undertone of something else in his statement wasn't lost on her.

Her face warmed. Yes, this was a date, but it was definitely time she took charge of the conversation again.

As another gray day turned grayer still, until not much light remained outside the windows, they talked about college, dream destinations, pets, siblings, and parents. That is to say, Andrew did most of the talking. Leah kept a firm hold of the topics after that near slide into unknown territory. If he noticed, he didn't say anything, and in the midst of one of his stories from college, the barista showed up at their table to let them know the place was closing.

"Already?" Andrew asked.

"Yeah, we close at ten," she said with a curt but firm smile.

Leah pulled out her phone. They'd been there over four hours. It felt like one at most.

They scrambled to put their dishes on the cart with a cursive "dishes here please" sign and exited the cafe with that sense of unreality that comes from having time-warped through a whole evening. Round-eyed and blinking at the darkness, they ambled toward the car, close together, but not quite touching.

"This was great," Andrew said. "Obviously."

"Yeah." Leah nodded, her eyes on the ground.

"Can we do it again?" He glanced her way. "I mean, maybe not right away. Or we don't have to. Unless you're up for it?"

His stumbling question was what finally gave Leah the courage to meet his eyes. She was up for it. More than made her comfortable. But she also didn't want to come off as overeager. "I might have some time later this week. How about I call you when I know my schedule?" As if she didn't already know.

"Great! For sure." He opened her car door and smiled. "Looking forward to it."

His words burrowed underneath her skin and settled there, warming her from within as they drove off toward home.

Another *pop* in her chest, and there it was again—that fracture in her defenses tearing further.

"Oh, that's right, I never told you about yesterday," she said after a minute of amicable silence. He still didn't know about the cottage.

They merged onto Woodinville-Duval Road. "Yeah, your interesting day. What happened?"

"So, turns out, Mom had a second property across the lake."

His head snapped toward her. "What?"

She was about to give him the details when a dark SUV sped past them, got in front, and hit the brakes, forcing Andrew to do the same.

He laid on the horn, the sudden blare causing Leah to jump.

"What the hell?" Another long and several shorter honks. "Fucking moron! Learn to drive, why don't you?"

"Hey, it's not a big de—" Leah's throat constricted on the last word, a wave of nausea forcing her to close her eyes. The memory of another drive years ago, another horn blaring, forced itself upon her—Neil speeding past what he deemed to be "Sunday drivers," the controlled fury in his voice as sirens approached in the rearview mirror. *If you hadn't dragged your feet and made us late, this would have never happened. It's like you wanted me to get pulled over.*

"Argh, it drives me nuts—these idiots think they own the road," Andrew ranted. He muttered another few curses under his breath.

Leah wanted to cry. She needed air; she needed out. She couldn't have a panic attack here. Palm to her belly button, she inhaled slowly through her nose. Flexed her toes, relaxed, tightened her calves, let go.

"You okay?" Andrew glanced her way, but she ignored him. Exhaled through her mouth.

"Leah?"

"I'm fine," she mumbled, leaning toward the window away from him. "Little car sick." *Just drive*, she thought. In Neil, something dark had lurked beneath the glittery surface. Was it the same with Andrew? She hadn't thought so, but what if she was wrong?

The sharp bark of his voice still rang in her ears as they pulled into their old neighborhood. If he was talking to her, she didn't hear it. She couldn't get out fast enough, and she closed the door behind her without a backwards glance. *Away, alone, safe. Away, alone, safe.*

"So, I'll talk to you later?" he called after her as she unlocked the front door. The same warm voice she'd listened to over coffee and paninis a lifetime ago.

Yes, she wanted to say. *Of course.* But the boogeyman was there, and he'd stolen away her ability to speak.

THIRTY-FIVE

JILLIAN

It was almost as if Seattle had never happened.

At 35,000 feet, soaring above the clouds, Jillian was back in her element. Escape came in different shapes for different people, but for her, nothing beat leaving the earth's surface for a few hours to reset her inner equilibrium. Somewhere down below was the wide expanse of the Atlantic Ocean, somewhere above the constellations Dad once taught her, but at the moment, neither mattered. She was in charge of a plane and roughly 360 passengers and crew, that was all. She was Captain Brady, not Jillian up here, and as such she was also allowed to let go of Jillian's problems.

"I'm going heads down for a minute," she told her first officer and pulled out her tablet. She and Audrey in Dublin had exchanged a few messages so far, but she wasn't twenty or naive enough to think a night meant anything but one night.

Ever seen the world from a cockpit? she typed. *You'd like it.*

There was no immediate response. Which was fine. In a few hours, she'd set them down in Frankfurt, but this was the present, and it hummed faintly around her outside the noise-canceling headphones, not making demands or posing queries.

A little slice of heaven.

Nothing offers a reality check like having to switch hotel rooms at 2 AM because of bedbugs. The hotel near Frankfurt Airport left much to be desired esthetically too, something Jillian might have forgiven, had it at least been sufficiently clean. Not so. Her small saving grace was that she'd checked the mattress before getting into bed, and the second room showed no sign of the tiny pests. But still—how was she supposed to relax now?

She thanked the embarrassed night manager and closed the door, wide awake.

Good thing she didn't have to fly tomorrow. She'd only ride along to Paris to be ready for the return on Friday. She could sleep until noon if she wanted to, provided she'd find a way to settle in.

She curled up at the bare-bones desk and opened her laptop to connect to the Wi-Fi. Might as well do some research to make time go by faster.

Since her conversation with Leah, Jillian had cautiously been looking into stories online of other single women hoping to become mothers. There were scores of them, many with situations similar to her own: approaching forty, financially solid, never found the right partner. But no matter how many forums she browsed and how many searches she did, all these women were overwhelmingly confident they'd be able to live up to their visions of motherhood "if only this IVF cycle worked." The closest thing to doubt Jillian had found were questions about loneliness without a partner, and meeting the practical demands of working and raising a child alone. No one questioned their capacity for loving that longed-for baby once it finally became a reality. Was that just her then? And if so, did that in itself mean her fears were justified?

As she had so many times before, she got stuck on that

thorny hurt that always simmered beneath the surface. What was it about her that had made Marion want little to do with her? She was born into a functioning family unit. A core middle-class family with two parents in a committed relationship. Two beloved daughters already. Marion hadn't wanted a boy (Dad had, he'd admitted once, but he'd changed his mind as soon as he saw Jillian). She wasn't a difficult baby—her sisters had assured her of that. She didn't add any sort of great expense seeing as how they had clothes and baby things already left from Alison and Leah. Postpartum depression would have passed eventually. Then what was it? What could it be, except something undefinable, unlovable? Something she might pass down.

Jillian flicked through her social-media pages but didn't linger on any one post for long.

An instant message from Carla popped up in the top-right corner:

When will you be back? I haven't seen you in ages. Dixie never wants to go out. Old fart.

Jillian smiled. It had been a while. Her roommates must be getting used to having the place to themselves. *Friday*, she typed. *Happy hour at Cold Cat?* It was their favorite hole-in-the-wall bar, and the best place for gratuitous carbs.

Better believe it!

Jill waited while Carla typed another message.

You're up late even for you. Jetlag?

Bedbugs.

Yikes. Go to sleep. Love you, Goose.

Jillian chuckled. *You too, Moo.*
She signed off and closed the laptop. Yawned.
Perhaps not completely unlovable.

THIRTY-SIX

ALISON

"Hi, Alison—come on in." Dr. Wezniak held her door open and nodded toward her room.

It was 9 AM on Wednesday morning. Alison had been up since four.

"How are you doing?" Dr. Wezniak asked after they sat down.

Alison forced her hands to be still in her lap. She'd subsisted mostly on coffee since Tyler had left, and now ants were crawling beneath her skin every time she stopped moving. She'd shown eight houses yesterday, and she had another seven scheduled for today—all with the same couple. As long as she immersed herself in work, she'd forget everything else.

"Fine," she said.

Dr. Wezniak stayed silent. After a moment, she tilted her head, pen perched against her notebook.

Alison sighed. *I know what you're doing,* she wanted to say. *I'm on to you.* Instead, she pulled one leg up under her and cracked her neck.

"Tyler left," she said. "Not *left* left, but he went to see his sister."

"Oh?" Dr. Wezniak's eyes narrowed. "When will he be back?"

"It's anybody's guess."

Dr. Wezniak put her pencil down.

Alison continued, "What I don't get is—how am I the bad guy here?"

"Who says you are?"

"Ty obviously feels that way." *Duh*. The good doctor was a little slow on the uptake today.

"He said so?"

"I'm paraphrasing. He says I have 'issues' I have to figure out." She used air quotes around the word, which wasn't nearly an adequate measure of how ludicrous this was. So she ran late sometimes—the point was, she was still there. She wasn't the one who'd left. "And he can't be around me until I do."

Dr. Wezniak studied her a moment. "And do you? Have issues?"

Alison flopped back against the seat. "Don't we all? He's the one who changed. He's completely forgotten what it's like to have responsibilities outside the house, how to have intelligent conversations, goals, other people who demand things from you."

"This is making you upset."

"You think? My husband left me because I got home later than I said. I'm the provider here. I'd lost a client and needed to replace them, and he's forgotten..." Alison blinked against the heat stinging behind her eyes. She would not cry about this. Not again. "He needs a fucking job."

"Okay, let's take a moment. Here." Dr. Wezniak poured Alison a glass of water and waited until she'd taken a sip. "If you don't mind, I'd like to go back to something Tyler said on Friday. About not knowing what he wants to do. How does that make you feel?"

Alison took another swallow of the water. "It's sort of out of the blue, I think. Why now? What's wrong with what he was doing before?"

"It's not entirely uncommon to question your path at this point in your life and career."

"But how is that my fault?"

"If Tyler had come to you eight months ago, right after he was laid off, and said he wasn't sure what to do next, what would you have done?"

Alison pictured that day. They'd known it was coming given all the restructuring the company had been going through after having been bought out by a competitor. He'd always liked his job. Would she have taken him seriously? "I don't know."

"How about if it was you and your job?"

That was easier. She'd always taken pride in being resourceful. Someone who didn't give up at the first sight of an obstacle. "I'd figure it out. There's career counseling, you can shadow someone in your network, connect with a mentor, talk it through with friends..."

"And this is something you'd be comfortable doing?"

"Of course." If you weren't prepared to help yourself, who would be?

"Would Tyler?"

Alison's mouth snapped closed.

"Don't take this the wrong way," Dr. Wezniak said. "I'm not taking sides. I'm merely asking questions." She waited.

"I don't know," Alison said eventually. Ty was great at mingling, at making people feel comfortable. Not as great at talking himself up. "I guess he's better at putting others in the spotlight."

"Hm. And does he have those things you mentioned? A network of people, a mentor?"

Ty's voice echoed in her mind—*I would have told you if you'd been around.* Was there something to that? She'd always loved her job, and he'd supported her in the past. Sure, she'd become busier over the years, and there was more at stake now, but she was still the same. They were both adults. Surely she hadn't neglected him. It couldn't be on her to always be available. Right?

"Alison?"

"Huh?" Alison met the counsellor's inquisitive gaze. She squinted to force her eyes to focus against the forming headache. "What was the question?"

"Are you sure you're feeling okay? You're a bit pale all of a sudden."

"I'm fine." Alison blinked. "Really. But ca... can I have some more water?"

She drank the full glass again and set it down on the table. "I'm not sleeping well," she said, wanting to explain. "I never sleep well when he's not home."

Dr. Wezniak leaned forward, resting her elbows on her knees. "Does he know that?"

Back in the car, Alison slumped behind the steering wheel. Was this what it felt like to be hit by a truck? It was like she couldn't catch her breath. She wanted so badly to close her eyes, but her first showing was only thirty minutes out. Dr. Wezniak's parting words echoed in her mind: *A marriage is choosing over and over to love another person for better or for worse. Sometimes the choice is easy; sometimes it's work. Regardless, you have to put in the time.* Nothing on where Alison would find that time though. There was only so much of her.

She took a sip from the to-go cup in the middle console and grimaced as the cold coffee made her tongue curl. Still, she finished the last few sips and popped a piece of gum in her mouth. *Okay, look alive.* Deep inhale.

She put the car in drive and glided out of the parking spot. She made a right onto the main road and allowed the flow of

traffic to sweep her along. Only problem was there were no
other directions clear in her mind. Alison, who normally knew
Seattle's neighborhoods and streets like the back of her hand,
drew a blank.

With a rising sense of panic, she pulled into the closest lot
and parked across two spots. Her hand shaking, she opened her
appointment calendar. There it was, address and all. She had a
GPS—this wasn't the end of the world. If only her head would
stop throbbing.

She pulled back out into traffic, and this time she made it to
her destination without complications. She was even fifteen
minutes early—enough time to check in with Bess on how dona-
tions were coming along for the fundraiser auction. Maybe they
needed a last push for sales. Alison wanted to dazzle her peers
with the turnout next Saturday. She may have lost the
Microsoft client, but that didn't define her.

As she dialed the office main line, she made a mental note to
follow up with anyone on the primary invite list they still hadn't
heard from. It would take a chunk of time out of her day, but it
needed to get done.

"Brady Realty, this is Bess speaking."

"Oh, hi. I was expecting Peter to answer—is he not in yet?"

"Oh my gosh, thank God." Bess sounded frantic. "Your
calendar said not to disturb you, so I didn't know if I should call
or not, but this is bad—really, really bad."

What now? Alison closed her eyes. If it was Peter messing
up a contract again, she didn't know what she'd do. "I have
clients in five. Are you sure it can't wait?"

"No! I think Peter quit."

"What?" Alison straightened. If he gave his notice now, she
wouldn't have time to train his replacement. They were ten
days out from the fundraiser, for God's sake. What was he
thinking? "Is he there? Can I talk to him?"

"No, he's not here, and there's a note on his desk that says

'Don't contact me.' Signed 'P.' He probably left it there last night. I only found it because I had to go in there to look up an invoice number from a vendor. They called and asked if we'd sent payment since they hadn't seen it on their end."

"Didn't we pay them all in May? I thought we did."

"So did I. But it wasn't in the system.'

"Did you call Peter and ask?"

"That's why you need to come in. His phone goes straight to voicemail, and when I started looking into it more, I found a stack of unopened mail in his bottom drawer, all invoices we should have paid over a month ago. Some as far back as four months."

The hairs on Alison's neck rose. "What are you saying?"

"Looks like he hasn't been doing his work for some time. I think we're in trouble."

THIRTY-SEVEN

LEAH

After the disastrous end to her date with Andrew, Leah had vowed to focus on the house and the house only, even though her therapist, ever the voice of reason, had cautioned her not to jump to conclusions.

"Did he yell at *you*?" she'd asked when Leah called her. And "Have you never cursed at another driver?" Well, he didn't, and she had, but that was beside the point. He may do odd things to her insides, but she didn't *know* him. Not really. It had been twenty years. Neil probably wasn't abusive in grade school either, and she wasn't at all sure this thing with Andrew was worth the gamble. Plus, if her reaction in the car said nothing else, surely it suggested she wasn't ready to lower the drawbridge even to someone who appeared to be waving a white flag. Not when she'd been so thoroughly duped into defeat previously.

Fortunately, manual labor was a great distraction, so here she was at eight in the morning at the home improvement store, pushing a cart full of items she'd never before used. There was a flat bar, a crowbar, several scrapers, a heat gun, a putty knife, a pair of worker gloves, a box of respirator masks, protective glasses, and a tarp. Today, a stretch of the wood paneling was coming off.

She'd been dismayed at first to find that the chair rail was glued on, which would make removal take longer, but by now she'd done enough googling to have a general idea of what she was taking on. It was exciting, really, actually *doing* something to contrast all that research.

She passed the paint section on her way to the registers and paused in front of the wall of swatches. When she and Neil had moved into the Chicago house, it was already pristine with a fresh coat of white paint on the walls. It would have been wasteful to spend money to make them the light blue she wanted. White was neutral, and they wouldn't have to repaint again for a while, Neil had decided. It had made sense. But now? The walls in the cottage were an odd beige and definitely not pristine.

It's not yours yet, a small voice whispered in the back of her head. Leah ignored it. It was hers—a third of it at least. She grabbed a handful of different swatches and put them in her purse.

Her phone rang as she was loading her purchases into the car. Typically, she didn't pick up unknown numbers, but she was expecting a call from the Chicago real estate agent she'd contacted.

"This is Leah."

The line was silent for a beat. "Um, hi."

Andrew. Leah straightened and grabbed on to the cart handle. *Crap.* "Hey." She bit down on her cheek. "Where are you calling from?"

"I'm at work. How's it going?"

His voice brought it all back, but surprisingly her mind settled on the good stuff: his dimpled smile, the way he squinted when he laughed, how he asked questions not for the sake of conversation but to know more.

"Fine." Leah tapped a quick rhythm on the plastic handle-bar. "Busy morning. You?"

He didn't respond right away, but eventually he cleared his throat. "Hey, are we okay? I texted. I thought— Why do I feel like you're mad at me or something?"

Leah closed her eyes. "Um..."

"Oh my God, you *are* mad. Was it something I said?"

You lost your temper. You scared me. The bitter taste of the past made the words stick in Leah's throat.

"Whatever I did, I'm sorry," he continued.

Was she really going to let Neil keep exerting power over her this way? She wasn't being fair; Andrew had a human reaction to a jerk driver, nothing else. Her grip on the phone tightened. "No, it's not... It's me—some personal stuff. And there's a lot to do with the houses." Above her, a few rays of sunlight ventured out from behind the cloud cover. She turned her face toward them. Inhaled. "I didn't mean to leave you hanging."

"You sure?"

"Yeah." Then with more conviction: "Yes. I'm sure." The truth, she realized.

His voice brightened. "Phew. Okay, cool."

His relief made her smile in spite of herself.

"Wow, I feel like we just worked through something there." He chuckled.

He was such a sweet man. How on earth had she even for a moment let him remind her of Neil?

"So, I know we said you'd let me know your schedule," he continued, "but I'll actually be out your way later to help Dad with a hole in the dog run, so would you maybe, I don't know, want to grab a bite? Busy or not, you'll need to eat at some point, right?"

She almost said yes without thinking. Now that she'd decided her therapist was right, she had to allow for the possibility that part of her had missed his company since Monday. But today wasn't ideal. She had no clue how long the demo would take, and if there was one thing she didn't want to do, it was to cancel on him last minute—especially after giving him the cold shoulder once already.

"A raincheck maybe?" she asked, after detailing her workload.

He hummed as if considering this. "Or how about we do something completely nuts and wing it? I'll finish work, you go do your thing, and if the timing works out later, then great. If not, we'll raincheck. But see, I still think you'll need food at some point, so I like my odds."

Leah laughed. His optimism was contagious, and now the clouds really were parting to blue skies. She agreed to his suggestion without pause. She could be spontaneous. Fake it until you make it, right?

Leah was covered in debris when her phone chimed around 6:30 that evening. The fruits of her labor lay in a pile on the tarp, and she'd uncovered enough wall that the inspector Alison was bringing the next day should be able to give a yay or nay on the drywall, but it had been a much more strenuous endeavor than she'd expected. And it wasn't looking great.

The chair rail hadn't just been glued to the wall but had somehow fused to it, and only after experimenting with a scraper and hammer to chisel it off had she made any sort of progress. There was also glue on the lower third of the paneling. None of the how-to videos Leah had watched had prepared her for that scenario. She had glue chips in her hair, dust from broken panel pieces all over her clothes, and she didn't exactly smell like a summer meadow. Thus, her first instinct when Andrew texted was to decline. She was tired and sweaty and preoccupied with what the inspector might say about the dark splotches she'd unveiled on the wall. She wouldn't be good company and she told him as much without flat out saying no.

I demand little and am not in a hurry, Andrew texted back. *Go home and freshen up. Take your time. If you're hungry, I can bring something over.*

She looked around at the mess she'd created—or rather, the progress she'd made. She was as good as done here for the day; she could head back to Mom's now and shower. Her stomach growled, answering the second part of his query. But to have him over for dinner, the two of them alone at the house? Did she want that?

Give me an hour, she typed. *Anything but pizza and sandwiches.*

When Andrew rang the doorbell an hour later to the minute, she was ready. That is, she was freshly showered and in clean clothes, but that was also the extent of the effort she'd put forth. Her hair was wet, she wore no make-up, and the sweat-pants she'd found in one of the closets upstairs definitely belonged to someone taller than her. She'd had to roll them up in order not to step on them.

"I have a few options," Andrew said after she'd let him in. He set two bags down on the kitchen counter. "This is from my favorite Mediterranean place in Redmond so there's a falafel plate, a kebab plate, a chicken shawarma sandwich, fries, and side salads."

Leah's mouth watered. She was hungrier than she'd real-ized, and with the scent of garlic and spices seeping through the air, she all but tore the bags open.

"You can pick one or we can split them up and sample all of it."

"The last option. Oh my gosh, this looks delicious." Leah

grabbed two plates and silverware and set them on the table while Andrew unpacked the goods. "Thank you so much for feeding me." Leah tore off a corner of flatbread and popped it into her mouth.

Andrew smiled. "It's my pleasure. Plus, selfishly, it was probably the only way I'd get you to meet up."

"Today at least," Leah added between bites.

"Oh? You'd have agreed to a proper date another day? Should I pack up and go?"

The devilish gleam in his eyes made Leah blush. It was a good thing she'd left the dimmer in the room on the low side.

"Would be a shame with all this food," she said. "But you do what you have to do."

He stared at her for a moment, a forkful of falafel halfway to his mouth. Then he chuckled. "Funny." He pointed the fork at her before putting it in his mouth. "You almost had me there. I wasn't prepared for that level of snark."

Leah's cheeks twitched. "I aim to please."

For a few minutes they ate in silence, Leah savoring every bite. Even though she'd specifically requested no sandwich, the shawarma wrap was her favorite, and she could have easily eaten the whole thing.

"So, you never told me about the other house," Andrew said. "What happened?"

Leah filled him in on all the details from Mr. Dunn disclosing the property at the funeral to the mystery of how Mom had come to own it.

"You said the name on the card was Catherine?" he asked. "I wonder..." He pulled out his phone and did a quick search before showing her the screen. "Is this her? The woman in the picture?"

The photo showed a headshot of a woman in her sixties. She had piercing blue eyes and soft gray curls that framed her face. While the photo at the house had been a couple of decades old and taken at a candid moment, Leah had no problem recognizing her.

"It is. How did you know?" Leah stared at him, wide-eyed.

"Everyone around here knows Catherine Anthony. She's a local celebrity. Fantastic artist. Very private though, and I haven't read anything about her in a long time. Of course, now we know she got sick." He scrolled through a few more pictures, lips pursed. "I wonder how Marion knew her."

"I think she was her caretaker," Leah said. "Jill and Ali don't, but why else would she move in with her when she already had a house. And it's not entirely uncommon that someone dies and leaves something in their will for a personal assistant. A house is a little extravagant perhaps, but it makes sense."

"Mm-hmm. It's a possibility." Andrew shook off his faraway look and closed the lid of one of the Styrofoam boxes with a dull snap. "No more fries for me or I'll wish I'd brought *my* comfy pants." He raised a brow.

What was it about him that made her insides go all squishy? "Are you hating on my sweats?"

"I'd never." His eyes glittered in the dim light. "They're really cute on you actually."

She tried not to smile but failed. "Thanks."

Their eyes locked across the table, and with that, the air shifted around them toward something much too unwieldy for Leah. She stood abruptly and started clearing what was left of the food.

"Do you mind if I keep the leftovers for tomorrow?" she asked, her back to him. "I've been so busy—I keep forgetting about meals." She dumped the napkins and containers in the garbage.

"Hey, Leah?" Andrew's voice was soft.

She turned, her heart speeding to a rhythm she'd thought lost to the past. "Yeah?"

"I like hanging out with you. And I think you like hanging out with me."

"Mm-hmm?" She was afraid to blink.

"I'm telling you so you don't have to wonder."

"Oh."

A crooked smile. "I have a feeling you're not too keen on ambiguity, and frankly, I'm too old for games."

What if she went to him there and then? Kissed him? The possibility glowed in gold around them for a brief moment, before Leah remembered herself. That wouldn't be fair to him; he had no idea of the baggage she carried. Would always carry. She ran her fingertips across her brow. She should tell him he was wrong, that there was nothing between them but friendship, but when she opened her mouth to speak, her lips were stiff and her tongue parched.

Andrew beat her to it, perhaps sensing her struggle. "You don't have to say anything. I know our life situations are different. You... had a husband, a kid..." He let out a dry laugh. "We live in different parts of the country for crying out loud."

"I'm thinking of moving here." The words were out before she had a chance to consider the implications. Of all the things to say...

Andrew's eyes widened. "Really?"

Great—now he was going to think she was a stalker. Surely there were better ways to drop that information than in a conversation about their hypothetical relationship. If that's what he was talking about.

"Yeah... the cottage..."

"But that's great. I mean, not just for me of course. New start. Closer to Alison. And it's a lot prettier out here than in flat Illinois." He pronounced the s as if to goad a reaction.

She ignored it and hurried to add, "There's no guarantee. This house has to sell, my house in Chicago has to sell, I have to convince Ali it's a good idea, find a new job..."

He leaned back in his chair, hands on his lap. "Many moving parts. I get it. But try not to worry too much. If there's anything I've learned, it's that life is easier if you roll with it. If you want it to, it'll work out."

She couldn't help but wonder if he was still talking about her moving plans—or something else entirely.

THIRTY-EIGHT

JILLIAN

Paris in June was an old friend. Once upon a time it had been one of the first cities Jillian visited for longer than a night's stopover, and it had forever since held a special place in her heart with that bustling urbanity set against a backdrop of centuries-old architecture. Time slowed among the patisseries and boutiques, perhaps because it was a city that had seen so much—had experienced an abundance of days and years already. *Rest with me*, it said. *Have a seat at my table*.

Jillian had taken the train from her hotel (bedbug free this time) into the city early enough in the morning that she had to compete with the regular commuters for space. That way, she'd have time for a temperate stroll through Montmartre before the tourists descended upon it in earnest. It was worth it—more than two hours of Paris uninterrupted. Now, however, it was nearing 10:30 AM and Hannah's train should be on approach, so Jillian reluctantly turned her back on the white domes of Sacré-Coeur and set her sights instead on the trains at Gare du Nord.

It had taken some convincing on Jillian's part to get Hannah to come out. Not that she didn't want to, but it appeared Chase was under the impression it would be a difficult trip to make in a day. Not until Jillian explained it was a shorter trek than from UMass to Boston did Hannah relax into the idea. Europe was a strange place that way—all those countries with different languages, histories, and currencies, yet no real physical distances between them.

Hannah's blond head was the first thing Jillian spotted from their meeting spot near the stairs.

"Aunt Jill!" Hannah ran the last few steps into Jillian's arms. "I was worried I wouldn't find you."

"Here I am." Jillian smiled at her niece, holding her at arm's-length for a moment. She hadn't seen her in person since her dad's funeral. Gone was the round-faced teenager, replaced instead by a young woman with the confidence to pull off a bright red lip. "God it's so good to see you, Hannah banana." They hugged again. "I can't believe this worked out."

"Right?" Hannah's gaze dodged away for the briefest of moments. An edge of seriousness marred her brows in a way Jillian didn't recognize, maybe the effects of early-morning travel.

"So..." Jillian hooked her arm through Hannah's. "Paris virgin. Do you know what you want to do today?"

They exited the station and stepped out onto the cobble-stoned street in front. Paris was fully awake now, and pedestrians and tourists hurried in all directions. The summer sun shone down on them from a blue sky. Hannah stopped and turned her face to it with a greedy tilt of the neck. Her features cleared in an instant as if an opaque varnish had melted away. "Anything." She let out a little laugh. "Everything."

"Everything in a day, huh?" Jillian cocked an eyebrow and pointed straight ahead. "We'd better get going then. The Metro is that way. How about we start with the essentials and take it from there?"

. . .

It was exactly the kind of Paris day one could while away in any one of the many parks around the city, but Jillian chose the Tuileries Garden because of its proximity to the Louvre and Arc de Triomphe. They wouldn't have time to go inside the museum—not with only one day at their disposal—but the building was impressive from the outside as well, and something about the symmetry and lushness of the Tuileries was undeniably Parisian. Of course, her plans also included the Eiffel Tower and Notre-Dame, but that was for later in the day.

As they strolled, Jillian quizzed Hannah on her year at UMass, her plans for the semester to come, and how she liked Brussels, and Hannah reciprocated by inquiring about everything that had gone down in Seattle.

"Mom didn't tell me half of this," she said when Jillian had finished relaying the drama surrounding Alison.

"In Tyler's defense, Ali isn't the easiest person to live with. I speak from experience."

Hannah fell quiet as they made their way toward Place de la Concorde.

"Your mom misses you. A lot," Jillian volunteered when the silence stretched too long. She was about to say something about the cottage when she remembered Leah's admonition not to worry Hannah with her moving plans yet. Instead she said, "She's getting your grandmother's house ready to go on the market. It's keeping her busy. She likes it though."

"She was always a fixer. I don't know anyone who figures things out like her." A flash of a smile across Hannah's face before it returned to that impassive mask from earlier. It reminded Jillian of how she'd looked at Neil's funeral. She'd wanted to tell Hannah she knew what it was like; that they had this in common—losing fathers who'd doted on them—but she'd never had the chance. Maybe Marion's death had brought up bad memories.

"Hey." Jillian stopped, forcing Hannah to do the same.

Tilted her head. "Something's up with you. Anything you want to talk about?"

Hannah shrugged and started walking again.

"I'm a pretty good listener," Jillian said. "Is it Marion? Are you worried about your mom?"

"No." For a moment it looked like Hannah was about to say more, but then she clamped her lips together.

What would Leah do? What would a Good Mom do in a situation like this? If she could figure out how to get Hannah to open up, maybe there was still hope for her.

"Want some ice cream?" she asked when they passed a vendor.

Hannah hesitated, but Jillian steered them both toward the temporary stand. "Come on. Sunny summer day in Paris. You can't not have some *glace à la fraise.*"

"Fine." A slight twinkle in Hannah's eye.

"Grab one of those tables and I'll bring the goods."

Everything tasted better in France. Better food regulations, better ingredients, better backdrop perhaps. They'd only had a few spoonfuls when Hannah leaned back in her chair with a contented sigh. "Ah, fuck it," she said, but renewed buoyancy to her tone softened the curse.

"Fuck what?" Jillian asked, mouth full of sugary cold.

"Chase and I had a fight last night. He's been acting weird lately."

So that's what was up. Jillian didn't say anything but made sure to put on her most sympathetic listening face.

"Brussels is nice and all, and I love the time he and I spend together, but he's so busy and I'm... well... not. He says all these things—"

"You're getting bored?"

"Yeah. Or not exactly. But it's like—here we are in Europe, and I want to see more of it. I figured we'd go travel around on weekends and stuff, but by then he wants to chill at home."

"Good thing I gave you an excuse to come here then."

Hannah's face darkened. "That's what the fight was about. He didn't like that I was going alone." She huffed. "All of a sudden, he was all—'we should do it together, babe; it's the city of romance, babe'—but there *are* other times. I wanted to see you."

Jillian's heart expanded. That was the nicest thing she'd heard in a long time.

"Right?" Hannah's question was posed in such earnest that for a moment she sounded again like a precocious ten-year-old.

"For sure."

"And he's been to Paris before with his family so it's not like I'm ruining his first trip or anything."

"And did he get that after you talked?"

"I don't know. He went to bed."

"Well, you're here. I'd consider that a battle won."

Hannah chewed on her lower lip while stirring what was left in her cup into a runny mess. "That's just it though. No one won, because he ended the discussion first. And"—she looked up, eyes dark in the shade of a large elm—"he may not exactly know I'm here."

Jillian stared at her. "Oh."

"Yeah. I left a note in case he comes home before me."

"Okay." Jillian tried to sort this out, still acutely aware of her role as advisor in the moment. "Well, if you ask me, it's not his business where you choose to go during the day, right? Do you know everything he does while at work?"

"No."

"We had one chance to do this. One day. He'll understand. It seems like he loves you very much, and in a way, it's kind of cute he wanted to experience it with you. You'll get home happy, full of new impressions, and he'll see how good it was for you."

Hannah nodded, silent for a moment before agreeing, "Yeah, no, yeah that makes sense."

"I wouldn't worry about it."

Hannah sucked in a long breath. "Yeah, okay."

She must really like this guy, Jillian thought. She'd never known Hannah to be a worrier.

"Want to get going? The Eiffel Tower awaits."

They'd walked a few yards when Hannah turned to Jillian. "Thanks for letting me vent. You're a good listener." She paused. "Just don't tell Mom about it, will you? I know she worries with me being all the way over here, and I don't want to make it worse."

Jillian, glowing from the compliment, put her arm around her niece's shoulders. "Of course. Not my business. No worries." If she could keep Leah's dealings to herself, she could do the same for Hannah.

It did strike her a little later, though, that mother and daughter might benefit from being a tad straighter with each other. But maybe that's what happened when you lost a husband and father—you got protective of those who were left.

THIRTY-NINE
ALISON

Alison and Bess sat on the floor of the office with stacks of mail surrounding them in a circle. It was worse than they'd thought. After going through Peter's office, they'd found more unopened mail behind his desk, a stack of phone messages never delivered, and several of the missing contracts Peter claimed had been lost in the mail. The sense of betrayal was overwhelming. She and Peter had worked together for over eight years.

"These messages are from the past three weeks," Bess said. "Might still be worth following up on them."

"Yeah, anything older let's keep and call only if we have time."

Time. As if Alison didn't already have enough to do. If she stopped to think about it all—new clients, old clients, leads, Tyler, the fundraiser, Mom's house, Leah and the cottage, the contest and conference, Dr. Wezniak—the room spun. So she tried not to.

"Were you able to log into the system and do a print-out of payables and receivables?" she asked.

Bess lifted two sheets of paper to her left and handed Alison a stapled bundle. "Here."

"Great. The number-one priority is to make sure the vendors for the fundraiser have been paid, and that no sales are compromised."

They worked well into the evening and, come nine o'clock, Alison sent Bess home. It wasn't her fault they were in a bind. Alison should have been on top of things. This was what she got for delegating.

She flipped through the fundraiser-related pile they'd created, put it down, and stretched. The good news was she'd paid the venue in full. The biggest question mark was the caterer, who'd left a message last week that Alison would need to follow up on first thing tomorrow. There was an emailed agreement, but as far as she could see, they had yet to pay the fee. It nauseated her to think she might have to try and find someone new with only a week's notice. Failure wasn't an option.

Alison lay in bed that night, having gone through the motions of her bedtime routine even though she knew it would be futile. She turned toward Tyler's empty pillow, wondering what he was doing. Sleeping most likely. He'd sleep through anything. He'd sent her a text to let her know he'd reached Idaho where his sister and her husband lived, but other than that, it had been radio silence. She hadn't tried to contact him either—didn't want to give him the chance not to respond.

She reached out a hand and rested it on his side of the bed. Why had that distance been untraversable when he was still here—as if the two of them were in different parts of the same labyrinth, unable to find a joint path? One would call out and the other wind their way further into the thickets. There had to be a ladder somewhere—a shortcut. He was it for her. Him or no one.

When they'd met, she'd been thirty-two and newly single

after a string of casual (and brief) relationships. She'd gone to a cocktail bar downtown to commemorate a new era in her life—one of autonomy, self-reliance, and independence—and Ty had been there with his coworkers. He'd asked if he could grab the chair next to her for his group but instead had ended up sitting down and never leaving. She'd known she was in trouble the moment he'd ordered a Cosmo with an olive—none of the suit-clad, image-obsessed men she normally fell for would ever do that.

With a threatening knot in her throat, Alison pushed all thoughts of Ty out of her head. Dwelling wasn't productive. Instead, she ran through tomorrow's schedule in her head—all the calls she had to make, the inspection at the cottage, the staging meeting she'd have with a client. Finally, as the night officially shifted into early morning, she gave up and brought a blanket with her into the office. She wrapped it around herself and opened her computer.

For a moment, she sat staring at the screen, hands poised above the keys while she waited for the noise in her head to quiet into a single thought. She typed in the address for the cottage and scanned the search results: some nearby listings, a county assessor page, and a map of the area. A paltry offering. Alison sighed. There must be something she could learn about the place. What was the name on that card Leah had found? Catherine?

She redid the search adding the name, and this time the top result was a link to the website for a Catherine Anthony. Alison straightened and clicked it. A minimalist page loaded.

Artist Catherine Anthony, the header announced. Next to the name were buttons for *Home, Gallery, About,* and *Shop.* Alison went straight for *About* and leaned closer to the screen.

Born and raised in Bremerton, Washington, Catherine Anthony grew up with a keen appreciation for the rich and varied hues of the Washington landscape, and an uncanny ability to capture them on canvas. Encouraged by her father, local photographer Edwin Bard, she pursued a fine arts degree from UCLA and has in the decades since made a name for herself in the Pacific Northwest for her contemplative water-color and ink portrayals of the Olympic peninsula's flora and fauna.

Currently, Catherine makes her home east of Seattle where she divides her time between her home studio and Whitman College, where she's been teaching since 2004.

Beneath the text was an old black-and-white photograph of a young woman in a polka-dotted shift dress à la 1960 surrounded by paints and brushes on the floor of a studio.

It could be her, Alison thought. East of Seattle fit. She quickly clicked the *Gallery* button and was met by row after neat row of landscape images—some a series study of the same motif, others random one-offs of a majestic stag or a hawk in flight. All shared the captivating tones of the paintings that hung on the walls at the cottage.

Alison wasn't tired anymore. As her brain fired up, she did another search, now for the name Catherine Anthony, and, as the results list populated, a thrill of excitement shot through her.

Painter Catherine Anthony named Seattle artist of the year, one read.

Local phenom C. Anthony to give commencement speech at UW, read another.

There were links to galleries that displayed her art, online stores that sold prints, a profile from the 1990s written by a big lifestyle magazine, and, toward the bottom of the first page, a *Seattle Times* obituary dated November 28 of last year. Alison opened the latter first and rifled across the words as if afraid settling too long on one would make the rest go away.

*Catherine Louise Anthony... Washington native... rise to
fame... admired teacher... beloved friend... retreated from
public life... after a long illness... preceded in death by her
parents and brother... dearly missed... private ceremony...
support cancer research instead of flowers.*

Not exactly a rich source of information.

As the sun came up outside, Alison scanned the other pages
with equal ardor, only stopping to grab a banana and a glass of
milk from the kitchen when her stomach got too loud. None of
the sources offered the kind of satisfying deep insight into the
private life of Catherine Anthony or her link to Mom that
Alison had hoped for. By all accounts she'd been a private
person, not much concerned with nurturing a public persona or
notions of fame. Alison respected that while at the same time
groaning in frustration at the few notes she'd scribbled on the
notepad next to her.

Still, after pouring over the virtual vaults for hours, there
were enough clues to make her confident she had the right
person. One interview mentioned a lakefront house, a
Redmond gallery housed several of her larger paintings, and,
most enlightening perhaps, the series of paintings that had cata-
pulted her into the spotlight in the 1980s was called *No Man's
Land*.

FORTY

LEAH

Leah was sore the next morning from all the demoing. She stayed in bed long after her alarm went off, willing her body to wake up, but her limbs were too heavy, and the bed was too soft.

Lingering in that light-blue area between sleep and consciousness, she replayed the evening before with Andrew. Regardless of how complicated the thought of an actual relationship seemed, there was no denying their chemistry. And no matter how convinced she was this was a passing fancy, she also didn't want to not see him. So here she was—another date set for tomorrow night. Dinner out this time. The real deal.

She forced herself to sit up and switched her phone out of silent mode. Several group messages from Jillian and Hannah, that had come in overnight, illuminated the screen.

Paris is awesome, Hannah announced. A photo of the two of them in front of the Eiffel Tower followed.

No Hunchback here, Jillian captioned another picture—this one of Hannah striking a pose in front of Notre-Dame.

Oh Hannah, her beautiful daughter. So confident, so grown-up.

Leah responded with ten heart emojis. *Wish I was there,* she typed. *But glad you were able to get together.*

She put the phone down then changed her mind and sent a separate text to Jill asking for her general assessment of Hannah —was she happy, healthy? Was she having the time of her life?

The three dots appeared instantly.

Had so much fun. She's great but misses you of course. Back to the States tomorrow morning. Talk then.

Leah let out a breath. All was well.

With that settled, she got out of bed.

The sun was finally making her return as Leah pulled up next to the cottage. She'd become used to arriving in the rain and making a run for the door, but this morning, she stopped at the gate and inhaled deeply. The bright, sweet scent of cut grass filled her nostrils. Everything sparkled, water droplets hanging like crystals off branches and leaves. A magical place.

She still had a half hour before Alison and the inspector were slated to show up, so she had time for one more sweep to make sure the house was as clean as possible. The last thing she wanted was for Alison to think she couldn't be trusted with the property.

As soon as she went inside, she smelled it—a musky, sick stink irritating the air. Her nose wrinkled. It was worse by the kitchen, but she found nothing but paper and plastic in the garbage can. The bathroom was fine too. It wasn't until she descended the stairs that she put two and two together. With each step, the smell grew stronger until she reached the bottom floor and remembered the stains on the drywall. Mold, probably, and likely worse than she'd thought. The paneling must have acted as an insulator, and now that she'd torn it off, the odor was set free.

Leah rushed to the sliding glass door and opened it, then

went into both bedrooms and opened the windows too. There wasn't much of a breeze outside, but within ten minutes the smell got better. That or she was getting used to it. She must have been like the proverbial frog in boiling water yesterday, not noticing it right away.

"Dammit," she muttered, surveying the demoed panels on the floor. How much would something like this cost to fix? She'd been prepared to replace some drywall, but what if there was mold behind it? Structural damage?

With a sigh, she went outside and sat down on the stairs leading from the deck to the lawn. The next hour would tell whether this had been a vain idea from the start. See, this was why she couldn't be an optimist like Andrew—as a realist you were always prepared. If the inspector offered bad news, she might have to walk away.

She rested her chin in her hands and stared out across the lake, which lay like a tranquil mirror in the mid-morning light. Realist or not, the dreamy "what ifs" wouldn't budge. She might get a kayak or a small rowboat. Out there in the middle of the lake, equidistant from each shore, the world would melt away, leaving only the sense of the water below and the skies above. She might even forego bringing a book.

This love for water was something she'd had in common with her mom. Alison had been terrified of the murky depths and the unknown below, and she'd always stayed seated in their dinghy growing up. Leah, on the other hand, felt more at home floating and diving until her skin pruned. She and her mother would often compare their ridged fingers at the end of a summer afternoon.

Mom and the lake...

Leah gnawed on her lip. Once that final fatal decision had been made, had her mother chosen the lake for comfort— because it was a friend? A safe place? Not that it made the choice any better.

A car came to a noisy stop on the other side of the house, dissolving the image in her mind.

They were here.

While Leah greeted Lars, the inspector, Alison's car pulled up next to them. She jumped out and rounded the hood, an unnatural grin plastered on her face. Her hand, when she extended it to Lars, missed as if she'd momentarily lost balance, but she didn't notice, instead correcting her stance with a lurch.

Leah squinted. It was hard to put a finger on something specific being wrong with her sister, but her general vibe was... off.

Alison gave Leah a hug. "Wait until you hear what I found out last night. Her eyes shone as if she was spiking a fever. "I know who Catherine is." She grabbed Leah's arm and moved toward the entry.

"Yeah, some famous artist, right? Catherine Anthony."

Alison expression turned sour. "Oh, you know."

"Andrew told me."

Alison stopped. "Andrew?"

Uh-oh. "I've... seen him... a few times."

"Oh."

Leah paused before opening the door for Lars. "I should let you know it was a little smelly in here this morning. I tried to air it out, but..." She opened the door.

Lars stopped in the middle of the hallway. "Oh yeah."

"It's downstairs," Leah said. "I'll show you."

"We'll get there." Lars pulled out his tablet. "I'll start up here. You said you two and your sister own the house."

Leah nodded. "Inheritance."

"Gotcha." He wandered off.

Alison deflated on the couch in the living room. Was she drunk?

"Are you feeling okay?" Leah asked from the doorway to the kitchen. "You seem weird."

Alison rewarded her with a glare. "Yeah, well. You would too if your husband left you and you couldn't sleep."

Leah stared at her.

"Shit." Alison grew paler still. "Sorry, I didn't mean—I know Neil... I'm sorry."

Leah waved her off and sat down in the chair next to the couch. "Tyler left you?"

Alison sighed. "Maybe. I don't know. He's at his sister's."

"What happened?"

"His version or mine?"

"They're different?"

Alison scoffed. "Either it's I have issues with priorities, or he needs to get a job."

Leah cocked her head to the side with a furrowed brow, choosing her words carefully. "Could it be some of both?" she asked.

Alison glared at her. "You would take his side," she muttered.

"What's that supposed to mean?"

Lars rounded the corner and moved toward the stairs. "This level looks great," he said. The windows are old, but they still have some life left. No outlet issues, no plumbing leaks. Heading downstairs now."

Leah stood, foregoing a possible response from Alison for the time being. "I'll join you."

As they descended the stairs, she explained the work she'd done. The remaining smell was faint now thanks to the open windows, but Lars still stopped in the middle of the common area to survey the space. "Yeah, I see the problem," he said.

Leah steeled herself. "How bad is it?"

He walked over to the wall and prodded the dark spots with his stylus. "It's not wet now. There might have been a leak at one time, but you'd have to remove all this"—he gestured to the length of the bared wall—"to know what we're dealing with."

He leaned close to the wall in a couple of spots as if sniffing it. "Here," he announced, marking a stretch of about three yards. "My guess is there's mold on the back of these."

"How expensive is that to fix?" Alison asked from the bottom of the stairs.

Lars rubbed at his jaw. "I couldn't say. You'd want new insulation too, and if any posts are compromised, those would need fixing."

"If you had to ballpark it?" Alison insisted.

Lars made a "phew" sound. "Ten grand maybe. Hopefully less."

Leah swallowed. Not great but also not terrible. In the grand scheme of all the transactions she was considering, that was small potatoes.

"I'd take care of it sooner than later if I were you," Lars said. "Especially if anyone is spending a considerable amount of time here." He passed Leah, continuing his tour. "Good job on the panels by the way. I hate dealing with old glue." He smiled.

Leah squared her shoulders at the compliment.

While Lars went through the bedrooms and the downstairs bath, Leah headed outside with Alison in tow. She pretended to inspect the flowerpots on a shelving unit by the wall, while sneaking glances at Alison, who was deep in thought at the edge of the deck, gaze somewhere far off in the distance. Her older sister usually didn't let things get to her like this. Whatever had happened with Tyler must have sent her for a spin.

After several minutes, she sidled up to Alison and said softly, "For the record, I'm not taking Tyler's side. I'm sorry if I came off like that."

"I know." Alison's shoulders slumped, and she turned to lean against the railing. "I thought..." she started, eyes on the floor. "We were fine, you know. Great even. Going about our lives. And now suddenly we're not."

She looked up and there was such confusion in her eyes that it took some effort for Leah not to reach out and hug her.

"He thinks I don't love him anymore, but I do. How does he not see that when I work so hard for us?"

Leah waited for Alison to continue, but this time her sister was expecting a response. She scrambled to find something helpful to say. Something that didn't send Alison spiraling even deeper. Ugh, she had nothing.

"Hey." Leah reached out and put her hand on Alison's arm, let it rest there a moment. "You'll figure it out. Marriage is… work. Compromise."

Alison sniffled. "I guess. Kind of hard to work on it when one party takes off though. I miss him."

Lars came outside. "Okay, I'm done in here. What you see is kind of what you get aside from that wall. The sink doesn't drain well, but I suspect a thorough cleaning will do the trick. Other than that, it's cosmetic stuff. It's old." He shrugged.

"That's good," Leah said, her dream firming up again.

"We'll check the exterior next, and I can already tell you the siding needs a new coat of paint, and the roof should be replaced within the next couple of years." He went down the steps to the lawn and backed up a few paces. "See where the shingles lift up? That's the sign. I'll do a lap around if you want to wait here."

After he left, Leah turned again to Alison. How could she bring her out of this gloom? "You said you did some research on Catherine? Find anything about Mom?"

Alison raised her brow and straightened on an inhale. "Oh. No, nothing like that. She won a bunch of awards, somewhat of a prodigy when she was younger, taught college classes, died of cancer in November."

"Hence the hospital bed."

Alison turned toward the lake. "Makes sense."

"Could they have met through work?"

"Maybe. But Catherine taught occasional classes at Whitman, not UW. Although she did give a speech there once. It was a big deal apparently. But that was decades ago, so it hardly fits."

Lars returned, tablet now at his side. "Yeah, nothing else. Siding and roof. Overall the property is in decent shape. I'd get the septic company out here for that. Did you want me to look at the guest house too?"

Leah squinted. "Guest house?"

Lars hoisted a thumb toward the water and the gray building next to the dock.

"You mean the shed?" Alison said. "Can't hurt."

Lars laughed. "Pretty fancy shed with water and electricity." He pointed to the wires that ran from a corner of the shed's roof to a post hidden by a large fir. "There's a water line coming from the north side of the house."

Leah gawked. With all that rain, they hadn't ventured down to the water before, but still, now that he'd pointed it out, she had no idea how they'd missed it. Maybe this was where they'd find answers. Maybe it had been right in front of them this whole time.

Together, the three of them crossed the lawn.

FORTY-ONE

ALISON

As soon as Lars said "water and electricity," a bell went off in Alison's head.

"I know what it is," she said under her breath to Leah as they approached the structure. It was one of the few things she'd written down during her early-morning research. "Catherine Anthony had a home studio. I bet that's what it is."

Leah's step faltered. "You're kidding? I figured it'd be gardening tools or something."

"You guys have a key?" Lars asked. "Door's locked."

Leah pulled out a keyring that held four keys—among them the ones to the main house and the mailbox—and handed the bundle to Lars. "Maybe it's one of these?"

He got in on the second try. "After you."

Alison was first across the threshold and stopped, gaping at the sight that met them. The wall facing the water was all glass—something that hadn't been visible from the main house—and it made the twelve-by-twelve space appear much larger than it was.

Lars, as if sensing the significance of the find, excused himself to check out the outside and left Leah and Alison alone.

A bank of cabinets ran the length of one of the walls, the counter ending in a stainless-steel sink, and on the opposite wall was an easel with a half-finished canvas perching on its ledge. A small secretary desk and chair sat in the corner by the glass wall, and there was a rug on the floor that took up half the space. Other than that, the room had no furniture.

Leah took a few more steps into the room. "Wow."

Alison silently agreed. A veritable treasure trove right under their noses. She joined Leah on the rug, scanning the multitude of canvases lined up around the perimeter of the room. How much would a posthumous Catherine Anthony bring in if she auctioned it off for the fundraiser?

Leah opened a large box in the corner and turned to Alison. "There are more in here. She was busy. Maybe we'll find the big square one in one of these."

"Not that I knew who she was until early this morning, but isn't it kind of fascinating to picture her working in here?" Alison asked. It was more than the faint smell of paint that permeated the air. The space breathed with life even though its owner had been gone for some time. It pulsated around her as if in wait of something or someone to take charge of it.

"Very," Leah agreed. "Hey, look at this one. It's the dock outside." The painting she held up was a fall motif of the lake framed by colorful trees with dramatic clouds rolling in from the right. A woman sat on the dock with her back to the painter, staring across the water. Perhaps it was a self-portrait.

"I can't believe I've lived here all my life and had no idea she existed. You'd think I'd have read about her in the paper or something." Alison ran her finger across the top of the canvas on the easel. It left a gray streak of dust, and she stared at her fingertip for a beat, a tremor starting somewhere deep inside. This woman's legacy was collecting dust. It didn't matter how prolific she'd been or how many accolades she'd collected—she was gone now. And the world kept turning anyway, like she'd never been there. Like Mom had never—

"We should tell Jill," Leah said before Alison could follow that tremor to its originating fault line. "She'll be excited to hear she can have more than one painting if she wants."

Alison hummed in agreement, still lost in thought. Tyler would find this place fascinating. A secret lair uncovered, the lifeblood of someone unearthed. A pang shot through her. Why was he in Idaho again? She should call him...

"I think this was Mom's," Leah said, pulling Alison's focus back. She held up a UW mug with a faint lipstick stain. "You don't think she painted too, do you? Maybe she took lessons?"

"No way." Alison joined her and together they examined the mug as if the discolored ceramic held the key to all their questions. "I think your personal-assistant theory is getting more and more likely though. An artist like Catherine would have wanted to keep painting even when she was sick."

"So Mom would have had to help her down here and then wait for her to finish," Leah filled in.

Lars stuck his head through the doorway, interrupting their speculation. "That about wraps it up." Addressing Alison, he continued, "Did you want to set up a time for the Queen Anne property?"

She blinked a few times as if that would help the transition into work mode. "Uh, yeah. Sure." She pulled out her phone. "I'll be outside," she told Leah, who was rummaging through the cabinets of art supplies. "Work stuff."

Leah didn't respond.

"We also need to look at Mom's house," Alison told Lars once outside. "Do you have time now?"

He glanced at his wristwatch. "Sorry, I have a twelve o'clock meeting." He scrolled through his calendar. "Tomorrow is also booked. How about first thing Monday?"

Next week was going to be intense with the fundraiser. Bess

was covering most initial client meetings—something Alison had agreed to out of sheer necessity—but there were still existing clients who needed attention. Way back when all of this started, Tyler had suggested she hire a meeting planner, and at this point she grudgingly admitted he might have had a point. But she was an expert juggler; she'd pull it off. The only thing she couldn't do was be in two places at once.

Leah came outside, brows knit. "The desk is locked. You haven't seen a small key anywhere, have you?"

"No. Maybe it's in the house somewhere. But I was about to call for you—are you around Monday morning? We're trying to schedule the inspection for Mom's house."

"Yeah, I'm here."

"Is 9 AM okay?" Lars asked.

It was set.

Maybe she could still swing by, Alison thought, her mind sorting to-dos on autopilot. If there's a will, there's a way. And speaking of to-dos, she needed to get going or she'd be late for Dr. Wezniak.

The discovered studio already fading to the back of her mind, she walked Lars to his car and dove into her day.

FORTY-TWO
LEAH

Andrew picked Leah up at six on Friday night. With their last ride together still fresh in her mind, she'd told him she didn't mind driving, but he'd insisted she was on the way to where they were going. In the end, she decided it wouldn't make sense to drive two cars.

Leah wasn't used to butterflies anywhere other than in the yard, but today they'd swarmed her insides from the moment she'd woken up. After a quick stop at the mall, she'd tried to keep busy at Mom's house. The weather had cooled off a little and was perfect for yard work, so she'd spent the afternoon weeding and spreading new mulch in the flowerbeds. If the inspection on Monday was positive, they'd have pictures taken midweek and the house listed shortly after. Leah was all for optimizing the chances it would sell quickly.

"You look nice," she said to Andrew as she slid into the car. He was wearing skinny jeans and a linen-texture sport coat over a striped button-down. Pretty hip compared to what she'd previously seen him in.

He glanced at her from the driver's seat, a smile playing on his lips. "Thanks, so do you. Your dress or something you found in a closet?"

"I got it this morning." She clamped her lips together. *Too much information.* Trying too hard.

"I'm honored."

She ventured a tentative smile. *Okay, good.* She let go of the seat belt and leaned her elbow against the door. Opened up her shoulders. "I figured my gardening jeans might be frowned upon."

He chuckled. "Good call."

She pushed a strand of hair out of her face and rested her head against her hand. "What about you? Is this your go-to date attire?"

"Ha!" It burst forth from his chest. "Maybe if dating was a regular occurrence in my life."

It took focus to keep a straight face at that. "It's not?"

"Not for a while."

"Why?" She hung on his every word, both wanting and not wanting an answer. This was uncharted territory for them.

"Um... It feels a little weird to go there now, but..." He sighed. "Fine. I was engaged a few years ago."

"Oh?" Her stomach dropped. "What happened?"

"Gretchen got a job in Singapore. Then a husband and a kid. Also in Singapore." He grimaced.

"Ouch."

"Yeah."

And you're still in love with her. She broke you for other women. You've sworn off love... Leah held her breath.

"But it was for the best. I mean, it took a while to figure stuff out, but now I think if it was meant to be, we would have been married sooner. We were together for eight years."

Yikes. Was that better or worse than the answers she'd expected?

"Turned me off dating for a bit though for sure, and then I just haven't found anyone I wanted to ask out."

Getting better... Should she dare say it? "Until now?"

He pulled to a stop at a red light and looked at her in earnest. "Until now."

She turned her face away to hide the grin that tugged at her cheeks. What was this even? She pinched her bottom lip with two fingers to settle the whirl of winged creatures inside her chest.

Andrew cleared his throat. "As long as we're being honest, I should probably tell you I used to have a huge crush on you when we were kids."

Leah chuckled. "I knew that."

His gaze cut to her. "You did? I thought I hid it so well."

A flashback to how his knuckles had lingered against hers even after that awkward first kiss had ended. "Nuh-uh. Everyone knew." She rubbed at her right hand as an electric thrill evoked by the memory skated up the back of it.

He let that sink in for a moment. "Damn."

"Yeah, sorry."

"But you didn't...?"

"No. You were just a good friend." She lifted one shoulder, then added under her breath, "Back then."

They drove another few minutes in silence before Andrew sucked in a deep breath. "Okay, so what about you then? Mom told me about your husband. That must have been hard."

Leah froze. *No. No, no, no, no, no.* Neil wasn't allowed here with them in this car. Not now. "You never considered going with Gretchen to Singapore?" she asked as if he hadn't spoken. "I hear it's a cool place."

He glanced at her, and she did her best to keep her face neutral. *Take the hint.*

The muscle in his jaw twitched once. "I didn't. I like it here."

"Ah." Leah nodded as if this was of great interest. "What do you like about it specifically?" How long until they reached the restaurant? The air in the small space was getting increasingly hard to breathe.

"What do I...?" He turned to her again. "Come on—you don't have to do that. Just say you don't want to talk about it. No big deal. I'm sorry if I overstepped."

Silence once again wrapped itself around them. Andrew kept his eyes firmly on the road now. Was he mad? Leah watched for signs—tightening knuckles, heightened coloring, deceptive calm.

But then he smiled again as if some hilarious thought crossed his mind.

"See that huge cedar over there?" He pointed up ahead on the right side of the road. "Junior year in high school, me and four other kids tee-peed it one night." He chuckled. "People were so pissed. They wrote about it in the paper."

Leah's eyes widened. "No way! That was you?"

"True story."

"Did you get in trouble?"

"No." He grinned. "No one ever found out. You're the first person I've told."

"Not even your parents?"

He cocked an eyebrow. "Especially not my parents."

Leah had no such stories of her own. She'd had friends and gone to parties, but she'd still followed the rules. Never missed a curfew, never got drunk, never failed to study for a test. There was only one thing...

"I smoked for two months my senior year."

"Two whole months?" His expression was one of exaggerated shock.

She swatted at him, and he pretended she'd got him good. "Whatever. I was badass."

"I'm sure."

"I was."

"Then why'd you quit?"

"It was gross."

"And...?"

How did he know there was an "and"? "And I didn't like sneaking around."

"Aha!" He smiled, clearly pleased with himself. "See, such a good girl. Can't tell a lie."

Leah scoffed, more bitterly than she'd intended. If he only knew what a great liar she was.

"What?" he asked, glancing over. "I didn't mean any offense. It would be totally fine if you weren't a good girl. I'm not trying to insinuate that women have to be good to—"

She put a hand up to interrupt his freakout. "You're fine. No offense taken." She tried a reassuring nod. "What's this place we're going to anyway?"

He paused for a beat as if considering whether or not to drop it.

"We're five minutes away," he said. "A buddy of mine is a co-owner in this farm-to-table place in Snohomish. Best food ever. The menu changes all the time based on what's available, and it books up weeks in advance—unless you have contacts." He winked at her. "I hope you'll like it."

Leah's stomach rumbled. "Sounds amazing."

The date was back on track.

Andrew hadn't lied—the food was out-of-this-world fantastic. For the first time in years, Leah also had half a glass of white wine with the salmon ceviche appetizer, and the slight beneath-the-skin glow that followed had allowed her to let go of any lingering tensions from the car ride.

She tried pâté with pickled red onions and coarse mustard, clams in garlic butter, a blue cheese and pear tart. Each mouthful was more exquisite than the one before, but when a plate with green foam was put in front of her, she balked.

"Um, no. This looks like it comes straight from the shallows in Cottage Lake."

Andrew just laughed. Didn't demand, coerce, ridicule. "It's matcha pudding." He took a bite. "It's good for you."

Aside from the food and the witty conversation, that's what Leah appreciated most about the evening—how Andrew never *insisted*. There was no urging her to drink more, or to have another bite. He deferred to her to make her own decisions and accepted them without argument. It was a revelation, and one that made room for boldness. The pudding was, of course, delicious.

They emerged from the restaurant late in the evening with full bellies but light steps and set a course toward the car. Neither was in a hurry, and when their arms brushed up against each other once, twice, three times, Leah took a deep breath and splayed her fingers toward his. The warmth of his hand as he took hold of hers billowed up her arm and down her back, goosebumps rising in tandem. Whatever this was, whatever was happening right now, Leah didn't want it to end. Not yet.

"If you want, I can show you the cottage," she said, the boldness of her words counterbalanced by a slight hesitation. Was that a presumptuous suggestion? Oh no, would he think she was inviting him to sleep over? "Unless you're tired. There's always another day." She groaned internally.

Andrew gave her hand a little squeeze. "It's only ten. I'd love to see the studio too, if that's cool with you."

Leah bit down on her lip to stifle a bubbling giddiness. "Sure. I'll give you the full tour. Be warned that the basement floor is smelly. I'd air it out but—"

"So you said. I'm sure I can handle it." They reached the car, and he opened the door for her. "Don't worry so much.

Easy breezy. We're hanging out. No expectations." He nodded once, eyebrows raised as if asking if she understood.

She smiled. "Easy breezy. Got it."

Man, was she in trouble with this one.

It was new, arriving at the cottage after dark, unlocking the door and turning on lights. For a moment, Leah floated outside herself, a spectator watching her returning from a night on the town, the image as clear as if she was already living here. It was a first as far as homecomings went, and doing it *not* alone imbued the air with possibility. That and mold spores...

"Wow," Andrew said, coming down the stairs after the initial tour of the first floor. "You weren't joking. Phew!" He waved a hand in front of his nose. "Let me know if you want any recommendations for remediators to help with that."

"Sorry." Leah wrinkled her nose. "Let's head over to the studio instead."

By now, the evening had grown impenetrable, and once they stepped outside the glow of light cast by the lamps inside, nothing but darkness remained.

"Should I go get a flashlight?" Leah asked as they took tentative steps in the general direction of the deck. How else would they traverse this ocean of black?

"Here." Andrew took out his phone and, before long, a cone of light illuminated their feet.

"Making yourself useful." Leah hooked her arm through his. "I like it."

If she'd been impressed with his resourcefulness, he displayed equal awe when she turned on the lights in the studio.

"No way," he said, standing in the doorway, much like Leah and Alison had the day before.

"I know." Leah showed him the easel with the half-finished

painting. "I mean, look at this. Have you ever seen something so heartbreaking?"

"It's beautiful though. I've seen her art before in the paper and stuff, but never like this."

"Wait, there's more." Leah grabbed a box they'd yet to unpack and opened it. She pulled out canvas after canvas and laid them on the floor.

Andrew perched on the stool by the easel, eyes fixed on the paintings surrounding Leah.

"It's like a window into her soul," he said after a while. They both looked up at that, found the other. The air quivered. "I mean, it's her life's work, right? But we don't know her. It's like a puzzle." He was leaning forward, elbows on his thighs. Intent, alert, lost.

Leah looked away first. "There's a big one here at the bottom. Help me get it out. It's wrapped in a towel or something."

He joined her, and Leah instantly realized her mistake. As long as there'd been distance, she could chalk up what was between them to the late hour, the wine, the pull of the lake even. She could ignore it. But once they were shoulder to shoulder, there was no escape. Her skin ignited where their arms touched.

"It's heavy." Andrew grunted as he tried to free the parcel from the box. It was a tight fit, even though the wrapping made it easier to get a good grip. "Feels like it's framed."

Leah tried to keep the box steady while Andrew wrestled with its contents. If he turned his head the slightest bit, they'd be face to face. No air between them. She wanted him to but hoped he wouldn't.

With a *whoosh*, the towel and its contents slid free of the cardboard, and Andrew stumbled back a step. He regained his balance and set the parcel down on the floor between them.

"Let me." Leah reached for a corner of the terry cloth the

frame was wrapped in and folded it back while Andrew steadied it. His fingers were long and slender but his grip firm. She grazed the back of his hand when she reached for the next corner, the need to touch him coming from some place deep inside.

His head jerked up as if she'd burned him. Should she apologize? Pretend nothing happened? As she scrambled for words, their eyes locked and, like earlier, the atmosphere changed. They were now only a foot apart, and Leah said a quiet prayer he wouldn't hear the rapid drumbeat of her heart. Then another prayer he would.

Neither of them looked away.

Screw it. Leah swallowed and moved her hand back to Andrew's. As their fingers interlaced, he let out a strangled breath. She was close enough to see his pupils dilate.

"I really want to kiss you right now," he whispered.

Not sure her voice would carry, she nodded once. Her lips parted as they rose up on their knees and together as if two breakers had given them the push they needed. His lips were soft but unwavering, and he tasted faintly of the red wine from earlier. At first their point of contact was tender, almost chaste, like there was a need to hold still and settle into this new nearness. But familiarity soon sparked an urge for more, and then he trailed his free hand across her jaw to deepen the kiss.

Leah wished she'd taken off her sweater; the room was suddenly too warm. Dizzyingly so. She melded into him even as the frame dug into her hips, preventing an even closer union. Andrew must have deemed it an annoyance too, because he slid it out from between them and tilted it onto the rug with a soft thud.

Oh Lord, that was better. She pulled him closer still—a feeding frenzy after nearly starving to death. His kisses were life, and she needed them like she needed air.

Their breaths were shallow and their faces flushed when they finally parted.

"We have to stop," Andrew whispered on an exhale. "Or I can't... You're so..." He placed a soft peck on the tip of her nose. "Whew. Better than seventh grade?"

Leah laughed as she sat back on her feet. "A lot." Good thing he was stronger of will than she was.

She looked down, and there was the painting, now almost free of its cloak. Leah gasped. Not only was it different than the others—only ink and water, and fully detailed while still maintaining the dreamy sense of surreptitious observation Leah had come to recognize as Catherine Anthony's trademark style—but it was also a perfect square. Steeling herself, she lifted the last fold out of the way to reveal the central motif and knew in an instant this was the missing painting from the house.

Andrew, who had followed her movement, leaned closer. "Is that...?"

Leah reached for the canvas, all the cogs in her mind grinding, spinning, then settling, finally, in place.

In front of her was a beautiful black-and-white rendition of two women—two half-naked women—amid folds of fabric that trailed off and morphed into swells of water. It looked like they were spooning, one of them embracing the other from behind, her face hidden in the delicate curve of the other's neck. But the woman at the forefront—the woman being embraced—stared into Leah's soul with eyes she saw every day when she looked in the mirror.

Mom hadn't been Catherine's caretaker; she'd been her lover.

FORTY-THREE

ALISON

"Calm down—you're not making any sense." Alison had the phone wedged underneath her chin while she gathered her dry cleaning in one hand and her travel mug in the other. Her laptop bag balanced precariously on one shoulder, threatening to fall off any moment as she tried prying the door handle to the garage open with her hip and elbow.

"God dammit," she muttered when the phone slipped and fell to the floor. "Hold on," she yelled to Leah on the other end of the line. "I'll be right back." She hurried to put her things in the car then went back for the phone.

"Are you still there? I'm running out the door. Hold on, let me put you on speaker." She got in the car and opened the windows. "There." It was a gorgeous day, and she needed all the fresh air she could get. She was still only sleeping a couple of hours max every night. A spray tan would be necessary if she wanted to avoid looking like a colorless zombie at the fundraiser. She added it to her mental to-do list for the week. "What were you saying? I couldn't hear you before. Take it from the beginning—what about the studio and Mom?"

This time, Leah's voice came out crisp and clear from the speakers. "It's big. I don't know if you should be driving."

Alison rolled her eyes. "Just tell me."

Leah was silent for a beat. "Okay fine. So we found a painting last night."

"We?"

"Andrew and I."

"Oh?" Had she finally done something about him then?

"I'll tell you later. Anyway, this painting..."

Alison groaned. "Spit it out."

"Catherine and Mom had a relationship. I think Mom was gay."

Alison slammed on the brake a split second before hitting the car in front of her. "What?"

"The painting is of her and Catherine. Together. You have to get out here. We have to figure this out."

Leah had lost her ever-loving mind. Mom hadn't been gay, and Alison told her so in no uncertain terms. "Just because you find a painting of two women doesn't mean it's her. Frankly, your theory about the personal assistant stuff was more realistic, and that's saying something."

"Fine—you don't believe me? Give me a second."

Alison stretched her neck until it cracked, waiting for traffic to move again. Her phone buzzed in its holder. A photo. She picked it up and opened the message.

"Believe me now?" Leah said.

The car behind Alison honked, but her eyes remained glued to the screen. Leah was telling the truth. It *was* Mom. And what's more, the date next to Catherine's signature in the lower right-hand corner said -96. As in 1996. As in over twenty years ago.

Alison started to sweat. "I'll be there in an hour."

. . .

Leah was pale like she'd struggled with sleep too, Alison thought when she arrived at the cottage. That or... Andrew?

"It's still in the studio," Leah said by way of greeting. "I wanted to wait for you before going through the rest." She led the way across the lawn.

"I don't have a ton of time, so you know. Did you tell Jill?"

"Not yet. I know she had some stuff to take care of today."

The painting was propped up on the easel, Leah having moved the half-finished one to the floor. Alison stopped short at the sight of it. Up close, it was even more obvious it was Mom looking back at them with inky eyes.

"I think this one is Mom too," Leah said, holding up the fall motif they'd found the other day. "I remember this sweater."

"Did you notice the date?" Alison asked.

"This one says 2015."

"No, I meant on this one." She nodded to the black-and-white one. "1996."

"Really?" Leah frowned and hurried to Alison's side. "I don't know how we missed that."

We again, huh? Alison glanced at her sister. "I'll be asking you about Andrew later, so you know. Don't think I'll let it go."

Leah pressed her lips together. "Fine," she said with practiced ease. "Not much to tell." She touched the signature on the painting. "What does this mean? They had a relationship for over twenty years, and no one knew?"

"At least that long." Hadn't she read about Catherine speaking at UW sometime in the eighties? What if that's when they met? And how long had Catherine owned this place? Had she bought it to be close to Mom? Alison pulled the stool closer. She needed to sit down.

"Maybe there's still another explanation," Leah tried. "Catherine might have used a face she knew for inspiration for that painting."

"That doesn't explain why Mom never mentioned her. No,

there must have been a good reason, and this fits. Plus, you have how this painting used to hang above the bed in the main bedroom, Mom's clothes in the closet, the fact that she inherited the house at all..."

Leah's brow furrowed. "All those weekends when she was away at a conference or working or whatever—she was here, right across the lake?"

"Who knows?"

The years spun in reverse through Alison's mind. All the way back to Dad getting sick. Had Mom already met Catherine back then? Memories from those years had murky corners, and Alison had shoved some less-than-pleasant particulars in there hoping to never drag them out into the light again. But they were there, lying in wait. After all, they were the reason why she knew that if Mom had found happiness with Catherine, she'd never hold it against her.

FORTY-FOUR

JILLIAN

No one was ever excited for an OB visit, and with the stakes so high this time, Jillian was dragging her feet. On the one hand, she needed the clean bill of health to start looking into donors. On the other hand, once she had it, she'd no longer have an excuse not to proceed. It would be all down to her. Making decisions. Admittedly, seeing Hannah had helped. Jillian had listened, offered advice, provided welcome distractions. And it hadn't been scary. Sure, Hannah was a young adult and not her own kid, but she'd known what to do. That was the point.

She pushed open the door to the clinic where she usually had her annual done. Her stomach sank a little further with each step she took toward the reception desk. What if Dr. Sanders thought this was a terrible idea? Still, she took a seat in the waiting area, surreptitiously eyeing the two pregnant women and their partners who were also there. Still, she rose to follow the nurse who called her name. And still, she undressed and hopped up into the examination chair covered by that crinkly sheet of paper that did its best to slip off her lap any chance it got. She yawned widely. She'd been back in New York less than twenty-four hours and jetlag was brutal.

"Jillian, I didn't expect you back so soon." Dr. Sanders entered the room with her affable smile. "It's not time for your annual yet, is it?"

Jillian tightened the thin robe around her torso. "No, not quite."

The spinning stool creaked as Dr. Sanders sat. "What can I do for you today? Everything all right?"

She should come right out and say it. Let the words flow and brace herself. "I'm thinking of having a baby." She fought to keep her eyes open. Closing them wouldn't hide the delicate nucleus of her soul she'd just bared. "By myself."

Dr. Sanders's expression didn't change. "I see. And this is something you've thought over carefully, I assume?"

If she only knew. "I have."

Dr. Sanders leaned forward and lowered her voice as if someone was listening in. "Between you and me, I don't doubt it. But I'm obliged to ask, you understand." She straightened. "Well, let's make sure everything is good, then I'll let you get dressed and we'll talk about your options."

That was it? Jillian lay back and tried to focus on the *Where's Waldo* scene someone had placed on the ceiling as distraction while the doctor did her thing. She must have been in this examination room before, because she found him right away.

"Are your cycles still regular?" Dr. Sanders asked as she pressed down gently on Jillian's stomach.

"Pretty much."

The doctor pulled down the paper sheet to cover Jillian's legs and rolled back on her stool. "All done. I'll give you a few minutes and then I'll be back." She left the room.

Jillian didn't waste any time getting dressed. This was it. Moment of truth. If everything was okay, she would try for a baby. Holy shit! The flutter in her belly turned into an avalanche at the thought, but she let it wash over her and was still breathing normally when Dr. Sanders returned a few minutes later, carrying a stack of brochures.

She fanned them out like a hand of cards and introduced each one. "These are two different sperm banks we recommend." She indicated the glossy trifolds. "Given your age and overall health, I think you're a good candidate for starting with home insemination. It's less expensive and has a decent success rate, especially if you start charting your ovulation.

"This one has contact information for our counselors should you need to talk this through with someone before getting started, and these last two are perhaps a bit premature, but I figured you might want to familiarize yourself with how to have a healthy pregnancy. There are some great links to online resources there too."

The simplicity of it all was what stood out the most. *Nothing about what to do once the baby arrived? Nothing about how to make sure you're not a bad parent?*

"You're quiet today," Dr. Sanders noted. "Do you have any questions for me?"

Jillian stared at the brochures. The words blended into complete nonsense whenever she tried to read a line. She chewed at her lower lip. "I could basically call up the sperm bank today and place an order, they'd ship it to me, and I'm good to go?"

"Pretty much. I'd encourage you to wait for the test results from today. We'll do a blood panel before you leave too. And you do need to know your fertile window in order to time delivery of the product, but generally, yes—you're good to go."

"It's that easy?"

"To do the actual insemination, yes. Keep in mind, though, that it takes an average of five tries for any woman to get pregnant. Don't expect success on your first try."

"Oh." Here she'd been trying so hard not to get pregnant for the past twenty years... "But if I do, I'd come back to see you?"

Dr. Sanders grinned. "You're free to pick any OB of course. But I'd love to be part of the journey when that day comes. It's my favorite part of the job."

Finally, Jillian's death grip on the brochures loosened. Maybe there was no judgment coming. She had to ask. "Do people... I mean... is it frowned upon?"

Dr. Sanders squinted. "Using a sperm donor?"

"No, having a baby without a partner. Alone."

Dr. Sanders shook her head. "I meet women like you here every week. It's much more common than you think, especially in a city like this. And if you ask me, there are plenty of couples who make worse parents than single people. It's not about the number." She crossed her hands in her lap. "That said, it can't hurt to prepare yourself that you'll meet people with strong opinions on the topic. Families come in all shapes and sizes these days, but some people find it hard to embrace change even when it's staring them in the face. But I'm sure you'll handle that just fine."

Jillian nodded. Except, what would she do if the dissenting voice came from within? It was so much easier leaving a conversation behind when it was external.

"Sometimes it's hard to think of questions in the moment. If anything comes to mind—anything at all—message me via the care portal and we'll schedule a call. As relatively easy as it is to reproduce, there's no such thing as overpreparing. A child is an enormous responsibility."

With those apt words ringing in her ears, Jillian left the office.

FORTY-FIVE

LEAH

Going through the remaining boxes, Leah and Alison found several more paintings where the female subject might have been their mother, but none so blatantly romantic.

Long after Alison left, Leah sat among the canvasses, willing them to tell their story. That profile over there, was that Mom? The tiny figure in the boat? One of Leah's favorites was a detailed study of a hand in close-up, holding a pen to paper. Judging by the rings and the fact that the subject was left-handed, she was sure it was her mother's hand. That one was dated *1990*. It boggled the mind. Dad was still alive then. Sick but alive. Had she cheated on him? True, he had been gone a lot, and not necessarily present when he was home, but so was Mom. They matched.

For the umpteenth time since discovering the painting, Leah had the urge to dismiss the theory of the two lovers altogether. There was no way. Mom wasn't that free-spirited, not open-minded enough to be not straight.

Her phone buzzed in her pocket—Jillian letting her know she'd seen her OB to get things rolling.

Fantastic, Leah typed. *So excited for you!*

A grinning emoji came back.

Her heart sank. She needed to tell Jill about all this, but how? Now that Leah knew exactly how much Jill's fraught relationship with their mom had hampered her adult life, how could she tell her that, oh by the way, Mom was also bisexual? The last thing Jill needed was another commonality.

The phone chimed again as she was about to put it away, but this time it was Andrew.

Want to watch a movie tonight?

Leah tensed. She was sitting in the exact spot where they'd kissed last night. In the stark light of day, that seemed less of a good idea and more of a disaster waiting to happen. Yes, she loved the time she spent with him, and the kissing had been mind-blowing, but the fact that he could tear down her defenses in this short amount of time reminded her of being stuck on the tilt-a-wheel at the fair in middle school. She was drawn to it, but as soon as the ride started, she wanted to get off. What if she wasn't ready?

She hesitated but then typed, *Sorry, can't tonight. House stuff.* She shrugged off her hoodie, flushing hot at the lie.

Anything I can help with?

Darn it.

It had been a good kiss. Great even. Leah's thumb trailed her lower lip. Maybe...

No. Too much, too soon.

Thanks, but Alison will be here.

She could always ask Ali to come over and make it true. She waited for the dots, but they took a while.

Okay no prob. Raincheck.

She sent a smiley emoji, hoping that would take the sting out of the rejection.

Hopefully he wouldn't be at his parents tonight, or she'd be so busted.

It was still dark out when Leah was startled awake by something shrill and insistent. She'd stayed up late watching a movie, and she'd not yet had enough sleep by far.

The noise stopped and she drifted, but then it started up again, and this time she couldn't tune it out. Who was calling at this ungodly hour, and why oh why had she forgotten to switch her cell to silent mode?

With a grunt, she swung her legs out of bed and stood, giving herself a head rush. Where was the phone? She rummaged through the pile of clothes on the chair and fished it out in time for a third round of signals to come through.

"Hello?"

"Yes hi, this is Kyle with Home Alarm Services. Is this Leah Sloane?"

"It is."

"Hi, Ms. Sloane. We're calling about an alarm going off at your house. Can you verify?"

"Um..." Leah blinked herself wide awake. At first, she thought he meant this house, then the coin dropped. The house in Chicago. "No, I can't actually. I'm not there at the moment."

"Is anyone else on the premises?"

"No."

"I see. And before we continue here, would you verify your password please?"

Leah did.

"Great. What would you like us to do, miss?"

Leah stared at her reflection in the window. How was she supposed to know? It could be battery failure—that had happened before. It was a frustrating downside to getting the alarm installed after Neil died. Then again, it might be a burglary in progress.

"Which window is it?" she asked. The one in the kitchen was the iffy one.

"Let's look." Kyle sounded much more chipper than what the situation warranted, Leah thought. "Garage entry."

The hairs on Leah's arms rose.

"Do you want us to check it out?"

Leah pictured masked robbers with crowbars sneaking around in her house like a sinister cartoon. "Yes, please do."

"Okay, dispatching a car now."

"What happens next?" Leah asked, pacing.

"You can stay on the line if you want or get a callback when I hear from the security officer."

"I'll take a callback." Nature was calling and she didn't want Kyle with her in the bathroom.

"Okay, five to ten minutes."

They hung up.

Leah's hands were shaking. What if someone was really there? What if she'd been home?

After doing her business, she went down to the kitchen to grab a glass of milk. The sky was starting to sport a few pink streaks, but the garden outside the window was still cloaked in night. She turned away from the window to escape the sight, a shudder running across her back.

The next five minutes dragged on. When the phone finally rang, Leah almost dropped it on the floor.

"This is Kyle again. I'm patching Officer Luca through."

Leah waited through some static.

"Ms. Sloane?" a deeper male voice said. "I'm Officer Luca; I'm here at your property. Do you have a daughter named

Hannah Josephine Sloane, born May 1?" The way he said it made it sound like he was reading the name off something.

What did Hannah have to do with this? "Yes."

Another, fainter voice in the background: "I told you. Now can I talk to her?"

Was that? No, not possible...

Officer Luca came back. "Hold on—she wants to talk to you."

Leah's mouth had gone dry, so she simply nodded as if he could see her. Hannah was there? Her baby girl wasn't supposed to be anywhere near Illinois.

"Mom, it's me. I'm really sorry."

With her daughter's sweet voice in her ear, Leah sank heavily into one of the kitchen chairs. If Hannah was home, something must have happened, and if something had happened, she needed to be there for her. There was no Alison, no Catherine, no house, no Andrew anymore—the only thing that mattered was how fast she could get back to Chicago.

FORTY-SIX

ALISON

Alison stared at her phone. Leah was doing what? The message had come in late the night before when it seemed her sister had remembered the inspection scheduled for this morning. "I'm so sorry," Leah said. "Hannah came home, and I need to go to her. I've been at the airport for hours trying to get on a flight and they finally fit me in. If you can't be there, maybe reschedule? I'll call you when I land."

Alison's scalp tightened. Another failed delegation. Why were people like this? Her pulse racing, she opened up her calendar for the day. She had a 9 AM call with the printer who was supposed to do programs for the fundraiser. He was one of the vendors Peter had failed to pay, and Alison had no idea if they'd be able to get it done in time. At 9:15 she had her Monday morning check-in with Bess, who was meeting two potential clients in the office; at 9:30 she was supposed to view a property in Madrona; and then she had a 10:30 with Dr. Wezniak. The afternoon was no better.

And now she also had to meet Lars at Mom's house...

She closed her eyes and willed her heart to slow. He'd understand if she canceled, but then everything would get delayed. And it wouldn't be fair to call with an hour's notice. Maybe if she called the printer a little early from the car, let Lars into the house and gave him a key to drop with Mrs. Carlisle, then called Bess on her way to the showing. If traffic wasn't too bad, she might make it. It would be tight, but it was worth a shot.

By the time Alison took her seat on Dr. Wezniak's couch ten minutes past the half hour, another headache was brewing. She'd downed a bottle of water and some ibuprofen in the car, but it had yet to kick in.

"What's going on today?" Dr. Wezniak asked, her eyes on Alison's bobbing foot.

Alison forced herself to be still. Sitting here was such an inconvenience when she had a million other things to take care of. But she'd promised Ty. If this was what would make him come back, she'd keep doing it.

"My sister left last minute and screwed up my schedule," Alison said. "So I'm short on time. The fundraiser is this weekend."

Dr. Wezniak asked more questions about that, and Alison answered them dutifully, not leaving any plans out. It brought her back. Her brain was made for lists; information automatically got stored in neat folders. When Dad returned from work trips, he'd always ask about the days he'd missed, and she'd taken pride in her detailed recaps. It had pleased him, and so it had pleased her too. Before things changed.

The phone rang in Alison's purse. They both looked at it.

"Do you want to turn that off?" Dr. Wezniak asked. "You know the policy."

Alison hurried to correct her mistake.

Dr. Wezniak leaned back in her chair. "It sounds like you're busy. Are you sleeping better at all?"

"I get a few hours."

"Have you talked to Tyler?"

"No."

Dr. Wezniak took a few notes but didn't speak.

"I've texted him, okay? He's texted back. But until I get this fundraiser out of the way..." That sounded bad. No matter how true it was, Alison wished she could take it back. "I can't drop everything. That's not realistic. I'll lose business and let a lot of people down."

"What about asking for help?"

Alison scoffed. "Like I did with Peter? Or Leah this morning? You want something done, you do it yourself."

"Like your mom used to say?"

Alison flinched.

Dr. Wezniak tilted her head and pursed her lips. "You've said it many times before. Look, I know you admired your mother. She sounds like she was an accomplished woman, practically raised you and your sisters alone, self-made, self-sufficient... But people aren't islands. We're connected. Relationships are what make us human. Your mom had your dad, she had you and your sisters, she had colleagues at the university. Friends, I'm sure."

Alison's palms started to sweat, and she wiped them on her slacks. Whenever she'd pictured Mom through the years, it was as a solid, solitary silhouette. An Atlas carrying her world alone. But the truth was, Mom had had Catherine. A partner through several decades if she was to believe the signs. The thought was reeling. She hadn't "done things herself" at all. At least not exclusively. What did that mean?

Alison opened her mouth, the question threatening to spill out, but at the last moment, she changed her mind. She had no interest in discussing her mom's love life here and now with so little time left of the session. It would be better to save it for next week when the fundraiser was done, and she'd have a clearer head with which to navigate those uncharted waters.

"What are you thinking?" Dr. Wezniak asked.

Alison paused then tried for a smile. "Nothing. You're probably right. That said, I know our time's not up yet, but if you don't mind, I need to get going. Get this day on track." She stood, hoping her expression relayed something like *"this session has been very helpful in readying me for the rest of this week."*

"It's up to you," Dr. Wezniak said, a small wrinkle lingering between her brows. "Same time next Monday?"

Alison agreed, then hurried toward her car, pulling out her phone to check what was next. She didn't notice the man lingering in the parking lot until she was about to open her car door and he addressed her.

"Alison Brady?"

She spun, grasping her purse at the same time. At the sight of his suit and tie, she relaxed her stance. "Yes?"

He pulled out a large Manila envelope from his briefcase and pushed it into her hands.

"Here you go, ma'am. You've been served."

FORTY-SEVEN

LEAH

You move heaven and earth for your kids. It's a truth for most mothers. Leah had gladly waited at the airport for a flight for seven hours, endured her snoring seat neighbor high up in the sky, and battled motion sickness in an Uber with broken suspension, because now she was back home in Chicago and about to see Hannah.

She paid the driver and tipped more than was deserved, then stood a moment at the curb. She'd been gone for two and a half weeks, but it felt like a year.

The front door opened and there she was—her daughter. It was 5 AM, but she was up, waiting.

Hannah flew into her arms, and, for a long moment, they just held each other.

"I thought you'd be asleep," Leah murmured into Hannah's hair. "You didn't have to get up for me."

Hannah grabbed Leah's carry-on and brought it inside. "I dozed on the couch. I'll sleep more later. Coffee?"

"Please."

The house smelled different. Clean. Neutral. Nothing at all like the more organic scents that come with older buildings that she'd recently grown used to. It was like an absence in her nose. Impersonal. No longer her.

Seated at the counter in the kitchen—her own tidy kitchen —she studied her daughter more carefully. Aside from sporting an attractive tan, she looked the same. A slight tension in the jaw perhaps. Leah cocked her head. Hannah hadn't said much on the phone—only that she had to cut the trip short, and that she and Chase had broken up. But she'd cried, and that wasn't like her, broken heart or not.

"How was the flight?" Hannah asked, sipping her coffee.

Nice try. "Fine, but I don't think that's what we're going to talk about right now."

"Mom..."

Leah shook her head to stop her. "What happened? I thought you were having a great time."

Hannah gnawed at her lip, her eyes darting down, then up as if unwilling to settle.

Leah reached out and put her hand on her daughter's. "Hannah," she said. "Tell me."

Finally, she made eye contact, her irises a flat gray. Then, slowly, she pulled one arm out of the sleeve of her sweater, pushed the fabric up over her shoulder, then looked down at the floor.

The bruise was dark and hand-shaped around her upper arm. Leah stared at it for a moment, all blood draining from her face. A sputtered breath. "Who?" she whispered, even though she already knew the answer.

A tear swelled and ran freely down Hannah's cheek. "He was so different there," she said, sniffling. "The first few days were fine, but then..."

"He hit you?" Leah could barely form the words.

"No, not really. It was more... He'd say things like, I was there for him, I represented him. He didn't want me to go out without him. He wanted to decide what I'd wear. I didn't want to embarrass him, so I went along with it at first, but—it was *Europe*. I didn't want to sit in that tiny apartment waiting for him all day. So we'd argue, and he'd get so angry." She wiped her cheek with the back of her hand. "But I didn't think he'd..." She sighed. "I was planning on leaving. It wasn't fun anymore. I was going to ask Aunt Jill about it actually, if she could get me on her flight back, but when we talked about it—"

"Wait, what?" Leah's eyebrows shot up. "You talked to Jill?" Her sister knew and hadn't said anything?

Hannah tilted her head back in exasperation. "Don't go all *Mom* on me, okay? I was in a funk because we'd had a fight about me going to Paris at all. She sniffed it out."

"Why couldn't she get you on the flight?"

"Mom, stop. I ended up not asking. After I told her about the argument, she made me realize maybe he was just protective. She said it was obvious how much he must love me and that he'd come around. I figured I might be overreacting. I mean, he was still sweet most of the time."

A loud whooshing noise in Leah's ears drowned Hannah out. Her own sister had sent her baby girl back to someone who would harm her. Had told her not to trust her instincts, that his behavior was love. She wanted to throw up.

"Except," Hannah said, her right hand drifting toward the purple mark on her left arm, "when I got back, he was waiting for me, and he... wasn't happy."

Leah's mouth had gone dry, and she took a big gulp of coffee as if that would help. Then she pulled Hannah to her. "I'm so sorry, sweetie," she said. "I'm so sorry." *Sorry for letting you go, sorry for not being able to protect you, sorry for not setting a better example, sorry for failing you.*

"So I left," Hannah said, matter-of-factly, once Leah let go. "I wasn't about to give him a second chance after that."

Like I did. Leah closed her eyes. *Second chance, third chance, tenth chance, thirty-fifth chance...* "You're stronger than

I was," she said, her voice shaky. Hannah's bruise was an imprint on her soul. The pain deep and dull. Lingering. She fought another wave of nausea.

That first time Neil had hit her—after Hannah's birthday party—he'd been filled with remorse. He'd had a few beers, he was stressed about work, he would never *intentionally* do anything to harm her, the person he loved most in the world. And she'd believed him. The second time had been three years later—enough time gone by to forget she'd promised herself to leave if it ever happened again. He groveled; she forgave. What people didn't understand was that abusers are seldom monsters through and through. He was a great dad to Hannah, a provider for their family, a man she'd committed herself to for better or for worse. And she'd loved him, in spite of it all—at least until Hannah was old enough to understand. After that she'd stayed only because she didn't know anything else. Call it weakness, or denial, or survival instinct—whatever it was, she'd stayed.

Thank God Hannah didn't.

"I don't know about that." Hannah pulled her sleeve back down and got up to put her mug away. "You're the strongest person I know. Anyway, I'm fine, I'm here. And sorry again about the alarm—you should have told me you changed the code."

Leah shrugged. Her mind was still foggy with images of Neil and Chase floating together. And Jill. Boy did she have a few choice words to say to her.

"I think I'm going to try to sleep a few more hours after all," Hannah said, covering a yawn. "You?"

"Maybe in a bit. You go up. We'll talk more later."

Hannah smiled and turned toward the hallway. "Love you, Mom," she called over her shoulder.

"Love you more," Leah responded.

Now, what time was it in New York?

. . .

Leah waited until everything was quiet upstairs before she pulled her phone out and sat down on the couch. Hannah's senior photos hung on the wall across from her, fanning the flames of fury that had ignited while Hannah told her story. She'd been hurt, and it might have been avoided if not for Jill. What right did she have giving advice on matters she knew nothing about? What right to keep Leah in the dark?

Jillian answered after two rings. "Hey, you're up early. Isn't it like four in the morning there?"

"Six. I'm home. In Chicago," Leah clarified.

"You are? Why?"

"Hannah came home unexpectedly." Leah's hand was shaking. She didn't do confrontations; life had taught her she never came out on top. But this time it was about Hannah.

"Oh? I thought she had another month in Brussels. Is she okay?"

Leah took a deep breath. Was she that clueless? "You were supposed to check up on her for me," she said, jaw tight.

Jillian was quiet for a moment. "Mm-hmm..."

"And instead you... you..." Leah's voice broke.

"What? Leah what's going on? You're scaring me."

Ha! That was rich. "He hurt her, okay? You sent her back to him, and he... *fucking* hurt her." Leah buried her face in one of the pillows to stifle the agony that wanted out.

"But I..."

"She told you he was being controlling, that he was angry. That she didn't tell him she went to Paris. And you said it was a sign of love?" Hearing the words out loud—the sheer ignorance of them—made Leah want to throw things. "She was going to ask you to fly her home and instead you talked her into going back."

"But, Leah, I didn't know. How could I—"

"You're the adult," Leah half-yelled. "Did it sound like a healthy relationship to you? She came to you and expressed worry about her boyfriend. And not only did you tell her to go back, but you let *me* believe everything was fine. I'm her mother. I would have known. But I guess that's the difference between a parent and someone who's not—I would never, ever presume to interfere with someone else's kid." The words were rising like bile up her throat, unstoppable even though they stung her lips and scorched the air around her. They wanted out, for Hannah. "You can't just tell them random things and hope for the best. Is that the kind of parent you'll be?"

"Come on now—you know I love Hannah—"

Leah ignored her. She was a runaway train. "No concern for her well-being. Like Mom was with you." Another figurative shard of glass appeared in her hand. "Oh, and by the way, turns out you do have more things in common. Catherine and Mom were in a relationship. Go figure!" A sharp cackle followed the diatribe. Leah didn't recognize it as her own until, suspended between them, it stretched into nothingness and the line went silent. Her chest caved in the moment she registered the absence of sound. She blinked the room back into focus. What had she said? Had she really outed Mom to get back at Jill?

"Okay," Jillian said, voice barely there. "Wow. Um... I need to go. I'm sorry about Hannah."

"No, Jill, wait."

But it was too late. Jillian had already hung up.

FORTY-EIGHT
JILLIAN

Jillian's whole body trembled. She'd been on her way out the door when Leah's call came in, and now she stood frozen in place in the foyer, one hand on her carry-on, the other clutching her phone. The room around her swirled in grayscale, and no sound penetrated the walls. When her lips parted with a small *tick*, it echoed in that odd cocoon that surrounded her. Before she knew it, she'd sunk to the floor. Only the grip on her bag offered a point of focus.

Leah's voice rang in her ears. It was a quiet static and at the same time a jet engine blasting her eardrums, but she could still pick out certain words—*sent back; hurt her; healthy relationship; no concern; like Mom*. Oh God, what had she done? Why had she ever thought she'd be the right person to offer relationship advice when she knew nothing but how to fail at them? They'd never forgive her for this. Jillian's fingers dug into the rug. She deserved every bit of Leah's wrath, but that thing about Marion and Catherine must have been made up. Surely their mother wasn't bisexual too.

She thought back to Alison's wedding—the day she'd come out as bi to Marion.

"No date?" she'd asked when had Jillian shown up alone. "That's unusual."

Jillian, who'd been in a somewhat steady relationship at the time, having dated the same girl for six months, had decided not to invite her because she didn't want to steal Alison's thunder, but at Marion's underhanded comment, she hadn't been able to keep her mouth shut.

"Yeah, my *girlfriend* had to work," she'd said and watched with satisfaction as the implication of her words sank in, and a pale shadow passed across Marion's carefully made-up features.

That's right, she'd thought, bracing for the comments that were sure to follow. *This is me—what're you going to do about it?*

But nothing had happened. Nothing memorable.

"Shame," Marion had simply said, before she'd turned on her heel and walked away.

At the time, Jillian had read it as *shame on you*—an expected but not overly creative retort. Now, in hindsight, she supposed Marion might have intended *that's a shame.* They'd never spoken of it after.

Was it possible she'd been bi too?

Jillian's phone buzzed, announcing for the second time that her ride was waiting downstairs. With a grunt of effort, she broke the paralysis and collected her things: captain's cap, keys, bag. She had a three-day turn lined up—New York to London and back. It was a good thing planes pretty much flew themselves these days.

She tried, but unfortunately compartmentalizing wasn't Jillian's strong suit. She was no Alison. Once at cruising altitude, Leah's words wanted in again, no matter how she tried to quiet them. She knew what Leah had implied; she shouldn't have kids. Look at what she'd done.

"Do you have a family?" she asked her first officer, Mitch, on impulse. She hadn't flown with him before, but he had an approachable demeanor, and they'd made small talk earlier at the gate.

"Nah," he said. "Haven't found the right gal. You?"

"No."

"It's hard with this job, isn't it?"

"Doesn't help."

"I heard you're up for a promotion."

Jillian looked at him. So, the jungle drums were beating.

When she didn't respond, he apologized. "None of my business—I get it. Feather in the hat to be thought of though."

That it was. Check Airman had been her dad's title and the summit of her aspirations since she'd enrolled in flight school. She was damn proud she'd had the offer at thirty-seven, and she'd shout it from the rooftops if things weren't so complicated. As it was, she'd already drafted a letter to decline the offer. She'd written it Saturday after seeing her OB. If she was going to have a kid, the promotion would have to wait. It would be too stressful, too hard to puzzle the two pieces together. There were other chances. No hurry.

She expected Mitch would disagree. Heck, she couldn't think of a single colleague who wouldn't.

Mitch adjusted his headset. "Looks a little rocky up ahead."

Jillian checked her instruments and turned on the seat-belt signs, then sent a quick thought to the passengers who might be scared of flying. Turbulence wasn't something she worried about, but she knew others did.

"Would you take it?" she asked Mitch. "The promotion?"

"I have a long way to go."

"If you didn't. Hypothetically."

"For sure. It's a lot more money. Recognition."

There was that. She was damn good at her job. It was a sure thing.

As she considered again the latest developments in the case of her fitness for parenthood, Jillian couldn't help but think it was a good thing she'd yet to send that letter.

Heavy clouds of a different kind trailed her into the hotel that night. It wasn't London's fault. They'd had an unusually mild spring, and the summer heat, with its accompanying smog, had yet to make its entrance. No, what was hanging over her was non-atmospherical, but no less threatening, earth-shattering changes.

She barely responded when the receptionist handed her the room key. She shampooed twice instead of using conditioner and consequently ended up pulling half her scalp out with the brush after. She forgot to put shoes on as she headed downstairs to the restaurant for a bite and had to ride the elevator back up to the seventh floor.

She'd thought she'd made her mind up. For so long, the question of having kids had come down to fear. She'd told herself she didn't need kids, that she was satisfied with her life the way it was, that not everyone was made for parenthood. She'd watched friends and colleagues settle down and start families, rejoiced with them, pushing her jealousy aside, knowing it wasn't for her. She'd mess up, ruin the kid, make them hate her. Fear had triumphed because of Marion, and when the longing had grown stronger—when that hateful biological clock had started ticking—she'd repeated that logic with increasing desperation. She couldn't. It wouldn't be right.

Until Greg and David.

Damn them for infiltrating her defenses. Damn Leah for offering a sense of possibility. Jillian should have known better. Leah had been right to rescind her encouragement.

The restaurant was empty, except for a family of four at a

table by the window and a couple of guys at the bar—one at either end, both engrossed in their phones.

Jillian took a seat mid-bar. "A ginger ale please," she said to the bartender. "And a menu."

One of the kids at the table yelled a loud, "No," to which his mother retorted something in a hushed voice. Jillian observed them from behind the menu. A nuclear family. Why was it called that anyway? Because of its propensity to explode and leave devastation in its wake?

She sighed. There was a pretty simple solution to all this—return to what she knew and settle for what she'd basically already decided up until a few weeks ago. She'd be a single, childless professional in New York City, focused on her career and personal well-being, with the freedom to go wherever and see whoever whenever she wanted. Not the worst thing. Hey, here she was in London. She took a swig of her ginger ale as if to toast herself.

Her stomach growled.

The man to her right had finished up his food and stood to pay the bill. He wore a wrinkled linen jacket and carried a briefcase. *Underpaid detective*, Jillian thought as he left. She practically heard the nineties soundtrack playing as he passed behind her.

"Is that fish and chips any good?" she asked the other man, pointing to his food.

He glanced up from his phone, startled to note he wasn't alone in the room. "Huh? Oh." His gaze flicked to his plate. "Ah yes, quite so," he said in the most proper Queen's English.

Jillian suppressed a smile. "I guess I'll have to give it a go then." She made eye contact with the bartender and ordered.

"American?" the man asked.

Oh, they were talking now? She made a corny salute. "Howdy."

He put his phone down and narrowed his eyes. "No, not a

southerner. I'd venture East Coast. New York perhaps? Lawyer? Advertising?"

Jillian relaxed. She'd played this game before and with people less attractive than this sandy-haired Brit. No wedding band. It might take her mind off things.

"Not a newbie to the States, I take it. Close. I work for East Coast Airlines, but yes, I'm based in New York." She'd learned the hard way not to lead with her title and position when flirting with men. They scared more easily than women. Now he'd assume she was a flight attendant, and the fantasy scenario would write itself.

He nodded. "Oh, splendid. I'm Harry by the way." He moved two seats closer to her, still leaving a chair between them, and extended his hand.

"Jill."

The bartender brought her food, and she took a moment to thank him and pick up a fry.

"Do you mind company?" Harry asked. "I don't want to impose. Perhaps you were looking forward to a quiet meal."

Polite to boot, huh? Maybe she didn't mind so much. "Go right ahead," she said, indicating the space next to her. Then, when he'd retrieved his glass: "So what do you do, Harry? What brings you to this fine establishment?"

Harry was an attorney in Brighton, with an early flight to Belfast to visit his sister. Jillian kept the conversation going by asking questions about his work and life, not leaving much space for him to reciprocate. She nibbled on her fried fish (which, indeed, was delicious), sipped her ginger ale, and soon found herself immersed in the lilt of Harry's accent and the finer details of what it was like being the only son in a family with six children. He was engaging to talk to, and she didn't regret inviting him over.

"Refill?" he asked when Jillian finished her second glass.

She checked the time on her phone. The bartender had

cleared her plate some time ago. "It's getting late," she said. "I have an early flight."

"No rest up in the air, huh?"

Jillian stood and gestured for the check. "Not for the captain." She winked at Harry and relished the way his eyes widened as the coin dropped. It never got old.

He didn't give her the usual "Really, *you* fly the plane?" follow-up though. Instead he raised his pint and gave her an appreciative smile. "Can't say I'm surprised. Good for you."

Jillian paid, adding a sizeable tip. She hadn't expected a good time when she'd come downstairs earlier. Maybe...

She took one more measure of Harry and made her decision. If this was the life she was supposed to have, she might as well go for it. "Hey, if you feel like company once you finish your drink, I'm in 702," she said. She made sure the bartender heard her—not to flaunt the invite but as a bare-minimum safeguard. If Harry was a creep, he'd be less likely to show up knowing there was a witness. Not that Jillian needed protection; she'd had enough self-defense training since moving to New York to be at ease even in sketchy situations. "No pressure. I've had a good time either way."

He knocked on her door twenty minutes later. The thrill up her spine was automatic, and at the same time, part of her was tired and had started to hope he wouldn't show.

She opened the door. "Hi."

His smile was genuine and made his eyes crinkle. "Hello."

She could have offered him a drink from the minibar, but since they both knew why he was there, she simply reached for his hand to pull him into the room. He was a gentleman, so she knew he'd expect her to set the pace. Which was fine. Some nights you needed to be thrown down onto the bed or pushed up against the wall. Not tonight.

Jillian touched his cheek lightly, the stubble scratching her fingertips, and then she kissed him. He tasted like breath mints, and when he pressed her to the hard plane of his chest, something at the core of her eased. It was soft and warm and hard and familiar. A moment's respite from the ambiguity of the day. She *knew* this.

Unfortunately, the moment of abandon only lasted so long. Her mind kept venturing one step ahead of them: next, she'd bury her hand in his hair to pull him closer, and he'd reciprocate. He might nibble on her lip, run a hand down her side. He was taller than her, and she liked that. He'd have to tilt her head back and lean down to kiss her throat. One hand here, one hand there, two steps to the right, knee on bed. Shirts off. It would be somewhat awkward as they were strangers, but Jillian knew what she liked and wasn't afraid to say so. She kept condoms in her toiletry bag just in case. They'd both have a good time. They'd say so, cuddle for a bit maybe. He'd leave. She'd sleep.

She stifled a yawn against his shoulder.

No, this wasn't going to work.

"Hey," Jillian said, pulling back. "Harry."

"Mm-hmm." The flicker of his pulse was visible in the light illuminating the side of his collared throat.

She swallowed. That want in his eyes nearly toppled her resolve.

"I can't do this." She took a step back. "I thought I could, but…"

He ran a hand through his hair, making it stand on end. "Did I do something wrong? If so, I—"

"No, you've been… lovely." Jillian willed her lips into a smile. "I'm dealing with some stuff, and this isn't right. Not now."

"Oh." He squared his shoulders. "I see. Well."

"Any other time, I would have…" Jillian moved toward the door. "It's really not you. I'm sorry."

He put his hands up. "Say no more." He sidled past her. "For what it's worth, I still had a great time tonight."

"Me too." She held the door for him.

"Good night then." He exited, then turned. "I hope you figure things out. And fly safely."

She closed the door and sank to the floor against the wall, tilting her head back. He was a perfectly nice guy, probably above average in bed if the kissing was anything to go by, *and* he could make conversation. She lived for this. The thrill, the temporary connection, feeling alive. But tonight, all it did was remind her of the rerun of a show you used to like when you were young and dumb. She wanted more. Meaning. Permanence.

As the tears started falling, she had no choice but to admit to herself that no matter how she fought it, she still wanted a baby. There was only one thing she could do to make that possibility go away. She had to accept the promotion.

FORTY-NINE

ALISON

Peter was suing her for wrongful termination. *He* was suing *her*. Alison didn't know whether to laugh or cry and she definitely didn't have time for this shit. She scrolled through all her email exchanges with him from the past six months scanning for anything and everything that might be helpful. He'd left the back office in complete disarray after not doing his job, and, somehow, she was in the wrong because she'd demoted him? No. Not today.

She moved several emails to a folder on her laptop, closed it with a snap, and stood. The room spun. She closed her eyes and curled her shoulders inward, willing this mess to go away.

She'd been able to get a meeting with her business attorney, Candace Merle, first thing this morning, by using the fundraiser as a plea to Candace's humanitarian side. This was an emergency. A lawsuit was nothing to brush off, no matter how ridiculous the claim.

She tried to create a timeline of Peter's last months at work in her head as she drove the few miles to her attorney's office. Normally, that wouldn't have given her trouble, but today she kept having to start over. Her thoughts were like branches in a wily bramble—looping and intertwining with invasive weeds. Eventually, she opened the dictation app on her phone and tried listing events there. It was a slight improvement.

Ugh, she needed more caffeine.

Candace was at her desk when Alison arrived, typing away at something.

"Did you bring me a coffee?" she asked, a glint in her eye. "You know I don't come in this early for just anyone."

Alison handed her the extra latte she'd picked up. She needed Candace amenable and on this. She'd buy her lunch too if needed.

"Ah, lifesaver."

They dove into the lawsuit, Candace asking questions, Alison answering them as best she could. She had to call Bess a couple of times to double-check details. When was the first time Peter had forgotten to send in a contract? What had his response been when Bess had taken over one of his client contacts? How many times had he been late?

An hour into the meeting, Candace leaned back and stretched her arms behind her back. "I'm not too worried," she said. "It's pretty obvious he left the job of his own accord. Yes, his responsibilities changed and it's your word against his whether this position change was formalized or not, but his salary stayed the same, so he can't argue it was a demotion."

Alison blotted her upper lip with a tissue. Did they have the heat on in here? "What do we do?"

"I think we can get him to drop it. I'll set up a mediation meeting with him and his council as soon as possible."

"I don't have a lot of time this week."

Candace narrowed her eyes. "Are you okay? You look pale."

Alison ignored her. "I'll try to move things around if I have to, but Friday is a no-go. What if he doesn't drop it?"

"You may have a case for a counter suit considering his negligence. We'd argue financial impact to the bottom line."

"No, I don't want to—"

Candace raised a hand. "Often all it takes is the threat of one. I doubt he wants to spend months in court any more than you do, and, unless his council is some strip-mall schmuck, they'll advise him his case is weak."

Alison slumped back. That was good news. She reached for her coffee but overshot and knocked the mug over instead. What was left of the brown liquid spilled all over the corner of the desk and started dripping onto the carpet.

Alison jumped up. "Dammit." She looked around for something to wipe with, but another headrush forced her instead to sit back down.

"I've got it," Candace said. She grabbed a handful of tissues from the box on the cabinet behind her and spread them across the desktop.

"Too early in the morning to be coordinated," Alison tried to joke. "I'm so sorry." Truth was, she really wasn't feeling well. Her arms were like jelly, and her head felt two sizes too big. Did they not have air conditioning in here?

"No harm done," Candace said, still eyeing Alison with poorly concealed concern. "Why don't you head back home and lie down? Seems like you could use it. I'll let you know when I hear back from Peter's lawyer."

"Yeah, maybe," Alison mumbled. Perhaps she'd sit in her car for a few minutes at least. Close her eyes.

"Are you okay to drive?"

"Of course. I'm fine. Like I said, it's a busy week." *Jeez.* She stood again, slower this time. Paused. It would probably be rude to ask how sure Candace was of her assessment of the situation. She hoisted her purse onto her shoulder.

"Don't worry—I'm on it," Candace said as if reading her mind. "Go do your thing."

.   .   .

The caterer was a slight, efficient woman with one eye on her phone the entire time they talked. Not until Alison asked what the vegetarian option would be did she pause to fully look up.

"You didn't request vegetarian," she said.

Alison wrinkled her forehead. She was sure she'd had this conversation before.

"Here." The caterer turned her tablet toward Alison. "See?"

Alison took it and read through the email on the screen. It was an estimated number of plates, dishes, courses, coffee, tea, wine. At least it was *supposed* to be the estimate, but the way it was phrased made it sound like the final count.

"No, no, no. This is one of the first emails we sent. There's supposed to be another one from two weeks ago with the final counts after ticket sales closed." She had sent it, hadn't she? Between Mom, Tyler, and Peter, she had to concede it was possible she'd forgotten. And last week, the relief at still having a caterer in spite of the late payment had taken precedence over double-checking the order. Damn.

"Hm." The caterer scrolled through her messages again. "I'm not seeing anything."

First the payment, now this. "Is it fixable?"

"In four days?"

Alison brought a palm to her clammy forehead. "I mean, this count isn't even accurate between the chicken and the fish. These numbers were a guess." Her heart went ka-dunk-dunk in an awkward summersault, forcing a cough up her throat. She rubbed at it without thinking. This was a disaster. The meal was essentially what the attendees were paying for. If she screwed that up...

"I'll see what I can do," the other woman said. "It's not ideal. Do you have the numbers on you?"

Alison pulled her laptop out, almost dropping it in the process. Her fingers were slick with sweat and tingly at the tip. She shook her hand out before starting her search. A phone was ringing somewhere nearby, an annoying trill that wouldn't stop. Why wasn't anyone answering?

"Yeah, here they are," she said. "I'll email them to you now." She was coming off like the epitome of disorganization. How embarrassing.

"You want to get that?" the caterer asked.

Alison glanced up from her email. "Excuse me?"

"Your phone is ringing."

Oh, that's what that was. Yes, she should answer her phone. Where was it? She turned her head right to glance over her shoulder. The movement felt sluggish, like she was treading through caramel. Tyler made the best homemade caramel sauce. She should ask him to make it soon.

"It's in your purse," the caterer said, a crease forming between her brows. She pointed at Alison's feet.

Somehow Alison reached it and answered. It was Bess, sounding chipper as usual. Like a little birdie. Alison smiled. "Hi, Bess. How's your Tuesday?" Her tongue scraped against the roof of her mouth as if it didn't fit right. She pressed it down behind her teeth, making a faint clicking noise in the process.

There was silence on the line for a moment before Bess responded. "Alison? Is that you?"

"Of course." *Who else?*

"Where are you?"

"With the caterer." Something nagged at her—that urgency in Bess's voice. "Why?"

"You were supposed to be at the Madison Park property ten minutes ago. The clients called and asked for you."

That cut through the fog somewhat. *Fuck!* This whole day was so strangely tinted.

"I have to go," she told the caterer while hanging up with Bess. "I'll have to call you later." She offered an apologetic smile and rushed off.

It took a minute to find her car since she had no memory of

parking it in the first place. Once inside, her hands trembled, entering the address into the navigation system. She'd tried to limit her coffee intake lately, but maybe she'd overdone it today. Why was it so hard to remember?

She merged onto the freeway, and the car behind her honked long and hard. She gave it a dismissive wave, turned her head to change lanes, and blinked as her vision was suddenly obscured by a flickering flash. A wave of heat rolled up her spine, then everything went black.

FIFTY

LEAH

Leah and Hannah were curled up in separate corners of the couch late Tuesday night, Leah with a cup of tea in her hands, Hannah with a pint of ice cream. They'd spent half the day at a nearby park, reading and enjoying the sun, and now they were done watching a movie to which Leah had only paid fleeting attention. There were still too many things unsaid between them. Questions to ask, truths to share. The light of day had made for a too-bright spotlight, but now it was dark. And it was time.

Leah reached for the remote and turned the TV off.

"Oh boy," Hannah said, a small smile playing on her lips.

"What?" Leah asked.

"You have that mom look on your face again. You put it on thirty minutes ago. Don't think I didn't notice."

"Did not."

"Oh yeah? How did the movie end?"

Leah stared at her, drawing a blank. Ah, what was the point? Hannah had always been able to see right through her. "Fine," she said. "There are things you should know. But first I want to talk about you. And I... I want you to know how proud I am of you." She switched the mug she was holding from one hand to the other. "That you left."

"Mom."

"No, I mean it. It makes me so... ashamed—that I didn't." Her eyes stung, and she let her eyelids close. "I should have. It wasn't fair to you."

"Mom, please stop." Hannah's face was flushed as she scooted closer to Leah. "It's not the same. It wasn't your fault. I know you think so, but it wasn't."

"But I've read that children who grow up with abusive parents often gravitate toward partners with those same traits. And look at you." She gestured toward Hannah's arm. "If I'd left when you were little..."

"Mom, this is exhausting. Don't. Dad was a manipulative asshole, and Chase is some version of that too. That's their problem. Not ours. I left him because he reminded me of dad. If I didn't know what dad did to you, I'd still be in Brussels. So let's not do this, okay?"

Leah sniffled. Her daughter was the best thing. Even with everything that had happened, she'd do it all again for Hannah. "Are you sure you're okay?" she asked.

Hannah reached for Leah's hand. "I'm fine. Are you?"

Leah took a deep breath. It was time. "I'm thinking of selling the house."

Hannah smiled. "Well, good riddance."

"Really? I was worried you'd miss it."

Hannah made a sputtering sound with her lips. "Not in a million years. And it's too big for you."

Emboldened by Hannah's unexpected support, Leah ventured further. "I might move out to Seattle."

Now, Hannah made big eyes.

"I know it's far, but I've realized over the past three weeks that I miss it—the trees and the mountains. Even the rain isn't so bad. And..." A tingle of excitement ran down her arms. "I might be able to get the cottage. I can't wait for you to see it. You'll love it—I know you will."

"Wow." Hannah nodded. "That's a big step."

Leah braced herself. "Too big?"

"You're kidding, right? I've only told you for the past year you need to get out more and live. Have fun, travel, date."

Leah flinched at the last word. Would Hannah really be okay with that or was it only something she said? She'd get along with Andrew though—Leah knew that much. He was easy to like, and Hannah was, as she'd already established, the best. To have the two of them together—

Hannah threw a pillow at her mom. "Oh my God, you've met someone."

"How... I..." Leah put her hands up in defense.

"Yeah, I see that smile. Holy cow. This is huge. Who is it? Someone I know?"

"Calm yourself," Leah said with a laugh. "We were friends growing up; he lived next door. Andrew Carlisle." It was impossible to say his name with a straight face.

Hannah's eyes went even wider. "Someone you used to know? A second-chance romance?" She was practically squealing.

Leah fanned her burning face. "We've only been on a couple of dates. I don't know yet." She knew she'd been vague when responding to messages he'd sent since Friday, and she owed him several rainchecks. He'd made it clear he wanted to see her again, and, while she wanted the same, it was harder than it should be to admit that. If she said it aloud, the dam might burst fully open, and she'd scare him off. It was easier, then, to hide behind everything else that was going on in her life.

"What do Alison and Jill think?" Hannah asked.

Jill. Leah cringed. She'd said some truly awful things to her sister the day before.

"Wait, let me get something to drink and then you tell me everything." Hannah jumped off the couch and rushed to the kitchen.

Leah ran her teeth across her lower lip. Not that she wasn't still mad at Jill, but she could have handled it better. She'd have to reach out in the next day or so. Apologize.

Hannah returned with Leah's phone in one hand and a soda bottle of water in the other. "You missed a call."

Leah checked the screen. Odd time for Tyler to be calling. She was about to text him when it rang again.

"I'll have to take it," she said to Hannah. Then into the phone: "Hi, Ty."

"Hey, sorry to call so late." His voice was shaky. "I hope I didn't wake you."

"Nope, what's going on?"

He sighed—a desolate, end-of-the-world rumble. "It's Alison," he said. "She's in the hospital. Can you come back?"

Last-minute flights, airports, quick goodbyes—was this her new normal? Leah didn't want to leave Hannah, not so soon after getting her back, but her daughter practically shoved her out the door with a promise to start sorting through the house.

Now, Leah's flight was touching down yet again at Sea-Tac.

Tyler was waiting for her at the exit, but to Leah's dismay, he wasn't alone. Leaning against the wall behind him was Jillian, still in her uniform. Leah's stride faltered as her sister tracked her approach with a watchful glint.

Tyler looked like he'd forgotten how to smile. His face was pale, and when he embraced Leah, he squeezed a little too hard, as if needing to steady himself.

"How is she doing?" Leah asked.

"She's stable. Awake."

"Let's go," Jillian said. "I want to see her."

"Hi, Jill." Leah glanced at her younger sister. Being next to her, it was much harder to hold on to her anger. It drained off her into an invisible puddle on the floor.

"Hi."

"I'm parked this way." Tyler led the way.

They left the airport in silence, joining the sparse midday traffic going north on 405. It started drizzling as they crossed the floating bridge, and Leah traced the droplets trailing down the passenger-side window with her finger, ever aware Jillian was behind her. This tension was her fault. She'd been cruel, and she had to figure out a way to undo it. If possible.

As if sensing the need for a distraction, Tyler started talking. "I'm sorry I left," he said. "You must think I'm a horrible person."

Leah turned toward him, about to object, but he kept talking.

"She wasn't listening. I thought I had to show her how serious I was. It was a mistake." A bitter laugh. "Clearly."

"But she'll be fine, right?" Jillian asked from the back seat. "You said she'll be fine."

"She will. The arrhythmia that caused it can be controlled. She'll have to make a few changes."

"Like what?" Leah asked.

"Eating better, keeping a regular schedule, less stress..."

When neither of them responded, he laughed again. "I know, right? Don't they know who we're talking about?" He shook his head. "She was damn lucky this time. Who faints on a four-lane highway and comes away with a few broken bones and a concussion?"

Leah nodded. Life was a series of curveballs that could take a turn with no warning. Lucky was the right word. Alison might have died, and then Leah and Jill would be the only ones left. She had to undo what she'd done before it was too late. "Jill, I'm really sorry," she blurted out, turning. "I shouldn't have said what I said. It was shitty, and I didn't mean it."

Jillian pursed her lips, her eyes dark as she met Leah's. "That's fine," she said, voice low. "We don't have to talk about it right now."

"All right. But I wanted you to know. Hannah is okay."

Jillian's lips parted as if on a sigh. Then she gave Leah a slight nod before turning back toward the window. Leah did the same, ignoring Tyler's quizzical glance. Life was so frail. At least if something happened to them now, things wouldn't be left completely unsaid.

FIFTY-ONE

JILLIAN

Jillian trailed several yards behind Leah and Tyler through the winding hospital corridor. Alison had been moved from the ICU to a regular room while Tyler was away, and it took them a few minutes to find their way to the right floor.

It was a relief to know Hannah was fine. Jillian hadn't fully realized how much that had weighed on her until Leah had said what she'd said in the car. She'd wanted to ask about her injuries, if she was in a lot of pain, but why make Leah paint the picture?

A commotion in the doorway of a room up ahead pulled her from her thoughts.

Tyler ran the last few steps. "What's going on?"

One of the nurses stopped him. "And you are?"

"Her husband. Tyler Larson."

"Oh." The nurse stepped aside. "Maybe you can help us convince her she needs to stay in bed then."

The three of them entered the room where a pale and bandaged Alison glared at the doctor who stood next to her bed. Everyone looked up to take in the newcomers.

"Your family I take it?" the doctor said to Alison before

turning to Tyler. "It's imperative that she rest as much as possible. We're monitoring her heart rate, and the broken ribs need at least a fighting chance."

"I'll do my best," Tyler said.

The doctor nodded and left, followed by the nurses. The last nurse to leave indicated the panel next to Alison's bed. "Call us if you need anything."

As soon as they were gone, Alison leaned into her pillow and closed her eyes. "This is stupid," she muttered. "I'm fine."

"Clearly." Jillian walked around the bed. It was new, seeing Alison in such a vulnerable state. Disconcerting. "I've never seen you so alive and well." Alison opened one eye in a pirate-like glower, but Jillian ignored it. "Ali, you could have died. Do you have any idea how lucky you are?"

"Yeah, I feel like I won a million bucks."

"Jill's not wrong." Leah stepped up next to Jillian.

Alison opened both eyes. "You're here too?"

"Of course."

Alison glanced toward the door. "Hannah?"

"Still in Chicago. She's okay. Long story."

Jillian turned her gaze to the floor. Leah hadn't told anyone then. It was something.

"It wasn't fair of me to take off on you like that," Leah continued. "I had to do it, but now I kind of feel like this is my fault—sticking you with the inspection when you were already busy."

Alison lifted a hand half off the bed. "Nah. I could have canceled."

"Still."

"Stop it," Alison said, sterner this time. They all fell quiet. "I know you just got here, but I need to rest. The pain meds are kicking in." She closed her eyes again.

Tyler turned to Leah and Jillian. "Maybe grab something to eat in the cafeteria? I'll let you know when she wakes up."

Leah nodded and looked to Jillian, a question in her eyes.

"Sure," Jillian said. Might as well get it over with.

They ordered coffee and found a table near a half-dry yucca palm tree by the window in the communal space. Jillian followed Leah with wary eyes as they took their seats. She'd sounded genuine when she'd apologized in the car, but Jill was still sweating in her uniform, wishing she'd changed out of it before coming here. Best to rip the Band-Aid off.

"You were right," she said before Leah had even emptied her pack of sweetener into her mug. "I overstepped, I... I gave Hannah terrible advice. It wasn't my place, and I should have never kept it from you. I don't know anything about parenting and never will. I'm so sorry. And I totally understand if you hate me."

Leah did that thing where her gaze bounced off Jillian's as if they were two repelling magnets. "Come on. I'd never hate you." She set her spoon down then picked it up again. Her eyes finally settled. "I meant what I said earlier. I was horrible. It wasn't your fault Chase was... abusive."

Poor Leah, she had a hard time even getting the word out. Jillian shook her head, tears threatening from equal parts relief and remorse. "I've replayed our conversation so many times and I promise—if, for a second, I'd thought Hannah was in danger, I'd have never told her to go back."

"I know."

A knot eased in Jillian's stomach. "Really?"

"Yeah." Leah sighed. "I still wish you would have told me what she said, but..." She shrugged. "Hannah is an adult. It wasn't fair of me to expect you to report on her. It's just—she's been my everything for a long time. The thought of her out there in the world, alone, is scary. I can't lose her. I wouldn't survive. You'll know when you have a kid."

"Yeah, about that..." Jillian stirred her coffee. It was too warm a day for a hot drink, but it gave her something to do with her hands. "I accepted the promotion instead. I think that's... that's the best thing for me. Let's face it—there's no scenario where I wouldn't screw a kid up." She let out a sad chuckle.

"But I thought... You saw the doctor and everything." Leah paled. "It's because of what I said, isn't it?"

Jill shrank back in her chair. Leah's words certainly hadn't helped. "Well..."

Leah leaned forward. "Again, I'm so sorry. If I could take it back... You know I didn't mean it. That was *my* issue. A gut reaction because of—" She shook her head rapidly. "I think you'll be a great mom."

"But you don't know. So why risk it?"

Both their phones chimed with a text at the same time. Tyler.

"She's awake again," Jillian said. "Should we head up?"

"Please. At least think about it," Leah said.

Jillian didn't respond. She'd thought about it enough.

FIFTY-TWO

LEAH

Acid burned the back of Leah's throat as she made her way to Alison's room the next morning where Tyler and Jillian were already seated. She'd gone back to her mom's house for the night, but this time, Jillian had opted to spend the night at Alison's instead. So much for a reconciliation. It was fair; she knew better than most the damage words could do, and yet she'd leveled volley after volley of fiery accusations at Jillian. The damage was obvious in the way her sister's shoulders still slumped and in the dark circles underneath her eyes. When struck at the chink in their armor, even the strongest fell.

Over the next hour, Alison, Jillian, and Tyler chatted intermittently around her, but all Leah did was think of how to fix what she'd broken.

When no one had spoken for some time and Alison was drifting back to sleep again, Tyler stood. "Okay, I'm off. You've got it covered until I'm back?"

"Yup, no problem," Jillian said.

"Where are you going?" Leah asked.

Tyler frowned. "To meet with Ali's lawyer. We were just talking about it."

"Lawyer?" She must have been spacing out.

"Yeah," Jill said. "Her coworker is suing her, but only because he's being a dick. He doesn't have a case."

"Ex-coworker," Alison mumbled from the bed.

Leah nodded as if it was coming back to her when, in fact, she'd missed the whole conversation.

"Want me to pick anything else up while I'm out?" Tyler asked. "Snacks? Magazines?"

They declined, and he left.

"That reminds me..." Jillian pulled a periodical out of her purse. "I picked this up at the airport. It's the one with Ali's interview."

Alison stirred properly at the mention of her name and asked for something to drink.

Leah got up and poured her some water. "The one with Gladys Malone?"

"Yeah." Jillian flipped through the pages until she found the spread.

"What picture did they use?" Alison asked, her voice groggy. "Show me."

Jillian held it up. The photo showed Alison perched on a low brick wall outside her office. She wore a blue pantsuit and looked every bit the hardcore businesswoman they knew her to be, but the photographer had also managed to capture a rare softness in her smile. It was a flattering combination.

Safe homes for everyone: From residence to refuge, the title read.

"Should I read it?" Jillian asked.

"You'd better," Ali said. "I'm going to close my eyes again, but I'm still listening."

"*'In the competitive world of Seattle realty, one woman has risen above the fray,'*" Jillian began. "*'We sat down with Alison Brady on a sunny May morning at her lakeside office to talk shop, female ambition, and charity as this housing juggernaut launches a collaboration with the Stepping Stone Foundation to help those in need in the community.'"*

"Wow." Leah couldn't believe it. An honest-to-goodness magazine feature about her sister. "This is like a real thing that people will read."

Alison smiled on her pillow. "So far so good," she said.

"Seriously," Jillian said. "This is so much bigger than I thought it would be."

She went on to read the initial questions and answers that were focused on Alison's path to becoming the professional she was today.

"I didn't know you won an award your first year," Jillian said. "That's cool."

Alison opened an eye. "Mom wasn't that keen on me doing real estate in the first place, so I had to show her I was serious one way or another. Seemed like a good place to start."

Jillian and Leah exchanged a knowing glance. Mom again.

Alison lifted a hand off the bed. "Keep going."

Next was a section on how success, like intelligence, had little meaning in and of itself unless you used it for something good.

"*'I'm not going to lie,'*" Jillian read, "*'I've done well for myself, and I love what I do. I could keep doing this until the day I die.'*"

"I know how that sounds under current circumstances," Alison said from the bed. "Obviously, I pictured that being way in the future."

Jillian continued, "*'But you'd have to be willfully ignorant not to notice the increasing disparities between those who have and those who don't have in a city like this. I see it every day driving around town. I figured, why not do something?'*"

Jillian read the next question about the charity Alison had chosen and her explanation of how they provided housing for women and children who fled unsafe home situations. "*'It's a hidden need, but a real one for too many women. If you're depen-dent on your abusive partner and you have small children —where are you going to go? The Stepping Stone Foundation offers a solution, but more than that, they empower indepen-dence and foster hope in the women who pass through their doors.'"*

Leah was on the edge of her seat, simultaneously hanging on Jillian's every word and ready for flight. This hit too close for comfort. She poured herself some water to remedy her dry mouth.

Jillian continued. *"'And what inspired you to choose this particular charity?' the interviewer asks."*

Alison opened her eyes and turned her head toward Jillian.

"'It wasn't a difficult choice, Gladys. While I've been blessed with an amazingly kind and supportive husband, I've witnessed first-hand, with someone close to me, what abusive relationships do to otherwise strong women. It's a cause that's been near to my heart ever since.'"

Leah stopped breathing. Alison knew? How?

Jillian continued reading, but Leah was no longer listening. The dam had cracked, and the secret she thought she'd kept so well hidden was now on the pages of this glossy magazine. People would put two and two together. They'd talk about her.

She looked at Alison, whose gaze was far away now, locked on someplace unpleasant in the past perhaps. Leah's past. How could she do this to her?

She waited until Jill was done reading, then summoned all the bravery she'd promised herself to employ. Alison's eyes were closed again, but, after having spent a few hours at her bedside, Leah knew her rest was never deep. She rose from her chair and perched instead next to her sister on the bed. Behind them, Jillian was still flipping through the magazine.

"Hey, Ali?"

Alison opened her eyes. "Mm."

Leah trapped her hands between her thighs to stop herself from wringing them. "How... how did you know?"

"Know what?" Alison drawled.

"About the... um... the abuse? You said in the article—"

"What are you guys talking about?" Jillian asked. "You're mumbling."

Leah glanced over her shoulder. One small room, both her sisters present. It was time. "I asked Ali about what she said in the interview—about someone close to her inspiring the choice of charity." She drew in a deep breath through her nose. "It's me." She turned back to Alison. "But I don't understand how you knew. And why you didn't say anything."

Alison stared at her, her lips slightly parted. The line between her eyebrows deepened by the moment.

"Wait, what?" Jillian said in the background.

"But it wasn't you." Alison looked at both of them in turn. "It was Mom."

Leah's vision narrowed until all she saw was Alison's face, her gaze now as present as ever. *Mom, Mom, Mom*, echoed in her head.

"What are you talking about?" Jillian sounded incensed.

Alison didn't turn away from Leah. "You were there, Leah," she said. "You don't remember?"

Leah blinked. Memories played like a reel inside her head. She ran through the house—through the hallway, kitchen, dining room, up the stairs, office, bedrooms. Dad was never there. Except he must have been. When she thought of him, all she remembered was a door closing, a packed bag. That couldn't be right.

She squeezed her eyes closed. Her memory-self walked over to the window in her room and looked out at the garden. Mom was on her knees with her back to the house. She was planting something—or weeding perhaps. Leah focused hard on the image. No, not weeding. She was crying. It had happened more than once.

"You guys are insane," Jillian said, louder this time. "Mom wasn't some abused woman."

Leah's fingers sought the spot where her wedding band used to be. How had she forgotten? Was it the child's way of blocking out the uncomfortable, the incomprehensible? And then she'd fallen for Neil. She turned to Jillian. "No, I think she's right. We were really young, but there was definitely something... going on."

"No." Jillian stood, roses blooming on her cheeks. "No way! Dad was a good man. It was Mom who..." Jillian's voice cracked. "No. You're wrong."

"I'm not wrong," Alison said from the bed. "You were seven when he got sick; I was thirteen. And the year before, I saw him grab her head and bang it against the side of the fridge when they were fighting. I wasn't supposed to be home. The student council meeting after school got canceled because half the kids were sick, so I got on the regular bus home. In a way, I think I already knew. She'd hardly ever wear make-up, and then all of a sudden, she'd have this caked-on foundation. And she was so different when he was home."

"But maybe you misread the situation." Jillian paced toward the window. "You were a kid too."

"I didn't. I asked her about it after he died and she didn't deny it, just told me never to bring it up again. I know you don't want to hear this, but—"

"That's where the dent came from," Leah said, more to herself than to her sisters. She'd polished that fridge so many times, she could picture exactly where Mom's head must have hit it. She shivered. Her own fridge had been built-in and dent free, but for the longest time they'd had a hole in the drywall in one spot of the basement courtesy of Neil's fist. She'd been two inches to the left. It was a good thing he'd only tried to scare her that time.

Alison reached across the sheet and took hold of one of Leah's hands. At the feeling of her cool fingers against her skin, Leah met her sister's gaze.

"You thought it was you," Alison said quietly. Paused. "Neil?"

A gasp to her right told Leah Jillian had finally put two and two together.

Leah pulled the truth close into a bundle at her core and held it there for a moment. Then she released it all with a small nod.

Alison's grasp tightened on her hand. "Why didn't you tell us?"

Leah let out a bitter laugh. "We haven't exactly been on speaking terms. And I was scared. Of everything." She shook her head. "My world... He made everything so small. Everyone loved him. If I'd left, he'd have taken Hannah." Something painful constricted her throat. "I was going to tell Mom; that's why I came out here. She never forgave me for eloping with him, and I wanted to tell her she was right. Instead..." Her voice broke. She'd been so dumb. All these years lost with Mom because she'd assumed the grudge was insurmountable, and then it turned out she, if anyone, would have truly understood.

"Hey." Alison squeezed Leah's hand. "It's okay. I'm so sorry."

It was such an unusual display of sympathy that Leah had to smile through her tears.

"I still don't get this," Jillian said by the window, interrupting them. "How did Dad...? And Neil?" She spun toward them, both hands pressed against her forehead. "I need some air."

She was out the door before they could stop her.

"That's exactly why I didn't tell her," Alison said. "With how Mom was, I figured I'd let her have Dad at least."

Leah looked at the door where Jillian had disappeared. "Do you think that's why Mom didn't like her—because she was close with Dad?"

"No idea. You'd think she'd have swooped in once Dad died if that was the case. But she didn't." Alison grunted as she tried to shift her position in bed.

"Careful," Leah admonished. "Can I get you anything?"

"Maybe ask about more meds. I'd be all for a nice drug-induced nap after this."

Leah rang for a nurse, who came and administered something intravenously.

"I have questions of course," Alison mumbled before drifting off. "Does Andrew know? I'm sorry I'm so out of it."

Andrew. Leah still hadn't told him she was back. After running away like she had, there was no easy segue back to Friday night. Once Alison was doing better, she'd call. By then she was sure she'd know which words would be the right ones.

Tyler returned a few minutes later, brows knit. "I ran into Jill in the lobby," he said. "Is everything all right here?"

Leah stood and stretched. "Ali is fine. There was some other stuff. I'll go talk to her." She turned on her way out. "How did it go?"

"It's looking good. They agreed to a mediation."

"Thank goodness."

"Hey, when you get a chance, let's talk about this fundraiser, okay? I don't want her to have to cancel." He nodded to Alison. "She's worked really hard. I was thinking maybe you, me, and Jill could take charge there."

His hopeful expression was contagious. Yes, this was what they needed—something to rally around, together.

FIFTY-THREE

JILLIAN

Leah's approach stirred up a sense of impending doom in Jillian. She wanted to forget what Alison had said about Dad, not talk about it. He'd been her person—the one she'd admired, the one who'd loved her, the one who'd made up for Marion being indifferent. If she'd so misread her whole childhood, was she right about anything at all?

"Hey." Leah sat down next to her.

"Hey."

"I know how you must be feeling—"

"Don't." Jillian shifted away.

Leah was quiet for a moment before speaking in a low voice. "It's totally fine for you to have good memories of Dad. Neil was a great parent to Hannah. He never hit her."

Jillian flinched. How pathetic she was to make this about her own feelings when Leah had dropped the biggest bomb about her marriage. None of this made sense.

"Like Ali said, you were only seven when he got sick," Leah continued. "I was older than you, and I'd completely pushed that stuff away. He was kind of a blank space for me. Maybe as a defense mechanism."

"But you think Alison is right?"

Leah looked down. "Some of my memories of Mom make a lot more sense knowing this. I remember her crying, and being different when Dad was home. Stiff—or jumpy kind of. I don't think I ever saw him hit her, but I believe Alison. I'm sorry."

Jillian sighed. Now she had two bad parental gene pools to contend with. Fucking awesome.

As if Leah had read Jillian's mind, she put her hand on her arm. "You. Are. Not. Them," she said, emphasizing each word. "Jill, you have to remember that Alison and I have the same parents. We're all completely different. Our parents don't define us. They don't predetermine who we'll be or how we'll act. I'm going to say it one more time and then I'll stay off your case. If you want a kid, you should have a kid. You're not going to either ignore it or abuse it, because that's not who you are."

"Some would say it's not who Mom was either. To you and Alison I mean."

"Yeah, I was thinking about that..." Leah hesitated, her lip sucked between her teeth. "What if... and I'm not saying this was it, but what if you weren't... planned... like Ali and me? Maybe that's why Mom couldn't connect with you."

"You mean I was an oops?" Was Mom so set on only two kids that a third had put her over the edge?

Something trembled across Leah's face. "Um, yeah, but even"—she swallowed hard—"a non-consensual one."

Jillian stared at her. No. No, that couldn't be it. A cold knot formed in the pit of her stomach.

"It happens," Leah mumbled. "It would explain a lot."

The next thought—how had Leah even come to think of this? Jillian's jaw slackened as she formed the question. "Did Neil?"

Leah tensed as if steeling herself against a great pain. Then her features softened. She inhaled. "Once. He... raped me once." She met Jillian's eyes. The word seemed a burden to pronounce, but she continued. "I didn't even know to call it that at the time. We were married. I thought... I don't know... husbands have rights. Or something. Things had petered out after Hannah." Her face flushed scarlet. "I've told myself so many lies throughout the years."

Jillian nodded. This was too much. Poor Leah. *Poor Mom.* Now that was a new feeling. If that was, in fact, how she'd come into this world, she'd have been a living, breathing reminder of that abuse every time her mother had laid eyes on her. A nail keeping the wound open. And Jillian's closeness with their dad would have been even more damaging. In that light, she could almost—*almost*—understand her mother's seeming inability to love her. If only she'd known.

"If that's true, it makes Dad even worse," she said glumly. "Even if he was good to me, how will I ever think of him the same way again?"

Leah took Jillian's hand. "Maybe you can't. I'm really sorry."

Jillian scoffed. Again, this shouldn't be about her. "*You're* sorry? I'm the one who should be sorry. Like forever and ever. Now I understand why you reacted the way you did about Hannah. It must have brought up some pretty bad stuff."

Leah offered a crooked smile. "Yeah. But fortunately my daughter is stronger than all of us together." She squeezed Jillian's hand. "Please don't give up. Who knows—if you do, you might well be robbing the world of another Hannah. Think about that."

A kernel of warmth ignited within Jillian at those words. Apparently, the embers she'd tried to extinguish still had some life left.

"Maybe," she conceded. She pulled Leah in for a hug. "Thank you."

FIFTY-FOUR

ALISON

Alison would never admit it in a million years, but it wasn't the worst thing in the world to be stuck to a hospital bed with people fussing over her. Not having to be places. Or, rather, having places to be but a legitimate reason not to think about them. She floated high on her painkillers, drifting in and out of sleep. The words from the interview swirled together with her sisters' faces, the beeps from the heart monitor, images of unpaid bills spread out on the floor, Tyler's steady grasp.

He was there when she woke up, holding her hand, so perhaps that part wasn't a dream.

"How are you feeling?" he asked before she even opened her eyes.

"Good," she murmured. "What day is it?"

"Friday. Nine in the morning."

Alison's eyes popped open. She'd been here four days already? The tendrils of rising panic snaked through her limp form, rallying her. She'd missed so much work. The fundraiser...

"And before you say anything, we've got it covered." Tyler placed a hand on her arm. "Bess has been rescheduling clients,

Jill and Leah are doing the walkthrough of the venue this morning and making last-minute calls, and I've got your play-by-play of the event here." He held up a black notebook from her desk at home.

"But I needed to confirm with the caterer. I never... The plates—"

"She called Wednesday. Bess and I were able to dig up the info. It's a good thing you keep notes on everything."

Alison fought the impulse to sit up. It still hurt too much to move without help. The nurse had made her walk to the bathroom the night before, and the experience had reminded her of one of those ninja-course shows Tyler sometimes watched. She searched the foggy corners of her mind. What else was she forgetting? "The band?"

"Will be there thirty minutes before to set up."

"Raffle?"

"Leah took on that one. It's covered."

"Check-in?"

"Jill and I will be at the door."

Alison relaxed into the pillows and squeezed his hand. "Thank you," she mumbled. He'd thought of everything.

"If you're up for it, we can ask the doctor if they'll consider discharging you tomorrow. You could give your speech."

Normally, the prospect of standing in front of an audience of two hundred people would have lit a fire in Alison's belly, but today it made her want to disappear beneath the sheets. She was a mess. No one wanted to see that.

"I don't think I could stand for that long," she said.

"So you sit," was Tyler's pragmatic solution. "Don't decide now. If you're too tired, I'll say a few words. But I know what this means to you."

Her heartbeat slowed and the tension in her muscles eased. She pulled his hand to her chest. He always knew exactly what to say to her. She didn't deserve him. Tears welled up unbidden, and for once, she didn't try to stop them. He was her husband. Her person. He'd dropped whatever he'd been doing in Idaho to be by her side, to take charge, to support. He was clearly not incapable of initiative, which meant the hunch she'd tried to dismiss was true—there *was* culpability on her part for where they'd ended up.

"I'm sorry," she said. "Really. About everything. I think I've forgotten how to not work." She wiped at her cheek with a heavy hand. "And you were right—I did stop listening. But not because I don't love you, because I do. It was like I had no room for being less than efficient."

"And I was the opposite of that." Tyler hung his head. "I'm sorry too. I know I've let this drag on too long. I got... complacent. Honestly, I think I just didn't want to deal with figuring out the next step. My sister thinks I'm depressed."

Alison nodded. "Then we'll figure it out. Together. I'm not exactly at my peak either." She smiled wryly.

He reached out to caress her cheek. "You'll get there." And with that, he leaned over and kissed her forehead.

Alison wore black slacks, a green blouse, and a sparkly black blazer that hid the sling her left arm would have to remain in for a few more weeks when she entered the hotel where the fundraiser was in full swing. Jillian had done her make-up earlier, and Bess had picked her up, but it was Tyler who escorted her through the doors and up onto the stage in front of a sea of tables and smiling faces.

The short walk made her legs wobble like jelly, and, for a moment, she was afraid she might crumple if Tyler let go of her arm, but he'd thought of everything. A chair waited where the podium might have been, and the mic stand had already been lowered.

She sat and took in the banquet room. The tablecloths were

white with purple centerpieces to denote domestic abuse awareness, and the signs above the raffle and auction tables were also purple. Every seat was taken, and every eye in the house was on her. To her surprise, Alison had to swallow away the lump that wanted to form in her throat. She scanned the room until her gaze fell on Leah and Jillian off to one side. They both gave her a thumbs up. She smiled.

"Six months ago, this night was only a nugget of an idea," Alison started. What was it Mom had told her? *Some successful people find ways to give back.* It was the closest she'd come to acknowledging Alison's achievements in her field—a backhanded compliment that suggested there was still more to do. But Alison had basked in it, run with it, and when she'd told Mom about Stepping Stone and what they did, there had been a long silence on the phone. "Sounds good," she'd said eventually —all Alison had needed to know she was on track.

Now, this night.

She spoke of the importance of having a safe place to retire at the end of the day, a door to lock, shelter from the elements. She spoke of surviving and emerging stronger after hardships, about the organization and how she hoped to partner with them for years to come. She spoke of community and the importance of asking for help when you need it.

"No one is an island," she said, echoing Dr. Wezniak. "No one should ever feel like they have to go it alone."

Tyler shifted his stance in her peripheral, and she glanced at him. He was beaming and nodding at her in encouragement. His smile flooded her with a sense of arrival. She took a moment to find her sisters again. She looked at Bess at one of the tables next to the other two realtors who shared her office space, and at business associates, former clients, and acquaintances she'd picked up through the years. They'd all come because she'd asked them. Her family had pulled the event itself off without her. The world hadn't stopped turning when she almost did.

She wasn't an island.

Not anymore.

FIFTY-FIVE

JILLIAN

Jillian was the last to wake up the following morning. They'd all stayed overnight at Alison's house after the fundraiser, and when she made her way downstairs to the kitchen, the others were already seated on the deck, empty plates and cups in front of them. Alison was wearing a robe, half lying in a recliner, but she was awake and alert, and color was starting to return to her cheeks.

"Good morning," Tyler said with a smile. "Sleep well?"

"Like a log." Jillian reached for a piece of apple from the cutting board at the center of the table.

"There's coffee inside," Tyler said. "And I picked up bagels."

"Carbs and caffeine," Jillian said, voice dreamy. "Marry me?"

After fetching provisions, she settled in the chair next to Leah's and put her feet up on an empty one. With her knees bent, only her toes reached past the edge of the shade cast by a large umbrella, and with the sunlight's warming tendrils unfurling across her skin, she closed her eyes and sighed. She could get used to this.

"Since we're all here now," Alison said, interrupting the peace, "I wanted to say a couple of things. Hon, help me up?" She waited until Tyler had raised the seatback for her before clearing her throat. It sounded like a tiny mouse squeak, and that broke the tension of the moment, making everyone giggle. The doctor had said it would be weeks before her ribs were healed enough to cough normally.

Alison rolled her eyes. "Yeah, yeah. Laugh at the invalid."

"Sorry," Leah said. "We'll be good."

"Anyway," Alison said, dragging out the A, "I want to say thank you." She looked down at her hands, but when Tyler took one of them in his, she raised her chin again and smiled at him. "This has been a... weird week. A weird several weeks. I've got some thinking to do. Clearly. But last night was a success. And I couldn't have done it without you."

"Hold up," Jillian said. "*You're* glad someone helped you? Stop the presses!"

They all chuckled again.

"Fine, I deserve that." Alison smiled. "You did it. Preliminary numbers are over $100,000."

Leah leaned forward. "What?"

"I know. So tease me all you want—today is a good day."

"Tyler did most of it," Leah said. "Jill and I followed directions."

"Come on—you did more than that," Tyler said.

"Nah, I'm with Leah," Jillian chimed in. "You knew where Ali had all the information and what to do with it. A toast to Tyler!" She raised her coffee mug, and Leah did the same. "Seriously, you should do more stuff like that," she said. "You're a natural."

He squirmed. "Oh, I don't know."

Alison looked at him in earnest. "It's not a bad idea," she said. "I want the company to do more of this. It's worth thinking about."

Jillian shared a wide-eyed glance with Leah. Had she helped?

"Nice job," Leah mouthed silently to her.

Jillian stretched and let the sun bathe her whole legs.

As the morning closed in on noon, Jillian and Leah cleaned up in the kitchen while Tyler helped Alison with a few urgent business-related bills.

"What are you doing today?" Leah asked as she wrung out the dishrag. "Want to help pack up some stuff at Mom's?"

Jillian was still floating high on the calm of the morning and had hoped to keep that up without any more navel gazing and family intrigue until it was time to leave. While she and Leah had risen above and worked fine together at the fundraiser, she wasn't entirely convinced her sister shared those aspirations.

"Not sure. I'm flying back tonight."

Leah's face fell. "Already?"

Jillian chuckled. "Not everyone has the summers off."

"But what about the painting you wanted to take home? And you haven't seen the studio. Please come with me. We'll be quick."

Leah's pleading eyes were hard to resist. She so rarely asked for anything. "No packing?"

"No packing."

"Um..." Tyler entered the kitchen, Alison's phone in hand. "Did either of you happen to get a call from the funeral home this week?"

"Not me," Leah said.

Jillian shook her head. "Why?"

"I guess Ali was supposed to pick the ashes up on Monday but forgot. They left a couple of voicemails," Tyler said. "No worries though, I'll get them tomorrow."

After he left, Leah turned to Jillian. "That's morbid. I never even thought about the ashes." She lit up. "Hey, if you stay a couple of days, Mom's birthday is Tuesday. We could spread them in the lake or something."

"I don't think that's allowed. And you can still do that without me."

"But—"

"Not having this conversation." Jillian closed the dishwasher with a snap. "I'll come with you to get the painting if you promise to stop pestering me, but I'm leaving tonight. End of story."

It was funny, watching Leah drive toward Cottage Lake. The closer they got, the more her face relaxed and the clearer her eyes grew.

"You love it here, don't you?" Jillian asked as they pulled up in front of *No Man's Land*.

Leah beamed. "I really do."

They walked up the path to the front door, but when she turned to face Jillian again, her features had darkened. "I feel like it's already mine, but I know that's not the case. I promise I'll get you and Ali your money one way or another." She unlocked the door.

Jillian was about to respond when a nasty odor slammed into her nostrils. "Phew," she said, waving her hand in front of her face.

"I know." Leah's nose wrinkled. "It's not as bad as before, but I still need to get someone out here. Andrew knows a guy, but I still have to call him." She walked deeper into the living room.

Andrew again, huh? Jillian was about to dig into that when Leah asked, "Was this the one you wanted?" She pointed to an 11x14 painting of an ominous sunrise above ink-stained fields.

The canvas was as striking as Jillian remembered. The

colors made her think of dawn above the clouds, isolation and beauty. She knew exactly where to hang it in her room back in New York. "Do you mind?" she asked.

In response, Leah unhooked it from the wall. "There are a few other ones in the studio you might want too. Come on."

The last time Jillian was there, it had been raining, so to walk through the yard toward the lake under a clear blue sky was like seeing it with brand new eyes. It was no mystery why Leah loved it so much.

"Ta-da." Leah swung the door to the small space open.

Sunlight bathed every inch of the floor in golden light through the wall of windows, and the space smelled like the art classroom had in high school. Erasers, paint, wet paper. Jillian took a few steps in but froze at the sight of the large painting on the easel. Marion with Catherine. *Mom*, she corrected herself. With sympathy had come an urge to humanize. If Leah was still talking, she didn't hear it.

The brushstrokes that delineated the shapes and curves of the two women had a dreamy quality—a spark of life wherever the lines intersected. *Mom had Catherine.* Somehow, her mother had loved this woman enough to stay with her for twenty, thirty years. Enough, perhaps, not to want to live when she was gone, especially with a cancer battle looming. Catherine might have been her only love. How do you contain devotion like that? How do you keep it a secret?

Jillian turned to Leah. There were too many secrets in this family. Enough was enough. "So what's going on with you and Andrew?" she asked.

Leah arched her eyebrows.

"I mean, clearly you're into each other. Alison said you've been on a few dates. He seems like a good guy."

Leah stared at her a moment, then her features relaxed. "I honestly don't know. Or I do. I like him a lot. He says he likes me too." She sucked in her lower lip. "But I haven't told him about... you know. It could change things."

"Or it doesn't."

"It's like—" Leah let out a frustrated groan. "I feel one way when I'm with him, but when I'm not, I'm second-guessing everything. My judgment let me down in the past—what's to say it isn't doing it now? How do I trust him?" She turned toward the lake. "How do I trust myself?"

Oh, Leah. A wave of rage swelled at Jillian's core on behalf of her sister. If Neil wasn't already dead, she'd fucking kill him.

She sidled up next to her, close enough that their arms touched. "Hey." She nudged her sister gently. "You know what happened wasn't your fault, right?"

"I know."

"There's nothing wrong with your judgment."

"But—"

"Nothing. You deserve to be happy. We've known Andrew and his family a long time, and they're good people. If you don't even give him a chance, Neil wins."

Leah turned to her. Smiled. "You know, I've had that same thought. And that would suck ass."

Jillian chuckled in surprise. Phew, there was life in the old girl yet. "Good for you!"

"Plus, he's an excellent kisser nowadays," Leah added under her breath.

"Wha— You kissed him?" Jillian swatted her arm. "Okay, it's time. Spill, sis. I need all the details."

Leah laughed, putting her arms up as if to fend off the questions, and as she moved, something familiar caught Jillian's eye. "Hey, that's my desk." She passed Leah to get to the corner with the old secretary desk. What was it doing here?

"That's yours?"

Jillian pulled it out from the wall and peeked behind it.

"Either that or someone else carved J.B. into the back of it. I thought Mom got rid of all my stuff. Oh, I loved this thing."

Something tugged at her heart as she ran her palm over the old wood. It was entirely possible Mom had kept the desk because of its utility. Likely even. *But...* Jillian didn't want to allow the thought in, yet there it was. *Leah and Alison had had desks too, but Mom had kept this one.* It could mean nothing of course. But it *could* also mean something.

"It's pretty," Leah agreed. "But useless until I can get a lock-smith out unfortunately."

"Ha!" Jillian shook off her sentimental speculations and reached behind her neck to unclasp the chain resting there. "That's what you think." There had been two keys at one point —small, ornate things, perfect for a charm necklace. She'd taken one with her when she'd moved to New York.

"You're kidding?" Leah came up next to her.

The lock clicked open, and Jillian lowered the drop lid.

They stared in silence at the contents.

FIFTY-SIX

JILLIAN

Jillian kept her eyes on the tarmac on the other side of the plane window as the engines roared to life. A tote they'd found at the house sat between her feet calling her name with a siren song so loud that, for once, she was thankful for the noisy machine. The tote was just big enough to hold some of the contents from the desk, as well as the wrapped-up sunrise painting, but she'd promised herself she wouldn't look at any of it until she was in the air.

"Cabin crew prepare for take-off," the captain said over the speaker.

Jillian knew the guy in passing, but she was in plain clothes today and had no intention of making herself known. She closed her eyes and sank deeper into the seat, ignoring the safety demonstration.

The plane shook its way to the runway, held there for a few minutes, and then they were off. Jillian counted—ten seconds, twenty, thirty. It would take about twenty minutes to reach cruising altitude. Her fingers itched to pull out the notebooks and letters that had filled the four drawers in the desk.

As soon as she'd unlocked it, it was obvious it had been

Mom's corner of Catherine's studio. A legal pad with the
University of Washington logo sat on top of a stack of several
thick Manila envelopes. A work desk, they'd thought at first,
which made sense considering the only office space in the house
had been converted to a makeshift hospice room for Catherine.
But then they'd opened the drawers, and things were no longer
so clear-cut. While the scribbles in the first notebook were
Mom's, the writing had nothing to do with her work.

Ding.

The seat-belt sign turned off, and all around her, people
started squirming out of their seats. It was amazing how people
could sit for hours at home on the couch watching TV, but force
them into a seat belt for twenty minutes and they couldn't wait
to get up.

She reached for the bag and pulled out three notebooks and
a stack of letters bound by twine that she set in her lap. The
letters were from Catherine to Mom, short notes mostly about
everyday things, as if the two women had been aware a third
party might be privy to their content. Only one of the letters,
dated five months before Jillian was born, stood out. Its envelope had no address and no postmark, just Marion's name, so it
was fair to assume it had been hand delivered. *I don't want to
fight*, it said. *And I won't tell you what to do—I won't be like
him. I'll keep wishing and hoping, even though I know a baby
changes things. Even if you feel you need to stay, I'm always here
for you, my love.*

Jillian stared at those words for a long time. Another clue,
perhaps, to her mother's antipathy toward her. If she'd planned
on leaving Dad then didn't dare when she fell pregnant, how
could she not have viewed Jillian as the obstacle to her freedom?

This was speculation of course, and it neither exonerated
her mother nor explained why things didn't get better for Jill
when their dad died, why Mom didn't pursue that happiness
then. The only thing Jill could think of was that Alison and

Leah were older at that time, and Mom had always worried about appearances. Easier, then, to maintain the secrecy. Maybe.

Two hours later, she put down the last of the three notebooks and tilted her face to the ceiling. Her neck was stiff from staying in the same position for so long, and she cracked it with a snap that sent a burst of warmth down her shoulder.

While the letters hadn't been written by her mom, the notebooks had, and it turned out Mom had been something of a poet. Jillian hadn't been sure what to think or feel as she'd read page after page of penned verses. They weren't the straightforward accounts she'd hoped for, that was for sure, but they were the closest thing they'd come to Mom's own account. And so much of it didn't fit the woman Jillian had known. There was self-doubt, pride, regret, dreams and hope, love, and deepest despair. A roller coaster of a life. More than *Marion*.

She let her fingers dance across the spine of the burgundy notebook then flipped through its pages again until she found the poem titled "In the Garden":

> *I made neat rows*
> *One and two*
> *Eight by eight*
> *And dropped the seeds therein*
> *A scattered few*
> *Careless hand*
> *Will of none*
> *Took hold outside the line*
> *I tended some*
> *Steady heart*
> *Hidden soul*
> *With water from within*
> *In sleep they grew*
> *Deep the roots*

Dark the bed
To see the light of day
By shadow cast
Ally worms
Beetle shell
The scattered breached the earth
To prove me wrong
Turn around
Open eye
They prospered fair by night
Two crops I sowed
Vanity
Circumstance
Intending but one yield
At harvest time
Staked and pared
Run-off vine
Both equal radiance showed

The words stayed on her tongue, tiny crystals of sweet and bitter, as she closed the book and turned toward the clouds outside. The flavor was a hint of something that would never be spelled out, not a plea for forgiveness necessarily, but perhaps a quest, at least, for understanding. She could be wrong—interpretive reading had never been her strength in school—but was it so farfetched to think she might be the scattered seed that grew in spite of intentions? The run-off vine. And if that was the case, Mom had thought her equal to Alison and Leah in the end. It was something; a sign, perhaps, that she should be open to shades in between black and white in her life. Maybe it wasn't promotion *or* kid—maybe it was both after all.

For such a long time, she'd lived in the past, had hardened herself to it even as it dictated much of her life. But in that moment, the future morphed into a new entity in her mind.

Separate, with unlimited possibility. She'd stepped across the threshold between before and after.

Jillian wiped her cheek with the back of her hand and found it wet. When had she started crying? A small chuckle shook her shoulders as the tears kept falling. *This* was why there were weddings, birthdays, graduation parties, and funerals. To mark transitions. Mom would have turned seventy-one on Tuesday, and her sisters were spreading her ashes then. What if Jillian was making a mistake not being there, not acknowledging the moment?

"Cabin crew prepare for landing," the captain said over the speaker.

Jillian's ears popped. Down below was home, friends, career, freedom, future, but it would be there tomorrow and the next day too.

By the time they touched down, she'd made her decision.

FIFTY-SEVEN

LEAH

Sunday evening, Leah sat in Mom's kitchen, boxes spread out around her. She had a roll of bubble wrap at her feet and stacks of plates and bowls out on the counter. This lot would get donated to the Stepping Stone Foundation, and she didn't want to risk chipping anything in transport. It would be another two weeks until the house would go on the market—plenty of time— but it felt good to get started.

As the sun set, the doorbell rang. She knew who it was, had both hoped he'd show up and dreaded it. An ambiguous tremor ran up her spine as she put the plate she was wrapping down and stood.

Andrew's smile was tentative when she opened the door.

"I saw your car," he said. "Sunday dinner." He nodded toward his parents' house. "Can I come in?"

"Sure." Leah held the door for him then led him toward the kitchen. "I'm packing. Or I've started at least."

Andrew stopped in the doorway to survey the mess. "So I see. Need help?"

Why not? Leah thought. It might be easier to get out what she had to tell him if their hands were busy doing something else. She handed him a pile of packing paper and pointed to the cabinet with coffee cups. "Want to do those?"

They worked in silence for a few minutes until the mounting tension became too much for Leah. No, this was weird, them packing up a kitchen together after not speaking for over a week. She pushed the box she'd been filling aside and turned toward him. "I'm sorry I didn't reach out when I got back."

Andrew looked up, a dainty coffee cup in his hand. He wrapped it slowly in a sheet of paper and placed it on the counter. "Yeah, why didn't you? I thought..." His voice trailed off. "Weren't we having a good time?"

"We were." Leah patted the table. "Come sit." She waited until he did. His hands rested idly on the tabletop. Gentle hands. She wanted to hold them.

"Then what?" Andrew asked. "What happened?"

Leah forced herself to meet his gaze. "A few things," she said, stalling. "Hannah needed me, then Alison's health scare, the fundraiser... I had a lot to deal with."

"I offered to be an extra pair of hands for the fundraiser. But you—"

"Didn't respond," Leah filled in. "I know."

He cocked his head. "If you ask me, I think it's about more than being busy."

Leah looked down at the table, biting her lip. *Trust him with the truth.*

"If I misread things, I want you to tell me. I can take it." He leaned back and moved his hands to his lap, shoulders squared as if opening his chest up to a firing squad. *I'm not scared of you,* it said. *Do your worst.*

He was expecting her to end it, she realized. He was giving her an out. Sure, it would mean one less complication in her life, but also—no way. The very thought made her want to reach across the table for him. "You didn't misread things," she said. "I... got scared."

"Of what? Us?"

She shook her head. "No. Not like you think anyway. I haven't done this in a long time. Dating. Feeling things..." Her cheeks warmed. "It's like I have this voice in my head telling me I shouldn't. That the ship has sailed." She tried to put a comedic spin on her words, but Andrew didn't smile. "I know it's silly," she mumbled.

"I don't know about silly," he said. "A little sad maybe." He dragged a fingertip across the tabletop. "Is this because of your husband? Because I can understand if you're not over him yet."

She'd seen it coming, braced for it, but now that the question was hanging between them, she needed more time. "I'm kind of thirsty," she said, getting up. "Are you thirsty?"

He reached out for her arm as she passed him and stopped her. "Leah, come on."

His touch slowed her thoughts, the warm pad of his thumb against her wrist keeping her firmly here. With him. She backtracked her steps and sat down again.

"I told you about Gretchen. Why can't we talk about him?"

"It's compl—"

"Complicated," he filled in with a sigh. "I get it. You lost him. I won't pretend I know what that feels like."

Leah stared down at her hand—at the spot where her wedding band had once been. She hadn't put it on since the funeral.

"It's not what you think," she said. Everything around her stilled. "For over a year now, everyone's been treating me like I'm some fragile, grieving widow. All I hear is how strong I am, how hard it must be, and what a wonderful man he was." She met Andrew's eyes. "The truth is..." She took a deep breath. "The truth is, I'm glad he's gone. He wasn't a good man, and he wasn't very nice to me." She scoffed at the understatement.

Andrew's lips parted. "You mean...?" The cogs turned behind those kind eyes. "He didn't hit you, did he?"

Leah felt sorry for him; he hadn't bargained for this.

He must have read the answer on her face. "That fucker." His voice dripped with loathing. He stood and paced to the counter.

At first, his agitation made her muscles tense. A gut reaction. She followed his movements warily until he stopped and turned, his gaze the same tender one she'd known since Ruby Mallard's closet. Her body eased. She knew this man, was falling for him if she was going to be honest with herself. His rage wasn't directed at her—it was on her behalf. For her protection. Nothing about him scared her. Well, nothing but the feelings she had for him. It would be a greater loss than she'd admitted to herself if this ended them.

"It's okay," she said. "I've done a lot of therapy this past year. He can't hurt me anymore." Never had the words resonated truer. Spelling out the secret—which, by the way, was Neil's secret not hers—stripped it of its last shreds of power. "It's one of the reasons I'm moving here. I can't stay in Chicago. Our friends were his friends. Our colleagues were his colleagues. He fooled everyone. I don't think anyone would believe me if I said something, and I'm tired of pretending. I'd rather start over."

Like Mom had done. Catherine had been her new start. Another life on the other side of the lake.

"I mean, holy shit." Andrew eyed her with a mix of horror and something that resembled awe.

"Now you know." She steeled herself, her insides pleading with him not to leave. "I know it's a lot."

He hurried across the floor and crouched down in front of her. Their intertwined fingers rested in her lap. "I'm so sorry," he said. "I had no idea. I shouldn't have pushed it." He leaned his forehead to hers. "You're amazing, you know that?" he whispered, lifting her hand to his lips. Not at all the reaction she'd pictured. "I totally understand if you need time, or, or..."

She leaned back to better see his face. "Time for what?"

"Well, you've been a bit distant, right? If we're moving too fast or you need space, I can back off."

There it was. The graceful bow out.

"If *you* want, that is," he continued. "Let me be crystal clear —I'd see you every day if it was up to me."

Or not. A smile tugged at the corner of Leah's mouth. "Really?"

"Are you kidding?"

Her smile widened. "I haven't scared you off?" It was a stupid thing to ask, but something about him made her forget to censor herself. "Even with all that?"

"Everyone has baggage. I wish you didn't have yours, but not for me—for you. That's an awfully heavy burden to bear alone."

She hadn't thought of it that way, but he was right. Was that why she felt so much lighter after sharing it? She nodded slowly. "I don't want you to back off."

"No?" His whole face lit up.

"Nuh-uh."

An understanding passed between them—one that erased all doubts. He held her steady with his gaze, and she let him. She wouldn't look away, not from this miracle of a man, not for anything.

"Can I kiss you?" Andrew asked, still smiling. "I don't want to push my luck here, but I'd beat myself up if I didn't at least ask. No pressure." He reached up and brushed a strand of hair off her eyebrow.

The trace of his fingertips glowed against her skin as she paused before leaning in to answer his question.

FIFTY-EIGHT

LEAH

I don't want to work; I just want to be with you, Andrew texted as Leah made her way to her sister's door at a quarter to two on Tuesday.

She'd kissed him the other night—a giant leap of faith tethered by bared hopes and wishes. It had felt like the kind of step that began a great journey, and the feeling had lingered. Funny how one honest conversation could change everything.

Sounds like a cheesy eighties song, she texted back, smiling.

Leah and Alison had rented a boat that would take them out onto the Puget Sound to spread Mom's ashes since that's where Catherine was—or so they'd deduced based on a journal among the books in the desk. It seemed appropriate the two were reunited.

Alison already looked so much better, and Leah told her as much when she opened the door. Her posture was straighter, and she didn't move as slowly as she had a few days ago.

"I can walk around the block now," she said proudly. "It takes like an hour, but still. Progress."

Tyler joined them and kissed Leah on the cheek. Then he handed Alison her phone. "Jill for you."

Alison frowned but took it and stepped into the office while Leah and Tyler went to the kitchen.

"I figured I'd pack a picnic," Tyler said. "Might as well make a day of it."

"A birthday celebration. I like it." Leah pulled a grape off its stem and popped it in her mouth.

As soon as Alison rejoined them, Tyler zipped the cooler bag closed. "Are we ready to go?"

"Actually, I need a few more minutes," Alison said, an odd expression on her face. "Um... bathroom. And I think I want to bring my yellow sweater in case it's cold on the water."

"It's eighty-eight degrees today," Tyler pointed out.

Alison pouted. "Please get it for me. It should be in my closet."

He left without another word.

"Thank you," she called after him.

Leah narrowed her eyes at Alison, who was perched on one of the counter stools. "I thought you needed the bathroom."

"Oh." Alison stood. "Right." She shuffled out into the hallway.

Leah's spider senses tingled. Something was going on.

"Got it." Tyler returned with the sweater, but Alison still wasn't back. "Hon, you okay in there?" he called.

"I'm good," came Alison's chipper voice. "Be right out."

Another several minutes passed before she emerged. "Now I'm ready."

They followed her through the front door to Tyler's Honda in the driveway, but before they had time to get in, a town car pulled up behind them, the doors flinging open in tandem.

Alison sidled up to Leah. "Surprise!"

Leah's confusion only lasted a moment, then one dark and one blond head became visible.

Jillian and Hannah.

"What on earth?" Leah exclaimed as Hannah rushed to hug

her. She looked over her daughter's shoulder to Jill, who was finishing up paying the driver.

When Jill turned to her, a self-deprecating smile bloomed on her lips. "It was the least I could do," she said. "I had some time on the flight home to think and I realized we should be here for this."

"What about work?"

"Eh, my turn to Dublin isn't until Thursday."

"She has a hot date," Hannah informed them with a wink at her aunt.

"Do not." Jill set about bringing their carry-ons inside, but not before Leah caught a glimpse of her fiery cheeks.

She made a mental note to ask later, then turned to Alison. "Were you in on it?"

"Only since she called. They were running late; she needed us to wait."

"Sneaky," Leah said, her arm around Hannah's shoulders. "Everything good?" she asked her daughter.

"Yep."

Jillian rejoined them, complexion back to normal. "So are we doing this or not?"

With the bustle of Seattle at their backs, the glittering surface of the Sound spread out before them, offering an illusion of seclusion only sporadically interrupted by the distant caw of a bird. The boat Tyler had rented was a nice-sized cruiser that came with a captain named Mark. Per Tyler's instructions he'd take them out about midway between North Seattle and Bainbridge where they'd lie at anchor long enough to give Mom a proper send-off. Leah had the urn with Mom's ashes in her lap, and she held on to it with both hands even as she tilted her face toward the sun. Next to her, Hannah did the same, until a cheerful jingle interrupted the peace.

"Whose phone is that?" Alison asked.

"Oh, it's mine." Hannah reached into her purse to turn it off. "I'll get it later."

When she straightened, she had something white in her hand and cleared her throat to get everyone's attention. "Might as well do this now, I guess," she said, looking around their small group.

"Do what?" Leah's pulse picked up speed at what Hannah was holding. *Was that...?*

"Um... I got a letter." Hannah held up the envelope. "From Grandma."

"What?" Alison exclaimed as Jill leaned forward in her seat.

In the general commotion of reactions, Leah held out her hand for it. "Let me see."

Hannah handed it over. "It looks like she sent it to Amherst and then it was forwarded to our house back home. That's why it took so long to get there. I only saw it yesterday because I knocked the mail pile to the floor with my backpack. I didn't expect there to be something addressed to me."

"What does it say?" Alison asked.

"I haven't opened it yet." Hannah took the letter back from Leah. "I figured... I don't know. I felt like I should wait, especially after Jill called me about coming here."

"Open it now." Leah hugged the urn closer.

Hannah nodded and dug her finger under the closed flap.

"Read it out loud." Jillian's voice was thin in the wind whipping around them. "Please."

Hannah took a deep breath and began. "'*Dearest Hannah, Are they very mad at me?*'" She looked up, hesitating, but when no one reacted, she continued. "'*If they are, I don't blame them. I was always a better grandmother than I was a mother, which is also why I'm penning this final note to you, who I've always felt such uncommon closeness to. I hope you enjoyed Europe by the way. What an adventure!*'"

Jill scoffed and mumbled, "If she only knew."

Alison hushed her with a sharp, "Shh."

"*'I'm ready for my next adventure too,'*" Hannah read. "*'That's how I choose to look at it. I'm getting older, sicker. I have no interest in what is left, and I will not be a burden. The only person who ever truly knew me is gone. If your mom and your aunts object to hearing this, they haven't been paying attention. I know they didn't know me, because I didn't let them. Please tell them there was no way for them to prevent this.'*"

Across from her, Alison sucked in what sounded like a choked sob before covering her mouth. Jillian reached out and grasped her free hand.

With a quick glance at Leah for reassurance, Hannah pressed on. "*'I know there must be questions, but at the end of the day, all anyone really needs to know is that I did what I had to do to survive. Each moment. Every moment. And that Catherine saved me. Yes, I was unfaithful to my husband, but Alison can attest he betrayed me in worse ways. I've made peace with my choices, because life is too short for regrets. May you always do the same with yours.*

"*'I can still hear them, you know.'*" Hannah stopped and frowned. "I'm assuming she means you guys here."

"That's okay, go on," Leah said.

"Okay. Um… '*I can still hear them, you know. Their footsteps, whispers, laughter, and tears. Their dreams reverberating against the walls of that house, trying to break out, break free. Does that make me sentimental? If so, it probably means I should wrap this up.*

"*'Oh my little Hannah. Take care of yourself. Make good choices or at least ones you can make peace with when you're old like me. And tell my daughters that I'm sorry. Remind them that they're sisters so that they might start acting as such. All my love, Grandma.'*"

Hannah dropped her hands and the letter into her lap and

looked up. At her side, Leah caressed the smooth side of the urn. Alison blinked at the sky as if surprised it was still daytime, while Jillian remained intent on the letter, her head moving up and down in a slow nod.

"Is that it then?" Jill asked.

Hannah turned the sheet of paper over. "That's it."

"It doesn't tell us much."

"It's something." Alison leaned into Tyler and rested her head on his shoulder.

"Very Mom," Leah agreed.

After that, they all got lost in their own thoughts. The boat was surprisingly quiet for its size, and as they rode further out on the glistening water, a new lightness came over Leah. Clarity. *We move forward, meet new challenges, self-determine, persist. We're not alone.*

She looked at her family and remembered the purpose of this trip. Mom had said her piece—now it was their turn. They weren't here for dwelling; they were here for closure.

"How about we each share a memory of Mom while we're still moving?" she suggested. She allowed a moment for the others to shake off their meditations and voice agreement before continuing. "Okay, I'll go first. Ninth grade—the article she got published in—"

Jillian and Alison filled in, "The *Journal of Memory and Language.*"

The three of them laughed, and like that, the mood on the boat shifted.

"It was a big deal," Leah explained to Tyler and Hannah, who looked confounded. "For six months it was the only thing she talked about." Leah sighed. "We laugh now, but she really was so smart." The others nodded. "Your turn, Jill. And it doesn't have to be a good memory," she added.

"Okay, in that case..." Jillian straightened. "Don't worry— I'll be gentle." Everyone chuckled. "We all know Mom wasn't famous for her culinary skills. Her efforts were good and, fortunately, not too adventurous. But the birthday cakes..."

Leah smiled. For some reason, Mom had always insisted on making their cakes, even though the only passable way she could contribute to bake sales and the like was to get store-bought cookies and transfer them to a different container.

"So my memory—something I'm *thankful* for—is that she always passed on baking mine and got muffins from the grocery store instead. Those things were addictive."

After a moment of tense silence, Alison chimed in. "They really were. God, you were so lucky."

Jillian met Leah's eye and winked. "It's all about the spin," she said. "Okay, who's next."

"Homework," Alison sighed. "All the freaking homework. Sometimes I still have nightmares about her circling my math in red, telling me I have to redo it." She lifted her chin. "But you know what? It worked. I wouldn't be where I am today without her."

"Bandaged and in a boat?" Hannah asked, making everyone laugh.

"Yeah, yeah. You know what I mean."

Leah reached for her bag. "Oh yeah, I meant to tell you..." She pulled a folded sheet of paper out of an envelope. "This was in my stack from Mom's desk. Does it mean anything to you?"

Alison took it and started reading. Her head jerked up, eyes wide.

"What is it?" Leah asked.

"The Education and Leadership Award," Alison mumbled.

"What?"

"Oh, it's a thing. I was nominated... The North American Women's Business League." She closed her eyes and gave a little shimmy as if focusing hard.

Tyler grasped her arm. "Hon?"

"No, I'm okay. I thought I'd forgotten I'd applied." A stunned laugh peeled from between her lips as she smoothed the sheet of paper in her lap. "Mom did it. She's the one who nominated me. It's a draft of the application."

"She said some nice things." Leah smiled. Maybe now Alison would finally be at peace, knowing Mom's true feelings. No more need to chase validation there.

"She did." Alison nodded, eyes glittering. "She did."

They sat with that in the wind for a long moment. Surf spray and closure.

"She welcomed me to the family right away," Tyler said when the minutes lengthened. "I'd heard all these stories about how scary she was, but that wasn't at all my impression when you introduced me." He took Alison's hand in his. "She told me right after the wedding that we were a great match. That she knew I'd be good to you. I'll never forget that."

His words brought a more subdued tenor to their party, and, in spite of herself, Leah's throat began to ache.

"She was a good listener," Hannah said, kicking her purse underneath her seat when it started buzzing again. "She always asked lots of questions when we talked." She put a hand on top of the urn and leaned her hand against Leah's shoulder. "I miss her."

"Aw, sweetie." Leah kissed her head. "She'd be so proud of you, you know." She looked around the boat. "Heck, I think she'd be proud of all of us. Sure, she didn't get along with everyone, she was judgy at times, and a workaholic, and she sure knew how to keep a secret. But she ended up living on her own terms. I'd like to think she was happy with Catherine all those years, that between a job she loved and her life with her at the cottage, she was fulfilled." Leah wiped away a stray tear. "She rewrote the beginning, and I kind of think we're doing the same. All of us."

A mumble of agreement swept through their small seating area.

"Speaking of which," Alison said, "Jill and I have something to tell you." She nodded toward Jillian, who grinned.

"We're going to give you our shares of the cottage. We don't need it, and it's clearly your home."

Leah stared at them, not comprehending.

"And don't you dare object," Alison added. "You deserve a new start more than anyone else here. It's done."

A sob escaped Leah's throat, then another. "You guys," was all she croaked before the tears came in earnest. She would make a life in the cottage. A new life. Next thing she knew, they were all hugging and crying.

"Is this spot good?" Mark hollered from the captain's chair, unaware of the sob-fest going on behind him.

Tyler, the only one able to still form words, told him it was.

On wobbly sea legs, they made their way from the docks to the car as the sun lengthened their shadows late that afternoon.

Mom was with Catherine now, as she should be. Leah couldn't wait to tell Andrew about it. What a novelty that was—to have someone to share such things with.

They rode in silence, each lost in their own thoughts, until again Hannah's purse began to buzz. She stared out the window as if she wasn't hearing it.

"You're still not going to answer?" Leah asked. "Who's calling you?"

Hannah turned to her, her forehead a little pink from being in the sun on the water. She wrinkled her nose. "I didn't want to tell you before with everything else going on. It's Chase. He's been calling for days now."

A fist tightened around Leah's heart. "What does he want?"

"To talk. To apologize."

"And?"

"Oh, I only listened to the first voicemail. I haven't actually picked up."

Leah let out a breath. "Good."

"Yeah, I figure if I ignore him, he'll stop eventually."

Her words wedged themselves sideways into Leah's brain. Because if she knew anything, it was that men like that weren't so easily dissuaded. Was this what Hannah's foreseeable future would be like then? For now he was still in Brussels, but what about when he came back? Would he look her up? Insist on meeting her? Stalk her online?

No.

No, that wouldn't do. Hannah deserved better.

When the phone rang again ten minutes later, Leah held out her hand. "Give it to me," she said.

Hannah's eyes widened. "Why?"

"Please. This stops now."

After a moment's hesitation, Hannah complied and gave Leah the angry mobile.

"Chase," Leah said in greeting, voice crisp.

A beat of silence on the line, then: "Oh, hi, Mrs. S. How are you doing?"

That smarmy voice. So polite, she'd thought at first—a mother's dream.

"You are going to stop calling my daughter," she said. "After we hang up, you will delete her number from your phone and move on with your life. If you ever contact her again, or if I ever hear about you hurting another woman—and believe me, I will keep tabs on you—I will make your life a living hell. Are we clear?"

"But, Mrs. S, I think—"

"Are. We. Clear? Your parents will know, your friends will know, your future employers will know, and the police will know." Leah's voice could have cut steel. "Raise your hand against a woman ever again, and I will personally end you."

She didn't wait for his response before she hung up.

She handed the phone back to Hannah and blinked as the car came back into focus. Four pairs of eyes were on her, four mouths agape.

Dear Lord, what just happened?

"Holy shit, Mom," Hannah said to her right.

Shaky from the adrenaline infusion, Leah took Hannah's hand to steady herself and leaned her head back. She might need a nap after that. Or to run a 5K. Her brain was sending conflicting signals. She smiled weakly. "It had to be said."

Alison grinned at her from the front seat. "I'd give you a hug, but my body doesn't move that way."

"I think you leveled up, sis," Jillian said to her left. "I'm really proud of you."

Was that what that feeling was, unfurling at her core? Pride? Whatever it was, Leah liked it—it made for a stark contrast to everything she'd once held true about herself.

Mom would be proud too, she thought. What was it she'd said about making peace with our choices?

"Can I see the letter again?" she asked Hannah.

"Sure."

As they headed north along the freeway, the water behind them, the future ahead, Leah pulled the letter out of its envelope, but this time a smaller note fluttered into her lap as she did. It must have been stuck to the envelope wall earlier. No one else noticed, so Leah picked it up and turned it over discreetly.

She read the poem several times, allowing her mother's words to wash over her. "Love Wins" Mom had called it. On the surface, it conjured the lake, the wildlife above and below, a boat drifting much like the one Leah had pictured herself in at the cottage. But beneath the linguistic effort Leah knew her mother had valued so greatly lay a truth of hopelessness and salvation that finally answered the question she had initially come here to ask. *Would Mom understand and forgive?* The answer was yes, and with that, a kinship she'd never felt with her mother while she was alive closed the hole she'd carried in her chest since leaving home all those years ago. Beyond a shadow of a doubt, she knew they would have made amends.

Leah looked around the car and smiled. Like Mom, none of them was defined by their past. No one's future was set in stone. Not only were they rewriting their beginnings, but doing it together, the stories of the Brady sisters would be forever changed for the better.

Love Wins

Caught unawares at sea with broken sail
The Ragged drifts 'tween crest and trench forlorn
A storm cloud in a glass, a wicked gale
That sunders hope 'til all the seagulls mourn
The depths conceal a many-handed brute
A specter lyin' in wait beneath the skin
To challenge it, a Sisyphus pursuit
To yield, a lure that beckons from within
She stares with milky gaze toward the sky
Her armor parched, with briny cracks bedecked
The arid clouds rush forth to petrify
An aimless heart, unmoored, undone, unchecked
But as the sun sets on horizon blue
She berths the distant shore that harbors you

ACKNOWLEDGEMENTS

Since my women's fiction consistently revolves around dysfunctional family relationships, I feel a sudden urge to begin this endnote by thanking my family for being absolutely nothing at all like the characters in my books. While I do have two sisters without whom I might not have written a novel *about* sisters, the fact that there's three of us is really the main thing we have in common with the protagonists in this story. If we sometimes go a long time without seeing each other, it's not because of contention, but because we live on three different continents. (Wild, right?) So thank you, family. I miss you. And thanks, Mom and Dad, for not stopping at one. I would have been (even more) obnoxious as an only child.

Next, my fabulous agent, Kimberley Cameron, without whom none of this would be possible. You are tenacity personified, and I'm so happy to have you in my court.

This is my first title with Bookouture, so I'm sending heaps of gratitude to my whole team there for welcoming me into their family with open arms and expert know-how. Of course, an extra special thank you goes to my editor, Claire Simmonds, whose enthusiasm, keen eye for detail, and general support and loveliness have made this book's journey a thrill ride where I didn't once fear for my (and my book's) safety. And I'll be honest—that's my favorite kind of ride. Safety first! I'm so excited to see what more we can do together!

A big, enormous thank you to my early readers for this book —Megan McGee, Jessica Holt, Vanessa Carnevale, Melissa

Wiesner, Sheri Taylor-Emery, Amy Jones, Julia Miller, and Lana Hrabal. I maintain that smart readers like you are the most important tool a writer can have in their toolbox. And big hearts to Rompire for having my back both writing-wise and otherwise. With friends like you, a girl can weather any storm.

Thank you also to Patrick Gillespie, Margie Fuston, and John Pollard, who patiently answered an abundance of questions about their respective jobs to lend authenticity to the sisters' professions in this book. Any mistakes remaining are mine and mine alone. What can I say? Sometimes authors go a little nuts with their imagination...

I'm forever grateful to my husband and kids, who are my biggest cheerleaders. Brian, if I'm able to write with authenticity a dreamboat hero whose grounded sense of self underlies the love, care, support, and respect they show their love interest, then you are the reason. You are still the best person I know. To my kids, who I love more than life itself—thank you for being unwitting teachers who help me grow every day on this crazy ride. I'm not saying you're the reason my hair is turning gray, but *if* you are, it's totally worth it. Be strong, be brave, and if you choose a creative career, make sure you find a second job to supplement your income.

Thank you to everyone—friends, family, strangers—who at any point have taken an interest in, talked up, emotionally supported, posted about, reviewed, and recommended my books. It means more than you know.

And as always, last but not least, thank you to my readers, whether you've just found me or you've been on this journey with me since it started. It is the most amazing feeling to think up a world full of imaginary people, choose the words that will do it most justice, then connect with strangers over the meaning of it all. Thank you for letting me do it again and again.

Made in the USA
Las Vegas, NV
21 September 2024